BURIED SMOKE

☆ *Made in the USA* ☆

BURIED SMOKE

☆ *Made in the USA* ☆

GA-NI-SA-NV TSU-GA-SV-S-DI

☆ *ga-le-ni-da-nv vhna a-ma a-ye-tli* ☆

E. ANN SHEEHAN

This novel is a work of fiction. The plot, characters, places and events are all a product of the imagination or are imaginatively referred to in this work of fiction. Character resemblances to actual persons, living or dead, is unintentional, but cited Cherokee personages, history and culture were carefully researched and authenticated. Special appreciation to Lisa LaRue Baker, contributing editor. Words not in English are in one of the many dialects of the Cherokee language, often referred to as Tsalagi. Unless otherwise attributed, all poems are by the author.

ISBN 978-1-7352889-6-3

Printed in the United States of America

Book design by TeaberryCreative.com

For Sandi
and her living-is-loving spirit
always in my heart
1964–2019

and

In honor of all Native Americans

Author's Note

Who doesn't like a good tale told round a fire?

BURIED SMOKE ☆ *Made in the USA* ☆ is a North Carolina woman describing her coming-of-age to Oklahoma Cherokees circled around a warming fire before the night's stomp dance. After her family homestead burns to the ground, the distraught heroine flees naked into the Smoky Mountains, survives a forest fire and wanders alone until rescued by three Cherokee men. So begins her long tale of self-discovery. But this is also a love story—between people who seem to be different yet discover a rich commonality. On another level, the story speaks to the very essence of American culture. As in the universal human cry, "Who am I," the heroine is seeking identity. Her search intertwines with Native Americans working out their own similar struggle.

The genesis for my story arises from a "quirk of coincidence." Some years ago, while writing a short story that happened to include Native Americans, I learned that General Winfield Scott, a nineteenth-century figure in American history, appeared on my family tree. Since Scott led the tragic march of Native Americans on the historic Trail of Tears, I was drawn to focusing on Cherokees and the enormous cultural transformation imposed upon them. For me, this is a small way of making amends.

Considerable research and generous assistance from many Cherokees helped produce the book. An initial course on Cherokee History and Culture with Dr. Barbara Duncan at the Cherokee Heritage Museum in Cherokee, North Carolina, led to extensive reading before I settled on the staunchly-traditional United Keetoowah Band of Cherokee Indians of Oklahoma. On my first visit to Tahlequah, Oklahoma, I met Lisa LaRue-Baker, who was working in cultural resources for the two Oklahoma tribes—the Keetoowah Band and Cherokee Nation. Over years, she kindly helped me understand and state traditional Cherokee history and culture, along with contributions from the beloved Keetoowah storyteller, Sequoyah Guess, and the talented Sammy Still. More recently, Cherokee Language and Lifeways Teacher, Lawrence Panther, and amazing cartographer, Aaron Carapella, of Tribal Nations Maps, helped me with the Cherokee language. Aaron allowed me to include his maps of original nations. Last, but never least, Cherokee National Treasure, Kituwah storyteller and tradition-keeper, Choogie Kingfisher, read the manuscript and counselled me on cultural accuracy.

I am not a Cherokee spokesperson, but I use their unique story to illustrate the importance of cultural identity to everyone. I have sought to be as true to Cherokee culture as I can and trust they understand my profound respect. I am honored by the faith put in me. Reference materials at the end of the book are worth using.

My sincerest appreciation goes to all readers and advisors who kindly critiqued my manuscript in its various manifestations: Assoc. Professor of History, Robyn Worthington (there at the beginning), Bettina Borders, Abra Degbor, Tom Lopes (and his beautiful mind), Robin Parsons, Janet Wing, Denise Portelance, Cheryl Stern, Leslie Stern, Michael Watson, Janet Wing, my daughter Alexandra Hartmann and her daughter, Jaime Stepansky (along the way), plus retired English Professor, Catherine McLaughlin (holding my hand near the end). I am eternally indebted to them and, of course, the biting wit of Mark Twain.

After sharing in this rite-of-passage, may you never think of fire the same.

—E. Ann Sheehan

Contents

Before the Fire

tsi-ni-ge-sv-na

*Once upon a time, perhaps as many as 700 million years before this mythical tale...*the location of this story was birthed in a giant cataclysmic event when a huge tectonic plate shift tore the American continents away from the African continent to form the Appalachian Mountains. Since then, this range has weathered into a majestic and mature mountain system stretching from Newfoundland and Labrador in the north to Alabama at the south, with individual ranges, like the White and Green Mountains of New England or the Blue Ridge and Great Smokies of the American South.

The Great Smokies are named for the moist air that hangs over the rich and diverse forests of eastern Tennessee and western North Carolina for most of the year. Each spring, a multitude of densely-colored oaks, hickories, poplars, hemlocks and pines shine aside flowering rhododendron and mountain laurel. Within this dramatic backdrop live abundant wildlife, such as bobcats, bears, wolves, snakes, foxes, deer, insects and a diverse bird population.

The area is also the traditional homeland of the Native people called the Cherokees.

It is quite possible the Americas have been inhabited for more than 50,000 years, always with different cultures coexisting in a vibrant trade economy—each with its unique history, social organization, language, laws, traditions, rituals, myths and customs. Pottery chards that were discovered in North Carolina were linked to a culture from 9,000 B.C. Think of it! Generation upon generation of human beings raising families, living and loving, cooking meals, managing the land, trading, birthing and dying in that location for over 11,000 years. But pre-conquest life on the American continent remains an enigma to us.

Who knows who visited before daring gold-seekers, such as Hernan Cortes, Vasco Nunez de Balboa, Amerigo Vespucci, Juan Ponce de Leon, Francisco Pizarro, Ferdinand Magellan and Cristobal Colon (i.e. Christopher Columbus)? We will never know the adventurous explorers, traders and settlers who came to make new beginnings, build homes, practice vocations, raise families, gain and lose riches, leave or stay in this part of the world over the many years that followed. Viking sagas tell us of adventurers, like Norway's Leif Ericson and Iceland's Thorfinn Karlsefni who traveled the east coast of North America around 1000 A.D. They portray boatloads of stalwart men and women with livestock and seeds spending years in places they named Markland, Cross Cape, Keel Cape, and Vinland. Intriguing remains exist of their constructions and possible stone writings in various locations from Labrador to Oklahoma.

Hernando DeSoto's 1540 expedition into what is now the southeastern United States described a densely-populated area with well-established roads and towns. Like the Vikings, DeSoto wrote of temples and earth-colored persons of apparent royalty. His later voyage introduced pigs to Florida—perhaps those carrying European diseases such as smallpox and measles, typhus and whooping cough, dysentery, tuberculosis and diphtheria, scarlet fever, mumps, influenza and syphilis. Some estimate the indigenous death rate in the century following Columbus' arrival at 90% or more. If this is anywhere near accurate, the culture in the Americas was undeniably altered before colonists arrived in the 1600 and 1700s. Native peoples were most probably in stark survival/recovery mode when the invasion and land-taking began. It is therefore obvious that, at best, a true understanding of our American legacy is limited. In this void, Native oral history, myth, legend and tradition must assume a paramount role.

BURIED SMOKE ☆ *Made in the USA* ☆ opens a door to a herstory—the kind of tale usually buried within history. Dressed in fictional female transformation, the story shines a spotlight on the universality of human experience within American diversity.

Your Plea to Me

Tell me a tale
not tall not stale
Tell me one true
Confidentially, you
help me to see
whatever might be
of interest to me
as opined by thee
Whatever it is
make it bubble and fizz
and roll off the plate
like marbles on slate
right into my lap
My attention you'll grab
Then hit me with truth
everlastingly sooth
Reach into my heart
Don't tear it apart
Imprint on it
as you fashion fit
and give me some hope
with which I can cope
and then you will see
a believer I'll be

Marco Polo was said to have told Kublai, "It is not the voice that commands a story, but Khan the ear." I suggest it's not all so terrible to hear this, a parable.

PART 1

Kindling

go-tv-s-do-di

OCTOBER 1974: Oh-h-h, why am I shivering? Guess maybe I'm nervous 'bout sharing my story with folks I don't know. But then again, it could be this chilly morning air. Anyways, it was just last year I sat in this circle for the first time. Today, I'm on a serious mission—to tell y'all how I came to be me. And I'm real grateful you're here to listen. C'mon, let's close in on this fire. I got my coffee and this here blanket's on my shoulders. I see some have yours over your legs. Whatever. I'm ready, Okies, are you?...

Back home, it was in April, 1960, when a majorly-big slamming of my front door actually done tore my house down. Oh, I see you smiling, but it really did and when my ugly old past went stomping off into the oncoming night is how my new life got born.

Rotted beams and ratty old timbers mixed with the newspapers we stuffed in the walls for insulation plus broken glass—all fell 'round my body as I stood hearing screeching wheels peel on down the drive. Most eerily, though, I remember Elvis' voice crooning *Don't Be Cruel* from the Victrola. Finally, I snapped to

1

and stepped over my Eddie Fisher and Teresa Brewer record collection afore sidestepping the corner cupboard that'd toppled over onto his dirty underwear. Pieces of my Gram's tea cups were clinging to her old gingham dress hanging off my body. And, when I tried brushing them, I noticed how the light breeze I stirred up caused chicken feathers to scamper. Ya see, I was fixing to cook a chicken for dinner. I blew feathers off my nose then set on out through my lavender front door that was hanging off to one side.

Even though it was a real nice day in the mountains, I could only take in the tall line of maple trees on the far side of the clearing that were showing off their spring-green. Crossing the overgrown weeds we joked was our lawn, I kicked hard down the dirt drive to the path through the trees. I dunno how my mind was working, but my bare feet dug deep all the way to Cee's house—'bout a quarter mile. After just a quick look, she gave me a long hug.

"It's over. Finally, finally over," was all I hadda say.

That night, loud thunderstorms belched overhead and morning brought a drenching rain. I lay on Cee's lumpy old mattress on her attic floor listening to Frank Sinatra down in the kitchen while the thudding on the roof kept beat to his "Come fly with me. Come fly, come fly away." I stuck my fingers in my ears when number one on the hit parade came on so I could drown out Paul Anka's *Lonely Boy* from the outside world and change it to "lonely girl" in my head.

'Round noon, the mountains were done with their morning bath and silence came on home. Looking out Cee's kitchen window, it seemed like steam was floating up beyond the grove of trees in line to my house. I explained as how my past was dead and my present empty, I hadda get on to my future. Cee'd heard plenty enough already. She encouraged the grace of God be with me, even though neither of us knew where I was headed.

On the Inside

Ideas bounce off walls
    reverberate
    ricochet, glance away
With no straight lines to Truth
    inside, no way to fathom
    how to calm the chaos
    echoing the screeching thought-twangs
How private is pain
    how seductive to slip into numbness
    and not fight for sanity, yet more

Retracing my steps, I wasn't in a mood for the what-all 'round me. Oh, it's true, the Smokies do hold spectacular scenes of what some folks call "sublime peaks and mist-filled overlooks" that often get buried under clouds. Ya see, spring mornings in the Smokies means the warm air in the valleys meets up with the colder hillsides and turns into lotsa mist. Last night's chill had made for a sweet and familiar aroma of burning apple wood, but I couldn't take in any of this. I was so intent on my feet touching the ground that my eyes popped when I broke outta the trees and saw what was left of my home had burned up. Or down. Whatever.

Ya think that hit me hard? No, I was really most pleased when I entered the smoldering shell. Even though this was my very own grandparents' farmhouse, one sorry sight after another lifted my spirits. First, was the dangling birdcage with a roasted carcass lying feet straight up. Oh, an evil thought popped right into my mind and I actually said out loud, "God, I always hated that noisy bird."

Then, my eyes rested on Gram's old stove—now almost unrecognizable. I allowed as it was the propane flame that musta lit up the chicken pot and, when it got dry, it heated the old ceiling that fell and fed the fire. Probably. Some wall supports were still standing and the chimney stuck out into the sky, but every sooty thing was dripping. I supposed God musta sent that rain to take care of that fire. Then came another mental delight and I spoke into my hand shielding my face from the "acrid"—yes, acrid smell, "Yukkshhh, this putrid odor's better 'n anything ever came outta my kitchen." You're laughing, but I wasn't.

At the doorway to our bedroom, I could see our sooty old bed and the only thing of any value—the pawn-shop candlesticks he gave me when we moved in—well, they were now a mangled mess on the floor. When my eyes landed on Momma's old dollhouse—the one Gram kept trying to get me to play with—I saw how it was now just charred wood.

I shook my head, "And I'll not be fixin' to use any of this anymore."

Most peculiarly though, I recall when those words popped outta my mouth a wee little humanoid creature appeared afore my eyes for maybe only a teeny second. I can't really describe it, but in swirling ashes at my feet I saw this thing standing at attention smiling and nodding its head at me. I blinked hard a few times to challenge the vision, but couldn't focus on it. Then, it was gone too quick and I made my decision quick, too. This all never meant anything anyway—better to leave it and walk away. I was done.

I dropped Cee's dungarees and blouse on the floor and began a search for the shower nozzle in the once-upon-a-time bathroom. The handle wouldn't turn, though—musta melted.

So, in my weird mental state, I figured on finding water by setting out. I know, I know. Later on, I'd look back and not believe myself, but it seemed so normal at the time.

First person I came on was Brant Steele. "Heidi, Brant. Today's my very own birthday," was what burst outta my mouth. Brant owned Forestland's Finest Service Station at the end of our dirt road where it met up with the back road into town. I could tell he was busy. He was slow to look up from some oily parts carefully arranged on the countertop. I guess I startled him when I said, "I just re-born myself, I did. And I'm meanin' to start over in a brand-new life." He gave me only a fast glance even though I musta been a stunning sight in his doorway. Right off, he set about studying his shoes.

"An... har-r-r you this fine day, Mz. Firestone?" came outta his mouth as he slowly poked mud off the heels of both shoes–first one, then the other.

"Well, thanks, I just busted outta my old shell, so I'm feelin' mighty special," I managed in the most natural tone of voice I could. But truly, I was mindlessly standing thar with my whole body glaring at him in the fresh light. Poor Brant bent down onto the darkness of the garage floor and picked up an oily rag, then walked to the back of the stall, put it in the waste basket and returned to the sink to slowly and most-thoroughly wash his hands with his back facing me.

My adrenalin was flowing and my words were spilling. "Fact is, Brant, for the first time ever, I'm feelin' fully, totally alive. I'm startin' out on my very own life today. A new person is what I am. It's why I need to wash up. I'm so-o-o soiled from my ugly old life, I can't begin to say. This time, I'm gonna start off fresh and clean. Hunh, guess that's what you'd call 'a clean start.' Anyways, after you're done thar, would you mind if I washed up a bit?"

Right. I was acting most strange and Brant surely needed to think this over. My request most likely struck him as peculiar, his sink being for only the dirtiest in his shop and most definitely the least fitting place for a woman to wash in. But he said he could look for a towel. Waiting on the hot water to gush, I scoured 'round in the darkness looking for some "amenities." I did find a clean piece of cardboard to sit on afore coming on a rubber stopper buried in a pile of junk. I was holding the plug down in the drain watching the sink fill when Brant came in with two old hand towels—hand-me-downs from his mother. Brant kept his eyes on the back wall as he stretched out his arms.

"Here y'ar-r-r, Mz. Firestone, it's all I could find fer ya. Hope they'll pass inspection."

I didn't bother to think on why he was so busy investigating the fly buzzing over the station wagon as I grabbed the towels to start cleaning the counter. Brant slid himself back under the Ford with his arms back up inside the vehicle. I could feel his mind racing, but I didn't know 'til later he was wondering why thar was no answer at the farm. *So, Delia can't remember if the Mister's workin' or not and Officer Mac said he'd be 20 minutes 'cuz of the accident on Soft Shoe Rd and Mr. Simpson's comin' in any time now and car's not ready. What am I gonna do?*

6

Yes, it's funny now, thinking how the corners of Brant's eyes watched me climb into his utility sink. Later, he told me he focused on my round butt and paid special mind as I lifted my legs into the sink, but turned away lest I catch him. Me? I was sitting on the counter with my feet in the sink intently watching the cool, clean refreshing water pour out.

"Oh Brant, I really hate to bother you, but would ya mind, I-I need some soap. Plain old water won't do the trick to make myself really, really clean for this new life."

His voice was a bit irritated as he announced there was liquid cleaner on the counter in a black bottle with a black top. I should look on my right for it.

"Oh, I saw that, Brant, but it smells horrible—it's like it's 'industrial.' Full of chemicals. My nose knows better. Dontcha have something else—maybe with a flowery smell? Maybe in your bathroom?"

"So-r-r-r-y, Mz. Firestone, this ain't my house; it's my repair shop—fer cars. Not a place fer fine ladies." Oh, he was steaming. He toned down later, but at that moment he wasn't coping well with this stress. He took a big breath. "And I don't much care fer flowery soap anyway. I use pure Ivory."

I saw him sneak another look at me on his garage counter. I was pouring water over my head and I saw his big grin. He told me later this picture "beat by a mile"–his words—the pinup calendar he put over the sink a few years afore.

I called out, "Yeah? Not me. That's one smell I can't stand. I won't let it in my house. My favorite flower is lily-of-the-valley and I just now got a thought. I'm starting over fresh in a new life, I am, and I have a mind to grow big, big fields of lilies-of-the-valley. I'm gonna make soap that smells real, real good and I'll give ya some."

My next words, "How's that sound?" musta gone into the sink because he called out real loud, "What?"

"Sorry. I said dontcha think that's a good idea?"

"Whatever" came back at me. But I wasn't 'bout to be discouraged.

"Right now, though, I gotta have something that smells better. This is the worst ever. No one startin' a new life—like I am—actually, no one ever should use stuff like this. Think. Dontcha have anything nicer?"

Brant shoved his work cart backwards with a jolt and pulled his lanky frame straight up, shaking off the rust dust settled on him, "Well, I don't rightly know. Guess I'll have ta take a look-see but I'm not at all sure that—" was all he got out. I think my splashing water on my breasts is what made him stagger outta the stall. When he returned with a single packet of hand cream he found in the bottom drawer of his desk—something he picked up on one of his cleanings in his restroom—I was speaking to his rat cat who came to inspect me.

"And aren't *you* the sweetest little thing? What's your name, pretty little kitty cat?"

He kept his eyes peeled on his cat as he messed with his hair with one hand and held the other out. "Perhaps if ya mix this packet with the soap it'll satisfy yer nose, Mz. Firestone. It's some new-fangled way fer women ta carry hand cream. 'Fraid it's all I could come up with. And this here kitty is Gotcha, named by my Uncle Seth."

Taking the tiny packet from him, I looked into his eyes with a quizzical tilt to my head, water dripping onto the floor, "Gotcha? Whyever would you name a cat that?"

So, just to be polite—I'm sure—he looked directly into my eyes. A big mistake. He started to explain how the stray cat proved herself a natural mouser, so his uncle said she'd named herself. But in the middle of his sentence, his voice cracked. He cleared his throat and looked at the floor, but stayed put.

I tried opening the packet with my teeth, but I couldn't. I silently held it out to him. As he reached for it, he brushed my fingers—by accident, I'm sure. Talking all the while 'bout the cat, he tore it open in one fell swoop so that thick, pink liquid gushed out. Oh, he knew how valuable every drop was for my testy nose and I was thankful he lurched forward so the precious pinkness would spill onto me instead of the floor. He plopped the packet into my cupped hands as he pointed his dripping fingers to the ceiling and drops of heavenly aroma ran down onto his palms.

"Oh, Brant, don't waste a drop of that precious stuff. And would ya mind rubbin' what's on your hands onto my back? I can't reach back thar and I need to clean my entire self."

Yes, y'all are smiling again. And, yes, I've thought back on this, many, many times. Retrospection is a most valuable thing, ya know. It's when we see things richer and clearer. I'm very lucky how it all worked out, but poor Brant—he should never have rubbed pink lotion on my wet skin. Ya see, I wasn't the only one to unravel that day. I think thar were two screeching voices in his head—one urging him to humor me and keep me occupied 'til I could be rescued—and another one.

Later, he told me he hadn't had a woman since his fiancé jilted him eighteen months afore. She took off with a car salesman and then, when she got jilted, he felt she got her "just desserts"—his words. Brant still looked forward to loving a woman, but she now hadda be a ten. One day, a ten would show up, he told hisself. In the meantime, he spent Saturday nights eating his mom's cooking and playing cards with his dad. The resta the week he kept to his garage. Only twenty-two, there was plenty of life ahead.

This day, though—with me the way I was—he slowly turned his hand so the stream of cream running down the outside of his fingers could run onto my back. Starting at my shoulder, he wiped the lotion from each finger—one at a time—afore sweeping his palm across my skin. It felt so good. I knew thar wasn't much to work with, so I handed the packet to him. Honestly, I wasn't myself. I dunno who I was.

My eyes pierced him as I watched him eyeing my knees. I knew he could feel my intense energy—in his hand when he took the packet, in his chest whar his heart was pounding and in his loins. He squeezed mosta the thick pink liquid between his palms. When I turned so my breasts faced him, I wasn't surprised when his hands rubbed both at the same time. It felt so good I put my head back. That probably told him I was his. Poor Brant musta been planning to leave at 4:30 to catch the baseball game afore I walked in, but not now. Me? For some reason or other, I was acting without any of the restrictions that had been *my whole life* up to then.

Where was my truck?... I'd no idea. Things moved fast now. He threw off his oily jeans jacket, handed it to me and pulled me to the back door. Gotcha took off, terrified. We jumped into his truck without a word and I thought to fasten the buttons on the jacket. In a flash, he pulled out his big key ring, revved the engine and sped 'round the garage. Now, the botha us were no longer of our worlds. First, Brant sped to his parents' house. He said he needed a stash of cash from his mother's cookie jar. He also grabbed two apples, a Ritz cracker box and a 6-pack of Bud, tossing them onto my lap. He called to his mom doing laundry in the cellar saying he was off to the cabin. We were tooling down the drive afore she got to the toppa the stairs. Passing the driveway to my smoldering house, we both caught the smell of wet smoke. He laid a hand gently on my knee. I closed my eyes and squirmed closer to him. My future had begun.

After a few minutes, I looked out at the passing vista. Rolling by were those misty hillsides abloom with mountain laurel and early azalea. The air was full of sweetness and I was sure I was alive and living in a fairy tale.

I asked, "Where we off to, anyways?"

He told me it was his secret surprise. Was that all right?

"'Course. Sure. It's all fine. I'm reborn into a wonderful new life and I'm gonna let things come as they will. You can go anywhars. I'll just go along for the ride."

"Oh-h-h, there're so many joys ta be had in this world— 'specially whar we're goin'," Brant whispered as he gave me a hug. I closed my eyes again and he grabbed a Bud.

At the general store, he apologized and would I please move my head? I sat listening to soothing 99.9 KISS country music—it's a great station—'til he returned with hamburger, buns and chips, cinnamon rolls, coffee and bananas, and a can of tuna, a small jar of mayo, a loaf of bread and another six-pack. I also noticed a bar of flowery soap that made me smile.

It wasn't season yet, so the gate wasn't open. Brant jumped out flashing his key ring. Slipping what he called his "big old silver bullet" into the receptive slot, he opened up the road to "Lil' Bit O' Heaven"—what the hand-carved sign said. He set his foot on the accelerator for the muddy climb up the hill and I reckoned I was indeed headed for heaven.

At first, the shadowy cabin seemed forlorn. Brant propped open windows with wooden sticks, lit a fire in the fireplace and fetched a pail of water from the nearby stream while I explored the loft with the ladder I found lying on the floor next to the back wall as well as the little kitchen separated from the large open area by a log railing. And then, thar was that inviting oversized fireplace that just screamed of simple luxury. It was all looking gorgeous.

Outside, I saw many trails promising mystery and adventure. Looking down one, I felt like I had been this way afore—sorta like what they call *déjà vu*—though I didn't pay it any mind at the time. Stooping to pass water, I surprised a spring toad looking up at me. I took giggly aim but missed. I loaded my arms with wood from the woodpile and returned inside to find my really plain, but suddenly handsome Adonis standing stark-naked in fronta the blazing fire. The wood thudded to the floor as I flew across the room and knocked him down. We lay laughing, panting and kissing while wriggling and worming our bodies as we followed our impulses. That fire witnessed our passion all night long and into the morning. We wanted and we needed nothing more and nothing from our old worlds entered the cabin.

As usual, next morning's fog melted into a misty sun 'round midday. We lay in fronta the fire in our own fog. With breakfast gone and the sun starting to heat the air, I grabbed the soap, declaring I was going down to the creek. I followed the trail next to the stream with a new flair—one that spoke of a new beginning. When I found a good place to sit, I let myself down into shallow, cool, crisp water and washed, then perched myself on a rock in the middle of the stream. I called Brant in what I guess what was a too-loud voice... He came tearing down to see if I was drowned or something. I laughed at his bouncing and flouncing and invited him to join me. We played like baby seals laughing and screaming into the trees 'til we could hardly stand, then found a warm, sandy spot 'til our bodies were covered with goose bumps. Once his adrenalin slowed, Brant suddenly bolted straight up in the air with bugged-out eyes.

"Ohmygodthefire—"

I followed him as fast as I could, cresting the hill in time to see the first flames shoot outta the door. The cabin was so aflame I think the right word is "inferno." Clearly, we couldn't enter to get anything—not the pail set on the other side of the fireplace, not his clothes, not his car keys. Poor Brant, he could only freeze into a statue and watch his family's precious, precious heirloom go up in flames. He stood 'til I screamed, "Holy Jesus, we gotta get outta here."

We looked at each other and our eyes said everything our hearts felt but couldn't put into words. Our hands clung together to seal the fierceness of our feelings as we resolved—or maybe dissolved—our relationship. We both ran toward the truck. He was scratching under the dash for the spare key as I passed him running down the road fast as I could. I dunno if I said out loud or just inside my head, "I'm gonna be free from now on. I gotta be free—gotta be strong in this life. I'll be needin' no one from here on." But I dedicated myself to these words. I'm not sure if I was afraid—I mighta been—probably was—but I never looked back. Just like my heavy life at Gram and Poppa's farm, I let go of this newfound happiness with the snap of a finger. I broke off a perfectly beautiful bond with a beautiful man without even a backward glance. Sprinting off the road on the first trail I came to, I was outta sight even afore his truck passed by, continuing to run as fast as the thick brush would allow—full of life, fully free, most likely afraid and all alone. I left a world where my government was sending weather satellites out into space and folks in Africa were rioting against an unjust government and here I was being sucked into a wilderness.

It was many years later that I heard what happened back thar. Things have a way of being passed 'round. Like Mark Twain once wrote, "Lies can travel 'round the world afore truth gets its shoes on." Perhaps the real story was different, I dunno. I heard he drove like the wind, his eyes ramrod straight past whar I entered the woods. The story is... instinct drove him back to the locked gate whar he sat trying to think through his nakedness, but thoughts wouldn't come. He was a stunned deer in the blinding light of the oncoming. No thoughts or answers. Just questions.

Sure, time plays tricks—we all know that. I heard that after one such time warp, Brant managed to uncover from the wayback some old blankets a stretch of frayed clothesline, a rusty and bent metal hanger, a coupla dollars in coins and handfuls of long black dog hair. Apparently, what was most helpful, that he also found, was a ripped swim suit. At the first house down and 'round the bend, he found old Oscar Hoyt at home and put together a buncha words that tried to explain the fire in the woods, his truck inside the locked gate and him wearing a swimsuit. Oscar called the volunteer fire department then drove Brant back to the gate.

That's why a most-somber Brant Steele spent the next three days alongside firemen and neighbors fighting the firestorm that raged over two counties and went on to scar 900 acres of forest afore a team of rangers and volunteers could get it under control—only with help from breakfronts and foam sprayed outta airplanes. It was headlines in the newspaper and evening news for at least a week. Brant was often interviewed. Some said his story got better and better.

That's how my old life left me and how I got lost in the woods afore I got to finding me. The next thing that happened was terrifying, but dontcha think we should stretch our legs afore I get onto that?...

Dontcha Know?

Dinne no one ever tell ya, young'n, life gets ya in thur end?
Yer ups 'n downs jest all increase as
years roll round the bend
Dinya never hear 'bout wearies, nor even 'bout loss?
Dinya never figger life would kick ya in the oss?
Where wuz ya when the preacher 'splained?
Where wuz ya when the old folks pained?
Where wuz yer mind when we was hurtin'?
Didya figure you was special, certain?

Well, now the devil's called 'n taken ya raight in
And now yer gittin' all that comes from livin' in yer sin
It's only fair an fittin' to see ya in yer pain
It's not that we don't love ya, but then agin my man
This's what'll happen when yer temptin' lady luck
Nothing good'll ever come of spittin' from yer truck
Nothing good'll ever happen when yer lookin' fer a fuck
From tartsy wimen peddlin' all the long night's dark

List'n to me good, boy, it's almost now too late
Yer much too old ta cry now, but not too old ta hate
Ta hate yer inner wicked, that poison layin' in ya
That's twistin' yer decisions 'n influencin' ya
Vomit up that poison 'n spit it ta the wind
Tongue the taste a rightness 'n drink it all right in
Toss on out yer hist'ry 'n write on in a new one
Open up a new life 'n set yer heart ta spin

PART 2

Ignition

a-tsi-li-do-di

Hi again. Well, as I already said, this is how things happening in my
life ended up changing me. I'm wondering if y'all ever thought 'bout
how the words "my story" and "mystery" are a strong coincidence
of sound? I have. It got me to wondering—maybe it's not just me—
maybe everybody's got a mystery. Anyways, I'm itching to burn
your ears off with mine, so let's go...

As you can understand, I was real traumatized coming outta
two fires in two days. Lots happened I can't remember, but
some things I surely do—like forging further and farther into
the forest, thrusting myself into dense vines and thickets and
brambles. I did that the whole day long. I dunno why I didn't follow the road or a path or trail—don't even remember if thar were
such. It was like thar was a reverend thing pushing me into the
deepest of the woods. And I mean trees—sorta like yers 'round
here, but—well, more! Just lotsa green growing all 'round.

17

All's I could think of was to widen the distance from that flaming tempest I couldn't put outta my mind. I'd pause, tilt my head and sniff the air, allowing how fire travels. I always chose to go with the wind in my face. I kept listening to my inside voice that kept repeating, *I wanna start fresh. I'm gonna find a new world. I can do it. Make another life. Live free this time. I gotta be free.* I guess that's how I got through the day.

Fear was surely motivating me. My heart pounded so hard and my breath come so fast, I felt like I was racing in a marathon. Probably, though, I was just plodding into the wind as I gave myself this pep talk. I tromped through wooded hillsides overgrown from years of finding their own newfound freedom. Ya see, I knew these hills had seen a lot of lumbering in the past and I allowed as they were now seeking freedom to create a new generation. I felt close to the forest.

I didn't know who I was sharing the woods with, though. And, not knowing whar to go—with no compass or even a trail—I was at sixes and sevens. I finally hadda trust myself. From time to time, my flitting eyes caught sight of a shadow shape—maybe another creature. But when I turned my head, thar was nothing. Sometimes, I shook my shoulders and trudged on, telling myself animals most surely had to be moving 'bout and all of them were most certainly savvier than me. Surely thar were gentle deers and probably bears and mountain lions and snakes—maybe ghosts, even. Who knows what else? And these whatevers could also be hungry and not especially friendly. I kept hanging onto one thought, though: *they* were the ones scared so *they* were retreating from *me.* I made myself see them running from the sounds I made—and also my smell. Who knows if this worked? But that whole day, I didn't bump into any animals.

I focused on keeping a sense of reality. What I mean is, sometimes I'd feel a sensation like hands and feet crawling inside my body—usually when I got to thinking 'bout the snakes that hadda be thar. That's when I'd tell myself I couldn't survive. And when it came on me, I learned to deal with it by just setting one foot in fronta the other and focusing on that.

When dusk came and the air dampened, I began to shiver. My naked body wasn't used to dealing with the elements all on its own. Probably my ego was naked, too—I think that's what made me dread the mysteries that come in the dark. Now I hadda go much slower. In the shadowy light, I came on a damped-down bed of soft pine needles—perhaps an animal's bed the night afore— I dunno. I couldn't resist dropping my shaking body down, but sleep wouldn't come. Instead, my mind was tuned into the woods' night sounds and the sky's night sights. My heart was pounding, but I could still grasp an unspeakable and overwhelming sense of awe and wonder. Ya know, being totally alone and at one with nature in the dark of night is magical. And I was beginning to get a wee bit comfortable in my new freedom. Instead of falling asleep, I stared into that sky full of wonder—and fortunately not socked in by clouds. My skin tingled even though my feet were aching from the day's wanderings. My stomach was crying in hunger and my tongue was begging for water, too. With so many full-body sensations, how could I sleep? Impossible!

I did detect foraging animals passing me by. Thar was one time a heavy-footed one snapped a branch that caused me to bolt upright and gasp out loud. In his rush to escape, he made an ever-fading rustle and my bug-eyes were left staring at that spot, which is how I happened to spy a tree that was glowing 'bout fifty yards away from me. Yes, a glowing tree! Believe me, I was stunned as I watched a twisting, writhing light show. It made no sounds, none at all, but did light up the woods. By this time, I couldn't hear sounds even if it was a symphony orchestra—the blood pounding in my temples and the mosquitoes buzzing 'round my head drowned out everything else. My imagination conjured up sinister stories to go with the light show, but after what seemed like—maybe—a big slice of forever, it was clear nothing more was gonna happen. So, I lay back down and blinked slower and slower, sometimes sneaking a peek at the yet-twisting vision.

I felt somewhat better when I repeated my favorite Psalm: *"The Lord is my shepherd I shall not want; he leadeth me aside the still waters; he restoreth my soul. Yea, though I walk through the valley of the shadow of death, I fear no evil. He comforts me. Surely goodness and mercy shall follow me all the days of my life and I shall dwell in the house of the Lord forever. Amen and Amen."* I memorized this when I was little and I still say it when it suits me. That night, it had a good effect and I eventually relaxed to the edge of sleep. When the grayness of early light returned, I knew I lost consciousness a bit. But that fiery vision—could it have been a dream? I still wonder 'bout that.

By now, my entire body was covered in welts and scratches, stripes of dry blood and mountains of itchy insect bites. And a large swelling under my left knee was painful when I touched it. I was so obsessed by these skin issues I forgot my overwhelming hunger or thirst. Instead, I made the decision I was finding water to clean up. Can ya believe it? It's true.

Getting going on this new day, I stumbled on damp earth a number of times. I just knew there hadda be water somewhars, but no matter how hard I searched, I couldn't find any to wash in. Conscious only of wanting to get clean, it was much later when I came to understand it was also my unconscious thirst to survive.

Ya know, being lost in the midst of a morning's mountain mist is altogether a different experience from seeing it outside a car window. As this was what my old English teacher called a "seminal" experience, I was gathering insights as I made my way through the dense growth. Moisture was clinging to me like everything else and droplets on my arms were invitations to lick. But I didn't like the taste of my dirty salty skin or the nasty coldness that followed. The mountain laurel and rhododendron bent over with dew were what called to me. I found licking their leaves far preferable, even though each moist gift was more like what I'd call a suggestion of water. I licked as many as I could, always choosing the most shimmery leaves and, at one point, I got to remembering the time when I was little and watched a hummingbird take a bath on laurel leaves. I had thought, even then, how every drop of water can be important to something or someone. And now, that someone was me.

I realized I was lucky in another respect, too. A month earlier and these woods woulda been touched by frost and, if I'd been tromping through then, it woulda been most inhospitable. But being as it was mid-spring, flowers were popping and newly-hatched leaves were stretching toward the sun all 'round me. The air had a freshness like at no other time—as if Mother Nature had put on her nicest perfume. The damp earth had a heady aroma of rotting leaves—maybe like the humus and sprouting vegetation was Mother Nature stepping outta her very own bath.

I told myself I was Eve back in the Garden of Eden. Yes, I surely resembled the mental image I have of Eve. Thar was only one problem with this Eden—it was a jungle. In school, they told how the Smokies give birth to nature's bounty, but I never truly understood it afore. This when I decided to find animal trails in the thick, lush overgrowth. Whenever I'd come across one, I'd follow it 'til it gave out or I got confused. Then, I'd start all over again. The cold morning soon became a warm, muggy noon. Even under the canopy of the trees—like hickories and maples and hemlocks and black cherries and so many others I didn't know—I could feel the sun bearing down. It made me glum 'cuz it meant thar'd be no more wet leaves that day. I also knew that even though our hills are captives of clouds, they don't hold many ponds or lakes.

I started thinking 'bout how I no longer knew whar the fire had been; I couldn't smell smoke anymore and couldn't see outside the heavy foliage to gain any sense of direction. The day afore, I let my impulses guide me to higher ground without caring whar I was headed—lengthening the distance from the fire was all that had mattered. This day was different. Now, I had a firm purpose of finding water.

I scouted out a rock ledge to catch my breath and get my bearings, but what I got was a whiff of smoke. Looking down, I was amazed and saddened at the extent of the still-smoldering damage. Two helicopters circled over lots and lots of charred trees. But the good news was the active fire was headed away from me and that meant I was a safe distance from discovery. I got excited 'cuz I'd escaped! I went and met a threat and beat it. I tell ya, this accomplishment feeling was mighty empowering.

But seeing how high I was in the mountains wearied me. It'd be harder to find water here. My good feelings were quickly beaten down. Ever since I was little, mountains have made me feel close to God. In Sunday School, I liked the Bible's emphasis on vertical places. Mrs. Jensen, my teacher, had always stressed the passage, *"I will lift up mine eyes unto the Lord from whence cometh my help."* I took this to mean, "I will lift up mine eyes unto the mountains from whence cometh my help" because Mrs. Jenson had also said the many temples and pyramids 'round the world were modeled after nature and human beings created sacred spaces to be like what God created. "Mountains evoke the divine," Mrs. Jensen had repeated over and over. I now contemplated the sacred mountains 'round me.

I was in this kinda religious trance when a most peculiar thing happened. After my wandering alone in the hills for this long, I suddenly stopped feeling human. Out thar on that precipice, I started feeling different—more like a raw animal. Being in those woods and on that spot, it seemed natural to revert to a sorta primitive. I dunno why. Without my meaning to, I took on the attitude of an animal—any animal—like the ones I was maybe sharing these woods with. I reckon I detached myself from human-ness and changed into something totally different.

Perched on my haunches at the edge of the outcropping, I opened my mouth and made an animal sound. The first time, I let out a moan in a low throaty voice that I thought sounded like nothing I ever heard afore. I have no idea why I felt this urge, but I repeated it over and over 'til it was more like a growl that got louder and louder. It felt so good I craved repeating it. Then, I got inspired to jump up and down and scrunch my face into a ferocious mask when I growled. And that felt great, too. Acting this way musta been some sort of emotional release, 'cuz tears started streaming down my face.

The more I cried, the more my growling became like howling then crying then howling then heart-wrenching sobbing and finally, finally, finally I fell into stillness. I think my body's biorhythms—or something—musta come to a standstill. In the loud silence that followed, the thought never entered my mind to move. I was like flinders of a shattered plate on a kitchen floor—or a popped birthday balloon.

Between Silence and Sound

What miracles lie between silence and sound
in oh-so-soft, precious spaces profound
where chatter and clatter are absent
and time with its pressures isn't
when life passes so swiftly
in momentous humility

I dunno how long I lay on the ground. I do know that's when I became aware of a new stillness that was like peace. It bathed me with healing powers. The quiet musta also given permission to nearby woodland creatures to pick up on their daily business. I reckon those forest creatures know to respect a fellow animal's angst. Once I pulled back into my body, they returned to their natural affairs and that's how I got to see a busy field mouse skitter by—probably scavenging for her brood back at the nest—and a hawk circling above—probably over a nearby carcass—afore coasting to a tall pine to stand guard afore swooping down again. I also spied a preoccupied porcupine waddling through the brush. I think the forest was revealing its true self.

Time passed. A clock mighta said an hour—but it felt like nothing more than fleeting moments to me. When I opened my puffy eyes, I was in the same place and not dreaming. Another day was progressing and I still had the same set of challenges with my energy sapped. What little was left, however, helped me get down the other side of the mountain from the fire. Even though my sore feet didn't wanna work, my rubbery legs did manage to hold me up. Soon, every painful step became a battle with a thorny thicket.

Eventually, lady luck found me. I came on what I think was a ruffled grouse nest in a huge, old decomposing log. I noticed it after flushing a squawking mother outta nearby grasses. Moving fast, she looked like a grouse anyways. Bending over to investigate the log, I realized how light-headed I was. I almost fell over. But, among all the worms and crawly things, I saw a most welcome sight—two warm eggs. Without any hesitation or guilt, I popped their insides into my mouth, one right after the other, afore dropping the shells back into the log for the insects to feast on. Then, not only my spirits lifted—so did my determination.

"I'm a proven and true survivor and I'm gonna make it. I'm gonna make it and I'm gonna live free in my world," I shouted for all the forest to hear. Feeling energized and giddy, I continued through the dense undergrowth on my search for some kinda meaningful buncha water. My mind stayed focused on always going downhill. I paid no heed to north, south, east or west. Just down, down, down to whar water hadda be.

I'm sure y'all can get how directions are hard to figure in the North Carolina mountains. Anyone plunging through dense underbrush, climbing over boulders and fallen tree trunks, dodging overhanging branches, prickers, spiderwebs and slick snail trails, finds herself in one dank and dusky holler after another afore ascending another stark granite outcropping or coming back into the heavy coolness of overhanging paw paws, red maples, birches, whatever. I can't tell you how many different kinds of trees are in those ridges. At times, I was surrounded by total silence that trees provide and then, at others, I was buried in the calls of birds. I mean multitudes of birds. Another thing—shadows that help tell time and direction are hard to find in dark heavy vegetation. So, it was my instinct and impulse that guided me.

It was late afternoon and I was still trudging through prickery shrubs in a basin on some animal trail I came on when the hairs on my naked body began to lift. My skin was feeling an ever-increasing coolness and, even though the day was still mild—the temperature agreeable and all—I was shivering. At first, I allowed as if it was excitement or fear. But thar was more than the softening ground that convinced me I was nearing water—it was that smell—musky, I guess you'd say. Gradually, I felt moisture in the air, too. When my feet got to feeling cold is when my heart skipped a beat and I speeded up my groping through thick bushes and blackberry brambles.

Then, my wandering eyes became wondering eyes feasting on what seemed a mirage. A mirage in a jungle? Well, it wasn't. What it was, was really blue-green water shimmering in the speckled sunlight that seeped through the overhanging branches. It didn't take me one single second to begin wading through the grasses on the shore. I carefully stepped out on the mud bottom far enough to sink my body. All my concentration was on that water. All that mattered in the world was thar.

My lucky wanderings had led me to a gorgeous, spring-fed pond—something rare in that part of the Smokies. Anyways, all's I know to do is what they call a breaststroke, so that's what I did as far and as long as the spirit moved me. I dipped my head under the surface, took in large gulps and gargled in sheer delight—sometimes kicking and splashing like a baby. I even laughed out loud, thinking how I finally did find my way to heaven. When I heard my laugh come back at me, I began imitating birdcalls and listened to them coming back afore trying out my growl. I laughed and laughed when I heard myself growling at myself. 'Course, my laughs echoed back, too. I didn't care how much noise I was making. I was having a ball.

After playing and drinking, diving and ducking, swimming and floating in the crisp water, I came to realize how I was shivering from head to foot—partly from cold and partly from feeling scared. So, I returned to that same spot and waded through the same grass back to that animal trail, taking just a moment to see my reflection in the water and notice the ripples radiating out from me, questioning if maybe I was inside a dream. I couldn't decide if my discarded life was the dream or this new existence was. I ended up telling myself it was more like I was between worlds—maybe even in two dreams at the same time.

I was shaking water from my hair when my eyes fell on something absolutely extraordinary I'd overlooked afore. It was an amazing spectacle, really—a lean-to next to a stocked woodpile—obviously an abandoned campsite. Somebody from the outside world had been here afore me—maybe running from what Walter Cronkite called "Communism" or that new invention, television. My heart pounding, I searched in the shadowy light for anything to eat, but 'course thar was nothing. The only lucky thing my hand fell on was a rusted old tin. After banging it on a rock, I was able to unscrew it and found inside three wooden matches safe and dry.

My heart jumped. I rushed 'round gathering a few dry leaves and a handful of twigs to jumpstart a fire. Once I got it lit, I fed it with nearby fallen branches 'til I made a solid blaze. After some time squatting and staring into the fire, my eyes began to sting from the dryness and the front of my hair got boiling hot. Hooving a sigh, I reflected on this day and swept myself up in self-praise. Whattaya know, I managed to make it through a second day of freedom all on my own. Indeed, I was a tried and true survivor. And now, even though fire destroyed my former life—here, in my new one, it was my blessed salvation.

Even though fire was second best to water, its warmth soothed my sorry body and made me realize how tired I was. I didn't have anything to cover my nakedness. I hadda spend the night tending the fire, turning from side to side to even out the cold-damp and hot-dry. And again this night, I was mostly awake—my mind full of wonder of both my personal dilemma and my new surroundings. I know I musta been in shock, but all's I felt then was a determination to find a way back to some kinda normal—to feeling good being me.

More'n once during that night, I got a glimpse of the truth that in this new life of mine things were coming at me in one extreme or another—either hot or cold, raw or overdone. Nothing was turning out to be mild, medium, or middle-of-the-road. Since then, I learned that many thoughts running together make a jumble, but this particular night taught me that, in this new life, it wasn't gonna do me any good to pit one extreme against the other. Thar was gonna be both good 'n bad and I shouldn't attach to just the bad.

And so, for the second time that day, I found strength inside myself. My isolation probably prompted these deep thoughts. Anyways, I settled into a gentler frame of mind and my aura—or whatever—musta showed that, 'cuz the animals tending to their nightly needs didn't bother me. I know—I spent the whole night listening to the frogs sing their hearts out.

So, here's where we better break, because what comes next was real different and it'll be a while afore y'all will wanna break. Grab another cup and come on back....

PART 3

Ablaze

a-da-we-li-di-s-gv

Oh my, did you happen to get some of that delicious frybread—what I call doughnuts? Mm-m, aren't they the best? Now, everybody, get real comfortable for a most amazing thing. Try to put yourself in my skin to see how I felt then and when it came back, ten years later. Okay?...

Early next morning, a mighty bird chorus reminded me whar I was. I jumped up from my bed of earth, sweeping myself clean of the clinging leaves and shaking my mess of hair pondering what I was gonna do next. I was muddling how to douse the coals so's not to start another fire, when my eyes fell on that pile of cut wood. Why, I could use a strip of bark to carry water from the pond! It was just then that my insides cramped—a real sharp pain, too. Something different was in the air—like danger—I—I could feel a new presence. I even tasted it in my mouth—almost smelled it. My skin started to crawl, then the backa my neck tingled and I shivered, which got worse when the hairs on my arms lifted. It was like I was sharing time and place with some other being. But how could that be? I was miles away from any road or house or town. Plenty of birds were 'round and most probably lotsa other animals I couldn't see. I even gave a hard look for snakes. Was I just feeling nervous 'bout being alone?

No-o-o, what I was getting was an energy. And I thought, if I was sensing a presence, the other must know 'bout me, too. Perhaps the other was watching me even if I couldn't see it. I reckoned I knew whar this energy was coming from, but a long consideration in that direction revealed nothing but bushes. It was like I was a storybook girl lost in the big bad woods with fero- cious animals, ya know, and I wanted to be rescued. Anyways, I opened my mouth again and again—I wanted to cry out, but noth- ing would come out. I suppose this was kinda funny—me standing staring at trees in all my nakedness with my mouth opening and shutting—but it wasn't to me. I could hear "Who's thar?" in my head, but my ears couldn't hear anything coming from my my mouth. And none of those trees were talking, neither.

Well, since absolutely nothing was happening, I tried speak- ing another time and, this time, from the backa my throat came a low—guess what you'd call a guttural sound—really more like a pathetic version of the growling I did already—but really more like Goldilocks pretending to be the big bad wolf. Thar was no reply. Finally, I put it in my mind that thar was nothing I could do 'bout this situation. Whatever was hiding hadda be a timid forest creature and it was best not to fret. After all, I was now a forest creature, too.

I busied myself peeling off from a dry log a nicely-curved strip of bark and then went and scooped outta the pond 'bout three cupfuls of water. Clutching the bark tightly between my arms, I hadda walk slowly and carefully, arms straight out in front and hands together plugging the other end, watching my every footstep. When I leaned over to spill the water on the hot coals, my breasts fell forward and that's when I distinctly heard a rustling in the bushes—sorta like they were shaking with laughter. And that was most disturbing. I can laugh now, too—but believe me—back then I froze with fear, 'cuz I was now one hundred percent sure the energy coming from those bushes was human.

Standing thar in the open, naked as a newborn baby, I could tell I was being watched. It came on me that I needed to pretend to *not* be nervous or terrified, like I really was. I hadda act confident, even if it meant faking it. So, on my next four trips, I made sure to spill my breasts over the dying fire and bob them up and down, bouncing them for every last drop. I was testing those bushes. And you're chuckling... But every time I came to the fire, I took pains to face the spot whar the rustling sound was. Yeah, I even chuckled at how I was maybe flirting with saplings. It did flash through my head maybe I was losing my mind—maybe from not having anything in my stomach. This sure was nothing I woulda *ever* done afore. By the time I got the ashes to hissing, only one more trip seemed necessary.

Approaching the fire the last time—all bent over—I was so concentrating on placing each step that I almost missed the totally-unexpected sight greeting me. Thar, on the fornenst of the fire—standing strong with their arms folded—were three men grinning at me. Honest.

Well, my nerves had been tested beyond their bounds and the shock had a most strange effect on me. I dropped my load I was laughing so hard. I was so relieved! I wanted to break the silence by saying something like, "Well, you're sure a welcome sight" or "Oh, can ya help me out please?" or "Hello, I'm-I'm, uh, I don't rightly know what to say—Guess ya can... well, call me Renee. Yep, I'm reborn, so I'm Renee. And, dear folks, who are y'all?" These and so many other thoughts raced 'round inside my head, but I was too choked up to let anything out.

The men stared at me, eyes twinkling, as I nodded my head to each of them but I got nothing back. Not knowing what else to do, I offered to shake hands, but their arms stayed folded. Here I was, not alone anymore, but my saviors just stood there silently. Finally, desperate to communicate, I rubbed my stomach and pretended to be chewing. That they got, 'course, and they mumbled to each other in soft strange sounds I couldn't understand afore they disappeared into the bushes and sprinted back with an animal carcass I couldn't identify. Its head was chopped off and the fly-covered fur gave off a ripe smell.

One glance stole my hunger, but the men went to work like they knew what they were doing and my stomach began growling as soon's the cooking aromas started. They brought my near-dead fire back to life afore peeling the skin off the raunchy being. Big chunks of flesh were skewered onto green branches and what looked like seasonings came outta the pouches hanging on their belts. With the meat cooking, they shook nuts down from trees— what looked like chestnuts to me—and roasted them. I giggled these were those things called appetizers. I didn't understand all what was going on, but surely enjoyed watching.

Right off, I envied their comfort with forest life and how they could work together without words. I sat by the fire pretending to be tending it even though I hadda keep moving my place—seems the fire was bent on sending its smoke direct to me wharever I sat. I tried to take in everything 'bout these beings discovered in the wilderness.

They all wore the same kinda jeans and vests and sandals, but each one was different—one kinda small, one middle-sized, and one kinda big. All had darkish skin and shiny, almost-black hair. Only the middle-sized one's hair was so long it was tied in a ponytail. Two had large dark-brown lively eyes, but the middle-sized man's face was lined and he had the most intense blue-gray-green eyes I ever laid eyes on. I could hardly take my eyes offa them. The largest had the biggest muscles and seemed to be in charge. The smallest was always smiling and nodding his head as he worked and he moved fast. The middle-sized one wore a shy smile as he quietly went 'bout. I just couldn't figure out how these handsome creatures happened to be here in this humungous forest in the first place. Besides which, how likely was it that they came along and saved me from starving? My brain was aching with thoughts. *Hunger's easy, but how can I ask 'em for help? We can't talk. Criminies, here it is 1960 in North Carolina in the United States of America, so whyever don't they speak English? Wherever can they come from?*

Something sprang from outta the backa my mind—something 'bout the universal appeal of music. I heard of it on the radio once. Maybe it was time to try out the theory. Anyways, I began humming something Gram used to sing to me—a sweet, simple, little tune. I actually found my voice—I did—and I sang softly. I noticed the men listening. Our mood relaxed. Then, the middle-sized man broke into a chant that caused the others to laugh and I laughed along with them. I dunno why. It just felt good.

I remember looking into the dancing flames and seeing a man without a face waving a large knife, writhing and turning, then rising up with the flames. When it seemed he was gonna leap out at me, I jumped back waving my arms like as if a spark had landed in my lap. I was most pleased to see all three men jump to help me. Nothing more happened with that, but I couldn't easily shake the image. I let my eyes again lose focus in the hypnotic flames.

When the smell of roasting meat became too delicious to resist, everyone gathered 'round on the ground. I wanted to dig right in, but the men didn't. I thought they weren't hungry, but their staring at me was like I was the answer to their dreams, maybe like their queen or goddess, I dunno. At first, I couldn't eat with all that staring. Far-off thunder sounded and they drummed the ground in answer, then spoke in words I'd never heard afore. I just couldn't wait any longer—I dove in. After what you could call my "harrowing escape" from two fires and all that happened afore that I haven't explained—yet—here I was with other humans and I was gonna live. I nibbled and gnawed at the tough fibers and smiled at them as they continued gazing.

After some time of polite smiling all 'round, the tallest one leaned over to me. I had meat in both hands and didn't move. He nodded his head and looked to the ground. I didn't know the right thing to do, so I nodded and smiled back and continued to chew. I figured we were expressing satisfaction with the food and I was being polite. When the others saw me nod, they jumped on the tall one, speaking gruffly in guttural phrases with "Whnh" sounds.* Then, afore I knew it and, totally unexpectedly, it was two against one wrestling next to the fire. At first, I was transfixed, but when the middle-sized man took the tallest one's head in his hands and banged it on the ground, a sudden terror arose in my chest. I shot up to the sky screaming at the toppa my lungs as I pulled my hair. Truly, I think I shot right into craziness. The men froze.

Holding my hair sideways, I blathered, "Stop! Stop! Stop it! Stop-p-p!" It's all I could say and I repeated it in pain. But I was thinking, *What's goin' on here? Nothing's worth killin' for. I'm sure not worth it. I'm just trouble. I'm always trouble. Everything gets ruined 'round me. Please, God, not again. Please let 'em go back to whatever they were doin' afore I came along. Get 'em away from me. I take it back, all back. Go, go, go. If you don't leave me, I'll leave you.* And then—without realizing I was 'bout to make a decision—I shouted for the whole world to hear, "That settles it. I'm outta here!"

Bawling and bug-eyed, nostrils flaring, I charged headlong into the woods—to what I didn't know and cared less. Behind me, the men wordlessly brushed theirselves off and tracked me. I led a parade through the woods with my voice loudly complaining to the trees and bushes and birds and anything else that might be 'round 'bout how this life was no better than the last, how things never ever got better for me no matter what I did, how disaster was attached to my body, how things were never gonna get better no matter whar I went, how I knew this now and how I hadda get

---

* Some of the listeners laughingly mutter to themselves, "Oh yes."

outta this life now, too. I was quite unaware they were following and listening to my "angst." What made my misery mighta been a mystery to them, but my pain was clear.

Since I didn't know the animal trail I was walking led me in a path circling the pond, what seemed to me to be another pond really wasn't. I walked right in again—this time, to rid myself of all the new toxicity I was carrying. You can see how washing was becoming a never-ending problem. Wading up to my waist, I jumped in and noticed hundreds of birds startle. Paddling along the shore made it easy to flush out those settling into cozy spots for the night. I swam directly toward one cluster that took off into the air chattering their complaints only to settle again at a safe distance.

Just when coldness came on me, something in the water grazed my foot ever-so-lightly, giving me a jolt. It wasn't hard enough to be a rock. I kicked again in the direction of the whatever, but didn't touch anything. Then, another underwater brush came against my leg, only this happened at the very same moment thar was a sudden clap of thunder. I panicked. I have no idea what that-all was, but I kicked frantically, screaming and swimming fast as I could. It wasn't 'til I was almost back at shore that I saw the middle-sized one jump in the water. Afore I knew it, he was with me and I was asking for his help.

He held onto me 'til we were outta the water. I was shaking so much the tall one took holda me and murmured in deep, low sounds strange to my ear some sorta explanation 'bout the thing in the water. 'Course I didn't understand a word he said. I was just glad to be back with them. Putting together when these strangers didn't understand my screaming 'round the fire and then at the water, I realized that even though they didn't know the source of my pain, they sure seemed like most-caring people. On toppa my exhaustion, this made me trust them.

We rubbed ourselves almost dry and filed back to the campfire to finish up the meat sheltered by the lean-to. Thunderstorms are never good for sleeping, though, and that was true that night. We lay on the ground to wait it out. Seems funny now—how we arranged ourselves so our heads were on others' bellies with our feet staying nicely outta faces. If a passerby had seen us, I'm sure we woulda looked like littermates.

Their warmth and strong energies were comforting. I relaxed. When the storm calmed, I sat up and pointed to my chest with both hands, "Renée. Renée. Renée." I liked this name—sure better than my old one. Stretching both my hands toward the tall one's chest, I lifted my eyebrows and turned my head sideways—like this. Laughing as the words came out, he answered, "Asha. Asha." I didn't pay mind to the others' chuckling. I repeated "Asha" with my hands on his chest afore returning my hands to mine and repeating my new name. He placed both his hands on my chest saying "Renee" and I figured we were introduced. I turned to the others and, without their touching me, they were most jovial saying they were "Aban" and "Atar." Soon's they did, Asha signaled me to follow him and I did.

I didn't know why the others stayed behind 'til the next day when I saw the place whar we had a fire, ate and waited out a storm—it looked like no one ever stepped foot. Right off, I learned that cleaning up after meals is most important to survival in the wilderness.

Asha led me up an animal trail on a path he clearly knew. On higher and drier ground, he guided me into a clearing where I spied a steep rock ledge. And you can bet that's when I halted. I could make out the trail was leading up to what looked like the opening of a cave high over the clearing. When he didn't hear me behind, he turned. I shook my head. He came back and wrapped me in his arms, rocking me back and forth, back and forth. Even though I was shivering, he made me feel enveloped inside a world of strength. Lost in his muscular arms and soothed by his body, my tears began to flow as he rhythmically crooned in a soft voice. We swayed back and forth 'til I was warm and soft inside. Hard rain began to bounce off our heads and shoulders, so he steered me ever-so-slowly up the ledge trail, never letting go of my hand 'til we were at the top and peering into the mouth of the cave. I followed him into the dark with my stomach in my mouth. It felt like I was in some strange dream.

Inside, he fluffed an animal hide over a cane mat on toppa some dried grasses mixed with leaves and downy feathers. At first, this all seemed more like a giant bird nest than anything, but when I fell down onto it I discovered it was the most comfortable bed I could want. I melted into it and was immediately warmed by a coupla pelts he set on toppa me. Soon, I was sleeping like a baby.

I woke up later and looked 'round in the dark. It wasn't possible to make out anything precisely, but I could hear three deep breathers. Looking up through a crack in the roof of the cave, I saw a tiny light. I faced the cave opening and spied a clear sky full of twinkling stars—a rare experience in our parts—then rolled over onto an anonymous warm friend. I pulled the pelt over my shoulders, tucking it under my chin with a full heart. I couldn't sleep, though, so I ventured another look outside and peered down on the scene below. My new bedroom was high over a clearing obviously made after some old trees fell. I could hear a small stream rippling and could see the moon's reflection in the moving water. It was the loveliest sky I ever did see. It got my mind wondering where I was and why and, most of all, who I was with. A passing cloud closed the curtain and I got to feeling cold and tired again.

Bejeweled

The night fell on my eyes
adorned in precious jewels
A pearly moon lit up the cobalt blue
crystalline and diamond-studded sky
A silver sheen cast on the glistening air
before opalescent clouds slid by

When I squeezed my eyes open next morning, all three were looking at me. I tried to rouse myself, but they crawled back into our bed. Again, I was swept up with this new feeling that the universe centered 'round me. Instinct told me what could happen. But I felt a call from nature, so I put on a serious frown and motioned to the doorway. Asha—always the gentleman—led me down the path and stayed 'round while I tended to my function. When I was done, he came to me with a buncha leaves he carried back to the cave.

I gotta admit I was beginning to like being the main attraction. I let them massage my body with the leaves. It felt like a spiritual bath. When we finally got up, all my anxiety was gone. We climbed down the ledge trail together and went back to the pond whar I watched the men face the sun and sing a song afore they waded in and washed. I watched the first day, copied them the second day and thrived on it every day after. This pleased them and they taught me the word for water, *A-ma*. I began using it right off. I began to feel honored witnessing their prayers and ceremonies, even though I had no idea what-all they meant. But thar was no doubt in my mind now—these men hadda be Indians (what I called 'em back then). After a short conference, the three formed a circle and performed another ceremony afore two left to search for food, as they motioned with their hands. Asha and I stayed to gather kindling.

I quickly found I could follow their thinking. They spoke in soft and low tones—softer than anybody in my family. I saw right off they spoke slower than I did and I was impressed at how good we were at communicating without a language. Watching them make rituals outta daily duties made me wonder how an alien watching me back home in my normal doings would see me? It's something to think 'bout, isn't it?

Asha, the big one I considered "my man" 'cuz of how things went—even though I wasn't drawn to him more'n the others—he became distracted trying to trap newts downstream. I got bored so I went back to the cave. I took the narrow trail up the side of the steep hill all by myself and sat down to think on my new life, but I couldn't concentrate. An inner voice said I needed flowers. So, I scurried back down the ledge—again by myself—on a search for some. Tromping through last year's grasses—a field where thar was enough sun for grass—I was on the lookout for anything blooming. I came across only a few small white flowers with tiny yellow centers and a kinda strong smell that didn't please me.

My search for flowers was fruitless, but I did find something really amazing. On the far side of the clearing, I entered a thicket and happened to spy under an old pine tree something odd-shaped that struck me as outta place. It was manmade. Up close, I could see it was a leather satchel with a broken strap. It'd obviously been thar a long time; the seams fell apart when I picked up the rotten old leather smelling like mold. My heart beat wildly when I investigated the insides. I found what hadda be more'n three hundred dollars in old bills, all lined up and packed neat and orderly—looked like they were put in thar brand new. Yes! Then I peered down deeper to see a neatly-folded, yellowed tablecloth and six matching napkins that looked like linen—probably also new when put in the bag—the folds seemed never to have been broken afore—and a ribbon made it into a bundle. I unwrapped the tablecloth, then wrapped it again—this time on me—like I was a Roman lady. I took a few minutes strutting 'round on my tippy toes, looking behind to see how it swirled. Never afore did any piece of cloth seem so special. I scooped it all up and—clutching my new cape 'round my neck—danced back to where Asha was still stalking.

He looked up startled and let out a loud guffaw. He rose to hug me and I held out the money begging him to "Look, look." My mind was full of food and soap we could buy, but he returned to his stakeout, totally uninterested. Let down, I took my treasure up to the cave and—smiling all the while—I folded the money inside the napkins inside the tablecloth and buried them all in the middle of the large nest-bed as safe-keeping for who-knew-what.

The others returned with a rabbit they killed with a blow gun—their hand signs said—and they set 'bout using their flint to start a cooking fire at the campsite. Dandelion greens, fiddleheads and ramps from the marsh near the pond made a tasty salad and we shared our yummy meat 'bout two hours later. As usual, the meal ended with a major clean-up. I came to understand a meal wasn't complete 'til the gound was returned to normal, which included sweeping it to remove footprints. I never got tired seeing how the men kept that area so undisturbed that nobody could possibly know they were ever thar. First, they dropped leftover bones and skins into the pond, then broke a reed from the water's edge and used the slimy insides to remove any animal scent on them. Later on, I saw hides from their kills hung up to dry in the trees. In everything they did, the men were... well, I guess the right word is "meticulous." It's probably why we were spared wild creatures visiting us.

And these men... Even now, thinking on each one, I smile. I admired and enjoyed them all in their own ways. Asha was sorta regal, probably why he was the leader. He walked upright with pride and dignity. His deep voice was confident and calm. It spoke of considerable experience and I saw the respect he got. Most importantly, he decided I was his. I liked that.

One thing I noticed was they didn't look me in the eye very much. Mostly, when they talked to me, they'd be looking to the ground or somewhere off. I say this 'cuz of Atar's eyes. He was the middle one and had his own look. Even though his hair was the same shiny, dark hair and his face had the same structure, his eyes were really different. They spoke of different genes. When he was tired, they seemed like... well, I guess I'd say "portals" to a deep soul. And when he got sexually roused, they became bottomless pools of passion. I hadda look to him when they were discussing things—his eyes flashed the meaning. Even when just talking, they sparkled. His eyes and the crinkly lines 'round them haunted me ever since. But more'n that—he was the most gentle, considerate and protective one. He treated me almost like a father. 'Course I didn't know how old any of 'em was; I just sensed he was the oldest. On the other hand, he was the most adventurous, too. He always got things done.

Last, but definitely not least, was Aban. His body was small, but he was large in generosity and kindness and thoughtfulness. He always responded the most to my moods and—when my depression took hold—he was the one to brighten my days. He could whistle like any bird in the forest and liked to attract birds into the campsite to entertain me. He made jokes that his buddies enjoyed. I liked his spirit, even though I couldn't understand his humor. The more I laughed, though, the more he tried to please me. He was what-you-call a trickster. His favorite trick was setting a frog or a toad loose under the covers after we made ourselves comfortable. Then, the frog or toad would come into my hair or my armpit or somewhar, making for so much fun and giggling. He coulda been like a caboose on a train—but no—his personality found a special spot in my heart that always skipped a beat when he came 'round.

Afore I tell you how I came to leave the woods, I wanna explain a bit more of what it was like. First off, the men went at life by sharing responsibilities. Right off, they made it my job to start each day shaking and airing out the bedding. I gladly accepted. That way, I could keep my buried treasure undiscovered. Luckily, Asha never seemed to remember it. I considered wearing the tablecloth, but decided to stay naked. It was doing its job of feeding my feeling of freedom. Also, 'cept for nights, it suited the mild weather. Sometimes my skin shivered with goose bumps, sometimes with itches or scratches, but I got to appreciate the energizing stimulation. Nights weren't a problem—the men and the mountain of hides kept me warm. Another positive part of being naked was how my new friends showed their approval with looks, smiles and touches. I was getting so much delight from all this that covering my body was a disappointing thought. As for money and linen napkins—they did seem kinda ridiculous in this world.

My happy and safe life went on like this for quite a few days— I dunno how many. I didn't have a place to go, so I didn't count. I needed time to heal and didn't want this to ever end. 'Bout the eleventh day, maybe, we woke up to pouring rain that lasted the whole day, so we stayed in the cave singing and playing a gambling game the men taught me. It was the first day I made love with them. It was beautiful and wonderful.

Every day, I could feel the days longer and the air warmer. Spring was in full bloom. The abundant birds made each day a spectacle and the animal sounds at night made them adventures. Seems the most common animal visitors were birds, deer and bears—leastwise, as far as I could tell. I heard bears somewhars in the distance lotsa times, but only once did one try to climb our rock cliff. The men were instantly up, shouting and banging on the rocks to scare him. I was relieved this wasn't fall when they most likely were looking for a place to hibernate. All in all, the animals were peace-loving 'round the pond.

One morning, I was airing the covers outside and found I was menstruating. Aban, the little one, came upon me as I was cleaning myself.

"Aban, look. I need—please."

"Whnh."

Ya know, I never gave a thought to the linen napkins stashed away in the cave. Guess that's how important they were!

I did use some English words with my friends from time to time, but they spoke to me in a kinda sign language, mixed sometimes with a few words in their language. They taught me some they used in daily life. Seeing blood running down my leg didn't require words, though. Aban raised a finger in the air and ran off to fetch some kind of spongy material. He showed me how to fasten this 'tween my legs and 'round my waist with vines. Then, he led me to the pond to perform a ceremony whar he washed hisself. He insisted I do it, too, afore returning to the cave—probably so thar'd be no animal visitors. I saw how during the next few days the men washed after being near me. Here again, I was always in awe at their skill and knowledge. In quieter moments, I sometimes wondered who they were and why they were in this place without somewhar's to go. It seemed so incredible I found them—or they found me. Whatever.

The night I got my period was sleepless for everyone. The men took turns staying by the mouth of the cave. The next day, as I was eating my wild berries and nuts, the men told me in motion and sound that had many "Whnhs" that they were leaving and wouldn't be back 'til sundown. I thought it was to get food and my hunger was aggravated by my period, so I looked forward to their success. I didn't know if they were truly in search of food or just wanted to keep their distance. Whatever. Atar left a sharpened pole for a weapon if I needed it and indicated I was to stay in the cave. The others set aromatic green branches in the doorway to disguise my scent. They left dried meat to chew on.

The day alone gave me plenty of time to ponder. I talked to myself just to hear my voice—I missed my language. And I also wanted to walk, so I ventured out—my stick in my hand—to get more familiar with the land 'round me.

On one swipe of the hill, I climbed up to a natural lookout rock whar I could see in three directions. Peering into the far-off mountaintops draped in light blue mist that day, I'm sure I saw farm fields and perhaps a twist of road. It was like I was in space. I saw a pick-up kick up dust afore it disappeared into another world. That caused me to recall Poppa's old pick-up that was left to me. I musta stayed in this spot for 'bout an hour, allowing what I left behind, remembering it through a different sorta mist.

I thought, *My body's sitting so near my past but my spirit's flying so far off.* This day helped me appreciate that my previous life was still inside me. Everything back thar pushed forth in a huge rush of awareness so fast that my brain couldn't match words to my feelings. I couldn't hang onto all the memories. The person I was becoming and the person I left behind were most different, but here I was connecting with what you could call the… "essence" of the person I used to be. It got me swept up into feeling like another person—a third one—sorta like the two had melted together to make somebody new. It was true, I really didn't know who I was and who I was supposed to be. And I couldn't help it—I let out long moans to the heavy unfeeling clouds.

Permission to Cry

It's okay to cry now
at last you're all alone
No one'll hear you moan
They can't hear the groans
oozing from your bones
It's okay to cry now
away from frights, painful nights, ugly fights
Your life is spared as if they cared
It's okay to cry now
to bare your inside
No sins to hide, no need for pride
no time to bide
It's okay to cry now
You won't lose face
no one in the place
not even near
Walls don't care. Can't even hear
So, it's okay to cry now
to take off the masks
that fake questions asked
a monumental task
Even better you cry now
to shed that inner tension
and pay yourself attention
not forgetting to mention
to discover the Why now

My mind spun into endless other questions like: *What does "being" mean? What is a human "being?" Are humans just animals? Can we "be" more than once? Have I lived afore as another "being?" Is it possible to connect to a former life and "be" in a new life?* I walked as I tried to understand it all. I think this is when I really started changing. Finally, the hours passed and the sun was 'bout to leave and my tired mind began to fight with an angry stomach. I picked a bunch of wild daisies and made a little puddle off the side of the stream to set their stems in afore climbing back up to the cave.

Sometime later, huddled up listening to the forest sounds, I heard feet climb up the rocks. In the pale moonlight from the doorway, I saw they were wearing laughter on their faces and success on their chests. Along with the familiar "Whnhs," they pushed in my face what seemed like a garden of greens and their pouches bulged with roots and fruits. They also produced a fish, a black snake and a fawn they hung high in a tree for a later time. It was quite a day for all of us.

The men made a smoke fire and smoked my body with tobacco afore our meal of nuts and greens. When they left to clean themselves at the water, I fell onto the bed, but even though my stomach and heart were feeling better, my mind remained tormented. That night, I went from one dream to another whar I was traveling strange roads in strange countries, passing through foreign cities, encountering all sortsa friendly and hostile people all speaking languages I couldn't understand. I mighta been thar, but they didn't see me. When I spoke, they acted like as if they couldn't hear me. I didn't find one place I could relate to.

My emotions mighta been changing a bit, but my body was still naked. And nakedness isn't easy. We humans cover up for a good reason—our skin is tender. By now, my body had gotten quite bruised, cut and scratched from one thing or another. My feet were sore and riddled with thorns and cuts and I was covered with insect bites. The best they could, my friends found remedies— like lemon balm to drive mosquitoes away and tea tree leaves to rub on my bites. I appreciated their considerateness, but my skin wasn't good. It wasn't being naked that was the problem—it was the problems that come from nakedness.

Thar were other nights I didn't sleep well, neither. Ya see, during dark hours, animals compete and fight and mate and stalk and kill and all these sounds echo in the trees. Then, too, my food wasn't what I was accustomed to and was hard on my digestion. Even the amount wasn't what I was used to. I learned to eat things I'd never thought to eat—even snakes. We had them a coupla times and I gotta say they weren't my favorite—too bony. Plants became better sources of food as days passed. Soon's the men taught me what plants to gather, another duty of mine was foraging while theirs was hunting. It was our routine. Only one day we couldn't find enough food to satisfy our tummies and hadda chew on insects and a few minnows scooped outta the stream that we steamed inside leaves over hot rocks. My body was slimming down on our diet, which was fine, but my stomach talked—especially in the night.

And it was then when pain came to live with me. Like my beautiful men, pains from my past came back unexpectedly— mostly at night, but some days too. My new friends, these three wonderful human beings in my new life, continued to provide for me. But still, I sometimes got to staring off in the woods or gaze down from my rocky perch onto the distant road looking for cars. One time, I broke into tears when I heard a plane in the sky. I sat for long hours, recalling hurts.

I don't remember revisiting the ugly memories from the farm—guess I wasn't ready for that—but I did remember the meanness of kids calling me Zebra for Zena—short for Zenobia. I could see the faces of the girls who shut me out on the playground. Silly me—I spent too much time wallowing in past miseries instead of drinking in my blissful present.

"I'm Renee Nada now 'cuz I'm not really here. Y'all can call me Renee Nada, now."

My pleas were to the trees, though; the men didn't seem to understand my complaints—in fact, they seemed not to hear any of it. They called me "Nene." I took that as a take-off on Renee and I liked it.

Even though I didn't shed my new sadness, I did try to distract myself by focusing on the men and their pure lust for all that came their way. I saw how they gave their full energies to everything they did—they truly "lived in the moment." Life as it should be, ya know? When we were all together, I felt whole and complete. That's when I decided every person in this new life from then on hadda be considered important, because every single one mattered. I still believe it.

One day, I woke up especially sour and wiped my tears in front of the men. Aban was the first to notice. Asha then made it clear that I should go with 'em on the day's outing. I think what they went for was cone flowers—which wasn't in bloom yet—but they needed the roots to rub on Atar's leg. He'd got bit by a snake. I was glad for a diversion. Afore heading out, we rubbed our bodies with lemon balm to repel insects, then some kinda grease to mask our scent. I just followed instructions.

I hope you don't mind me repeating how I admired the way they solved problems and went 'bout their work—like how they led me through the overgrowth that day. Ya see, we weren't following a trail and—as they indicated in body language—we hadda move "under a whisper." They mostly used nature's sounds to avoid being discovered—like rain and wind and moving water. This day, however, they weren't stalking—just going to new places. We, or rather they, found the plant that looked to me like coneflower and Atar did get better. Also, being included turned my mood 'round.

Here's an upsetting part. We were sleeping one morning when the men startled me by bolting up and cocking their heads to the side. I finally heard the sounds, too. We stayed put, hiding from the deep voices 'til it was clear the visitors were gone. Asha climbed down to investigate and whistled when it was safe to join him. The campsite had been what you'd say "ransacked" and the matches taken. Plus, there was a human mess laying right thar atop the ground with insects buzzing all 'round. I saw disgust on the men's faces and heard in their voices how upset they were. We put the place back to order.

I learned so much from the men. Perhaps the most important lesson was that fire is a friend and also a tool. We always put our fires out after cooking, but sometimes took hot rocks back to the cave for cold or wet nights. That was nice. When I discovered a pile of dry wood under a rock overhang, they were stern I couldn't touch it and they let me tend a cooking fire only after one of them built it. I didn't understand what I know now—that this is an important tradition. Then, it only seemed they wanted to keep the smoke down and I didn't know to do that. They sure did. When insects hovered over one of their bloody kills, they also knew how to smoke 'em away. Anyways, fire had left me nasty memories, so I never gave any argument 'bout tending them. Luckily, the weather was on a warming trend and fire was more for cooking than warming.

I'm close to the end of the woodland part of my story, but I wanna tell you a coupla more things. Like I said, thar were a few days I didn't feel well—mostly in my stomach. The others usually made satisfied sounds while we were eating—anything, like if it was roast venison, fresh greens or grilled frogs—but I had lotsa belly problems after eating only steamed fiddlehead ferns or roasted cattails or—once—just rattlesnake meat. My stomach liked it when they made pennyroyal tea by placing hot rocks in a hollowed log. Most of all, I liked a roasted animal, when we all sat 'round the fire for a good while picking the bones off this creature who gave its life for us.

For fun? Well, sometimes we took breaks—ya know, like wrestling competitions when I'd be the audience. One evening afore dark we held a talent show inside the cave. The men took turns telling stories with arm movements and sound effects—each ending with a "Whnh" and the others answering "Whoa." It seemed I was almost like a fly on the wall or a hawk in the sky and it came back to me that in my former life Bud woulda said I was hanging out with nasty critters and here I was knowing that wasn't true. I thought of that hawk looking down with insight—it could see reality and truth like I was and we could share this understanding. Oh, how I wished I could explain this to my new friends. Once I got control of my giggles it was my turn to perform, but I didn't know what to do. Then, I remembered singing the first night and began grandma's song again. This time, the men hummed along. It was beautiful and unforgettable—makes me teary to think back.

Mostly I was happy, but I was getting restless. I had conversations with myself trying to talk away the bad thoughts, but truth was I was lonely as a pine tree in a parking lot. I did learn to communicate without speaking English and that was a thing I'd ever be grateful for and I did figure out some meanings of their words watching Atar's eyes—never allowing I'd ever use 'em again. Still, I yearned to talk to somebody—just to talk. I asked myself why was I struggling against simple happiness. Why couldn't I accept things the way they were? Now, I reckon it was because I was afraid of the future.

Well, I guess my "romantic odyssey"—like some say—went on for a day or two more and abruptly came to a halt one morning afore dawn when two riders charged into the clearing, each with two tethered horses following behind. They stopped right under the cave like they knew whar they were. The sound of approaching hoofs had got us all to the cave door, but my men whistled and called to the visitors like they knew them. This discovery that thar were more like mine really shocked me. I done totally blotted outta my mind that my men—my whole new life—that thar were others like 'em—that my men might belong with others. I took them in to have and hold for myself for as long as I wanted and needed and my bubble had just busted.

Why, I could never survive alone! What was gonna happen to me if my men left? Strangers came into my world and made me feel like an alien. My legs quivered. In my new life, I was supposed to live without fear. I was supposed to feel power in my freedom. I retreated inside the cave, feeling dizzy, but I peeked down to see them patting each other on their shoulders. Male voices making friendly sounds I couldn't understand told me the men were happy together. Just as clearly, though, I saw no place for me in this group.

Suddenly, I hadda do something, so I marched down the ledge to face my enemy—naked as a jaybird. Asha smiled and put his arm 'round me like he owned me while the newcomers' eyes twinkled as they looked me over. I shook off Asha's arm and waded into the water, walking upstream—sobbing—my head full of questions. *Who can they be? Then again, who am I? Who am I to them or to anyone? I thought I belonged to Asha. Aren't I special to him... or am I just a plaything again?* I walked in the cold water 'til my feet were numb.

The horses watched me with sad eyes, but it was Asha who came and took me by the hand up to the cave whar he set me down on the deerskin. The whole group squeezed in and it was tight in the cave. He tried to settle me down, but closer to the new men now, I didn't like their smells. I was used to the smells of my men. I didn't want these. My three brought out the leaves. Aban used his flirty wiles and Atar's eyes pierced my heart. Asha stroked my hair and around my ears. But things just didn't feel right. They left. After listening to them go off on the horses, I listened to the trickling of the stream; but it failed to charm me like usual. I couldn't get beyond emptiness. I finally fell asleep when the outside got as dark as inside and didn't hear them slip in.

Next morning, change hung heavy on the air. We went our separate ways. When Asha tried to give me a hug, I slipped from him. My world was under attack; I dunno why I couldn't adapt. I still wonder if there's a limit to love. What's so scary 'bout new stuff, anyways? Well, that's what happened and how I was. I aired the bedding, but I didn't leave the cave. I guess that's why I didn't see 'em go. In the quiet 'round midday, I climbed down to search for something to eat. I heard the gently-rippling stream and the occasional birdcalls echoing through the trees, but nothing else. It was quiet as never afore.

The sound of moving grass caused me a start. It was one of the horses, his tether dragging on the ground. The gentle way the pinto moved his well-groomed body told me he was friendly. I approached him and patted his fetters, talking softly, and he nuzzled my shoulder. I felt he would let me mount him. Then, like a real-life Lady Godiva, I rode across the clearing and into the woods to search for my family.

Coupla hours later, my horse found its way back to home base whar I let it graze. Two hours more and I was nibbling watercress from the stream. A coupla hours after that, I returned to the cave to sleep, but woke in the night to crawl to the doorway. Fireflies were flickering everywhar and, every time one lit up a spot of darkness, another thought flitted through my brain. I pondered who-all and what-all is out thar, how earth came to be, whar life comes from, whar we go after death, what heaven and hell are. I didn't sleep all night.

After one more long, lonely and hungry day, I left the safety of my home atop the horse I knew in my heart had been left for me. My eyes wide and wild, I set out naked—'cept for that tablecloth flowing backa me and what looked like a padded bra. One hand clinging to the horse's mane and the other grabbing the tablecloth at my neck, I musta made quite a picture.

Now, that's what happened in the woods, best I can recall. I think you can see how it affected me. It was dreamlike, but it really did lead to the next totally life-changing thing that transformed my life the most—afore all the bits and pieces started coming together. Come back to circle in ten minutes and I'll tell you 'bout it. During the break, I'll answer any questions I can...

PART 4

Smoke

u-ga-sv-s-da

Looks like most y'all are back now, so let's get right to this most-important part of my life. Ya know, I hear folks say "history was being made" in May 1960, 'cuz President Eisenhower went and signed the Civil Rights Act; but that meant nothing in my life—I didn't even know it happened. History gets wrote down 'bout some stuff and not others. My history was gonna be made on an Ashland farm, but no one'll ever read that in a book…

Folks tell me I'm a "hillbilly storyteller," but all's I wanna talk 'bout here is how the unforgettable Sophie Connors put the most influence into my life. Sophie called herself a "typical Ashlander," which she said meant "hard-working, dedicated to family and involved in the community." She was sitting at her kitchen table in the late afternoon, her head hanging forward and a widow's hump quite obvious, when I peeked in her back door and knocked.

"Whoosssat?"

My muffled words went unanswered, so I gave a second knock.

"G'wan. Don't want none." She whipped her head 'round to me—a most sorry sight. Jumping backwards at my unkempt shock of hair and wild bug-eyes popping outta my very tan face on the other side of the screen, she knocked her chair to the floor and placed her hands on the counter in backa her. "Git on outta here, witch, afore I call the po-lice," she yelled as she reached into the sink for the butcher knife she had the presence of mind to remember.

I wanted to explain, "Please. Wait. Wait, please. I'm not here to hurt you," but no words would come to me. I could only wave my hands back and forth and shake my head sideways.

"Git! Git out. Outta my house. Just git. Leave me alone. Out. Outta here!"

She shook and shouted and swept the air with the knife, but I set my heels on her stone stoop. She made her way across the room to close and lock the inner door, I guess, then got a better glimpse of me—most pathetic. She stopped. Like I said, I was as freaky as you could imagine—my dirty hair flying 'round my head and an old tablecloth tied 'round my shoulders. Oh, you can laugh, but the old lady sure didn't. She stuck her head forward like a turtle 'bout to pounce, then squinted at something in the distance afore realizing it was a horse munching on her flowers.

"Jist what-all are ya doin' here? Whattaya want anyways?" Her weapon continued to wave at the ceiling, her eyes the size of saucers.

Words still escaped me, but a wail did come out—a deep, long release of pain I couldn't stop. Sobbing took all my energy and I collapsed to my knees. I guess it was reconnecting with society that brought bubbling up to the surface my pent-up feelings. I

dunno. All's I know is I was near the end. The old woman waiting on the inside of the screen door seemed like she didn't know
what to do 'bout this odd circumstance. Even in my grief, I could
see on her creased face her keen eyes were blinking real fast. She
pushed her glasses back up to the bridge of her nose to squint
again at my splotchy pinto.

"Lookee here—that animal of yers, leastwise I'm thinkin' he's
yers—he's eatin' up all the flowers I set out only two days ago.
Lawsie, cain't ya see? Cain't ya git on out thar 'n stop him?"

You can believe I bolted like shot from a cannon. My horse,
'course, then bolted himself 'bout as far as from here to the cars
over thar. He was headed to the woods afore he stopped and
looked back, then continued grazing. I returned to her door to
stand tall in front of the old lady, tears streaming down my face,
my chapped lips chattering.

"What's goin' on anyways? Are ya here 'cuz ya needs somethin' or are ya in trouble or what?"

I nodded. Moments that seemed like hours passed while a
bevy of birds commented on the weather, the location of their
nests, the current food supply, passing predators, whatever. Thar
were so many—Baltimore orioles, nuthatches, barn swallows, ya
know—all sharing important messages that we didn't hear—botha
us being caught up in the silence.

Sophie finally sputtered, "Well, seems anyway—if ya needs
something simple like water or eats—ya better say it."

My answer was more to the ground than to her, "Yes'm. Just
a drink—drinkin' water, ma'am."

"Whah? Speak-on up girl!"

"I said I just need some cold water to drink and my horse—he needs it more'n I do."

"Well, if I'm hearin' ya right—'course, I'm never altogether sure 'bout that—why, lawzie, yer welcome ta water from my well. Heavens ta Betsy, that's jist a common rule of farm folk. See that thar bucket on the ground? Glory be, go 'n help yerself, both you 'n yer horse, if that's all ya want. Then, if ya tether him ta that thar post out in backa the barn, he won't get inta trouble with me no more. He can graze yonder—the grass is too high thar anyways—jist like he's doin' now. Fine by me. Then ya can come on back ta this door. I think I can find something fer ya ta eat, too. Looks like ya can use it."

Right then, something special happened between us. I think it slipped inside Sophie's empty and aching heart like it did mine. I saw her move with a sudden bursta energy I don't think she knew she had. Sophie later told me she hadn't experienced such as this in all her ninety-three years and she wasn't prepared to face such a shock as I was. Thar was only one time when a man's car had gone off the road and rolled upside down a quarter of a mile from her house—when he came to her door asking if he could use her phone. Otherwise, no one else had ever landed on her stoop.

I couldn't tease my horse to come, so I gave up the idea and chose to drink long and hard from the old woman's well afore I set out a bucket for him. I returned to her door feeling a bit calmer with my face and hands somewhat cleaner.

I totally forgot how clever a person on the inside of a country door could be. Sophie's generous spirit took me by surprise. I stood studying through the screen what manner of woman was scurrying 'round the kitchen. Considering the fact that she was somewhat frail, she slid her feet across the floor from fridge to cupboard to table to stove to sink almost as if she was doing a shuffle dance. 'Course I didn't know yet that Sophie's body was ravaged by arthritis—that she was a good four inches shorter than when she was my age. I noticed how she held her white-haired head forward as she peered through the thick lenses atop her nose and saw her clothes hanging on her like still in the closet. Her what you'd call "wizened" face wore a stern look as she muttered to herself. I watched her face light up as if she saw an angel, then go blank again.

Familiar signs jumped out at me, like water spitting outta a faucet; food outta an ice box—oops—fridge; dishes and silverware lifted from drawers and cupboards. It pleased me she made a setting for one on the oilcloth. Best of all, though, was the butter dropped onto her hot frying pan that made a mouth-watering aroma all the way to the door.

Without looking, Sophie knew I was back. "Well, whiskerkittens—don't just stand thar, young'n, come on in. This here's jist 'bout ready."

Feeling bashful 'bout my bare body inside her house, I wrapped my cape tightly 'round me and slid into a seat at the old wooden table afore Mrs. Connors placed two sunny-side-ups on a chipped white plate along with two slices of toast slathered with homemade strawberry jam. I searched for long-ago words like "daily bread" and "gratitude" from my former life and recalled the mysterious sounds my forest friends uttered at each meal, but just then my stomach let out an enormous growl and I dove right in.

Sophie's bent-over frame leaned against the sink as she watched me eat. She kept taking off her thick glasses to use her gnarled fingers to wipe her eyes with a dishtowel. She put both hands up to her temples to sweep stray strands of hair back from her face as if that would return them to the bun on the backa her neck. Guess she finally realized she wasn't imagining the scene, because she fetched an open package of store-bought cinnamon buns. Leaning over my shoulder, she set one on my empty plate and whispered in my ear, "Thar now, bless my soul, this'll make ya feel like ya died 'n went ta heaven."

That's when I found my voice. Instead of stuffing my mouth as I was most anxious to do, I looked up for the first time and peered into her eyes to sputter, "From the bottom of my heart I wanna thank ya for everything you just now went and did for me. Yer the most-kindest person thar ever was."

Sophie passed this off with a shrug. But, now that I had my voice, I couldn't stop. "I never thought to find such goodness when I came to your door, ma'am. Truly, I didn't know what to expect, but then I found what's gotta be the nicest person in the whole world and now I'm wearied I'm a bother to you. I'm nothin' but trouble, ya know."

"Yer whah? Speak on up. Cain't hear ya."

"I said I'm nothin' but a hunka trouble, ma'am—it's what I been all my days."

Sophie instinctively laughed, but then checked herself afore answering, "I think ya went and said yer trouble. Now, don't go sayin' things like that. That's jist bunk. Besides, it's personal. That business is yer'n, not mine."

Again, she rubbed her eyes, then her forehead and then the soft skin hanging off her upper arms. She stood hugging herself as she smiled at me devouring both buns, one right after the other.

I could see she was pondering what to say or do with me. She stood shaking her head.

Finally, her words came tumbling like over a waterfall. "I dunno what yer thinkin', young'n, but ya needs ta know y'ain't trouble ta me. Lands sake, I been standin' here, thinkin', and it's come onta me that it jist may be yer my messenger—what I been prayin' fer. Why, glory be, the more I think on it, the more it seems so. All's I need is ta hear yer message. I been waitin' too long."

"Messenger? Message? Me? No-o-o-o, I don't rightly think so, ma'am. Thank ya kindly. I surely am not a messenger. Not for anyone. Nope. Truly. To be frank, if thar's any messages to go 'round, I'm the one in need of 'em. So, if I did have any, I'd surely give 'em to myself. I do wish I had something good for you in return for your kindness, though."

Sophie Connors wasn't one to be easily put off. Again, she laughed and started to say that she hadda sudden strong feeling why I was thar and what I had to tell her, but then stopped in the middle of her sentence—her finger still pointing to the ceiling. Later, she told me it was because in that instant it came into her awareness that she was hearing herself laughing. In fact, it was the second time she'd laughed since I got thar. Laughing for the first time since she couldn't remember, but certainly since afore her best friend's funeral, and she now realized she didn't have the slightest desire to cry. She wasn't thinking of her circumstances anymore, but 'bout this mystery event inside her very own house.

Sophie's eyes brightened into a twinkle and her face softened as if she was what you'd say "rejuvenated." She acted with another burst of unexpected energy as I watched her turn to the sink, sweep up the soapy dishpan in her arms and shuffle 'cross the floor to the back door. She elbowed it open far enough to fling the iridescent water in a rainbow arc on toppa the wintered-over grass out back beyond the stoop, then came back to lean over me again.

She took in a big breath and said, "Lands, I see it's gittin' on in the day so's it'd make me most happy if ya'd stay the night here in my house with me, young'n."

Those generous words echoed through the insides of my empty heart. I looked up into the old lady's sweet and kind face afore letting the unexpected wave of pure goodness wash over and through me 'til my whole body was overcome by a sense of worth and welcome. Gone were the feelings of abandonment and betrayal. It was like a simple coming to home.

I jumped up and threw my arms 'round the old woman, but that was definitely not a good idea. The suddenness nearly knocked her to the floor and she reacted by hooving herself up in the air, her arms seeking to fend me off.

"Well'nbetold, girl, I must say yer a body badly in need of cleanin'."

Nothing but nothing the old lady coulda said could possibly have affected me more'n those words. I pulled my arms back and slid my feet 'cross the floor fast as a jackrabbit.

Sophie immediately raised her hand, pointed her finger and shouted, "Wait. Stop."

I did, 'course.

Sophie continued with her hand in fronta her, her finger bobbing up and down to punctuate her words, "Jist a minute, now. Who do ya think y'are ta show up on me from outta nowhars, droppin' yerself inta my house, gettin' me all excited jist ta slink off 'cuz ya don't like something I said, hm-m-m? Who are ya, anyways, 'n whar-all do ya hearken from? And jist what-all are ya after?"

I took a deep breath, then with a guilty look on my face and a similar tone in my voice, I replied "Renee" and mumbled something 'bout living in Forestland at some point. Sophie interrupted and asked me to raise my voice so I could be heard. This time, I loudly claimed I was from the forest out back and was just passing through—in need of a helping hand.

"Well 'n so, Miss young Renee—or whatever—I'm Sophie Connors. That'd be Mrs. Connors to ya. I'm mighty proud ta be the eldest and—I might add—the most respected person in these here parts. Why, heavens ta Betsy, fer the past two years, I been named Queen-of-the-Day at the County Fair... with a crown, even, 'n a big buncha flowers, settin' and wavin' ta folks from a convertible at the front of the pee-rade. So, ya see, I'm mighty used ta gettin' respect. Yep, I spent a lifetime workin' fer it and after what-all I done fer ya today I don't think ya should jist turn 'n walk out on me. I'm ver-r-ry serious 'bout that."

I nodded. Here I went and made another stupid mistake, like always. I mumbled to the floor, "I'm most sorry, Mrs. Connors. Yer right, 'course. After what ya went and did for me I should be more gracious. Indeed, I'm most grateful. I apologize for being rude to one so kind and generous as you."

I'm not sure Sophie could hear all my words, but she most definitely could read my body. "Okee dokey then. Lookee here, ya don't know what-all's been goin' on in my life so's—as it says in the good book—yer sins are forgiven. But I jist don't want disappointment today. Not today." Her voice caught for a moment. "Today's been a hard one. Y'have no idea. So, it'd make me most happy if ya'd get yerself clean and have a good sleep—here. Ya know ya need these things, raight?"

Again, I nodded as my eyes inspected my toes.

"What I'm thinkin' is ta start with a bath. In a tub. A bubble bath even. No woman should ever be in the condition yer in. Lawzie, I may be old with not very good eyes and my hearin'— well, it aint anywhar's what it used ta be, but I can still smell fine—and girl, you reek of horses 'n sweat 'n smoke 'n I don't know what-all else. Well, it's not very pleasant. And ya ain't wearin' much, neither."

I'm sure I was offensive. I couldn't even smell my own body and couldn't measure my filth—a sorry place to be. I accepted the old woman's suggestion. She guided me to her bathroom. Now, I don't think thar's any more intimate place than a person's bathroom. That's whar our most personal habits and tastes lie. Yes, I see you nodding… Anyways, I found right off that during Sophie Connors' ninety-three years she developed many strong habits and tastes. She told me that for the last twenty-five, as her eyesight failed, she done turned to rely more on other senses. That meant once I got into her bathroom I discovered what hadda be my soulmate.

The room sat between the kitchen and the front parlor whar Sophie now slept. It was the size of any ordinary farm bathroom— not large, not small. Fornenst the door was a window with old pullback curtains in a yellow-brown flowery print and a weathered shade pulled halfway down. On the dingy windowsill were some small flowerpots with little struggling plants trying to survive dim light and no fertilizer—most depressing after weeks in my wonderland. The floor was once painted to match the yellowy-green walls, but was now badly scuffed and stained. The toilet hadn't seen a cleaning in a long time and a leak in the sink faucet left a rusty ring 'round the drain. I didn't see anything wrong with any of it, though, because as Sophie closed the door in backa me, my eyes focused on the bright spot in the room—a big old white bathtub sitting high off the floor on toppa huge claws.

It had a "massive" copper faucet and antique handles, but it was the deep tub that said this bath was gonna be unforgettable. I turned both hot and cold taps full force afore I spied a fluffy white towel folded over a rack over the tub. I couldn't resist smothering my face in it to feel its soft-yet-rough texture on my skin and recall long-ago baths at my grandparent's farm. Listening to the tune of water filling a tub and feeling the texture of the towel made tears well up.

"Oh, Miss Renee, I been thinkin'... Take a look in the cabinet whar I keep my special soaps and the bubble bath. Ya really should take a bubble bath, so g'wan 'n help yerself. There's plenty ta pick from. And also, it's very important ta light a tallow when yer in the tub. It lets yer spirits heal. Jist do it. There's lotsa tallows lyin' 'round. I know 'cuz I make 'em. Matches in the cabinet."

Inside the standing cabinet, I discovered matches and candles as well as many scents, lotions, soaps, oils, whatever. I stared in disbelief then mentally asked myself in the mirror, *Why'd I ever stumble on this particular house? How could she know? This must be a dream.* I couldn't resist fingering every bottle and packet, smelling each more than once. When the tub was almost full, I picked the lily-of-the-valley bubble bath * and soap and shampoo

---

* One listener whispered loud enough for all to hear, "I knew she'd pick that one."

set and lit a large, yellow, homemade candle on the back of the toilet afore I slipped into the water.

My muscles collapsed immediately and I melted down 'til my hair was floating on top of the crackling bubbles afore it, too, settled into the wetness. The effect of the water was like as if I returned inside my momma. I sunk my head back so that only my nose was sticking out. The air bubbling up the back of my neck and through my hair tickled me. For only a moment or two, I heard the plin-n-nk and plon-n-nk from the faucet afore I lost consciousness. Musta been maybe twenty-five minutes later when Sophie knocked on the door to say I could wear the housecoat on the floor. I smiled and found myself smiling all while I washed my hair and my body. I left the bathroom smelling sweet as could be, covered up in Sophie's summer housecoat—a multicolored flowery thing that snapped down the front.

"Whiskerkittens and beet juice, child, yer jist gorgeous! Lookee at that housecoat on ya! Why, it fits ya like snakeskin—like ya were made fer it, dontcha think? And dontcha feel good with somethin' decent on, hm-m-m? So, now that ya put yerself together, why dontcha sit yerself right down here 'n tell me what ya have ta tell me? I want ya please ta give me my message—ya know, the one from heaven I been waitin' on."

I held my tongue 'bout that housecoat, but it did occur to me that Sophie was probably, more comfortable not looking at a naked body anymore and, besides, I didn't see the tablecloth and napkins on the bathroom floor. I insisted, "Mrs. Connors, I'm sorry, but I don't have a message for you. Really, I don't even know why I'm here. I can't even figure, actually, why I'm still walkin' the earth."

"Young'n, did I hear ya sayin' ya cain't figure why yer livin'?"

"Yes ma'am. I can't."

"Why, sure as shootin', girl, yer not usin' yer noodle. Must be a long lacka food or somethin' ta cause ya ta say that. I'm not gonna listen ta such. Jist go on, take yer time 'n then come ta tellin' me what I need ta know. I can feel it in my heart of hearts, thanks be ta God. I been havin' this feelin' in my bones lately I'd hear soon. Jist didn't know how soon."

"Mrs. Connors, I don't reckon I know what you're talkin' 'bout. Ya see, I'm so lost. Ya have no idea. No one does. I didn't even know whar I was goin' when I came up to your house today. I been ridin' and ridin' on trails and paths through those hills out back for two days. I came on that thar clear cut out back, but I dunno how. I don't even know whar I am. Could you please tell me whar I'm at?"

"Well, this's the Connors' family farm, thanks be. That clear cut out back is a firebreak put in by the county, years ago, so's ta stop any forest fires from gittin' on down here 'n also so's the Ashland Fire Brigade can git into the woods ta help rangers—in case of a real bad one, ya know—like that lulu over in Forestland a few weeks ago."

I let that remark pass as I melted into my seat to take in the woman's facial expressions and hand gestures. I wanted these sweet moments to last forever. I looked deep into Sophie's face. It was defined by lines. I could see long days spent outdoors and lots of laughter in the deep squint lines 'round her eyes. Long nights of pondering problems had probably molded those lines that looked of maturity and wisdom—sorta like a veteran of a lifelong war. When she spoke, her face was rich with expression.

Behind her thick glasses, her light brown eyes were still bright and fiery, though. They sparkled her words.

"So, Great Grandpa Connors—that's great grandpa ta my Jasper—he left New York state and came ta these parts to become a Tar Heel. Built this house with his own hands. Yep, 'n Connors have been livin' here ever since. Seems I'm ta be the last. Can ya believe it? I cain't. My Jason—my only one—he moved his family ta Midway. Story goes his wife wanted better schools fer their boys—leastwise that's what he done said. But he's a good son—calls me every Sunday. Stops in as much as he can. But, when I go ta heaven—'n that won't be long now—this place is goin' ta the town fer back taxes. That's the sorry truth. I couldn't pay my taxes fer ten years, now, so my Jason went ta Ashland town hall and made this agreement. Lord a mighty, 'tis a horrible thing ta happen at the end of life."

"Ma'am? Sorry—I'm a bit groggy. Did ya say Ashland? This's whar I'm at? I'm sorry, Mrs. Connors, I can't get over this—I'm really in Ashland?"

"Truth is, this here's actually jist outside Ashland. It's Hope County out here 'n my road is County Rd #4. I'm seven miles outta town. But the post office says Ashland, so's I s'pose it's whar yer at."

"Why, I know Ashland. I came here to the outdoor theater. Is it still here?"

"Land sakes, girl, I wouldn't know such. I don't go out 'cept maybe ta grange meetings, sometimes, or church at Christmas and Easter, when someone comes ta git me—'n Ellie, too. Only then. But since I don't get 'round I don't know any more what all's goin' on. My eyes ain't so good 'n my body's gotten stiff as a rod.

It's tough gettin' old, young'n. Also, my dear Ellie—her house's jist over thar 'round the bend in the road—well, she up 'n died last week. Hers was the one place I liked ta walk on a fine day. Now, thar's no reason ta git outta the house. I jist sit here in the evenin' like we're doin' 'n listen ta the birds, waiting on bedtime. Speakin' of that, don't ya think it's gittin' time fer bed? Y'all stay the night, raight? I need someone in the house. I lost my last livin' friend 'n I'm feelin' mighty lonely."

"Oh, Mrs. Connors, you're so kind. I'd be happy to stay the night. I have no place to go. And I can pay for this, too."

"What-t-t? I'm not wantin' money, Miss Whatever, I'm wantin' company."

"Ma'am, please call me Renee. That's my new name. Afore that, I was Zena Firestone. Zena's short for Zenobia, my great-great-great grandmother. In Ireland. For the first parta my life I was Zenobia Wood. My father and his parents were Woods. I got to be Zena Firestone when I was—well—sorta married, but that doesn't matter now."

"What-t-t? Didya jist say bein' married don't matter?"

"Yes'm, that's what I said. For me, it's the truth."

"Heaven's ta Betsy, how can ya say sucha thing? Why, if my Jasper could hear ya now he'd jump up 'n go on outside fearin' he'd lose his temper. He was a very strong-minded man, mighty yes—especially on this subject. Mind ya, I agree with him, too. Marriage is most important. Jist what-all did ya mean by sorta married, hm-m-m?"

"Oh, it's a long, sad story I'm not up to—not tonight. I'm really tired and you really don't wanna hear it. It doesn't have a happy ending."

"Oh-h-h-h, one of those marriages whar everyone don't get everything everyone wants. Oh-h-h, I'm not one of those naïve farm wimen. I know 'bout such stuff. Wasn't born yesterday. Stars 'n garters, Jasper 'n I—we had nearly forty-six years ta work things out, which we jist 'bout did afore he up 'n died on me."

"I'm sorry, Mrs. Connors, I just can't talk more. I'm way too tired. After that delicious bath, I think I'm gonna collapse on your floor. I can explain in the morning."

Sophie and I walked to the stairs at the front of the house. She pointed out the parlor whar she slept and invited me in to pet Glitters, a fat tiger cat curled up on her bed—guess ever since I arrived. Glitters was too old to do much but sleep. I watched her go through one of those cat rituals—ya know, opening an eye, stretching a paw, licking it, sniffing at my hand then licking her paw once more and putting her chin back down.

"She's certainly a cutie pie, but why's she called Glitters?"

"Oh, that's an easy one. Jason, my son—he felt I needed company here, so's he went out ta the animal farm 'n saw her settin' in a cage. They found her feedin' herself out backa Winn's Finest—scrawny 'n all. Anyways, Jason said as he gave me it, 'Ya know, Momma, ya might need money more'n a cat, but then again ya always told me 'all that glitters ain't gold.' We jist laughed 'n laughed on that. Guess it was meant ta be, glory be."

Sophie said the room I could have was the door on the left at the toppa the stairs. The light was burnt out and I said I could replace the bulb in the morning. I felt my way up the creaky stairs and smelled the dankness of the upper level that hadn't seen fresh air in a long time. My fingers found the doorframe and I entered the room whar the strawberry moon guided me to the window. I opened it right off, gulping in delicious lungfuls of the cool, night air. Leaning on the windowsill, my eyes feasted on the silhouetted trees and the glorious flashing fireflies, but my tiredness took over. I fell onto the soft lumpy bed whar I never did know how to find the pillow. I don't think I moved 'til after 11:00 the next morning. Never heard the dawn crow fight outside my window and never smelled the coffee perking at 7:00. It wasn't 'til Mrs. Connors' voice came at me from the bottom of the stairs that I came to.

"Hello-o-o up thar, Missy. Can ya hear me? Are y'all right? It's gettin' ta be so late in the mornin' it's gettin' ta be afternoon."

"Hello and morning to ya, Mrs. Connors. Be right down," but I couldn't move. On my feet was the heavy weight of a sleeping cat. I could only look at the ceiling and think on my precious situation as I listened to the air blowing the leaves in the trees outside my window. A cricket called for a mate and then I heard a distant tractor working a field somewhars and a far-off dog barking. These all mixed in my head with house sounds, the purring cat and the downstairs radio and... *What?... Could that be?* I lifted my head and cocked it to one side to hear Sophie's voice better, then bolted upright. No doubt 'bout it—that was Gram's song she was humming. I bounded downstairs—causing Glitter consternation—and rushed outta the bathroom excited to speak of this to Sophie, but she took charge. Sweeping her claw-like hands overhead to emphasize her words, she was a work of fury.

"And, mind ya, jist whar's that horse of yers?? Been outside two, three times now 'n looked all over fer him but he ain't nowhars. Ya didn't tether him fer the night, did ya?"

Oh, Sophie was madder'n a red hen. But, truth is, I'd totally forgot my loyal friend. Guess he took care of hisself. I scoured the wooded area out backa the barn. *He coulda heard a familiar voice; it coulda been a whistle spoke to him—maybe a familiar whinny—maybe he just tired of waitin' on me. Could be he's homesick, or—I dunno—maybe thar's no more reason for him to stay.* My heart ached. I felt abandoned again.

"Mrs. Connors, you're right 'bout my horse gone missin'. He didn't come to my whistles or calls, neither. Now I realize I'm missin' my robe or cape—ya know, that sheet thing I took off last night."

Sophie was working at the sink with the water running. Her back to the door, she squinched up her face as she turned, "Hunh? What 'bout fast light?"

I repeated my words. She said, "Well'nbetold, ya surely won't be needin' that old thing no more. Ya know, dearie, that cloth is settin' ta fall apart 'n my closet's full of stuff I don't need. Ya can fit into any of 'em, that's fer sure. G'wan. Take a look 'n help yerself. Any young woman as good lookin' as you should go 'round lookin' good. 'Bout that old rag... I put it out ta the incinerator so's ta burn it next—"

"What-t-t? You did wha—Whar's the incinerator?"

"Why, bless yer heart, it's out backa the barn. On the other side from the well whar ya cain't see it—whar yer not *s'posed* ta see it."

The door slammed behind me as I raced to the incinerator. I sucked in a breath only after I found my stuff lying thar on the ground ready to be made into dust. Inside the rolled-up tablecloth was my so-called bra. Apparently, Sophie didn't see it—all the

76

money seemed to be thar. I stuffed the bills in the pockets of the housecoat and returned to the kitchen that was now filled with the delicious smell of vegetable soup in the making.

Over lunch, Sophie studied me. I could tell she was seeing the pain I wore. I could feel her heart aching on the other side of the table. I think so's not to press me, she started chattering 'bout her family—of Jason's difficult birth and his childhood and his wedding and her twin grandsons, Junior and JJ—really Jason Jasper Jr. and Jasper Jason.

She told me of her husband's slow death from congestive heart failure and then described her lifelong hobby, which was making candles—even stopped to show her supplies in the pantry—then went on 'bout the different pets through the years. She bounced from one thing to another to another and I listened to her sweet voice soaking in the warm sharing. All my life I loved storytelling and I loved her stories. Sophie talked away the better part of the afternoon 'til we did the dishes and collected the laundry off the line. We were both stunned to see the sun setting so soon. We agreed the day was one of those magical times when a body can lose time.

When I returned to the kitchen from the bathroom, I saw Sophie out in her vegetable garden, so I walked down the long sloping driveway to get a look at country road #4. The farmhouse sat up on a slight knoll, so walking in any direction was down. I wanted to see if anything on the road triggered a memory, but what I saw was just a rolling dirt road disappearing over a rise. On both sides were trees. Returning back, I figured I needed a place like this. It wearied me, though, that I might be a burden to Sophie. My head was spinning. I was surely free now, but freedom didn't seem as important. *Freedom feels good—better'n afore—but I dunno whar I'm headed. I thought freedom was the answer, but I'm scared—I need a safe place.*

I asked to stay the night. Sophie tossed her head and shrugged her shoulders as she replied she done expected it. "That's that, mighty so." She made it clear she needed my companionship and maybe I could be a help to her. That settled, we went to bed early. I felt free of a huge weight and I slept well with Glitters on my feet.

Next morning, I think Sophie took a cue from the dark sky hanging over our heads. She asked me to look her in the eyes. She said she could read pain thar. I allowed as it was true, but better not to go into it. I said I'd rather share my adventure in the wilderness—only after the cabin fire, that is. So, as I talked, my whole self sorta slipped back into the person I was in the woods and I took off Sophie's housecoat, sitting thar talking without anything on. I didn't plan to do it—it just came naturally. Later, when I was thirsty, I went to the sink for water and, when I cried, I walked to the back door to throw my tissue in the trash. Everything I did as naked as the moment I was born. Sophie's lively eyes missed nothing. They twinkled, but she made no mention of it. I guess it was most clear from my words and actions that my forest experience had birthed a new me and that talking 'bout it brought out my new spirit.

Just think on this... Sophie was from another century and—my goodness—she spent most all her life on this farm. She never did have such experiences like I did. I didn't allow this at the time—too busy telling my story. But her understanding and accepting of my forest adventure was rather amazing. She hooted and howled at the men's doings, never once pressuring me 'bout my nakedness. Oh, the hand waving and foot stomping when she learned 'bout all the things that happened out backa her house. And Aban's tricks made botha us scream 'til our stomachs ached. Later, I realized I spilled this all without thinking it out and I was most thankful Sophie reacted with laughter—not righteousness.

Our overly-long breakfast lasted to an overcast noon. Standing at the sink scouring the soup pot scorched the day afore, Sophie suddenly pulled both hands outta the soapy water, dried them on her apron and turned to me wearing her robe—still hadn't got to looking in her closet yet. She put one gnarled hand over the other on toppa my chest—just over my heart. And with her eyes closed, she lifted her head so's I could see her face wearing a saintly look. I waited, appreciating the healing warmth of her hands afore closing my eyes, too. We stayed like that 'til Sophie spoke in almost a whisper.

"After my little Jason was born, we started callin' my mama Mammy and then—later—remember I told ya Mammy came ta live with us?" I nodded, my heart racing, not knowing what was gonna happen. "Well, she was always a one with wise sayin's from the old country—these told ta me when I was a young'n and then again ta Jason as he growed up. Yep, I heard 'em all many, many times. I got a mind thar's one of them fer ya now, Miss Renee-of-the-Forest. Better yet, ya know, I been thinkin' ta call ya Sylvia deForest. It's a mighty fine soundin' name, dontcha think? Kinda says it all. Anyways, are ya ready ta hear it—Mammy's sayin'?"

Now, as Sylvia-Renee or Renee-Sylvia I couldn't say—my head down and my eyes closed—I nodded again. I felt my loose hair brush Sophie's arm as she whispered, "Well then, jist this... 'Tis the head seeks Truth, but 'tis the heart finds it.' That's all, mighty yes. That's all thar is to it. And in my opinion, it's a good one fer ya ta think on. How's that sound?"

I opened my eyes, but could find no words other than it was fine. We worked on Sophie's candle-making all afternoon with Sophie instructing me on how to use the equipment, guiding me through the prep and set-up we were to use the next day. Sophie was like a natural school marm. I washed the molds and dried them thoroughly, separated the dyes from their containers and cut the blocks of paraffin into good-sized chunks to melt in the humungous pot Sophie cleaned. She taught me how to cut the wicks just so and we laid out everything on the countertop for the production. When done to her satisfaction, she said it was quitting time.

By then, our stomachs were growly, so we heated leftover vegetable soup and dipped stale bread in it. Sophie then brought out the surprise she'd been saving all day—fresh strawberries— last of the year. She done skipped out back to the berry patch and came up with just enough for the two of us. We poured sugar and cream over the juicy ripe berries and grinned at each other as we licked our lips. I put my spoon down next to my bowl, reached across the table and took Sophie's hand in mine.

"I don't see as how you can know this, but this has been the best day of my life, Mrs. Connors, and I'm wantin' to call you Sophie—if that'd be all right."

Sophie nodded her head vigorously, eyes twinkling, so I continued with heartfelt words as if a hole had burst open the dammed-up dark memories, "I dunno how to find the words to thank you for being so kind. I never had such in my life. See, my momma went and had me when she was fifteen—not married even—and she left me with my Gram 'n Poppa 'cuz she fell in love with a banjo player who traveled all 'round the country. She done chose him over me, leavin' me with her folks who were way too old to have a frisky kid."

"Oh, dearie, what-all do ya know 'bout your momma?"

"Not a whole lot. She dropped in from time to time, when she was passin' through, but I was sad the whole time. She mighta been my momma, but she was a stranger to me. I always felt like a doll she set on the shelf when she was tired of playin' with it. I knew she was my momma, 'course, but I thought she was a sassy lady who had loads of adventures in what she called 'the real world.' If she was in a mood, she'd pull me onto her lap for a few minutes afore jumpin' up for something.

"Then, thar was the way Gram 'n Poppa gave her all their attention. I mean all-l-l. Why, their eyes'd beam up when she came like no other time. None. They got all hepped up listenin' to her stories. And she knew how to make 'em laugh, too. I even wondered, sometimes, if they went on livin' just for her visits. I always learned the most 'bout 'em when she came by. I kept busy watchin' them. It's how my jealousy began."

I saw Sophie blink a few times, but kept on gushing, "I figured my truest feelin' fer my momma was jealousy. As the years passed 'n thar were new men, it got more like hatred. I guess I did 'n still do hate the one who gave me life afore rejectin' me."

Uttering this "blasphemy"—no other word for it—was more'n Sophie could take. She jumped up and pointed a finger at me. She raised her voice saying that nothing in her religious upbringing prepared her for such an idea and ended, "Ya jist cain't mean that!"

"But, Sophie, listen ta me. She picked vagabonds over her own creation. How else could I feel? I think I hated her 'specially for leavin' me alone in what was like an old folks' prison."

I watched Sophie go to the sink and ask if I wanted a glass of water afore she found words. That's when she let go on me saying she felt she hadda mention what happens inside adults through the years. She explained how old people carry inside the young'ns they once were, but don't understand how they aged so fast. She pointed out young people have in them the maturity they eventually acquire, even if they aren't in touch with it. She stressed how important it is to keep connected with the other parts of the whole self. She said human lives are not really long, that old people aren't so very different from young'ns, that we only get so many years to appreciate what she called "the eternal flow of events in the universe." She went on and on saying that we place tiny moments in a puzzle we call time, but we do that to try to understand eternity. With gentle truths, she tried to ease the horrible pain oozing outta me by explaining how difficult it musta been for my mother to be separated without the joy of seeing me develop into—what she said—"a young lady pretty as a peach." And then she actually tried to put meaning to what I called a prison. Oh, I could see Sophie's intention was to give me consolation and I did take in her words as much as I could afore more pain started tumbling out.

"I know, I know. You're sayin' a bunch of truths and what ya say 'bout my momma is right—she did miss out on kin, like when cousins came for summer reunions. They were the best. Uncle

Bert and his family were real nice. They drove up in their big old truck, kids hangin' off the back, and thar'd be eight kids runnin' 'round the house for the day and it got crazy. Aunt Moira lived only a few miles away so she came in with as many kids as she could. I think she had five.

"Betty-Lee—her birthday was 'round the same time as mine— and when I turned five she turned fifteen. She'd come and she was real good to me—liked to fix my hair. I loved that, 'cuz Gram—well, all her fingers could do was set a barrette. But Betty-Lee—she made braids and put ribbons in. I liked 'em so much I wouldn't take 'em out 'til next Saturday's bath. And when I turned nine, Betty-Lee gave me her old Viewmaster I loved the summer afore so much that I cried when she left. Guess Aunt Moira made her do it. After that, the Viewmaster was mine and I spent hours turnin' the black knob, peerin' through the window into my escape world. Yes, Betty-Lee was my favorite cousin.

"Then thar was Aunt Penny. She always had money problems— probably shouldn'a had that name. She could only take off from work sometimes, so I didn't get to see them much. Our family was… See, my mother was the youngest of seven kids. They were so much older that mosta my cousins were 'bout my mother's age. They called me 'Baby' and treated me like it.

"Thar was another aunt, Dora. She never came. She married a northerner and they lived up thar somewhars, dunno whar. Only time I ever saw her was at Poppa's and Gram's funeral, but she called Gram sometimes to talk 'bout her kids."

"But it sounds like ya had some good times as a young'n."

"Well, it was those summer reunions I felt I had kin and that was good. I can still see Gram standin' at the porch door wavin' to everybody gettin' in their cars callin' out, 'See y'all next year, good Lord willin' and creek don't rise,' afore their cars rolled down the drive—the kids all laughin' 'bout that powerful creek. Then, the three of us would go back inside laughin' as the door slammed for another year. Yeah, those were good times."

The clock in the other room struck the hour as we let my words sit on the table. I took a big breath afore I continued, "Tell the truth, Gram 'n Poppa probably did put up with me best they could. Gram cooked and fixed Momma's clothes over. 'Course, she woulda been happier to do it if she'd been twenty years younger. But it was clear they didn't really care to have me 'round. I always heard 'em sigh when they hooved theirselves up to do for me. I knew they tried to find that not necessary. They always moaned and complained 'bout their creaky bones. I think it was just to make me feel guilty for askin'."

"Naw, it was probably 'cuz they couldn't help theirselves from makin' those sounds. I know how it is."

"True, Poppa wasn't in good shape. He was old when I came and did have a tender back after the 1925 coal mine explosion."

"My, my dearie—hope yer not talkin' 'bout that Coal Glen Mine over in Comnock."

"Yeah, that's the name. Gram told me how Poppa was talked into workin' thar by his cousin, Chuck or Claude or something. He convinced him thar was more money thar than anywhars else, so Poppa went on over to Comnock soon's the weather broke. Guess he was makin' good money, too, but that day he was just off his shift, hangin' 'round talkin' when the first explosion hit. It knocked him back onto the rocks and that made his back problems."

"Dearie, I suspect he's mighty fortunate ta have his life. That was the worst disaster we ever did have in North Carolina. Ya know, it was dynamite that done sent him onta those rocks, dontcha?"

"I only know it was horrible. Poppa never did wanna talk 'bout it; he said it wasn't a story for young ladies' ears. Thar was lots he didn't wanna tell me. But, it was the last job he ever did have and he was pretty bitter 'bout it. Also, his feet hurt and walkin' was hard and his head ached all the time. Too bad—he was healthy when he was young and worked the land."

Sophie looked distracted—probably recollecting how folks all over North Carolina—many of them relatives and friends—all whose lives were changed by the accident. "As I'm thinkin' on it, I don't rightly recall that company cared fer their workers the way they shoulda—not the way they'd hafta do today, fer sure. I think they went broke after. Did yer father's cousin make it out?"

"No. He was down in the mine when it blew. I know, 'cuz Gram 'n Poppa always sent his widow money at Christmas. She had a hard time raisin' her kids."

Now, Sophie couldn't contain her flooding memories. "Oh, young'n, how old are ya?"

"Me? I'm thirty. Why?"

"Well, okay, so ya cain't imagine how different it was afore the fifties when folks didn't have no health care. Back then, we jist learned ta live with illness and pain. Never thought different. 'Course, gettin' cared fer was simpler then—we didn't have no medicines even if we coulda paid fer 'em. No penicillin even—least not 'til after The War. Lands, even consumption didn't have a cure and afore the forties lotsa folks all over hadda suffer the resta their days from that. Today's young'ns jist don't know what sufferin' is."

"I guess. I dunno what-all was Poppa's pain. It's just… the way he felt in a day was all. Any concern of mine got a 'We'll see' or 'In a minute'."

Sophie laughed, saying she used to put Jason off with those same words. She seemed lost in her own past 'til I said, "I growed up on 'Hold back, girlie, hold back.' One way or other, the answer always meant no. Poppa's most used was, 'Wee Thistle'—it's what he called me mosta the time—'Wee Thistle, whyn't ya go on out and sing with the birds'?"

Sophie was laughing out loud, but I wasn't 'bout to be distracted. "I actually think he woulda liked it if I done flew away. Plain simple fact is he never had any interest in me. Gram and I liked to sit at the kitchen table and listen to *The Lone Ranger* or *Stella Dallas* or my very favorite, *The Shadow*. We sometimes raised our eyebrows or covered our mouths to giggle when we really wanted to shout or bang the table, but we couldn't disturb Poppa in the parlor. I liked the shows, though. Remember the old radio days?"

Sophie was bent over in her seat, head tilted to the side with a big smile on her face and her eyes twinkled at the warm memories. She nodded as I continued to reminisce.

"Radio was my friend and the voices inside that big old console were friends, too. I remember Jack Benny used to say 'Well!' and the audience would laugh. And George Burns ended his show sayin' to Gracie Allen, 'Say Goodnight, Gracie' and she'd answer, 'Goodnight, Gracie.' Remember?… Oh, after that show I'd go on up to bed callin' down 'Say Goodnight, Gram' and she'd answer, 'Goodnight, Gram' so's we ended the day laughin' like that."

Sophie was giggling so much her head was on her knees, even though the memories suddenly made me sad. "But Poppa—he never was with us. Never. No, instead, he'd call Gram in to sit with him 'cuz he was lonely or bored or wanted her. That made me feel left out. But it was lucky he didn't want me—I could hear the end of the show. I think the only thing interestin' to Poppa—besides his comfort—was The War. I can still see him sittin' in the glider next to the big console that had the deep bass sound—sittin' thar every night, listenin' to that announcer with his deep voice—I think he was Edward R... Murrow?"

"Yasss, that's who everybody listened to, every night. Ya got a good memory, child."

"It was probably 'cuz Uncle Jake was hurt in Europe and Will was killed—I dunno—but whenever President Roosevelt gave a fireside talk, Poppa'd sit with his head cocked, hangin' on every word, puffin' on his fat cigar and shakin' his head—no, always no. When I was 'bout thirteen, I remember him sayin' 'son-of-a-witch' like I didn't know what he meant. He didn't agree with the New Deal or The War or anything what the President said."

Sophie's body sometimes shivered like as she was purging thoughts and feelings and memories. I could tell she had lots. Everybody did, right? Anyways, I kept going.

"And I remember ration cards and pullin' the shades down and turnin' out all the lights at night. Funny, that didn't seem scary—probably just 'cuz I didn't know better. 'Course, livin' on a farm and all, I didn't know how many soldiers were overseas or how women hadda go to work in the factories and make the guns. Me? I just helped in the garden with the vegetables and tended the chickens and pigs, gathered up the eggs—that sorta thing. Poppa took it all to the farmer's market and that's how we made out."

Sophie said she survived that way, too—said everybody hadda do what hadda be done. After all, it was wartime.

"But Poppa's buddies—Petey and Mikey—Mr. Brady and Mr. Millar ta me, 'course. They came 'round the house a lot. They liked to sit and smoke their fags with Poppa. He always had a cigar in his mouth. And they always got hepped up over the Japs and the Krauts and the whole world bein' in a hash. I never understood it all. Sometimes, when their talk was loud and rude, Gram turned up the radio so's we could sing along with songs like "Pennsylvania 6-5-0-0-0," ya know? I knew she was tryin' to drown out the nastiness on the front porch. Really, their house was meant for grown-ups only."

"But, little one, I'm settin' here listenin' 'n thinkin' these were yer Grands who were doin' the best they could 'n their hearts were full of love." She was leaning in on me with all earnestness, but I jumped to my feet when she said that. I was full of righteousness.

"Love? Oh, no! I've thought 'bout that plenty, Sophie. I'm ver-r-ry sure they loved their own babies, but not me. What they did for me was outta love and loyalty to my momma. I *never* felt love. Sure never was told it. I growed up feelin' I was a heavy burden."

Then, because I knew I was gonna need to be closer to Sophie for what I was gonna say, I sat back down, "In bed at night, I'd squeeze my eyes tight like this to tell God what I did that day and how I was tryin' to be a good girl. My words would usually turn into 'God, forgive me for bein' alive. I know I'm not supposed to be. Poppa doesn't love me and Gram's too old and I make too much noise. I'll get outta their way soon's I can, but I'm only seven, or eight or nine—whatever—and I can't take care of myself yet. I promise to get out so's they can relax aand be old. I know I'm just a bother. I should be someone else, somewhars else. But I don't know whar to go.' Then, after I got such outta my head, I'd curl up in a ball and cry myself to sleep."

I wasn't crying now, though. I was sitting tall and composed, my face confirming my words. I watched Sophie watching me drink almost a whole glass of water, wondering if she was looking back on her own childhood. When she didn't say anything, I asked if she wanted to hear more. She looked at me sadly and said it was okay if I wanted to say more. Well, I needed to.

"At school, I always felt like the fringe on the other kids' blankets. Ya know, the name Zenobia is a gift ta kids! 'Zenobia, Zenobia, has another phobia' or 'Zena the Zebra. What, a bra? Doesn't needa.' Lotsa stuff like that. Gram told me I should be proud carryin' the name Zenobia—she was a Greek Queen of the East—and Gram also said it was an honor to carry a royal name as well as a family name. I was named after her grandmother. But the kids didn't see it that way. And, sometimes they kidded me 'bout my clothes, too. I was shy, so the more they did these things, the more I wanted to hang in the corners of the playground. I didn't know how to defend myself or even defend bein' alive. None. Then, when I was 'bout ten, Cee's family moved ta town and Cee had, let's see... yeah, six brothers and sisters."

"Dear girl, I'm a bit hard of hearin', ya know. Did ya say C or Z?"

"Oh, I'm sorry, she was Colleen Catherine Cunningham, but everybody called her Cee. When Cee arrived, things started gettin' better. She was in my class but lived on the other side of town, so I only got to see her at school unless I was invited for an overnight. That was pure heaven. Her house was noisy and messy and it was okay to be a kid. At Gram and Poppa's, things hadda be 'proper 'n fittin'—as Gram always said. So, for almost five years, it was only at Cee's I was happy."

Even though Sophie was hard of hearing, she was a good listener. She jumped outta her chair and into my story.

"And sure as shootin' Cee turned out ta be yer best friend!"

"How'd ya know?"

"Ha, wasn't born yesterday! Sure glad ta hear ya weren't miserable all yer days."

Sophie got busy at the sink, so I excused myself for a moment's privacy. When I came back, I couldn't stop myself. Now that I had a loving listener, I just hadda give her a better picture of my pain. We settled back down again.

"In seventh and eighth grades, Cee and I were together all the time. We were called 'The Inseparables.' Then, when I was fourteen and she was fifteen, we both got married—more or less." I saw Sophie's face drop, but kept on going. "First, I was maid of honor at her little wedding, then she came to my fake ceremony a few months later." I saw Sophie startle, but she still didn't interrupt. "She hadda marry a guy in tenth-grade—Jethro, real nice. He done got her pregnant at the end of the summer and they both dropped outta school in October. Jethro was real lucky 'cuz Cee's father gave him a job in his furniture store. And her parents let 'em live at home a while, so that was a big help. Then he went into the service. When he came home, they started havin' babies one right after the other—which is why they moved to 'bout a half-mile down the road from my grandparents' farm."

"So y'all were best neighbors?"

"Not really. That woulda been so-o-o good, but ya see, it goes back to ninth grade when I hadda stay home 'bout half the year—tendin' Poppa mostly. By then, botha them got so's they couldn't do for theirselves. I was miserable. The very day I turned fourteen, I told myself I hadda get outta the house. As it turned out, that's the same day Bud Firestone first noticed me—and that's how my heart near broke."

My voice cracked and I choked. Sophie waited patiently with her eyebrows lifted. I hooved a big sigh afore I continued, "Poppa knew Bud from the KKK. Afore his legs gave out, Poppa went to their meetings. It's whar he met Petey and Mikey. All of 'em liked to say they'd never forgive or forget. I heard 'em raise their voices on that so many times.... Then Poppa pushed me onto this ugly man I didn't even know."

Sophie's mouth dropped open and her eyes bugged. She shook her head like she was rejecting the urge to speak.

"One night, I was up in my bedroom when I heard his voice in the kitchen. I listened at the toppa the stairs and I heard... I heard Poppa offer him money for me! Can you believe?"

Sophie put both hands over her mouth, but still sat silently waiting.

"When I think 'bout it, even now, I still can't. Everything got clear as a bell in my head that Poppa wanted to rid his-self of me. Right 'bout then, I stopped thinkin' straight and got to thinkin'—well—movin' into town, startin' a new life, gettin' outta the house... It seemed like an escape was possible. Besides, thar was someone—a grown man even—who wanted me. A man wanted me. Me! And I thought 'bout Cee and me both bein' married—we'd get on with our lives—be friends—have babies together. I was a dreamy fourteen-year-old—'course that's how

I thought So, he was thirty-four and I was fourteen? That didn't bother me. I kinda liked that he could care for me like nobody else did. I thought I could make a life I wanted. Little did I know.

"One day, I was washin' the kitchen floor when I heard Poppa out on the front porch say, 'Top of the morning to ya' and Bud's, 'Same ta you.' I crept into the parlor on the floor real quiet. No one could see me and I could hear them whisperin'. After hearin' more than I cared to, I crawled outta the back door and ran to the barn to bawl. But, dang it, I still let Poppa talk me into tryin' out marriage—ya know, livin' with him like as if I was his wife—to see if it was okay. Poppa made pretend marriage sound good and right. I never did get over how my own Poppa wanted me to do this."

A long silence hung in the air as I sat thar shaking my head. Sophie left to get a hankie outta her bureau. When she returned, she kept busy folding and unfolding it or swirling her cold coffee. I guess she was wondering what to say. I dunno. I do know I had more to say.

"Well, he did and I did and soon's I was fifteen, I went to 'play house' with Mr. Firestone in his apartment over The Ordinairy Bar and Tavern. 'Course I didn't know the real Bud Firestone. I didn't know then how bad his drinkin' was or that he had a gamblin' problem or that he didn't know the first thing 'bout runnin' a business or that he wasn't a nice man, neither. He was—and he still is—de-spic-a-ble."

"Despicable! Now that's as fancy a word as I ever did hear, honey-one. Mighty strong sentiment 'bout yer very own husband."

"Yeah, I know. It's the best word I got to say how I feel 'bout that man who was *not* my husband. Remember that. Oh, everybody else mighta called us married, but it was all a big fake. A fake. I can't express myself right 'bout all this, but the bitterest pill I hadda swallow was that Poppa sold me."

The tears that had been dribbling down my cheeks started to flow freely and I hadda stop talking to put my head on my arms on the table leaving Sophie to mull things over. I knew I done said enough. Later, she said she was thinking I was like what Matthew described in the Bible—'*Wise as serpents and innocent as doves.*' But she didn't say anything just yet. Instead, she reached over and gave me her hankie and stroked my hair softly and lovingly with her bony, old-lady fingers. After a while, she whispered soothingly, "Aw-w-w, it's all right... all right. Livin' in misery can make a body crazy. Anyone'll tell ya that. Naw, naw. Yer okay... Yer okay. Yass'm, yer gonna be jist fine 'n dandy 'cuz it's over now. All over. Yer here 'n yer safe."

That night, my head on my pillow, I relived the discussion like in a "catharsis," I guess. It lifted my heavy heart to set aside the ugly memories of Bud Firestone and all the rejections and abandonments in my life. I focused on Sophie's precious words and held them inside as the inspiration I'd been longing for. I lay on my back feeling again her fingers that spoke of long years of hard work as they rested gently on my chest, feeding warmth into my heart. I placed my own hands on that same spot to better recall her touch and repeated in my head the words she done whispered. Like a sorta mantra, I kept saying, *Tis the head seeks truth, but only the heart finds it.* That night, it wasn't clear to me what I was gonna do with this, but the words seemed important. Truly, I knew I was the one who done got a strong message that day.

During the wee hours, I woke from another one of my dreams. I can still remember it. I was walking through the forest on my hands and feet like a wild animal—like I was a jaguar stalking in the moonlight, on the prowl for Truth. My stomach was empty, so my need was ravenous. I looked left and right as I cautiously made my way and my piercing eyes missed nothing in the misty light. Approaching an open field where the cool moon glimmered on every blade of grass, my heart started racing—I knew I was 'bout to find Truth. This was in the front of my mind when I woke up on all fours, looking directly into my pillow. It took a long while looking out the window at my friend—the moon—afore I could settle down again.

The next morning began like so many others in the Smokies, with dew frosting every leaf and blade of grass and mist so heavy it was like the earth was wrapped in clouds. It was comforting. Inside, I felt like I was crossing a threshold. And as the day continued, it still seemed like something in me had changed. Anyways, I greeted Sophie's "Morning sunshine" with a request to hear more 'bout Mammy.

Sophie said she wanted to tell me, but only if I'd help with the beans that needed picking. I was surprised we weren't gonna work on the candles, but her morning visit outside told her they couldn't wait and the candles?... Well, we could make those another day. So, the two of us—different in years but alike in need—trotted on down to the vegetable garden with baskets swinging on our arms.

Bent over side-by-side for more'n an hour, Sophie told me 'bout her mother. Mammy was born into the Alcyon family back in the

1800s and lived in Ashland working as a seamstress. She met her first husband when he came into her shop needing his overcoat fixed. Three years later, he done got killed in a tractor accident. Mammy then dedicated herself to church work, which sure turned out to be a good move—it's how she met the minister who came back to town from his schooling, an army stint and another church assignment. Mammy sized him up and made an immediate move on him. After they got married, they became a dynamo duo making Ashland People's Church the social center. Church was their life 'til twin daughters—Sophie and Sonya—came along. When Sonia got married, she and her husband raised their family near Nashville for more'n fifty years afore he made her a widow. Then, she moved in with one of her kids, near Knoxville. The sisters got too old to travel, but wrote letters or talked on the phone.

Sophie said having a mother with a personality like Mammy's was always difficult—being her daughters, they hadda work to find their place in the world. Mammy was a strong widow, too. Sophie was a spinster 'til she was almost forty and met Jasper Connors in the department store whar she worked. He asked her to a square dance and they got married only a few months later. Jason blessed them when she was forty-two. She was so was proud to be a mother at that age, she doted on her son. Five years later, Mammy moved in and Sophie lost her place in her own home. She resented her mother's strength, skills, confidence and—the word she used—"dynamism." It was only after Mammy died that Sophie could see what a jewel her mother had been. Only then, could she see her mother as others saw her and let Mammy's wisdom sink in sorta like ink in a blotter. I think she was brave to tell me all this.

We snapped beans from stems, filled our baskets and pulled weeds while Sophie told me intimacies she didn't share with any other living soul. She confided that in her old age—with Mammy and her husband and now Ellie all gone—she was tormented by living a long life of 'too little too late'—her words. She now wearied over opportunities she wasn't ready for. Her only challenge now was to keep going 'til the end—which was near—and the nearer it got the less it mattered how long life lasted. She said time wasn't making her life more meaningful, just longer.

I know letting these feelings out was good for Sophie, but I was getting the more outta this. True, the hot sun was beating on my back and mosquitoes were buzzing in my ears, but I was thinking that this looking into the heart and soul of another person was feeding my soul like Sophie's food had filled my stomach. It's hard to put words to how I felt. I came to see that all that happened to me in the past few days had opened a door to a place inside I didn't ever know afore—a place of caring. For the first time, I wasn't thinking 'bout myself, my situation or my problems. I was outside them, feeling truly alive. Sophie's caring and sharing drew me outta myself. Now, her life story was seeming more important than mine.

And more… I-I could see that this sweet, old, wounded Sophie was feeling the same way. She was carrying personal pain saved up over too many years, but still she was the one to reach out to me when I done showed up at her door. It seemed weirdly beautiful that any old, emotionally-scarred person could find the strength to help a pathetic unknown—me. Her words crooning like a song weren't as important as my own thoughts now spinning inside my head.

Sophie continued to drone on 'bout the painful days since her friend Ellie was put to rest, but in my mind I was realizing thar was hardly a difference between us. Yes, we were two different people with two different life stories, but we were like one in this moment. I remember thinking, *I feel so close to her I can't find words for it. My gosh, it's just like back in the forest when those kind men tended me. I drank in their carin' and what they did for me made me care back. And I did—so much. Whyever did they leave me?* I spent the next few moments recalling the happy forest days, the lonely ones that followed, the frightened ones after and then my stumbling onto Sophie's world.

When I came to, Sophie was commenting how this year's crop was affected by the spring weather, but my reveries returned: *Gram always said things like 'Love's the most important thing' and 'Love makes the world go 'round' and 'If ya have love in your life then ya have all that matters' and all that. But I think love is inside a person's heart—it's that person who knows that feelin'. Love's a very special joy, but the loved person wants and needs a showin' of love, meanin' they wanna feel cared for. So, I don't think it's love I'm lookin' for in this life. I really want and need somebody to care for me. Like Sophie's carin' makes me wanna care back. Love can be a one-way, but carin' means both people feel the love.* That's when a door to understanding opened up and my face beamed. I straightened up over my basket and arched my back to wipe my forehead.

Sophie never missed a thing, "Okie dokie, I say 'nough fer now. Quittin' time."

I gave her no argument. My heart was full as I hooked both baskets over one arm and took Sophie's hand with the other. We climbed the path back to the house, our feet in step.

Please Hold My Hand

Take my hand softly in yours
　　wrap it in warmth
　　so I may know I am not alone
Let me feel the wondrous experience
　　of pulsing inhalations
　　enwrapped fingers and intimate palms
I wish this life moment to wash my soul
　　so to know the all of eternity
　　through a simple act of human kindness

"Lando'goshen, lookee the sky, Sylvie! Sure is fulla weather."

"Yeah. Kinda scary. We probably oughta close the windows. Hey Sophie, I been wonderin'... Those expressions of yours—like 'Lando'goshen' and all—are they, by any chance, Mammy's?"

Sophie smiled, "Why, bless my soul, yer dern tootin' that most surely was."

Putting up the greens took the rest of that day, what with sterilizing the jars and lids, cleaning and blanching the greens, burying them in Sophie's special recipe and sealing the jars in the pressure cooker. I did this sorta thing many times with Gram and I enjoyed learning Sophie's style of canning. Suppertime fell on us quickly, so we had a simple farm meal of scrambled eggs and cinnamon-sugar toast. Her radio couldn't pick up a station without drowning our ears with static from area storms. Thar was no mention of my leaving.

We washed the dishes while I told Sophie what I knew of how Gram 'n Poppa got together in the first place, after the fire that burnt down her family's home. Before I could finish, Sophie said she desperately needed a bath and asked if I could please hold my thoughts. 'Course I could, but that gave me the same idea, so next came mine. Then, since botha our heads were spanking clean, we played with each other's hair. My curly, thick, long locks needed firm brushing to untangle the knots left from my woodland days. Sophie's long, needle-thin white hair needed gentle handling, but I was able to weave it into a long braid that hung down her back. That delighted her. Thar'd been many years since she could work her hair without her fingers going numb.

We turned on the radio again and, for some reason, thar wasn't much interference now. So, we listened to the country's top ten—laughing and singing along if we knew the words. And if we didn't, we made 'em up, which was even more fun. But then another storm unleashed its fury right over the Connors' farm. With an echoing boom, the lights chattered and went black. Thar we were in the last few moments of twilight giggling as we lit candles. We sat in the parlor telling more of ourselves in the dark. I even got to finish the story of how Gram was only fifteen when she got married after her fire. We sang together what I call "Gram's Song," laughing and hugging afore deciding to call it a day. I stopped in Sophie's room to gather Glitters for the night as was now our custom.

I cracked the bedroom window only a little bit, lest another thunderhead pass by. I took off the housecoat 'cuz of the closeness—but then got a chill—so I crawled under the top sheet for the first time. Its slipperiness against my bare skin was a pleasant surprise and I was quite content and cozy listening to the area storms echoing through the mountains. The best way to describe the sound is "cacophony."

I think back on this night lots, but I've never been able to figure why Sophie decided to come upstairs. Lying in bed, mighty booms and crackles played with my imagination, but in the loud mess of sounds I convinced myself I could hear creaking in the hall. Frowning, I wondered if Sophie would actually climb those steep steps under these circumstances or could it be that somebody else was in the house? I craned my neck toward the doorway whar I saw a flickering light and then heard Sophie's voice.

"Oh Sylvie, dear. It's not been too long so I'm hopin' yer probably not sleepin' yet."

"Ya got that right."

"Well, if ya don't mind, I jist gotta come on up. I got a question ta ask 'n it…"

And then, with my head crooked and tilted to the side to hear better, I heard the most unforgivable, unforgettable sounds that echoed through every crevice of my brain over and over and over. Noise to stop time and place. Louder and louder came the ugly sounds of a weight falling and tumbling, backward and downward, Sophie's voice calling, cloth ripping and then the worst of all—an unmistakable hard thud and deep moan. My mind denied the reality, but my body instinctively flew to the door and down the stairs in the pitch dark. On the way, thinking left me. My mind shut down, but my heart moved my mouth, "Sophie, Sophie, Sophie, dear one—thar now, sweet Sophie, aww it's all right."

After my hands felt their way down to my friend, a sudden bolt of lightning gave me an ever-so-brief glimpse of how she was lying on the floor and I got a fleeting look, too, at the tallow lying a few feet away and the blood creeping across the floor toward a small puddle of wax. Once again in blackness, my body moved 'til it was right over Sophie and my head was on her chest. I froze in this position for what seemed like eternity and listened for any sound of breathing. I heard only slight rattles. I tried over and over to feel for a pulse, but no.

My life experience didn't prepare me for this. I'd no idea what to do. I just lifted my head, my hair and tears falling in fronta me and placed my two hands, one over the other, on toppa Sophie's heart and—without thinking or hesitating—gave Sophie in my most crystal-clear voice the message she was waiting on. I remember it like yesterday.

"Dear, dear, sweet and kind good friend, I think you're 'bout to leave me. Oh, dear God, forgive my words. More'n anything I want you to pass on with peace in your heart, 'cuz you were a true friend ta me—me, a pathetic, needy, most-unworthy stranger who done showed up at your door. With all the gratitude I can dig from my insides, I wanna thank you for savin' me. You're the one who made me wanna go on livin'... and I do now. I'm gonna stay by your side and stand witness to your passin'. I'm stayin' here with you, Sophie, and I'm gonna tell you how I feel.

"Just you bein' you these past few days—you done gave me the strength ta go on in my new life. Just by bein' your very own self, you went and saved a human being—me. Like magic, you performed a miracle—without tryin' and without knowin'. I reckon you saved my soul. Now you're passin' on and that means you're leavin' a huge hole inside me that nobody else can ever fill. No one ever will. But please understand that, 'cuz of you, I'm gonna be all right—I am. I can go on now—'cuz of you. Your patient understandin'—acceptin' me, listenin' to me, your givin' me hope, your kindnesses, your generous and carin' ways—all these made the difference 'tween life and death to me. I was walkin' death afore you performed your miracle. Above everything else, it's been your carin' that's meant the most.

"Somewhars inside of me I know you're gonna be all right 'cuz you're gonna start fresh. You're goin' to a new place whar your beautiful heart can reach out and touch others like it did mine. You're gonna be at the right hand of God whar you can be an angel to others like you were to me. I can go on here without you, now. And as I'm losin' you, my heart is sendin' you on in peace and devotion and with all the good wishes I have in me.

"Dearest sweet Sophie, friend for a lifetime, I'll always cherish your memory. Bless you. Bless your sweet heart and sweet ways. You were the best ever in my life and I feel real privilege in knowin' you. I'm so grateful, so grateful. Peace be with you. Blessings on you. Bless your heart. Bless your soul."

The words didn't come out like that—ya know—all at once. Thar were many pauses and sobs and silences, but that was the message from my heart that I spilled onto the lifeless body lying on the floor in fronta me.

From my darkest depths, I expressed to Sophie and to myself emotions and thoughts I didn't even know I had. Even more, I think my words came outta somewhars else—like from some universal intelligence, whar I think thar must be an endless pool of sorrow. My words were just one person's attempt—mine—to fill that hole between life and death, between the one left behind and the one going on, between new purpose and overbearing loss, between hope and hopelessness. I dunno, somehow, in the pitch dark of that awful awesome night, I found the light to bear witness to what I guess you'd call Sophie's "agonal" moments. I never gave a thought to rescuing or saving her. I couldn't bear the idea of causing her more pain. The thought of moving beyond the moment never came to me. I just wanted to be with Sophie as long as I could—what felt, then, like forever.

Te Kore

Daytime's details distract
coming to life in light
calling our attention
taking us outside our selves
blinding our minds
distracting, deceiving, diminishing
Yea, hearken, listeners all
Truth births in blackness
comes to life within deepest-dark lacunae
Discovery Blooms Black
bemoan not the dark spaces and secret places
Te Kore harbors life's darkest depth

I lay on the floor next to my wonderful friend for a long while, then sat either with my hand on her heart or upright with my head against the wall, holding her hand. My wish was to be as close as possible—to drink in her warmth and inhale her sweet aroma as long as they lasted—to absorb her positive energy as long as I could. Thar was nothing that could pry me from Sophie's side the whole nightlong. I felt the passing of Sophie's soul hadda be marked by tenderness and gentleness and compassion.

When the next day came creeping over the horizon, I saw ugliness at my feet and felt repulsed by signs of a bloody night. Standing over Sophie, I saw alligator-skin legs sticking out from under a ripped and wrinkled nightgown. I couldn't stop staring at spider veins splattered across blue-white, wrinkly thighs. A small black spider had come in the darkness. It caught my attention as it busily put the finishing touches on its snare over her body. I couldn't see whar the web started or ended, my larger-than-life Sophie suddenly caught in a spider web.

Then, in a flash, my own predicament washed over me. What happened to Sophie was gonna be news to the outside world. Any time now, some Presbyterian or other "ist" could show up. 'Course they'd wanna see her, talk with her, check up on her. And who'd believe my story? No church member or Ashlander would understand or welcome me in this house—especially now. Me—dressed in Sophie's clothes or not dressed—didn't matter. I hadda tell myself it really happened—Sophie really did fall downstairs and die from her injuries. It's true. What good would it do to be here when somebody comes? I'd only complicate things.

It was easy to decide to leave, but I knew I needed to take a gift from Sophie—I hadda be dressed in that outside world. And since I wanted to cling to her, the idea was actually appealing. I felt Sophie's aura around me as I moved quickly and quietly 'bout the house investigating closets and straightening bedcovers. Sniffing and sobbing, my heart felt cold and empty. 'Course I didn't come on any of those stylish miniskirts, so I settled on one of Sophie's summer dresses and managed to push my suffering feet into some old scuffs that didn't really fit, then set down on the kitchen floor an extra-large bowl for Glitters. I gave the confused cat a hug and helped her nestle into a pillow on Sophie's bed afore stuffing my money into a handbag from the closet shelf.

The sky outside was steamy, as skies in our part of the world often are, but in moving 'round the house I noted an increasing brightness in the rooms. Combing my hair at the bathroom mirror, I saw the sun peek out and something more—a double rainbow outside the window that made me gasp. Its beauty and symbolism made me smile as Reverend Lundborg's expression, "Rainbows are a sign of God's love," streamed through my head.

I gained purpose as I calmly busied myself checking things both upstairs and down. When the phone rang, I didn't answer it, but it prompted me to move faster. I found an address book in her desk and stuffed it into the same purse whar I done stuffed my old money. Soon's I felt the house lacked any hint of my presence, I kneeled down and gave the cold, gray body a long, tender kiss and stroked the long, tangled braid. I was somber as I let myself outta the kitchen door and headed on down the drive.

County road #4 was quiet. I turned right not knowing why. My head didn't feel like it was attached to my neck. I was too busy focusing on how I was once again striking out alone on my new life path—like walking away from trauma was getting to be a habit in this life. I remember I did think on how walking a path is not only *from* something but also *to* something. Really, though, I was mostly numb.

When county #4 met up with a busier road, this one paved, I stood wondering which way to turn and then a big old Greyhound bore down on me. Seemed a good idea to get a ride, so I waved it down and offered to pay the full fare from Ashland to the next stop. The driver took one look and nodded me aboard. Inside I could see why. Thar were only 'bout thirteen passengers—an Indian couple and their three kids, an elder couple and some raggedy hippies. It probably took 'bout twenty to make a trip worth it. The driver tried to be friendly saying he'd take me all the way to New Orleans if I wanted, but I wasn't in the mood to joke. I said I was pleased for a ride to the next stop.

I slumped down onto a cracked cushion near the back and let myself sink into the bouncing vibrations. I tried looking out the window but as I settled into the ride the spectacular beauty of the passing hillsides had no power over me and my eyes never gotta glimpse of Clingman's Dome or the bridge over the Tuckasegee River that hadda be raging then. My nerves were raging too, but exhaustion was setting in—almost like a cold wind sweeping through my insides. Looking back, I'd say it was probably fear causing that coldness, but I was only aware of emptiness. Being with Sophie had given me a warm feeling of being alive, of hope, and now it was like halfa me was on the floor back thar. The other half was pushing me forward, telling me what I hadda do.

Yes, I was alone again and that was how life was to be. Sad and lost, but free. I shivered at the thought that this new life wasn't turning out to be so simple. What was past was past and I didn't know what was to become of me. After shedding a ton of tears, I gave in to the steady hum of the tires spinning on the road and my head fell against the fingerprinted glass under the spell of the hypnotic vibrations.

So, that's what happened with Sophie Connors. Can ya see why I needed to share it? I learned from Sophie I could make it. I think we don't always understand how God works. And now that I see food's ready, I'm starving. Aren't y'all? Even bigger stuff lies ahead, so come on back after lunch....

Smoke

ever-spiraling skyward
earth-made clouds gift the skies
ethereal blue light in incessant motion
swirling, twirling
around off and away
free from capture
freezing or freeze-framing
Unknowable Spirits
guide our life paths
whisperering
Truth

PART 5

Dancing Flames

a-li-s-gi-s-gi u-da-we-la-dv-i

M-m-m, I'm loving this beautiful October afternoon fire. I see many of y'all are keeping your blankets, too. Leona, many thanks for tending our stomachs today. You outdid yourself, girl.... So, while we were eating, some of you asked 'bout Sophie's passing and I told 'em same as I say now—it was like so much else that happened on my way to finding myself. I can't say it any better'n Mark Twain. He said, "When I was fourteen, my father was so ignorant I could hardly stand it; but when I got to be twenty-one, I was astonished at how much he learned." Sophie turned my life 'round and her dying was— well—monumental. And 'bout losing my voice.... Way I see it, it came on me after so much trauma and I was at the bottom of low. I dunno, seems words can pop right outta my mouth so easily and then, at other times, they get all jammed up inside. It's a part of me I still don't get. So, are you thinking the next thing is how things all came together and I got to live happily ever after? Not exactly. Ten years flew by and I growed up a lot, but stuff sure got complicated. Lemme explain...

Back in 1960, my insides were all tore up as I bumbled 'round naked in the mountains afore stumbling on those beautiful men who gave me the strength to get to Sophie. Then, after her giving me the will to go on living, I got myself on the bus. My pieces and parts mighta been glued together, but my insides were shaky.

The bus eased into the tiny Midway terminal, whar I could hardly recognize who was looking back at me from the ladies' room mirror. I splashed cold water on my face and plugged coins from the bus driver's change into a machine that spat out a clever little package I never did see afore. It held a tiny blue comb, a mini toothbrush and a teeny tube of tooth paste. Once I made a bitta difference in my looks, I stepped out onto Main Street, blinking into a bright sun. I was back in the world I done left and it felt mighty strange in all its familiarity.

Somehow, Sophie's scuffs hit the road and got me to the address I asked 'bout. I came on a big old fifty-ish man bent over tomato plants out back of a yellow bungalow sorely needing paint. His pants drooped down onto his hips showing his inside-out underwear. The lower part of his back was rosy red and sweat had soaked his shirt.

"Excuse me, sir. I'm wondering… Does a Jason Connors live 'round here?"

Without bothering to stand up, his head spun 'round as he asked, "And who might be wantin' to know?"

"Well, I do, for one."

Jason used both hands to push hisself up off his knees. His face wore a tired but friendly smile as he held muddy hands out. "And who might this *I* be, hm-m-m?"

"Uh, I went and had a few names up to this point. Most recently, it was Sylvia de Forest—given to me by Sophie Connors."

"Ah-h-h, so ya know Sophie. Well, then, I'm Sophie's son, Jason. Mighty pleased ta meet you, Sylvia. From the church? How's Mom doin'? 'Fraid my car's been outta service and I haven't been over ta see her in a coupla weeks."

"Mr. Connors, I'm here ta speak to you 'bout that."

"Y'are? Well, just so ya know, I called her this morning but thar was no answer. I figured she's doin' what I oughta and that's what got me out here in this heat. I'll try later."

"I'm most sorry to disturb you, but what I gotta say is serious and might take a while. Can we find a place to sit down, please?"

As you can imagine, this was most difficult. My voice got subdued describing my three days in his mother's house. It got even lower when I described Sophie's fall. I reached across the kitchen table and touched his arm. He flinched. I explained how, since the phones weren't back yet, I hadda choose if to go to Ashland for help or look him up. I decided if I was the one lying on the floor I'd want family, so I came to him. He nodded. I suggested he go his mother and he suggested I go with him.

He explained he picked up his car from the repair shop the day afore, whar it was waiting over a week on parts, which was why he couldn't take Sophie to her friend's funeral. Jason's beautiful sky-blue Studebaker Sky Hawk was fit-as-a-fiddle now, though, so I settled myself into the passenger seat as Jason took off.

My mind was made up—I hadda challenge him. Once we got on the road, I cleared my throat a bit and swallowed hard. "Mr. Connors, I sure didn't know your momma very long, but in the few precious days I was lucky to spend with her, I became very fond of her. She was exceptionally kind, caring and givin' ta me."

"Ohmygod, ya can say that again. Thar's not a one better. Heart of gold. Everybody agrees she's the best. Always has been. Sorry if I can't accept what ya said back thar. I-I got a hunch she's still alive. If we go fast enough, maybe we can get her to the hospital."

"Mm-m-m, I understand how you feel, Mr. Connors, I do. Oh, and I wish it wasn't like this. But, I'm 'fraid you'll see what I was sayin' when we get thar. I wish I wasn't the one to give you this news. You shouldn't have to hear it from a stranger. It's wrenchin' for me. For you, I can hardly imagine." My voice trailed off as I sucked in a sob. We rode in silence a bit afore I changed the subject. "Perhaps, you could help me—uh—understand something?"

"Understand something?"

"Yeah."

"Well, what-all do you need ta understand?"

"You see, sir, I'm findin' it kinda difficult to... to get... why... Oh-h-h I can't do this. Never mind." I shook my head and hands fiercely side-to-side and slunk down into my seat staring hard at a smudge on the console that looked like old chocolate—like as if somebody'd tried to open the glove compartment with sticky fingers. My resolve left me. All's I wanted to think on now was old chocolate.

"Naw, g'wan. I can tell ya got something on your mind. Say it."

"Yeah, I do have something, but nah—it's too hard to choose the right words." I shook my head again and slunk down more.

He hadda know I had something hard to say, but I don't think he figured what was coming. After a quiet minute or two, I just couldn't stop myself. I let him have it. "Rats, guess I just have to come out with it. I'm so upset I dunno if I'm thinkin' straight."

"Yeah?"

"Yeah, ya see, I just don't get why your mama was livin' in that house all by herself. And at ninety-three. How come no one—like yourself—was carin' for her? I-I just don't get it."

"So, Sylvia, I think that's it. Right?... That your name?"

"Ha! Your mama said it should be Sylvia—or Sylvie—so I guess that's it, mighty yes."

He smiled, "Ahah, Sylvie, I see ya listened ta Mom very well. I understand yer questionin' her situation, I do. The true 'n honest answer's a long story and I think ya want the honest answer. Am I right?"

I nodded, but kept my eyes on that dirty console.

"So, what you need to know is my mother's situation is related to mine and my personal life has been a secret fer years."

He paused to gather his thoughts, check his rearview mirror and study the road ahead. I used these moments to find words to hide my embarrassment. "Well, listen, ya don't have to go and tell me personal stuff, ya know. That's your business. I just been stewin' 'bout Sophie bein' in that house all by herself and then me—a perfect stranger—comin' in on her and bein' the only one thar when she passed. That's all."

He stared straight ahead and let out a long sigh. "Yeah. And it's not easy fer me ta separate her from my life, so can I tell ya in my own way?"

113

Charlie Boy

Hey, Charlie boy, little tyke,
Hurry up and come.
Mama's waiting. Mama's waiting.
Put away your teddy and your trike.
Where's your truck? Where's your ball? Where's your bug?
Whatsa matter? Whatsa matter?
Time for stories. Time for kisses. Time for bed.
Mama's calling...

Hey, Charlie! whatsa matter, cantcha hear me, Mama's calling.
Hurry home.
You're in trouble. You're in trouble. Very late.
Mama's calling. Mama's waiting. Mama's mad.
Whatsa matter with your teacher, with
your puppy, with your skate?
Dontcha hear me, dontcha wanta, dontcha care?
Mama's arms are open. Mama's eyes are closed.
Time for learning. Time for laughing. Time for listening.
Mama's calling...

Hey, Charlie! whatsa matter, cantcha hear me, Mama's calling.
Where've you been to, out so late?
Who've you been with, on a date?
Mama's calling. Mama's waiting. Mama's worried.
Where's you mind to? Where's the car at? What's that smell?

Toss away the toys of adolescence.
Time for joking. Time for hoping. Time for loving.
Hurry home to Mama.
Cantcha hear her calling?
Cantcha care?...

Hey, Charlie! whatsa matter, cantcha hear me, Mama's calling.
Mr. Charlie, Mr. proper distant man,
So, where've you been?
Whatsa matter with the phone, with the car, with the pen?
Where's the present? Where's the smile? Where's the hug?
Mama's lonely. Mama's angry. Mama's there.
Cast aside the lady spell upon you. Find your way to home.
Time for Mama. Time to cherish. Time to go.
Dontcha know?
Mama's failing...

Hey, Charlie! whatsa matter, cantcha hear me, Mama's calling.
Been too long now, Charlie Charles,
Hurry back to childhood. Hurry now.
Mama's calling. Cantcha hear her? Mama's sad.
Where're your manners? Where's your
heart? Where's your conscience?
Shed the toys of decadence.
Time for holding. Time for trembling. Time for framing.
Hurry home to Mama's bed.
Cantcha hear me? What's the matter's
Mama's dead.

I felt kinda chastened or chastised—whatever. I pulled myself back up into the seat to stare through the windshield at that never-ending white line speeding toward us, vowing to hold my tongue. That's how Jason's story came out.

"Well, ya see, my family 'n I—that's my wife 'n our two boys—we lived a coupla miles down the road from Mom 'til 'bout ten years ago. Those days, I could keep an eye on her—her 'n Dad, both. And I did. One especially good thing was my boys could get off the school bus at their house and spend a few hours with 'em in the afternoon. Ah-h-h, the good old days. Back then, we were close and it was great. But thar's my wife. I met her when I was in the service and brought her home when I got out. We got married in my parents' church thinkin' ta spend our lives in Ashland. But, well, she 'n I—w-we had an ugly secret that we worked hard ta keep from my parents. Ya see, my wife was—hunh, still is... best way ta say it is she's a wanderer, if ya get my drift. Truth is, she didn't want just me in her life—she wanted more. She had un-con-troll-able urges. Still can't control 'em.

"That means when we were tryin' ta work things out in Ashland—it's a very small place, ya know—and ya probably don't know, but the Connors name is like gold thar. Oh, we had lotsa pressure on us. My wife felt it more'n I did. After a while, though, I knew it was only a matter of time before the Connors name would get dragged through the mud. But, dang it, I couldn't let my kids or my parents carry that burden. It wasn't their fault. Sure woulda broke Dad's heart. He was a very proud man—very big on impressions. Had lotsa pride."

The moment he started speaking I started to get it. Thar was more to the Connors family than anyone—maybe even the

Connors—knew. What an eye-opener! I was noticing beautiful Clingman 'bout then—wondering whar it was when I passed it afore—thinking on how so much gets past us in life when we're not paying attention.

"Wife 'n I... we decided ta get outta Ashland. We chose Midway 'cuz the school system had a good reputation and we could use that for why we up 'n left. But then, Dad died. After that, I never did get round ta tellin' Mom. I don't think either of 'em ever found out—hope not anyway."

I assured him I was certain Sophie didn't know. I did remember, though, how something in her voice hinted thar mighta been more to them leaving Ashland; but I wanted to believe Sophie woulda told me. I also didn't want to upset him more.

"Wife 'n I... we couldn't make things work, after all. We got divorced three, three 'n a half years ago. I didn't tell Mom. I didn't know how without tellin' her everything. I wanted her ta be happy in her old age. She didn't need ta know. I wanted her ta be proud, ya know?"

He looked over at me but I stared through the windshield, sensing he had more of a long-dammed-up story that needed to be let out, like I did, so I let the words flow.

"Now, my Jason Jr... Been at college the last two years—and my young one—JJ... he just finished high school. Did real well, too—goin' into the army, like his old man. So, thar's nothing left for me in Midway. I stayed fer the boys—wasn't plannin' on stayin' forever. My heart's always been in Ashland. I been thinkin' ta move back—waitin' fer the right time."

I nodded as I listened. After what I'd heard from Sophie, this all made sense and I was stunned by how unexpected simple truth can sometimes be. It doesn't have to be complicated. But, Jason's need to talk wasn't satisfied.

"I dunno if yer married or not..." I knew he looked over at me again, but I didn't wanna get into that with him, so I continued to stare straight ahead. "But I always felt my parents measured me as an adult by how well my marriage was goin'." My head was now swimming inside the memories of my own so-called marriage and how thar were no parents to approve or disapprove. A vision of Poppa flashed afore my eyes afore I returned to what Jason was saying.

"I worried they'd never understand me havin' a failed marriage. Ya see, Mom 'n Dad—they brought me up ta feel strong about promises—any promises. They always made an especially big deal 'bout the marriage pledge. And boy, were they a hard act to follow. Why, it put the fear of God into me thinkin' 'bout sharin' personal problems with 'em. I think it's why I started makin' excuses fer our family—why we didn't all come ta visit. I created fake stories of my hard-workin' wife always tellin' me to apologize for not bein' able to get away. She always sent her love—always had me bring a birthday present or a Mother's Day card. As fer Mom—my wife was still family even though she stopped comin' ta visit.

"Jr. 'n JJ knew, 'course, and they went along with my fakin' it. But it was real hard on 'em. Whew, I can't believe the relief I'm feelin'. If what ya say is true—if Mom's not alive—I won't have to continue the charade anymore."

The more he talked the more I was surprised by the turnabout in my feelings. I done worked myself up to think he was a no-good bum who abandoned his mother in her failing years. Now, his life pain was echoing mine.

Jason pulled into a filling station just outside Ashland. Botha us sat quietly as the owner filled the tank and cleaned the windshield. It felt really weird to ride in a car again—in a convertible, even—and with a stranger, too. My eyes settled on a telephone booth in fronta the station and that triggered a memory of the time I was called outta eighth-grade science class to go to the principal's office. There was an emergency at home. I could hear Jessie's voice in my ear, "Gotcha babe—let's jist give Grammy a jingle—lessee, yer two rings, raight?" Thinking back, it was more'n fifteen years afore and I was amazed at how much technology change thar was. Why, phone booths put in just the year afore made it so folks could call now with pocket change—no need to even speak with an operator. And people could dial directly from home, too. I got to wondering what happened to all those out-of-work telephone operators?

Anyways, I was mulling these things over when Jason stepped out to get his wallet from his back pocket. I glanced at the back and noticed a book on the seat—*Brigit, Celtic Goddess of Healing.* When Jason got in, I asked 'bout it. He got all fired up explaining that he tended a grocery store part-time, but still had too much time on his hands—so, he was taking a night class. It was a ten-week course called "Celtic Crosses to Bear" 'bout important people in Celtic history. His face lit up telling 'bout his growing interest in his heritage. He described the report he was writing on Brigit, both pagan goddess and Catholic saint.

Sophie's drive appeared just as he finished telling me 'bout his report and, once he turned in, we got mute. Entering by the back door, we went straight to her. She was just like I left her. Jason immediately let out a gasp; it was altogether clear she done passed. We took turns stroking the stone body and murmuring to her spirit. I smoothed her skirt over her legs. After a few frozen moments, one of us muttered something 'bout candles and we went on a search. We used Sophie's own candles to form a circle of light 'round her rigid body on the front hall floor, careful to avoid a most-elaborate spider web.

Later, over cups of tea, few words went far. Guess you could say each of us was lost in the past. Jason opened up cupboards to see what thar was to eat. We ended up with the last of Sophie's vegetable soup. With toast, it seemed just right. Jason mentioned the need to drive into town since the power was still out. He thought to go to the hospital. Would I go with him? Well, as you can imagine, I sure didn't wanna be alone in the house with Sophie's wandering spirit. I guess, maybe, I was also being drawn to the living pulse of Ashland.

Going was enormous for me. I looked at everything and every-one like as for the very first time. Sounds were amplified. Smells were overwhelming. Voices told of personalities. When Jason was speaking to the hospital receptionist, he mentioned he was accompanied by a friend from Midway and waved his arm in my direction.

"Yes, hello, I'm Brigit."

Waiting for an important someone from the main office to appear from behind a closed door, Jason gave me a sly smile and wink. "So, my mysterious friend, ya got some explainin' ta do," was all he managed afore all the people and questions and deci-sions that followed.

Time went into overdrive, I think you could say. Things began to happen afore we were ready—our time and attention gobbled up in a storm of town officials and well-meaning folks. During the following days, we stayed in the farmhouse. I slept upstairs in "my" room and he stayed in Sophie's front room. I asked permission to wear Sophie's clothes and he agreed. Each time I put on a Sophie dress, I closed my eyes, buried my nose and drank in Sophie's essence. Her scents were like tonics to me.

Two days later, thar was a lovely service for People's Church members and friends. The female soloist sang three of Sophie's favorite hymns as well as Grandma's Song—my request. It made the congregation laugh. And Rev. Munson, their serious young minister, read a passage from the first chapter of the Book of Ruth 'cuz Jason done told him my feelings for Sophie.

The minister never got to know Sophie well. Seems she didn't go to church more'n three or four times during his term. He did remember the one time he visited her at home—when he described the previous Sunday sermon on the lesson taught to Moses—that 'bout an angel who spoke from the midst of a burning bush on Mount Sinai and how the angel instructed Moses to walk barefoot on the hallowed ground in front of the bush. He repeated to Sophie the lesson he told the churchgoers—to remember God is holy and whar He is is also holy. He said Sophie listened carefully to every word afore saying—in her opinion—the bush was burning but not consumed by its flames, so the message to Moses was that thar can be no limit to God's power—it is eternal, endless, everlasting. Her mental state made a great impression on the preacher and he admitted that no lesson he could give her was as

121

good as her ability to think for herself. He had nothing but praise for her. I hadda chuckle.

I liked being Brigit. At the little social hour back at the house, Brigit got to meet Lureen, daughter of the late Ellie Knopf, Sophie's dear friend and neighbor. Lureen lived next door to her mother and obviously suffered from shaking palsy. She worked part-time at the Ashland Five and Dime during the week and also took care of her Mongolian son at home. I asked if that was the same as Down's Syndrome, but Lureen didn't know. Soon's I met her I wanted to know her better and hear more 'bout Sophie—if Lureen should ever find the time.

After all the well-wishers had gone home and Jr. and JJ had set off on their drive to Midway, Jason and I sat across the kitchen table from each other. Everything needing to be said had been. All the kind words 'bout Sophie and the Connors family and the happy memories had their effect on Jason. The emptiness of loss got replaced by a sense of fulfillment. But the day had been special to me, too, because the Sophie I came to know this day was the same I carried in my heart. As I'd listened to the stories, my heart had overflowed with admiration.

We sat drinking in the deep quiet in the empty house. Sometimes silence says the most, dontcha think? The air hung heavy and the hall clock ticked the time as Sophie's aura hovered over us. I was not wanting to think 'bout what I was gonna do next, but it kept creeping into my mind. All of a sudden, Jason glanced up from his hands folded on the table to stare at me afore he broke into a kinda half smile that warmed my heart. I returned it. Without any thought or intention, we both just got up and crossed the space to wrap our arms 'round each other and buried our heads on each other's shoulders to bawl.

Our sobbing released deep sorrow—and that was good—but the physical touching opened a door. I think our emotional release that day helped Jason's years of rejection and frustration connect with my years of rejection and abuse. We reached out to the other intimately. At first, it was just hugging, then we kissed, then we moved toward the stairs—not talking and not thinking. I guess you could say we buried Sophie that day and sorrow that night. Yes, we continued mourning her loss, but we were so excited to share something other than death. It was as if a force was pulling us together. I dunno, maybe a magical magnet?

It's true, we were both free. But neither of us wanted to be alone. We stayed in the house as many days as thar was food, then went into town to buy more. Then, we stayed in the house to settle Sophie's affairs.* Eventually, Jason hadda return home to pay bills, but returned soon's he could and stayed 'til the following Sunday night when we began talking of the future. We were two lonely people who got befriended by loss.

We talked almost nonstop 'til he hadda return to work at the convenience store. I told Jason the stories Sophie had shared of his childhood and Jason filled in the blanks with his own memories. Naturally, I told him of Gram 'n Poppa and my invisible Momma. I helped him understand how loneliness and rejection had stayed with me ever since. I explained how my physically-mature fourteen-year-old body fooled everybody into thinking

---

* Some listeners in the circle whisper to each other, "And to have their own."

า or nineteen and how, when Bud Firestone was
ม to me, he didn't know my real age—how he was
the one to approach Poppa asking to see me and Poppa jumped
at the suggestion. I explained it was actually Poppa who pushed
me onto Bud and convinced me it was time to get on with life.
I also described the beginning of our pretend marriage back in
1945. Bud wasn't in the War; he was declared 4-F 'cuz one leg
was shorter than the other. I think that and also because he was
a small, heavy-built man is why he was a bully.

When we first went to live in his apartment over The Ordinairy,
he had a list of rules—the most important was to stay outta the
bar when he had customers. Fine by me—I didn't wanna be 'round
drunken men hanging over stools blubbering into Wild Turkey
as they watched Bud fix his specialties—those fancy Manhattans
topped with a bright red cherry. Bud's main idea was for me to
clean his bar every morning and I went along with it. So, almost
every morning for the next ten years, I was allowed into the large,
dark, dingy, musty bar—every day except Monday, laundry day. I
opened up the shuttered windows to let out the stale smoky air,
turned on the lights and the radio so's I could sing pop tunes as I
tried to undo the day afore by collecting and cleaning all the ash
trays then sweeping the dirt and wiping down the overturned
chairs. Some days, I washed the sticky floor. The men's room was
last. It was all dirty work, but I always felt a sense of accomplishment 'bout 11:00-11:30. That's when Bud came stumbling in with
a steaming mug of coffee. It amazed me how he always managed
to be on his feet when the first regular or deliveryman came. By
then, I'd be upstairs wolfing down my breakfast.

Oh, I gotta tell y'all 'bout Bud's television, a 12" Philco he got in 1950. He decided he hadda have this for the men coming back to the hills after traveling 'round the world. Television was gonna bring the world to their doorsteps, he bragged. He was right. Thar weren't too many who could afford television sets of their own and they couldn't get any reception in those mountains no matter how much they played with the rabbit ears. Same's for Bud. But soon's he found a snowy screen doesn't draw customers, he got hisself a big, old roof antenna. On account of the mountains and the weather, it didn't ever solve all his reception problems, but it was better'n nothing. And it drew a steady stream of damaged souls to come and drape theirselves over his bar to stare at the little black and white picture. I see many of y'all are remembering those screens, too. Anyways, every year, thar were more shows and more men at that bar and Bud's TV did the trick. It was frustrating to me, though. I could only see it when I did my morning cleaning. I got so sick of looking at that test pattern I smacked the screen every time I passed it by. Only 'bout 1952 did the morning test pattern go away so we could get morning shows.

I only knew the evening shows when I squatted at the toppa the stairs. My so-called husband mighta had a fancy TV, but I sure didn't. At the market, I sometimes heard 'bout the candy-factory scene on the *I Love Lucy Show* or that ventriloquist— Senor Wenchez, I think—on *The Ed Sullivan Show* or the Texaco quartet on *The Milton Berle Show*. Whatever. I remember one night when the *Lucy* show was on, Bud surprised me at the bottom of the stairs. Later, he stormed up threatening like he always did when he got angry—"Lissen up girl." This time he screamed, "Lissen up real good." We had a terrible row—which I didn't win, 'course—but TV was put out for discussion. Finally, I convinced him to let me come down far enough to see the screen as long as I didn't go inside the all-male bar—actually the all-*white*-male bar. Those were the Cold War years, remember, when some man from the Soviet Union—can't remember his name right now—he threatened President Eisenhower and our whole country shook with fear that we could get into a hot war again, so those evening shows were a good distraction. I only started to learn of the serious problems in the world when *The Today Show* started. I learned then how complicated the world was and how decisions in Washington affected my life in the mountains. When I tried talking to Bud 'bout such, he'd throw things at me. I stopped trying.

I explained how my life with Bud slid downhill after he got deep into gambling and his drinking got worse. It's why he lost the business and we moved to Gram 'n Poppa's farm. They done passed. Bud tried hog farming and I tried to help him, but he just wouldn't spend money on the hogs. I never could bring myself—ever—to tell Jason how bad things got and I can't tell y'all either. Sometimes, healing can take forever.

I gotta say Jason was a good listener. He asked questions—that's how I knew he was tuned in. Any storyteller loves a good listener. He also said he loved me. He felt his mother was bringing us together. We talked a lot 'bout our age difference. He kept saying that didn't worry him. After all, I was married to an older man afore and he was the one getting the better of the deal—yes, that's what he said! He said why not get married and I agreed. It seemed meant to be.

Jason's trips home continued for a few more weeks with me staying alone waiting for his return every Friday. I began to tune up the place as I thought Sophie would want. She was in and on my mind day and night. I asked for her guidance and called Jason every night. He called me whenever he could during the day. Every weekend he showed up so we could share more and more of ourselves. Sundays, when he left, he made me promise not to disappear on him and I agreed. I couldn't imagine leaving. After all, this was my safe haven and he was my man. Five weeks later, he arrived with a UHAUL and never left.

His first day back, I came to see how little I knew 'bout him. He was lying on the sofa looking up at the ceiling and I was flipping pages of a magazine by the window. It was all quiet 'til he suddenly jumped up and broke out in what I can only say was "oratory." Waving his arms to embellish his words, he gave a speech that came outta nowhars. I have a copy from my bedroom wall whar it's been ever since:

Thomas the Rhymer

"True Thomas lay on Huntlie bank
A ferlie he spied wi' his eye
And there he saw a lady bright
Come riding down by the Eildon Tree
Her skirt was o' the grass-green silk
Her mantle o' the velvet fine
At ilka tett of her horse's mane
Hung fifty siller bells and nine.
True Thomas he pulled aff his cap
And louted low down on his knee
'Hail to thee, Mary, Queen of Heaven

For thy peer on earth could never be.'
'O no, O no, Thomas,' she said
'That name does not belang to me
I'm but the Queen o' fair Elfland,
That am hither come to visit thee.
'Harp and carp, Thomas,' she said
"Harp and carp along wi' me;
And if ye dare to kiss my lips,
Sure of your bodie I will be.'
'Betide me weal, betide me woe,
That weird shall never daunten me.'
Syne he has kissed her rosy lips
All underneath the Eildon Tree.
'Now ye maun go wi' me,' she said
'True Thomas, ye maun go wi' me.
And ye maun serve me seven years,
Though weal or woe as may chance to be.
She's mounted on her milk-white steed,
She's ta'en true Thomas up behind
And aye, whene'er her bridle rang,
The steed gaed swifter that the wind.
O they rade on and farther on
The steed gaed swifter than the wind
Until they reached a desert wide,
And living land was left behind.
'Light down, light down now, true Thomas
And lean your head upon my knee
Abide ye there a little space
And I will show you ferlies three.

'O see ye not yon narrow road
So thick beset wi' thorns and briers
That is the Path of Righteousness
Though after it but few inquiries.
And see ye not yon braid, braid road
That lies across the lily leven?
That's the Path of Wickedness
Though some call it the Road to Heaven.
'And see ye not yon bonny road
That winds about the fernie brae?
That's the road to fair Elfland,
Where thou and I this night might maun gae.
'But, Thomas, ye shall haud your tongue,
Whate'er ye may hear or see
For speak ye word in Elfyn-land,
Ye'll ne'er win back to you ain countrie.'
O they rade on and farther on
And they waded river abune the knee
And they saw neither sun nor moon
But they heard the roaring of the sea.
It was mirk, mirk night, there was nae starlight
They waded through red blude to the knee
For a' the blude that's shed on the earth
Rins through the springs o' that countrie."

Okay, now, you can all stop laughing. I gotta say I put on that
accent best I could. Hope it worked. Back then, though, I didn't
laugh—I only stared for maybe a whole minute afore asking 'bout
this intellectual explosion. I never did hear such in my life.

"Oh, it's just a wee thing I put ta memory during my lonely years. It's a really old Scottish poem I came on in an antique store. Supposedly, thar's a Scottish 'some man named Thomas the Rhymer and this maybe tells somethin' 'bout his life. I think thar're other versions, too, but I dunno. Nobody really knows whar this came from."

"But why'd ya go and memorize it? I don't get it."

"I dunno—I liked it, that's all. It's got that eternal feminine wisdom and it speaks of a fairyland whar's thar's a mite bit of magic 'n whole lotta faith 'n truth. Kinda romantic, too. I like the feel, the rhythm, the mystery. Maybe the Scot in me yearns fer the ol' sod."

"Would ya ever wanna see Scotland?"

"'Twould warm the cockles of me heart, fair lady."

"I dunno, not sure I would. I got harsh memories of my grandparents' Scottish ways. I always tried to deny bein' a Scot. Seems such a hard way to live."

"I think that's in yer mind, little one. The Scots are a great people. I read that maybe a dozen of our Presidents came from Ulster stock. That's pretty impressive, isn't it? And thar's plenty others who helped make our country what it is today. Take John Muir."

"Who's he?"

"John Muir? He was one Scotsman, he was. Back in the 1800s, he explored out west 'n kept a diary. He got so caught up by the beauty he found everywhar's he went that he done dedicated his life ta convincing Congress to establish a national park system. And they did. Just one man—a Scot—made a huge difference to our country. Now, we have a big beautiful system of national parks. Girl, ya gotta think the best of yer own or who can ya think the best of?"

I shook my head and flipped a coupla pages. *Jason's right. Gotta think well of your own—something I never thought to do afore.*

The following day, I was telling Jason how amazing it was he memorized that poem and he allowed as having memorized another one, too. Yes! He said this one was by Sir Walter Scott. I remember the title, "My Own, My Native Land" 'cuz we used ta say over 'n over "Breathes thar a man with soul so dead who never to hisself has said..." and some of y'all can probably help me finish it with—"this is my own, my native land." Oh, then we made jokes with that last line, replacing it with all sortsa things, ya know. Whatta fun memory! Anyways, he finished the whole thing while I held back my laughing. Ya know, self-education always impressed me—it tells a person's sense of self-worth—which is my problem. I was so impressed by Sophie's wonderful only one.

One day, he disappeared for a coupla hours and came back with a pair of new shoes that fit me and a book on Mark Twain. He explained how Mark Twain was such a wise old American and also Scots-Irish, like me. He said I oughtta get familiar with the man's writing. That was just the thing. Soon's as it was in my hands, I did what I liked to do with my schoolbooks—flipped the pages 'til one spot fell open by itself. I took my first look and can still remember what it said. "Everybody's a moon and has a dark side which he never shows to anybody" and "I done lived through some terrible things in my life, some of which happened." Those were the first sayings I read. I kept that book at the side of my bed for years; it kept my spirits up lots and lotsa times. I'm sure Jason was hoping I'd think kinder of my own. Well, it worked.

Probably doesn't surprise you we got married three weeks after he moved in. Yes—me, a thirty-year-old adventurer or—like they say now—"adventuress," in a simple green dress and Jason—a fifty-year-old retiree—wearing a matching green shirt. We stood together afore the Ashland Justice of the Peace on Saturday, September third, 1960. After Jason showed his birth certificate, I told the Justice I was Brigit Celt—that's who I decided I was, even though it wasn't how I was born—and I said I was born at home so didn't have papers, which was true. It was lucky he accepted all that. We said our vows afore eating dinner at The Village Inn. Our table sat under a garland of plastic flowers... pink, I think. It seemed so romantic. Jason's sons came to visit when they could. It was clear they loved their dad and they seemed to approve of me. I think this is when healing began to take hold.

'Course I couldn't wait to share the news with my dear friend, Cee. I called her two days after our ceremony. As the phone was ringing in Cee's sunny house, my imagination saw her chewing on a carrot or something as she came to answer her wall phone in the front hall. I could see her wiping her hands on the backa her blue jeans as she picked it up.

"Hey-lo."

"Hi Cee."

"Ah-h-h, long time no hear, Zee."

"Long time no see, Cee."

"Long time no talk."

"Long time no walk."

"Long time on clock."

"Tick tock."

"Minutes."

"Hours."

"Years."

"Mine."

"Gold."

"Ring."

"Engagement."

"Weddin'."

"Divorce."

"Weddin'."

"Wait a cotton-pickin' minute, girl! What're ya sayin'?"

"Weddin'."

"Yeah?"

"Yeah 'n fer real this time."

"C'mon, how can that be? Ya walked out only six months ago—disappeared—up 'n vanished. And now, with yer backsides not even cold, yer tellin' me yer married? Sounds more like ya went and jumped outta the fryin' pan into the fiarrr."

"Well, Cee, thar's lots 'n lots ta tell. We gotta get together."

"Ya can say that again."

"We gotta get together."

"Oh git off it. So, how're ya anyways?"

"Just 'bout excellent."

"Oh Zee, I been so worried. Why'd ya leave me hangin'? Ya know I love ya more'n anything."

"Cee, honey, right now I can't begin ta tell you what I been through. Ya know I couldn't go back to my old life."

"I know, I know. 'Course not. But thar's somethin' ya gotta know—"

"That be?"

"That be he's comin' round. Fact is, he was here again jist last week—drunk as a skunk—coon owl, even."

"No-o-o-o. Why's he comin' 'round thar, anyways?"

"Lookin fer y'all, silly! He's been makin' quite a fuss hereabouts ever since ya went missin'. Seems he can't let go of the fact that yer body didn't show up at the burnt farm and that must mean yer feet are still walkin' the earth. He's after ya and naturally he thinks I know something."

"Naturally."

"But, 'course, I didn't know nothin'. I kept on tellin' him it. Then again, he never did believe anythin' I ever said, anyways. But he kept on sayin' no woman could walk out on him and live ta talk 'bout it 'n such. Packin' his .22, too. Must say, it was mighty scary!"

"He didn't threaten you or the kids or anything, did he?"

"Not in so many words. But ya know how it is with him. He's so creepy."

"Oh, yeah."

"So's, anyways, he stayed here, hangin' round, swiggin' from a big old Wild Turkey—even put a hole in Justin's diaper on the line. When Jeth peeled in and found him in his stinkin' state, staggerin' 'n slobberin', he started in screamin' ta git on outta here, never come back onta our property and we don't never wanna see him again 'n all that. He got hisself in his pickup and took off like a monkey gone mad. He's not come back yet. I gotta tell ya, though, I was sure glad Jeth wasn't on the road same time he was. I'm hopin' he's ridda us, but with him ya can never know."

"You just said a mouthful, girl. But now ya got me feelin' upset and worried."

"Well, the only thing is that .22 under the seat."

"Oh, he always had that."

"Yeah, but he's runnin' on fury nowadays and if he so much as gets a sniff of y'all, I think ya better say yer prayers."

"But I'm not thar—and y'all are. I didn't think he'd be goin' for you when I up and left."

"Honey, ya wasn't thinkin' 'bout nothin' when ya up 'n left. I remember that day very well."

"Yeah, I'm sure you do and now, all of a sudden, so do I. But, Cee, it's worked out so good. I'm in a new place in a really new world. I got a brand-new life and it's so good."

"So, why're ya callin' me, then?"

"'Cuz I want ya in my new life, hon. I miss you."

"Ynh, ya probably want yer old life back."

"Oh, no I don't. All's I want is for you to meet my personal white knight in shinin' armor—and, as of yesterday—my honest and true husband."

"Yer sayin' ya went and married a man and then called me? I don't git it. What's goin' on with ya anyways and whar're ya callin' from?"

"I'm in heaven, on toppa cloud nine, and like Vaughn Munroe says, *'I'm sittin' on top of the world, just rollin' alon-n-ng, just rolling alon-n-n-ng.'*"

"Zee, cut it out! If yer gonna dance in circles wastin' my time I'm gonna set this phone on toppa the fridge and finish hangin' out the laundry. I'm busier'n a hornet in honey. I got kids, ya know, lotsa kids, and lots ta do."

"Sorry, I know. How's everybody anyways?"

"We're all jist fine. Justin's gettin' over the measles so's he's only tolerable, but everybody else's had 'em already. We're ok. I gotta go in a minute 'cuz—"

"Right, but just one little thing."

"What?"

"Lone Ranger."

"Tonto."

"Pronto."

"Hurry."

"Rush."

"Relax."

"Sleep."

"Can't. Too much ta do. Bye. Call me again sometime. Soon."

"Next week. Love ya, hon."

So, as ya can see, Cee was my dearest friend 'n that's how it was with us. We got back together and our husbands enjoyed each other and the Hawkins kids called us Mr. and Mrs. Connors. All but baby Justin answered me, "Yes ma'am." Justin just stared. The hardest part of being back together was getting Cee to remember my name wasn't Zena anymore. Actually, it took her years. When the kids let go of the Mrs. and said "Brigit" was when Cee let go of Zena.

It bothered me lots that Bud was after Cee and Jethro, but didn't surprise me really—that's the kinda sick person he was—and is. After the call, I put my mind to thinking positive. I wanted to believe Jethro had scared off Bud, so I talked myself into thinking that was the end of things. But it wasn't the end. Things got worse.

Ya know, my story is how I got transformed into the "me" you see here, but really there's lotsa stories inside that. Altogether, stories inside stories make a life history and when I put "my" and "story" together, look what I get!...

Anyways, I quickly found how easy it can be to have babies—Jason and I got two in our first two years. Our little boy, Jasper Wood Connors, came first. We called him Sparky. Less than twelve months later, our daughter came along. Jason and I agreed she hadda be Sophie, but he wanted Sylvia included—fine with me—but I said she hadda be called Nene. I didn't have any problems having these babies, sure a relief after my experiences with Bud. This part of my life was so wonderful I don't have words for it. Botha them were born perfectly and were perfectly healthy. We agreed—Jason's job was to bring 'em up knowing of Mammy and I was to tell 'em Mammy's sayings. I think time stood still for a while.

Thar was only one little negative. When I was carrying Sparky, I began recalling my miscarriages in those years with Bud and feared it might happen again. I never told Jason, but did tell my doctor. He said I probably miscarried because I was depressed. Lying in the hospital bed after Sparky's wonderful birth, I couldn't help thinking of the stillborn we named Robbie—the very one whose sickening death caused me to stop having sex with Bud.

Anyways, with two kids, a husband and a home, I turned into Sophie's idea of a typical Ashlander—hardworking, devoted to my family and busy in the community. I settled into living so quiet I never thought to growl, never even remembered doing it. I woke in the morning praying only to shower love and support on my family and went to bed every night thanking the Lord for the extraordinary joy they gave me. I spent the days focusing on my family and shutting out the distressing, dreary, outside world.

Remember how the 'sixties tried to rob us of peace and sanity—with all the riots and killings, that war in Vietnam and all the violence everywhere you looked? Whew. Then, President Kennedy and his brother—and Martin Luther King, too—they all got assassinated and so many thousands of soldiers got killed in Vietnam. Oh, I can't find words for it all. Then Detroit and Chicago got "incinerated" with young'ns protesting on the streets and police pounding 'em with billy clubs and fire hoses. Seems the world went mad for a while thar. But not in our house. Oh no—I made sure of that. I made cookies and candles, read stories and wrote poems, made love and wrote recipes. Thar was no grand plan. I just did what I could to blot out the ugly and make my new life what I wanted it to be—safe and happy. Honestly, I forgot 'bout the free part. *The Sunday Telegraph Bulletin* was dropped at the end of our driveway, but the front page always had big bloody pictures. I fixed that—I closed my eyes and turned right to the home section and department store ads. My mind got too overwhelmed knowing of the brutality thar was in the world. Pain wasn't welcome this time 'round. But Jason felt he hadda keep up on the war and support JJ. Seems a soldier thinks 'bout war all his life.

Soon's our kids could walk we began exploring the animal trails out back. We all loved picnics. Sometimes the kids raced back home to see who could win a new book at the next book sale. Jason tugged 'em into Ashland Town Library to get circulation cards, so after Saturday morning story hour they could go home with three books for the week.

Perhaps you can see how I—once a suffering Zena—was turning into a nurturing Brigit. I baked bread, made curtains, potty-trained, patched scuffed knees, cut hair, sewed doll clothes, played hide-and-seek and flew kites. And I set in lilies-of-the-valley, raked leaves, shoveled snow, unplugged toilets, cut grass, mended fences, grew potato plants on window sills, strung popcorn on Christmas trees, colored eggs and played Monopoly. You get the idea, right? My new life—our life—was like outta a storybook for a few years. Seemed things were working out. Jason and I tried to be the best parents we could and I was sure I found what I planned and intended. I wouldn't let my old life get in the way of that. But it was too good to be true.

The first problem was Jason's eyes began to fade right after the babies came. I noticed it the Christmas I gave him those new-fangled disposable razor blades and realized it wasn't his razor's fault why he couldn't do a good job in the morning. We learned it was cataracts and that's what made me his link to the outside world—I started reading to him. On our sixth anniversary, he couldn't work at the library anymore and that's when reading the paper got real hard. I only did it when I could stomach it.

It wasn't all bad, though. Jason's wisdom and presence anchored our family. As the kids also learned to be his eyes, their vocabularies grew; he encouraged them with word games and riddles and jokes. Hearing them chatter in the next room, my heart was warmed. Never did I complain 'bout his infirmity. I could accept whatever this life offered. I think I learned that in the woods—every day I thanked God for that grand adventure—and Sophie, too, 'course. Jason was sweet to resurrect the Connors' tradition of smoking meats and cheese. He rebuilt the old smoke house out backa the barn and spent hours bartering with farmers for slaughtered and cleaned hogs. He tried to match his grandfather, who was a master smoker. He hadda give it up, but only after managing to learn how to make pretty good ribs.

One of his best ideas was teaching me to drive. He was what you call a pragmatist. Me? I never thought of it afore, so I didn't take to it too good. But it worked out better'n I thought. A thirty-something-year-old-learner can be mighty silly; I went back and forth between fear and humor behind the wheel of that Studebaker. But thar was a real need for me to take over the driving and we both knew it. Sunday afternoon rides became a family ritual. Coming home from church, Jason tutored me on the fine points of driving and these were the worst times in our marriage. I found it hard to learn how to match the clutch pedal to the gas pedal every time I hadda shift. It'd make me anxious and I'd burst into tears and that would go 'n upset the kids. It got to be general craziness 'til we'd bury the memory with ice cream cones. I—I did pass my license, though, and turned into a pretty good driver. Lucky, too, for my driving soon became necessary. I still love driving those beautiful hills—turning up the radio and singing. In those days it was with Sonny and Cher or the Weavers or Elvis. My heart felt full. I was alive and felt powerful and I thanked Jason from the bottom of my heart.

Here's where I gotta admit another habit of mine—this one most peculiar. It's what I took up right after Sophie died. It wasn't so much the hobby that was peculiar—more the way I did it. After lighting those first candles with Jason, I hadda continue—probably for the same reason folks all over the world do it—I just hadda memorialize Sophie and her life. Keeping her spirit alive was important, so I always kept a burning candle on the mantle—still do. At first, it was outta respect for her, but later it included everybody I cared 'bout—like even my Indian friends. Even now, when I go past my eternal flame, I give thanks to all my life guides. A candle glows in our home day and night, winter and summer, every day. 'Course, then I hadda make 'em. When I started donating them to the hospital gift shop, I called 'em Brigit's Candles and—over time—folks sought 'em out. They drove out to the Connor's Farm 'round April when the lilies-of-the-valley were blooming and rolled down their windows to breathe the delicious air. Then, some would even tap on our front door and peek through the curtains to see if the rumors were true—that Brigit Connors made her candles naked! They were right, but they never did manage to see me—I was way too clever.

Making candles naked might seem strange to you—or to anyone, actually—but to me, it was a reminder of how I got a second chance at living—a new start. I still give Sophie the credit for that—she's the one who made me wanna go on. It seemed so clear and obvious I never doubted it. I knew—however—no one 'cept Jason would get it. It's why I kept it secret. So, it was most disturbing when Nene came home from first-grade saying the kids were teasing her 'bout how her mother took all her clothes off when she made her candles.

"But Momma, ya don't do that, raight?"

"Oh, honey, they're just foolin' with ya. Remember not to take silly talk seriously."

"Momma, when I told 'em it, they said everybody knows."

"Oh, do they now? Well, we'll see 'bout that. I'll go have a talk with Mrs. Mallory. She'll speak to the class 'bout unkind teasin'. Don't worry your sweet little head, I'll see this is stopped. Everything'll be all right."

I wasn't ready to explain to Nene. Not yet. Only many years later could I talk 'bout it. I wearied 'bout who knew to spread this news, but never did find out. I did go see the teacher.

And Mrs. Mallory tried to put out the fire, she did, but my kids hadda bear up to taunting and teasing for years. I kept a strong denial, but kept on doing it one Sunday night a month—after the kids went to sleep, 'course.

Suddenly, I'm remembering the time when I was working on my candles and a stray cat showed up at the back door. It reminded me of when I appeared at that same door. I couldn't refuse it. It looked such a mess we named it Mess. Then we discovered she was pregnant, so we changed her name to Messenger. Messenger's four little messages we called Faith, Hope, Charity and Love. After Messenger got spayed, we renamed her Sweetness and she sweetened our lives for seven years that sped by in a twinkling. I'm sure y'all get it. These were years of a satisfying bond between Jason and me, but I gotta admit that as his health declined we became—well, there's no other way to say it—platonic.

Then, lickety-split, the world got 'bout as crazy as when the President got killed... 1968 came along. Jason proudly explained to me all 'bout how many years the Communists in North Vietnam done tried to take over South Vietnam and how our country finally got into it and tried to stop them. But we lost hope right at the start of 1968. So many of our soldiers had died and were still dying and all for nothing. Why, every year, more and more were sent over thar to die—and that's when the war protestors got fierce. Then, after Dr. King got assassinated, thar were more street riots and it seemed the whole world was in a hash. Plus, that George Wallace person stirred up the John Birch Society and that awful Mr. Nixon went and got elected. It was so hard to read the news to Jason that whole year. When I got to the summer Olympics in Mexico and hadda describe the two American medal winners standing in their bare feet, heads down and fists pushed up in the air with the national anthem playing, I almost threw up. But Jason wanted to hear everything. 1968 was real hard to keep outta the house.

Simmering

What began
Hot Hot Hot
Flaming attraction
Burning desire
Sparking the fire
Blazing through years
Fueling and generating
Consuming and devouring
Scorching out and insides
Softens into cinders
No more searing flames
Mere warm, loyal remains
Love turned down low
Simmering through time

I managed pretty good 'til right after the election. I took the kids to have their teeth checked. Our appointment was with Dr.

Otterman, a Midway Orthodontist who came to Ashland 3-7 one afternoon a month. He was gonna look at a coupla Sparky's second teeth that were crooked. He was running late. When he got to us and explained his treatment plan, he said it was gonna cost $3,000. I said Sparky had inherited his bite from his father's side and they all did fine without intervention, thank you, and that much money was outta the question. I had a flashback of my grandparents putting their uppers in water glasses aside of their beds at night and watching them finger 'em out the next morning. I was sick thinking what Sparky might look like someday, but we couldn't spend a fortune on just teeth. I was grouchy pulling my kids to the car.

It was 'bout six o'clock and getting dark and we all were anxious to get home for supper, homework and bed. I tooled along 'bout six miles of foggy, country road playing with the radio dial 'til I could get a station without static. I turned up the volume so we could sing along to what we called in our house "the Smoky Mountain National Anthem:" "*Let the sun shine, let the sun shine in, the su-u-u-un shine in. Let the sun shine, let the sun shine in, the su-u-u-un shine in.*" We all loved the melody and the repetition of the words and always sang it as loud as we could.

The ride was carefree, those "tribulations" at the dentist were over and we were almost home. The music was perfect and the road—well, this was the kids' all-time favorite, with its thank-you-ma'ams and twisty turns that gave them a taste of weightlessness and also an excuse to tumble over each other. Seven-year-old Sparky was ready for his favorite thank-you-ma'am. He was straddling the hump in the middle of the floor, hanging onto the front seat and singing with abandon as his head bounced up and down with the car. Nene had got herself so to soften the flip in her stomach by pressing her feet into the backa my seat. That way, she could also protect herself from what Sparky was gonna do when he fell.

And me behind the wheel? My heart was feeling all that sunshine. I played the road to the kids' best enjoyment, accelerating over the rise so their stomachs turned over and then coasting down the other side. I was singing at the toppa my lungs, too, 'bout that golden sun melting itself into and through our lives when—in the darkness at the bottom of the dip—I caught in my headlights two deer eyes. I swerved the wheel to avoid him then pulled the car sharply for the turn, but the two abrupt twists of the wheel made the car wobbly. I knew I couldn't correct again or then completely lose control. That's when I saw the tree.

Gripping the wheel with both hands, I slammed on the brakes as hard as I could and came to a screeching halt just popping slightly into the tree trunk. Sparky's bobbing little body shot like a missile into the dashboard while the radio blared "su-u-u-n shine in." I lifted my precious boy's head and blood gushed from his mouth. Gathering him to my chest, I learned Nene's bracing had saved her, so I moved the car afore somebody else came over the rise. Obviously, Sparky had bit through his tongue as well as his upper lip and his nose looked broken. I drove straight to the emergency room whar Sparky's lip got stitched. Dr. Otterman was called back to sew his front teeth back into his gums and that began a long series of orthodontic appointments, ending up costing way over $3,000.

I didn't handle it well for a long while. Jason was most understanding—never laying any guilt on me—and Sparky quickly bounced back to his usual happy-go-lucky self. But I couldn't let go of the fact I was responsible. I couldn't get behind the wheel of a car all that winter. I resigned from the Church Guild Luncheon Committee and the planning committee for the annual Christmas bazaar. I took a leave-of-absence from the hospital pink ladies and told everybody I needed to tend to my kids.

I gave Sparky extra treats, like strawberry milkshakes, red Jello and Kool-Aid popsicles. After his mouth healed and the red scar on his lip mellowed to pink, I started making jokes 'bout how he'd look with a mustache or 'bout being a world-class prizefighter. I tried to laugh 'bout it. I framed last year's school picture so the new one wouldn't need to be put up. I couldn't look at his smile. I couldn't for the life of me see the dear little person I gave birth to and loved with all my heart. Even now, that day is one of the lowest points of my life. I still can't pass that spot without recalling the horror and haven't ever enjoyed the sunshine song since.

So, I went back to writing poetry. It was a time to release some emotions. Mentioning this to Sparky's teacher got me invited me to read poems to his class. One thing led to another and soon I was heading up a monthly poetry group for people suffering loss and grief. I threw myself into this 'til life at home changed.

Jason got wearied; he felt I took the accident too seriously and insisted I get counseling. The five sessions didn't make me a new person, even though Rev. Munson did say some helpful things. In his quiet and calm way, he assured me it was impossible to bring up kids perfectly. He reminded me of what my grandparents musta gone through raising two generations. I got many ideas in his office and did learn to accept better my own imperfections.

Rev. Munson said what happened to me was just one of those things that can happen to anyone.

I also got help from Cee and Jethro, but working out my feelings with just Cee was different. We'd be talking 'bout raising kids and life, in general, then afore I'd know it my dear friend would be telling me 'bout Bud like she always did. Over the years, she kept me up on his rantings, even though I tried tossing 'em off. She was now shopping at the supermarket in the new mall and didn't go into town much, so she wasn't bumping into Bud much. It was Jethro's buddies who told her he was still hanging 'round the general store blubbering 'bout me. Seems he was considered the town drunk and his biggest obsession was *me*. He was sure I hadda be alive and he wanted me back. Dead or alive, he said. He bragged he personally wanted to stick that big old knife on his belt into me. I believed he woulda, too, if he coulda. It was his next words that were the worst, though, and I couldn't ever shake. He said he wanted to stick the knife into me and twist it round and round. Whenever I thought 'bout that, I felt like throwing up. It terrified me.

Unfortunately, some folks liked to play with him, so they done told him rumors from relatives or a friend of a friend or something. That didn't help, 'course. Bud never got on with my family, so I knew they'd have nothing to do with him. Cee was the only one he'd go for. He was a one to settle old scores and me being missing was giving him a reason to keep on living.

I started obsessing over my kids. I didn't go near Forestland so didn't go to Cee and Jethro's twentieth anniversary party and never looked up anybody from school or church. Always in the backa my mind—no matter what I did—was the fear he could show up on my doorstep. I thanked God I had a new identity—what was protecting me now. I asked how Bud supported hisself. Cee heard his family got together and took him in on condition he got help. Apparently, he did, but he also stayed with the clan and that surely fed his anger.

I couldn't bring myself to tell Jason. Ya see, he was really starting to slow down. Placing such a heavy burden on him seemed too much. Besides, the problem was mine and he couldn't do anything 'cept weary. I wanted to throw Bud off track and get his sick mind dealing with something else. But how? Cee was as sympathetic as a good friend can be, but our discussions went 'round and 'round. Night times, I tossed and turned seeking inspiration from Sophie, but I sure didn't get any. Some nights, Mark Twain's words helped a bit. "The two most important days in one's life are the day you're born and the day you find out why" and "The world owes you nothing. It was here first." They were like little glimpses of light in the dark.

Then, life really changed the year Sparky turned eight and Nene seven. Jason had his first chest pains. More followed—off and on—for over a year, but I didn't know. He didn't wanna pay attention to them, which is why he didn't mention them. So, I was really shocked 'round 11:00 on a damp, drizzly March night, back in 1970, when he couldn't get hisself ready for bed because of the pain. He asked me to take him to the hospital. I woke the kids, told 'em to lock the door and helped him into the warm car. I was scared to death, but I never, never, never imagined what was 'bout to happen.

Sitting in the emergency waiting area—heart pounding—I was flipping magazine pages fast as I could while he lay on a hard table behind the closed double doors. Thar was no space in the cramped exam room so I was back with the old plastic settees and even older magazines. Time was really dragging and I was beside myself. I finally tossed the magazines aside to stare at the posters on the faded walls. I couldn't think straight. I brushed every single dog hair off my pajama bottoms that peeped out below my raincoat and let my eyes drift aimlessly.

I got 'round to noticing thar were five others in the room. First was a sleepy, overweight woman opposite me wearing slippers and a housecoat. I noticed deep sadness in her eyes. A little boy was off and on trying to sleep with his head on her lap. An old man next to her was stooped over, his arms resting on his knees as he stared at the floor. A few seats away to my left was a couple just walked in. The man looking to be Indian was facing the opposite wall holding in his lap a black cowboy hat with an eagle feather. Even though his eyes were closed, he sat up straight. His long dark hair was mussed and matted and the cheek facing me had a huge bloody gash. His whole face looked badly swollen and dried blood covered his torn and dirty clothes. It looked like he'd been in a nasty accident.

When the woman with him was called to the desk, I recognized her. She was a volunteer in the hospital gift shop, but her regular job was in the Ashville Social Services Office. Here, in the emergency room 'bout one in the morning, I was bumping into nice Sally Lowney with a bloody Indian. That's when I glanced back at the man and felt a lightning bolt shoot through me. *What the... why, that Indian!* In a flash, everything in the room went fuzzy and the walls began to spin. I planted my hands on my knees and hung my head for a few moments—I needed to stop the spinning. Finally, I dared sneak another look sideways at the torn-up face. Yes. Yes. I knew him very well, but from another time, another place, another life.

Nothing could hold me back. You understand, no power on earth could stop me. My dear husband mighta been behind those doors in the middle of a heart attack, but I was in this room in a complete other world. My body was here, but my head was transported back to the woods—sucked back by a massive, invisible force—back to the life afore this one—like I was in another one of those time warps. Then and now came together. Brigit and Renee were one.

I knew this man was Atar. I could never forget that nose, that pose, that poise. From somewhars deep inside, I recalled his unique smell and let out a gasp. He glanced at me afore setting his head straight again. A second later, though, he turned and our eyes locked for a few seconds. No doubt. Those eyes—those piercing deep wells of emotion—those sparkling, twinkling, dancing blue-green eyes now so badly swollen and pained—they were his'n, for sure. He was the only one to ever have those eyes.

'Course I hadda find out more. So, after Mrs. Lowney returned to her seat, I lifted my goosebumpy body up and made my shaky legs walk right past Atar—I couldn't figure how to talk to him. My heart pounded so hard I could feel my neck pumping and I looked 'round to see if anybody else in the room heard it.

"Why, hello, Sally. Remember me, Brigit Connors from the hospital gift shop? I make the candles."

"My goodness, yas-s-s, 'course. And how are ya, dearie? Whatever brings ya here in the middle of the night? Nothin' serious, I hope."

I explained 'bout Jason and Sally explained how she was on call and hadda bring in a hit-and-run victim—this man. Seems he was run over by a motorcycle and the night patrol officer came on him lying alongside the road. They called her 'cuz the Indian couldn't speak English. She agreed to take him to the hospital since the officer hadda take another call. Now, she was just waiting on the doctor to finish with a heart attack patient afore looking at him.

At a pause in the conversation, I smiled, leaned over and casually murmured, "O-si-yo." It was just 'bout the only word I could think of right then.

Atar looked up with a sad and soulful look on his face and answered in that same sweet-soft voice with one of the words I remembered, "Wa-do."

Sally's eyes bugged. "Goodness gracious, what's goin' on? What-all didya say ta him?"

"Oh, nothing. Nothing, really. I said 'Hello' in his language and he thanked me."

"Why, I'll be hog-tied. Are ya tellin' me ya can speak Injun? I'd no idea. Why, y'all cain't possibly know this man, can ya?"

"Well, I did learn a coupla Indian words years ago and, yeah—strange enough—I do think I remember this man. Fact is, he and some of his friends done saved my life afore they taught me some words in their language. I was very fond of 'em, but we-we lost touch. Strange, I haven't seen him in years and can't say I know him now—know nothin' 'bout his life."

"But y'all can speak ta him and that's so-o-o helpful. Fer some reason I don't git he don't seem ta speak English. It's most clear, though, he does understand what I say. That's 'bout it. Nobody knows yet what happened out thar on the road. Why, I'd be ever so grateful if ya could git something outta him."

"I'd dearly love ta help, I would. It's just that I don't rightly know what's in store for me, what with my husband and all. Why don't we see how things go?"

"'Course, dear, 'course. I'm sorry, I understand. But if yer waitin' still when they come fer his intake, perhaps ya could be present?"

I nodded and returned to my seat to stare at the turquoise wall, this time split right down the middle with halfa me breathing in sweet fresh air, stepping on the earth in bare feet, listening to birds singing. Sometimes it's not possible to hang onto the present—that was one.

Jason was finally transferred to a room with an I.V. in his arm and an oxygen mask on his face and I was walking alongside his gurney with the nurse and she was explaining how Jason's condition was stable and I could go on home. After his transfer into bed, I kissed him and told him I'd come back in the morning. Then, I went and found Atar being treated for cuts and bruises, a broken jaw and a lacerated face requiring ten stitches—oh, and a displaced shoulder. Very few words would come to mind. I think I was in shock and my emotions on overload. I couldn't put medical questions to him and couldn't get a personal history. I mixed simple words and sign language and learned he was walking into town when he was hit from behind by a motorcyclist. I kept asking, "*do-hi-tsu?*" and he always answered like his state-of-mind meant nothing to him, "*do-na-da-go-hv'-i.*" *

When the treatment was over, Mrs. Lowney took the man everyone was calling Mister Red Man—which I found very insulting—she took him in her van to spend the night in the town shelter. I dunno how I found my way home. I kept thinking back to my "adventure in the woods"—what I always called it. Many times over the years, I considered how wonderful it was those kind men had saved me so I could go on sorta confident after. But never did I have such a rush of raw emotion as then—never afore did the old feelings, smells and excitement consume me like now. It took a long time to climb into my lonely bed.

I'm sure nobody's ever ready to have their safe and serene life tore up. I know I wasn't ready to have my past crash into my present—especially since my present just went and fell into turmoil and my future was looking mighty shaky. This wasn't at all what I wanted for this life.

With Jason, it was supposed to be orderly and smooth, protected. I done worked hard living like I reckoned was "normal"—hard to get at Sophie's "quintessential Ashland life." I didn't ever wanna give it up—but I didn't think to consider the matter of change.

Oh yes, there were other unanticipated things—like when Sparky fell off the swing and broke his arm during his birthday party and the time when Nene's fever reached 104 and her, convulsion drove me insane for a few hours—and then that time I

---

* Listeners smile at "Are you ok?" and again at "Let's see each other again."

messed up in the car. Oh yes, those all fitted into what anybody's gotta expect in a lifetime. And I was used to some things from my Zena life—like Bud and all—giving me trouble in this one, but I never gave a thought to Renee coming back to haunt me—and certainly not in the middle of my husband's heart attack. I ask why, when we're not ready and don't expect them, do hauntings return?

Anyways, I called the hospital three times the next day to hear Jason was sleeping and to let him rest. I visited that evening while the kids did their homework and sat next to him as he dozed, looking long into the lined face I knew so well. Soon's I got permission, I scooped up the kids to visit their father and kept a smiley face, speaking of how we could weather the setback just fine, how it was nothing to be concerned 'bout, how Daddy was a strong man and he was gonna get better. I put out jokes to make him smile and held his hand and fixed his hair. I allowed as I was the family team captain. Nobody had any inkling of the inner turmoil ripping me apart. And I never told a soul 'til now.

Fact is, though—seeing Atar dug up from deep inside something I thought I done buried when I rode outta those woods. Now, I was being eaten up by confusion and drawn down to that place inside whar nobody else goes. I was pretty good at play-acting in fronta others. I left my demons for private times. An old saying Sophie gave me—probably one of Mammy's—kept passing through my mind, "Life happens while we're busy making plans." Inside, I returned to Renee, the lonely survivor. I spent time in my bathtub holding long talks with Sophie, trusting her wisdom would help me be what she called "stalwart." Sophie's words the first day we met kept echoing through my mind, "Being married don't matter?" and "Oh, one of those marriages whar everyone don't get everything everyone wants?" Like it was the day afore, I heard her voice and her laugh sitting at the kitchen table and remembered her saying, "Caring is caring, no matter who, what, when or why." Most importantly, I also heard, "Tis the head that seeks truth, but only the heart finds it."

In my mind, I could see the frail, old arthritic body shuffling 'round the house like under an outer layer of heavenly "ethereal" light. Then, it all got to seeming more like flower parts I studied in school—with the Connors family folded 'round Sophie like petals while as she was what I think they call the "pedicel." I could see an outer calyx being like Ashland and a sepal being her ancestors guiding her. I tried writing a poem 'bout this vision, but never got satisfied. I just carried it in my head and heart. Oh well.

Meantime, the kids hung on news of Jason's improvement and his return home. When we got wrapped under our covers that first night, I-I was way too wound up to slip into my spooning position. Instead, I lay facing him with my head on his barrel chest listening to his thump *thump*... thump *thump*... thump *thump*... afore I realized my pulse was beating with his. I think they call that "synchrony." It relaxed me enough to let go my grip on him. During the next coupla days, I kept busy tending to Jason while the kids kept our spirits up. Yes, the whole family worked for days at recouping and regrouping, but the unspoken weary on all our minds was the future. We made it through the emergency and now we hadda reexamine our lives with our rock—Jason— knocked down. Then something huge happened.

I got a call from the head of Ashland Social Services, Sarah Ferguson. She was wondering, since I could communicate with that vagrant Indian, could I help them out by putting him to work 'round the farm 'til he was well? The town would pay. I broke into tears at such providence. Along with everything else in my head, I'd been stewing 'bout how I was gonna plant the garden plus prepare and paint one side of the house that Jason and I were gonna get done that year. But Jason was told he couldn't ever do heavy work again. Then, this phone call came like in answer to my prayers. Mrs. Ferguson said she could bring the man by on Friday and he could start work on Monday.

Whenever I thought back on my time in the woods, I questioned if it mighta been a dream or what they call a "hallucination." Perhaps it never happened. Perhaps I'd been so very hungry my mind done made it up. No matter—I was sure I could never understand it. But now, Atar was an actual living person who remembered me, so this—I guess you could say—"authenticated" my memories. My dream in the woods really happened.

I could hardly wait for Friday. I wanted to hear all 'bout my saviors—who they were, why they were thar in the first place and so much more. My nerves were frayed—how was I ever gonna get all my questions answered? If only he could speak English!

When the car pulled up the drive, I was in the kitchen setting out my candle-making supplies. My heart jumped and I gave a friendly wave to Atar. He nodded, but didn't wave back—didn't even turn his head, just faced the barn sitting in the beat-up, wood paneled station wagon while Sarah stepped up to the back door. We spoke a minute afore Sarah called him to join us. He ambled up to shake my hand.

"Brigit, I don't guess I have ta introduce ya ta Mr. Raymond Redman, do I?"

I think she was so conscious of her own nervous laugh that Sarah didn't pick up on my startled response. I hoped she didn't notice my trembling confusion as I reached my hand out to this familiar stranger with a puzzled look on my face. I knew he wouldn't miss it, though. I didn't say a word how strange this name was to me.

Soon's the car went down the drive, I tried to blurt out the few Cherokee words I'd practiced, but quickly gave it up because— are ya ready?—he made it very clear, right off, he spoke perfect English. Yes! And in that same, sweet-soft voice I remembered so well, he spoke gentle soothing English telling me just that. I dunno how I managed to stay standing.

"So, yer really Raymond Redman, then?"

He nodded and smiled.

"Well, I'm sure you can figure why I'm bustin' ta know who's Atar?"

"I understand, I-I do, but Raymond Redman is my birth name. Really, though, I'm Blue."

"Whatsa matter?"

"Nothing," as he shook his head.

"Then why're ya blue?"

"Oh, I mean you can call me Blue. My friends do. Nowadays some call me Ray, too."

"Excuse me?"

"You can call me Blue or Ray. Both are fine."

Now shaking my head, "Blue? Ray? Atar? I don't think I can keep all this straight."

"No need to. Just call me Blue. It's simpler. Atar was only the name I used when we met—a q-quirk of coincidence."

"A quirk of coincidence? What on earth are you talkin' 'bout?"

First, he smiled to the ground, then he looked into my eyes. Oh, that made my head pound and my heart melt. "Well, just before you came along in the woods, I was telling the others about a terrific book I read on Zoroastrianism."

"On what-t-t??" My eyes were popping outta my head. I couldn't believe my ears.

"Zoro-astrian-ism."

"Ya know, I don't know what-all you're sayin'."

"It's a religion based on the writings of a man who lived in Persia, a long time ago—no one knows exactly when. He was named Zarathustra, from a place called Azerbaijan."

"Look, I'm so confused. Whar in the world is Azerba... whatever?"

"Okay, Azerbaijan is in the Mideast near Pakistan and Iran. And Zoroastrianism... ach-h, I can tell you about that later, if you really want to know. All you need to know now is... for Zoroastrians, *Atar* is the word for fire, both what you know and see and then the invisible fire—the one we all carry inside us, whnh. They worship in fire temples and their medium for the Creator is thermal energy, sort of like the force inside us—our inner fire—our personal Atar. I always wondered how different cultures thought of fire, so I-I got this book from the library and learned Zoroastrians and I think a lot alike."

My eyes were still bugging and my jaw was literally hanging open. Who was this man I thought I once knew? I said, "This isn't goin' at all the way I thought it would."

"Well, okay, lemme explain. Just before you showed up at the pond, I told the others about th-this *Atar* along with other things from the book—like *Aban*, which is water to Zoroastrians. That means it's the source of life and nourishment, of course. Then there's other things, like *Asha* that means righteousness in their language—but I got interrupted, so—"

"So y'all weren't bein' honest with me right from the beginnin'? Those were fake names?"

"Well, actually, Scoop started it. He's the one who made the mistake."

"Scoop? Mistake? I'm beggin' you. Please, can ya help me out here?"

"Okie dokie. Look, remember h-how you were trying to get us to talk and you said you were Renee?"

"Uh-huh."

"And Asha answered saying he was Asha, right?"

"Uh-huh."

"Well, his real name was Scoop."

"So, whyever did he say he was Asha?"

"Theng is... he was trying to be funny. And he was thenking to name himself the Creator—as a kinda joke. He knew you wouldn't get it, but we would. But, then, he-he got the names mixed up—said Asha instead of Atar. Oh, he was so mad later when I told him. He really wanted to be Atar, but I got to be that instead."

"He wanted to be the big cheese?"

"Naturally. But you knew that."

"Right. Instead, he was what?"

"Righteousness."

"Okay—guess that fits. But you ended up bein' the big cheese?"

"It was only right and fitting. When he chose righteousness, it left me to be the Creator."

He shrugged his shoulders and laughed.

"I guess I can understand why y'all wouldn't wanna tell me who you really were, not knowin' who I was 'n all. I did that too, so I can't criticize. But your really-real name is Raymond Redman or Blue Raymond Redman… or Raymond Blue… or what? I wanna know the truth." I leaned in on him.

"Okay. Here's the true story. When I was born, my family gave me the name Raymond Redman, but they called me Blue—ya know, my eyes. Then, one of my teachers changed that to Red for a while."

"Blue to Red? Well, I'll be. Seems there's no end to this."

"It's all the truth."

"How'd it get from Raymond to Blue… no, I get that. But from Blue to Red?"

"Well, it was her first day teaching. Can't remember her name—she came with her head all full of herself. Cocky. She had us line up to meet her—formally, with handshakes and all. She was teaching us how important it was to look others in the eye and make a good first impression. So, when I told her I was Ray Blue Redman, she looked me in the eye and said I was a very colorful kid—ya know, Blue 'n Red together. Then later, she gave us a spelling quiz. She was going up and down the rows and—whnh—when she got to me she said, 'Okay Red, how do you spell the verb *does* as in 'the boy does well in school, not the Duz your mother uses in her washing machine?' Well, none of our mothers had washing machines back then; they all scrubbed clothes in wash tubs. But anyway…"

"Didya know?"

"Oh, I knew how to spell d-o-e-s, but I reacted to my name instead. I tried to tell her I was Blue, not Red, but she barked I had only one chance to give the correct answer and not to change the subject. I tried again, but she interrupted and shouted 'Next.' Gave me a zero in spelling the first day of school."

"That's rotten. She didn't even listen to you."

"Right. But, the worst part was what the kids did. They had fun changing my name again. This time to Purple. The whole year they teased me with purpley-girl jokes."

"Oh, goodness sakes! Did Purple stick?" This had me laughing out loud, now.

"No-o-o, fortunately. But that teacher changed my identity and I became Red for years. Funny I forgot her name. I was only Blue Redman again after high school. That's how everybody knows me now, even though Raymond Redman is my CDIB card. Some newer folks call me Ray."

"What if I call you Blue-Ray?" I asked sarcastically.

"I g-guess that's okay," was how he settled it.

"Oh dear, thar's so much swirlin' in my head, I dunno whar to start. But, whyever didn't ya speak English back then or—for cryin' out loud—at the hospital? And besides, in the hospital it was your life. Then again, why are ya speakin' it now? This is all so confusing."

"Well, whnh, it's not so simple. First off, you have to know about spiritual missions and I don't thenk you do. That's for another time. As for now—because of my accident and having to stay put for a while—I hadda interrupt my mission so that frees me to speak English. When Mrs. Ferguson mentioned maybe working for you, I kept silent so it could happen. In the woods, it's best you believe me—we couldn't break our vows—we were on a spiritual mission."

161

"Oh-h-h, I never gave a thought to anything like that. Oh, my goodness, me-oh-my. But, hold on, thar's much more I been losin' sleep on for ten years. Remember how y'all stayed with me and took care of me and—all the while—seemed happy to be with me? Then, when the other men rode in, y'all just up and left like I was nothing. Ya know, y'all abandoned me."

"Yes. I'm sorry. Leaving was very difficult for all of us—especially me. But when the others showed up, Scoop—or Asha—decided you were d-done with your job—what you were there for—and we were done, too. So, you were going back to *Selu* and we hadda let go of our attachment."

Selu? Well, I couldn't begin to take in all what he was saying. I just shook my head more, shuddering at the memory of my trust being betrayed at the very beginning of my new existence. I didn't stop his story.

"I'm sorry. There's so much to tell. That mission didn't go smoothly. See, there were seven of us who were to meet up at the pond, but my brothers and I—well, we'd been waiting three days an..."

"Wait just a minute here! I didn't ever dream y'all were *brothers*. Why, ya didn't look at all like you were from the same family."

"Oh, we don't have the same mothers or fathers. No, no. It's just that us Cherokees—we're all brothers." Blue shook his shoulders and waved away my question. I saw when he said he was Cherokee he sat taller. "So, anyway, the three of us were waiting to meet up for a farewell ceremony before starting back home when the most beautiful apparition a guy could imagine appeared. And on Sprouting Grass Moon. Not only that, sh-she was a stark-naked woman who flirted and wiggled her butt and bobbed her breasts. Why, she was the answer to any man's dream."

I giggled as he brought back buried memories with his body movements and word emphasis. Our eyes locked as we smiled.

"We were on a spiritual mission, though, and we knew we shouldn't respond as we naturally wanted—not right off, anyway. Scoop decided you were sent by *Selu* as a messenger from the ancestors."

I jumped when he was said I was a messenger. Again? Me? A messenger? From someone named *Selu*? My heart was pounding as I waited for more information, busting with questions.

"Either that or a gift or maybe a lesson. Only problem was, whnh, w-we didn't know which, so we waited a while. We finally figured—no matter what—you were there to keep us there. You were either a gift or a distraction to take our minds off waiting. Then, when the others showed up and told us what happened, we got to thenking we made the right decision."

"Who is the person that supposedly sent me?" I was hanging on his every word.

"*Selu*? She's our First Woman, our corn mother. Ya know, when we came on you in the woods, skin-walking, and then watched you swimming and singing with the birds, it seemed like you were one with the spirits. We were mesmerized."

"Y'all saw me walkin' in the woods and swimmin' the day afore?"

"We did."

"And ya kept your distance 'til the next day?"

"Uh-huh."

"Were you nearby durin' the night?"

"We were."

"Why'ncha make yourselves known, for heaven's sake?"

"We were working the meaning of you being there. And, besides... all thengs in their time, I guess."

"I guess."

That was all for then. I introduced Blue to Jason, sitting on the living room glider whar he liked to listen to the radio or flip pages of National Geographic or talk to one of his sons on the phone. After that, I took some time for a business talk and we arranged for Blue-Ray to begin prepping for painting as his first project. Sarah Ferguson came and stayed long enough to ask how things were going. I told her, "Jist fine." She drove him down the drive as I fixed lunch.

Jason's afternoon nap usually gave me some time to myself afore the kids came home. This day, however, I couldn't muster the energy to concentrate on anything. Besides, the bright sunlight streaming through the double windows in the parlor invited me to curl up on the handy window seat Jason done made. The sun would feel good. I spied old Eeyo—from "Old Macdonald's Farm" —a big old lumbering ball of fur. He already took my idea and had the entire seat to hisself. But I was determined, so first I opened wide the lace curtains, then squeezed myself alongside him, snuggling up to my blind, deaf and lame friend. Eeyo lifted his doggy head then planted his chin on my hip with a sigh afore going back to his dreams. My eyes closed as I focused on the healing warmth.

At first, I concentrated on the heat across my back. Eventually, this got me to recalling a childhood memory whar I was feeling much like this—secure. I drifted off to my pine hideaway, whar I rested on toppa soft pine needles under an old tree out back whenever I couldn't handle the pressures in the house. Now, I pretended to smell the blended aromas of pinesap and dank earth as my mind relaxed into this hideaway that I accidentally discovered chasing a chipmunk. I felt like I was squeezed under pine boughs, wrapped in bright sunlight and dog paws.

Afore I knew it, my reveries shifted to the day when Momma returned with a kewpie doll her male friend had won in some arcade. She was sitting at the kitchen table, her nails painted bright red, chewing a big wad of pink gum as Gram was fixin' dinner. I heard in my head the exact high pitch of her giddy voice, fast-talking 'bout one thing or another and then her high-pitched giggly laugh and her snapping bubbles. I remembered her blowing such a huge bubble that it stuck bright pink stuff onto her nose when it broke. I watched her peel the gum off and stuff it back in her mouth and continue chewing as Gram 'n Poppa took in every little thing she said. Five-year-old Zenobia knew no one would notice if she slipped out the back door and no one did 'til supper was on the table. A shrill "Ze-e-e-n-i-e" came outta the back door, but supper was over afore I appeared. It all came back to me now clear as a bell. My pine hut with ants and other crawly things is whar I went to calm the chaos in my head. The soothing smell of pine mixed with the earth always overpowering everything. That day and that place and this day all became the same with warm sunshine falling on my back. It melted me into sleep.

And I fell into a dream. I was floating in warm water, but couldn't move my arms or legs or see whar I was. My first sensations were of warmth and floating on toppa some liquid. I was sunning myself on a sandy beach and the sand changed from soft to hard—like a hard rock—and I was in the middle of sleeping seals—all just like me. I lifted my head over, flapped a flipper and startled the pup resting on my flank. The pup rearranged itself and nestled back down just like Eeyo would do. Then, a sudden beam of those lights they call "kliegs"—some popping like bubbles—they turned into footlights blinking and flashing and that quickly changed into moonlight flickering behind bare branches that were blowing in the wind. I hold this dream clear in my mind to this day. I still see the full moon breaking through, shining warmth down on me.

The next thing I knew, another flipper was stroking my neck and hair. This one gave me a jolt, though, and I became conscious of a tingling and a familiar smell. Eeyo lifted his head, gave a sniff then set his head back down, but I squinted one eye open to see crystalline aqua pools. I gasped, "H-how did ya get here?"

"Getting's not a problem now I know where you're at."

"But—"

"No buts now."

He was shaking his injured head slowly side to side. And I saw his gorgeous eyes come closer and I felt his swollen lips on mine. I closed my eyes to better inhale his aroma. Just one long, tender kiss on my mouth afore I felt a cold breeze on my neck. I sat up, but he was nowhars. Gasping and sweating, my legs kicked up to the ceiling then hit the floor and I ran to the window.

When I saw his backside swooping down the drive, a door to my heart flew open. The short nap I snatched was the only sleep that whole weekend. I stayed up making candles for two nights. Monday, Blue-Ray returned to paint the house and change my life.

Monday and Tuesday passed businesslike. Blue took advantage of the mild weather to scrape and sand. On Wednesday, a morning thunderstorm gave us a chance to slip inside the barn and return to the mystery of how we met. Right off, Blue thrilled me explaining who *Nene* was—some Cherokee creature with magic powers who lived in the Smokies. And I was supposedly her!

"After we heard you laughing and singing in the pond, we started guessing who you were and how and why you were there. We were looking for a sign, anyway, and Aban suggested maybe you were carrying *Nene's* spirit. Then, when you made a game of meeting us, teasing and all… well, we were thenking you were from the ancestors and they were communicating through you. We talked a lot about it and decided to observe you a while before doing anytheng. The way you put out the fire convinced us you were there to keep us there—one way or another—and we hoped that meant our mission would be successful."

"What mission?" I had so many questions I couldn't stand being quiet longer.

"The short story? We were planning with elders for a Cherokee reunification. That's it. I mean, some of us—we been wanting it for a very long time. Cherokees have been separated and broken up—I mean, spread out way too long and the years have split us in too many ways. It's a long story, but just know we treasure our homeland—it's central to our culture and mainly why I'm here again. I represent the United Keetoowah Band from Tahlequah, Oklahoma."

I musta worn a puzzled look, 'cuz after glancing at me he said, "Tahlequah's a town in northeastern Oklahoma. It's where I'm from."

"Uh, okay. But I still wanna hear more on this mission that kept ya from speakin' English. You're sayin' that's what did it?"

"Yes."

"I don't get it."

"Okay, look, we all spoke English and understood every word you said, but—well—our whole mission was based on tradition—strict Cherokee tradition—meaning we hadda speak our language—and only our language. To break this vow would've corrupted all we were working on and all we intended. We wouldn't do that—I mean—we believe in our ways. We're a proud people. Some of us want reunification, but it must be done right—must be pure."

"Lemme get this straight, now. Back then, y'all thought I was sent to you?"

"We did."

"And I was meant to do everything I did—even have sex with you?"

"Oh, yes. Remember you made the first move. Be honest now. Thenk back on how you were. Oh, don't get me wrong, we enjoyed your invitation. It wasn't easy to resist, whnh, but the way we were thenking—you were definitely a diversion—to make us want to stay longer." Blue nodded as he agreed with his own words, smiling to the ground. I gave him another flirty look and he grinned back.

"Well, I thank you for the kind words. I must say, it sure was my pleasure to please you. Can't exactly say I know why I acted like I did. I didn't ever think like that afore my house burnt, but I was attracted to y'all for some reason—maybe it was loneliness or bein' scared or... I dunno, but I never looked back with regret bein' intimate with you. Every one of you was most kind and gentle—but we were awful groupie—guess that means we weren't too intimate." I tilted my head and looked sideways at him. We shared a hearty laugh afore I confessed, "I only minded at the end when the new men came. I didn't understand what was goin' on and I couldn't go along with them in our group. Ta me, you three came together, but thar couldn't be others."

"Oh yeah, we got that loud and clear. We also knew Aban was right when he said the way you acted proved you were only a diversion and the time had come to leave. Well, and also because the others showed up and told us why they were so late. It was clear we were supposed to wait for them, but the time was up. You were telling us the ancestors were calling you, too."

"Oh, Aban—"

"Oh, Aban what?"

"I was just thinkin' 'bout him. Why isn't he here? And whar's Asha?"

Blue sat shaking his head, "Hunh, there's so much to tell."

"You could start right now. I been waitin' and waitin' for ten years. And your words are nothin' but a big jigsaw puzzle."

"I know. It's complicated when you don't know Cherokee history or culture. I don't want to b-bore you."

"I promise I won't be bored."

"Okay. Just say something if you don't understand."

And, in a slow, gentle way, Blue explained, "Six of us met up in the woods. Scoop—your Asha—representing Cherokee Nation and me from the United Keetoowah Band—we came in from Tahlequah. Your Aban was from the Tennessee Chickamaugas. George Walnut came up from the United Free Nation in Florida and Randy Wild Rice came in from the Echotas in Alabama. That leaves Lee Stillwater—he was from the Georgia Tribe in Cumming.

We didn't know each other before, so this was new for us all. We came together to join Bernie Crow. He was our seventh member, from the eastern Cherokees in the Qualla Boundary, near here. See, only three Cherokee governments are recognized—our two in Tahlequah and the one at the Qualla Boundary. There's plenty others around the country and how authentic they are is up for question. Anyway, Bernie Crow chose the pond as our meeting place so we could unify our group at the start of working on the larger project."

Blue was sober looking off into the distance as his voice trailed. After he took in a big breath, he continued."W-we were headed for *Ki-tu-wah*—that's our ancestral home that we made for ourselves after leaving the Senacas and Iroquois long, long ago—but that's another story. Anyway, our goal was to rekindle our mutual fire and it was our first trip when we met up with you. We were pretty nervous."

With all the new words and ideas jangling in my head, I couldn't help myself, "Wait a cotton-picking minute, what's the difference between this *Kit-u-wha* place and what else I think you said—sounded something like Keetoowee?"

"Um, well, *Ki-tu-wah*'s not far from here. It's our Mother Town. Before Europeans, we had seven major towns, but after fighting with the British and years of growing corn... Well, after so much history, *Kituwah*'s now just a low mound in the earth. To us, though, it'll always be a spiritual place. We don't build monuments. We cherish the earth."

"Got it."

"So, Keetoowah... I'm a Keetoowah Cherokee from Adair County, Oklahoma, and I belong to the United Keetoowah Band of Cherokees. You can just say UKB. It's easier."

"But I still hear those two soundin' pretty much the same."

"Yes, you do, but please—I want to finish one thought before I go to another, okay?"

I made a face and we grinned at each other afore he looked off into the trees to gather his thoughts. That's when I realized how seriously he took the subject.

"A little more information is necessary. To you, I'm an Indian and you call me Cherokee. But I say *Gaduwa*. Same theng. Many of us *Gaduwas* want to keep the traditional ways of our people, not white society's. You know our culture is thousands of years old, right?"

I raised my eyebrows and my eyes got big as saucers. He just kept going. "So, we pay respect to the seven directions in the circle of life and that's why there were seven for this mission. Seven for many other reasons, too, like we're all born into one of seven clans, the one from our mothers. Clans are a vital part of our ceremonies and traditions."

I was concentrating on his words, but the number seven never had meant so much afore and it was beginning to sound like a really important number. I saw the rain done let up and the sun was trying to come out. Steam rising from the ground told me it was gonna be a warm one and I thought of putting the clothes out on the line hoping to dry them afore the sun disappeared. I heard in the distance a truck grinding its gears going up a hill and the far-off signal from a freight train. I knew I better look at a spot on the barn floor—a stain from some old oil can—to hold my attention.

"... The seven of us came together because we believe that in the center of every life is a sacred fire we carry in our hearts, which means... Are you listening to me?"

I nodded I was, but continued to look down.

"... because—this is important—we all carry a fire that's the center of all there is."

My head popped up at those words. "Wow, that sounds like-like those Zoro-whatevers."

"Yes-s-s. Now can you see why I was so interested in that book?"

Believe me, I did. This was getting interesting.

"... And, for a while back there in the woods, I could really say I was *Atar.*"

My eyes mighta been aimed at the floor of the barn, but they were bugging out now. This man was amazing. My ears were picking up every intake of his breath and outta the corners of my eyes I could see his hands embellishing his words as he wrapped up his story.

"Around our central fire is a cross formed by north, south, east, west extending out from the center. They represent the life forces that come at us from the four directions and they're symbolized by four colors—red, blue, black and white. But it's the smoke from the fire that rises up, up, up to the sky that's our spiritual connection to the Creator. Altogether, they're part of the seven directions in the circle of life for every one of us."

I was nodding my head again as I heard this. It all made sense. I looked up to see in his wounded face a kinda serenity I didn't notice afore. We both decided this was a good place to leave off and get some work done. I knew we'd come back to it.

We started working on the house and the garden got planted, but weather in the Smokies can make planning difficult, so we always hadda "go with the flow." 'Course thar were other jobs I needed help with and sometimes Jason asked Blue to do something he thought of—like change the oil in the car or clean the gutters, ya know. I immediately realized how much help it was to have another pair of hands for the chores that never ended, rain or shine.

But going back to this talk... a little later, we were back inside the barn when Blue asked if I knew anything 'bout clans. Ha, that was a joke.

"Well, clans are very important. The seven of us in our group represented our seven clans that formed after seven wise elders received the first Sacred Fire on Clingman's Dome."

I thought, *Thar goes seven again,* but my words were, "Oh-h-h-h, Clingman's Dome?"

"Yep. Clans have names. Wanna hear them? They'll sound strange to you."

"Sure. Why not?"

"Okay. First, there's mine—*A-ni-wo-di*—the Paint Clan. We're considered the healers and wise men. I like to thenk of myself that way.

"*A-ni-wo-di,*" I repeated.

"Yes, very good. That's the Paint Clan. Next, there's the Wolf Clan—or *A-ni-wa-ya*—that's Scoo... Asha's—and they're the protectors. You can see him like that, right?"

"Oh yes."

"So, there's also Aban's clan. It's the *A-ni-sa-ho-ni*—Blue Clan—they take care of children."

"That's all they do?"

"No, of course not. But it's their special responsibility and it's important. It protects the future."

"'Course."

"Then, there's the Wild Potato Clan—or *A-ni-ga-to-ge-wi*—keepers of the earth—a very important duty. That leaves the *A-ni-gi-lo-hi*—or the Long Hair Clan, who take in those we adopt."

I interrupted him by waving my hand. "You adopt?"

"Of course we do. We take in people for all sorts of reasons and we take good care of them. For you, it's like immigrants."

"Wow."

"And there's the *A-ni-a-wi*—or Deer Clan—the runner messengers."

"Huh?" I musta been in a daze.

Blue gave me a funny look as he remarked, "Remember, these clans began before electricity" and then went right on to finish up with, "Last is the *A-ni-tsi-s-qua*—the Bird Clan—or scribe messengers."

"And they keep records?"

"You got it."

"Wow" I repeated. "Can you pick which clan to be in?" I asked. I didn't think it was so funny even though Blue laughed and laughed.

"No, no. We're born into our clans."

These words satisfied me at the time, but the question did occur how that all came 'bout. The words that jumped outta my mouth were, "This is better'n school. Can ya tell me more?"

As Blue smiled to himself and said "Okay, if you like," he settled himself and looked off into the distance with that special dreamy look of his.

"Long ago, we had spiritual healers who traveled around the countryside—yes, we've always been spread out—performing rituals for the progress of humans on the path from birth to death. These medicine people don't exist anymore, b-but our clans still relate to the seven levels of spiritual progression in life. Clans keep the necessary balance and prepare us to enter the spirit world. All clans are equal—no one is better than another—and all are needed to keep balance. In fact, we can't have a ceremony at the Sacred Fire unless all are represented. You can see now why we had to have seven for our mission."

"Exactly seven?" This number was amazing me.

"Oh, yes, exactly seven. Elders tell stories of how we came out of the sky from the *A-ni-tsu:-tsa,* the seven star brothers. We're known as the Principal People or *A-ni-yv-wi-ya.* And our tribal flag has a seven-pointed star as our symbol."

"Listen Blue, I really do wanna hear more, but... I'm sorry, I just realized I'm expectin' a call from the doctor and I can hear the phone ringin'."

I ran to the house as fast as I could but missed the call, 'course, then checked in with Jason who was sleeping. I returned with apple juice and cookies—I was starving. I also came back with a huge chunk of curiosity. "Ya know, I'm still tryin' to sort things out. You're both Cherokee and Kee-too-wee and Gaduwa, right?"

Blue smiled, then continued at a slower pace. "Yes, ya know I'm a Cherokee from Oklahoma, member of the Keetoowah Band.

And because I'm Cherokee, I say *Gaduwa*. You aren't, so you say Cherokee."

"Alright, I guess. But then thar's that town that sounds the same."

"It does. Yes. As I said, *Kituwah* is a sacred place near here. We can go see it if you like. I'm thenking of writing a book on the variations of our name. Heard plenty through the years. Grandparents say we used to call ourselves the *A-ni-ga-du-wa-gi*, meaning the Keetoowah people. Other nations called us all sorts of thengs—like the Creeks had a word, *Chilokee*, that translates to sometheng like 'people who speak a different tongue' and the Choctaws used *Chiluki* which meant 'cave dwellers.' That Spaniard, De Soto, called us *Chelaque* or sometheng and I don't know what that means. No matter, we're 'The Fire People.' Someday, let's talk more about names. They fascinate me. But I wanna finish answering the question you asked days ago."

You can tell the atmosphere was warming up. I smiled and the look on his face said he was enjoying himself. The phone rang again. This time I caught it and it was Sarah Ferguson saying she was running late—was that okay? I told her it sure was, even though I didn't know Blue would use up all the time explaining more of his mission. Apparently, a Planning Council was wanting his help.

"Ya see, this is historic. Some work had already been done on a proposal for a self-determination bill to submit to Congress. We're a separate nation. You know that, right?"

I shrugged, "But you're in the United States and that's a nation. How can thar be a nation inside another one?"

"Simple. Just by existing. I-I mean, I was born of Native parents. And listen, our nation was here first. This is our homeland.

Native peoples had governments before Europeans showed up and took our land from us in lopsided treaties. And th-these treaties and documents were between separate nations—even though the United States hasn't honored it since. Just because our land was taken doesn't mean the people aren't a nation."

He went on to explain how the U. S. government took control of all Natives, even passing a law saying they could continue living their own way only if they bought the land they were living on under some kind of formula called an "allotment."

"Did they?"

"Well, it's not so simple. If Cherokees on government lists had half or more Cherokee blood, the government labelled them 'incompetent'."

"What-t-t?"

"Yeah. They weren't able to make decisions about the land they had to buy and a white person was assigned to make decisions about their land."

"No-o-o."

My reaction stirred him. He threw his hands in the air and his voice rose. I never heard him speak so loud afore. "Yes-s-s. That's how many lost their new homes—that is, the ones they made *after* they were kicked out of their original homes back East."

"You gotta be kiddin'."

Blue settled down again and softened his demearnor. "I'm not kidding. I mean, there's so much to know. To begin with, we believe everytheng in the Cosmos is connected and human life comes out of the cosmic order of the Sky World. We're here on Mother Earth to populate the Middle World and care for it. We call our Mother Earth *Elohi*. Our attitude toward life on earth is how we keep balance with the Underworld that's full of chaos and change, whnh."

"That's beautiful."

"Yes it is. But when statehood came along, Gaduwas who never ever had thought of owning any part of Mother Earth and couldn't conceive of doing anytheng like that to *Elohi*... Why, they felt *Elohi* had loaned the land and they were to take care of it. Well, see, they were told by the federal government that they had to pay a tax to live on the land. This being the very same land granted to them by treaty to live in traditional ways, under their own rule. They expected to live on the new land under *Gaduwa* laws and customs—can't blame 'em for that, whnh. No wonder they didn't thenk of anything like a land tax—it really doesn't make any sense. Taxes are white man's ways—*yo-ne-ga* ways. Not ours. You can guess what happened."

"They lost their land?"

Blue nodded and I gasped, putting my hands to my mouth with an instant flashback of Sophie telling me how her heart was near broke fearing the loss of the Connors' family farm for back taxes. I had a sudden understanding of what that musta been like for those Cherokees. I remember this moment was like a bridge between worlds. I sat looking at this gorgeous man from a totally different world telling me almost the same thing as a dear old soul from yet another world. At that moment, I realized how thar was an amazing bond that connected all of us even when we don't know it. I couldn't put words to it—still can't—but I feel it in my heart.

"There's so much to tell, Brigit. Is it okay if I call you that?"

"Oh yes. Whatever. Just don't call me Nene. One of them is enough."

"Okay. It's Brigit, then."

I lost touch with what time it was or how hungry Jason must be or what else thar was to get done—I was so anxious to know what Blue was getting to. I came to realize very fast that he had a deep soul and I wanted to learn as much as I could from him.

"There are Cherokee groups around the country, like in Alabama, Tennessee, Georgia, ya know. The federal government doesn't recognize them and, truthfully, maybe it shouldn't—but that's another story. The problem is the Cherokee government was broken up back in the 1800s and we've not figured out how to p-put it back together again."

"Like Humpty Dumpty?"

"This isn't funny, ya know."

"I know, but I just gotta share something that flitted through my mind—a sayin' by Mark Twain. Know 'bout him?"

Blue sighed, "Not really. Why?"

"Well, he had a good take on life and his words help me a lot with unpleasantness. This sadness you're speakin' of reminds me he said something like, 'We humans have only one effective weapon—laughter'."

"Yeah, okay. Thanks for the comic relief. But listen, I want you to know that the ones who stayed in their homes back east and didn't go to Indian Territory... they lost tribal citizenship. That's the first reason why many of us are out of touch today. Even though we're disjointed, many of us still want to follow traditions—like using fairness and community to honor our ancestors, the *Ani-yv-wi-ya*. So-o-o, we were coming together because we were trying to organize to take back the right to live as we see fit. And *that's* the answer to why we were there and why we came on you in the woods."

"Oh-h-h, I see."

Sarah Ferguson's station wagon pulled up just as my lesson ended and my mind blown.

I slept poorly that night. I remembered dreaming 'bout all sortsa Native people all over the world having to leave their homes—all kinds of homes—and all kinds of sorrow. Blue's words had stirred things up in me. By nine the next morning, though, I was ready for his return. He was coming an extra day to help clean out the mess in the barn. We worked well together 'til almost noon, when Sarah was to pick him up. We agreed to keep our talk to a minimum, so I was startled when he suddenly stood up and asked, "I can't remember what year it was when we met. Can you?"

His question hung on the air and the sun's rays sticking into the barn reflected off a rusty pitchfork leaning on the wall. I was reminded of all the work yet to be done, but didn't need time to think 'bout my answer, "It hadda be 1960, 'cuz that's when Jason and I done got married."

"Oh, yeah-h-h."

"Why'd ya ask?"

"I been thenking there's sometheng I need to finish. Yes, it was when President Kennedy got elected that we started making plans to return our Sacred Fire. During the exodus in the 1800s, it was taken to Indian Territory but it needed to go back, back to *Kituwah*. That and it being our first trip—well, it made our meeting especially important. Remember, I told you we had two personal days at the end, before we were going to hold a farewell ceremony at the pond?... Oh, by the way, that pond is *A-ta-ga-hi*. Stories call it a magical healing place."

"Well, it was special, that's for sure, but why magical?"

"I dunno really, but legend says there's magic there. All three of us came to believe it because of you. And a healing place, too—also because of you."

"Oh, get off it."

"I mean that. When it got to be the third day of waiting, we were worried. Then, you suddenly appeared and it seemed you were saying we should wait longer. We all fell in love with you."

I blushed. It was suddenly uncomfortable to think back on our intimacies.

"Remember that first night when all of us were fighting and you screamed and ran off?"

"Sure do."

"We were fighting over you. I started it. Right off, I was thenking you and I were meant for each other. When I said so, Scoop claimed that since he was in charge of thengs that year, it included you, whnh. But w-we Gaduwas know it's the woman's place to choose who she courts and it seemed to be all of us back then."

I nodded. It seemed that way to me, too.

"... And also, to choose who she'd settle with, which probably now is me, ennit?"

Oh, the look he gave me then was priceless! I just sat for a moment or two looking him over, noticing his nervouosness, nodding my head as I twisted my lips into strange places.

"Yeah. Guess you're right 'bout pickin' you—now, anyway— but probably from the first. Your eyes always got me. What you say must be true—I'm blushin' all over. But tell me 'bout Asha—I mean Scoop—and Aban. Are they comin' this year? And what's Aban's real name?"

"Oh yes. Nope, neither of 'em. So, for Scoop—he heard the call to join up soon after that meeting and he was sent off to 'Nam and he gave his life slogging in the rice fields."

Tears flooded my eyes. We sat silently staring at each other while I absorbed this.

He continued, "I might have the newspaper article still. Maybe I can find it. Like too many others, he went to serve our country. Never came back. Whole theng makes me sick."

"Me, too. Why we were ever over thar in the first place I'll never get. I hate to think we lost him for that."

"Hunh, there was no way I'd go to 'Nam, I knew that. I took off for Canada."

"Ya did?"

"Yep. Left in '62. Stayed 'til I was too old to be called."

"How'd ya do it?"

"I connected with the Friends Society. They were advising men who didn't wanna kill and they helped me get hooked up with the Blood Tribe in a place called Standoff, in Alberta. That's where I went."

"What'd ya do thar?"

"Herded cattle."

"Ya like it?"

"Better'n killing for a living."

"That's for sure."

"I worked off the land—cared for animals and felt a beautiful sense of purpose."

I sat nodding my head. What else was thar to say?

"Your dear Aban was called up, too. But he was spared because of his size. That's one good theng about being small."

"Good for him. So, what's his real name? And whar's he at?"

"Sorry to say he isn't doing this anymore—gave it up couple years ago—am thenking it cost too much. Each time we go, we have to give up work for almost a month and he had a kid with special needs he liked to do for. Don't thenk this means as much to him any more. We called him Crook Glory—now that you mention it, I never did know his real name."

"Oh, I miss him, no matter what his name is."

"Me too. Ya know, he was another one to change names. Made jokes constantly. Kept us in stitches. Remember how he was?... He used to say, 'Call me Smoking Gun' or 'Limp Rod' or 'Damp Dream.' He was in a good mood a lot of the time when we were worried—kept us laughing—mostly with off-color jokes. Sometimes he'd go out to find the 'Dangerous Man of Cherokee Legend' and come back with tall tales. What a character."

"Yeah, I remember how much fun he was, even if I didn't understand his words or jokes. I'm so sorry I won't get to see either of 'em again. The others who came later—why were they late?"

"Oh, well, whnh... remember the horse we left you?"

"How could I forget? It's how I got outta the woods."

"Good, that's what we wanted. It was Lee Stillwater's. He rode her in from Georgia, but when he got near the pond the horse stumbled. Lee fell and broke a leg. We cared for him best we could 'til we got to town. A medicine man worked on him, but it'd been three days and it was infected. The bone was through the skin. They treated him with traditional herbs and he took part in everytheng—even seemed to be improving. Said he was anyway. He was t-tough. But he got a fever and the medicine man decided Lee needed the hospital.

"So, after Randy Wild Rice and George Walnut visited family, they were planning to meet up with Lee at his uncle's farm in Big Cove, but when they got there no one had seen him. A day or so later, they heard he was in hospital and the gangrene was worse. So, they stayed with the family and helped with the ceremony. There was no way to reach us at the pond and we were all pledged to follow tradition, anyway. They would'na phoned even if they could. We were all committed—I mean, that's how it was."

I got goosebumps listening to him. It took a long time for Sarah to arrive and she apologized, but I explained the extra time was helpful in getting to know Mr. Redman and his English was improving every day. I encouraged her to talk with him so she could see for herself. She remarked how happy she was at his placement. I gave her a big smile.

So, this is how Blue and I were getting to know each other—with a little bit of work and a good bit of talk. For example, the next time he came, we were scraping the side of the house and he asked how come I lived in Ashland with a husband and a family.

I had plenty of time to explain that, after Sophie, it seemed like ending one part of my life led me on to another and another— like things never really ended but just kept moving on to another something on a higher level—sorta like in a spiral. I was bubbling over with words and ideas and couldn't stop chattering. Looking back, I remember feeling so cocky, thinking I had life's answers, that day. Now, it's like as if I was only making sense of things best

I could. But thar were so many thoughts held tight for so long, I just hadda spill 'em out to this dear soul. He came into my life right when I needed him.

He only interrupted with a few comments 'bout the Cherokee circle of life. He hadda bite his tongue, though—I wasn't in a mood for listening that day—didn't know how much I had to learn. We ended up not getting much work done. A rainstorm moved in. Sitting on the back steps waiting on Sarah, I asked if he could drive.

"Yes, *usti* or little *u-da-li-tu-gi,* I have a license, if that's what you mean. Just don't wanna use it."

"Did ya just say you have a license, but you don't wanna drive?"

"Right. I—"

"What're ya really sayin'?"

"Well, uh—I, uh… Lets just say it's bad for my k-karma."

"What-all does that mean?"

"It means it's… well, maybe I find driving a waste of time. Life's too short anyway, so why spend precious time maneuvering a big hunka metal all around? I'd rather spend my time appreciating the Creator's abundance or the amazing sun and its messenger shadows, the clouds. All that means more to me than staring at macadam and other chunks of metal. Besides, being a passenger gives me a chance to see the future come to me as the present slips into the past."

"Interesting."

Later that week at the dinner table, I announced how Blue's scars were improving. They did fade some by the end of the summer, but the red rawness still gave his face a kinda rough edge. Sparky and Nene asked if they could call him "Scurfus." I reckoned a nickname could soften his image with the kids. I suggested they check with him. He said he was delighted.

"Cherokee parents give a baby an English name—like Raymond. But the mother's mother can give the baby a Cherokee name that's used in the family. It's how I got to be Blue. My father's family told me I could change my name if there was a strong reason— like if I was wounded. Then, changing it can heal the wound. But scars are the mark of a warrior and I'm proud to be a warrior, I think Scurfus is fitting. *Wa-do*, as they say "thank you" around here. Back home, we say *"Sgi."* Blue said his scars spoke of a life well lived, proving "victory over adversity"—his words. I silently wondered if interior scars—like mine—did the same. Later, Nene told me when Sparky heard what Blue said, he whispered in her ear, "He's one cool dude, ya know." Blue's attitude helped Sparky with his own scars. But "Scurfus" didn't stick.

Blue made a big impression on Sparky in lotsa ways. He did things boys like to do. He was real good at puzzling things and could climb trees and jump streams. He could shoot a gun or throw stones better and farther than anybody. He could start a fire without a match. That really impressed Sparky who tried lotsa times. Once, when they went to the back field to burn dry grass in the pumpkin patch, Sparky brought matches. Blue suggested they start the fire "the Cherokee way." Sparky told me how it went.

"Holy mackerel, ya make it look so easy. It's never that easy when Dad 'n I do it."

"Everytheng's easy when you know how, *Chooch*. Just pay attention and you'll learn. Then, it'll be easy for you, too."

"Gosh, ya know so much. How'd ya learn ta do everything— college? And whattaya do when yer back home, anyways?"

"I certainly did not go to college, whnh. But in my job, I do the exact opposite of what we're doing right now."

"Whattya mean?"

"Can't you guess?"

"Nope."

"I'm a f-firefighter. I work for the Oklahoma Forestry Service."

"Really? So ya know how ta start fires and stop 'em? Wow!"

Like I said, Sunday nights were for candle-making. That Sunday, I focused on an order from the hospital and turned out three dozen tapers plus four dozen votives for my personally-designed spider-shaped votive holders. They were my creation the first year after Sophie passed. I got the idea from the spider that built a web on toppa her. In mine, a burning candle cast a spider shape moving around on a dark wall. They were popular in the gift shop. I gave one to Blue. I was impressed when he went and bought a book for the kids, *The First Fire or How the Water Spider Captured Fire*.

He said he wanted to introduce them to Cherokee storytelling—saying, though, that true storytelling doesn't come outta books, but from elders who sit down 'n take the time to share their wisdom. Our family took turns reading to Jason the Cherokee story 'bout *Kananesgi*, the old female spider who, after many other animals had tried and failed, was the only one who could bring part of the first fire that was in the middle of a river to the cold Cherokees on the shore. She was the tiniest being, but she could weave a bowl on her back to hold the hot coals and tie them down with her own thread.

We agreed we wanted to read more Cherokee folk tales. Coupla days later, Blue won Nene's heart telling 'bout the little people—like the Laurels and the Rocks and the Dogwoods. But the ones who got her were the wee little ones, the *Na-n-ye-hi*, who live in underground caves in the mountains 'round us. Cherokee grandfathers say they lived in our area longer than anybody and they had supernatural powers and were invisible 'til they wanted to be seen. Yes—and they could be near our farm at that very moment! And they'd show up to help if we needed. Well, eight-year-old Nene needed help lotsa times, so she bugged me 'til I found a *Na-n-ye-hi* doll for her collection. She hoped it brought a little magic into the house.

Blue's coming along changed all our lives. He made the kids feel privileged just being with him. I think it was his dignity and self-confidence that drew them in. They loved his sayings—like "The grandfathers told me how nothing in life is meant to be perfect—anytheng that's perfect has its spirit trapped inside and spirit's not meant to be trapped. Thengs need to be imperfect so the inner spirit has a way to shine out." Bit by bit, he worked his way into our hearts and that's how things got complicated.

Ya see, as soon as Jason got sick, I made plans for the kids to go to the First Baptist Summer Day Camp. I heard so many good things 'bout this program and didn't want my little ones spending the summer hanging on Jason's illness. So, every weekday morning at eight, they hopped on an orange school bus and appeared at the end of the drive 'round four. My plan was to do projects in between. That's what was s'posed to happen, but what did happen was... Well, with Blue 'round, I was totally unable to separate myself from wherever he was. If the weather was sunny and he was work on painting the house, I checked on him up the ladder. I brought water or lemonade or sweet tea. I called him into the house for lunch. I stopped to remark on the condition of the paint or the roof or the weather. I found all kinds of excuses for passing by. I said I wanted to recall his language and we practiced. I didn't want him to get too much sun or get too hot or too wet. Whatever. When it rained, he came inside to do odd jobs or worked in the barn on repairs.

He got on well with Jason. They were mostly cordial, but stiff. Botha them had trouble with easy talk. 'Course I done told Jason 'bout the men in the woods and he knew Blue was in the group, so why should he ever wanna get close? Why should he even want him 'round the house? But this was how it was and seemed the way it was meant to be. They were two very different men with the only thing in common being me. One day in July, a passing storm damaged some shingles on the barn roof, so we asked Blue to do an emergency repair. It took longer than we expected and he stayed for supper. That's how they got into a testy discussion on fire-fighting.

"Hey, Ray—back in World War II, we learned how to fight fires. Lord knows we soldiers hadda expect to encounter such as them. And those kinds of things ya never forget, ya know. I done made it a point to keep up on fire-fighting techniques over the years and I know how the Navy developed an advanced aqeous foam. It's more pliable than earlier ones—can even spread over fuel fires. Are ya familiar with that? Maybe use it?"

Blue listened, keeping his eyes on Jason afore he cleared his throat and put his fork down. He nodded and said, "I heard of it being used in warfare. It's 'specially good for situations like crash landings. Not so much in the field, though. Ya know, we gotta be equipped to deal with dramatic changes in the course of a fire 'cuz of wind, structures or terrain. So, we carry heavy equipment, like suits and helmets, boots, goggles, radio, shovels and more. And our teams must be able to construct fire lanes and escape routes, lookouts, ya know? We don't want anyone to get trapped behind and we have to be prepared to make fire shelters. It's a dynamic environment. We use a foam that was developed in the sixties. It's a fluoroprotein with a longer blanket effect."

Both were most courteous, but I could tell they were competing. I noticed Jason calling Blue, "Ray." Nobody else did, so I wondered why, but never asked. It was lucky Sparky asked Blue to share some fire-fighting stories and the subject drifted.

All in all, Jason did his best to make me feel special, that summer. Praise came from the living room glider every day. He told me he didn't know what he woulda done without me and how wonderful I was to care for him. I did appreciate his kindness, but I also couldn't help recalling similar childhood memories that clashed with the sense of self-worth I was working so hard on. Once, I caught myself asking Sparky "Would ya take this cup of tea in to Poppa?" Uch, Jason—my one-time rock and salvation—he was now setting me off kilter, while as Blue was offering me calm, sane hope. I could feel myself becoming dependent on him day by day.

I sometimes breezed past the ladder. "Hi. How're ya doin' up thar?"

"Fine, thanks. It's getting pretty warm, though. Thenk I'll take a break in a few minutes."

"Good, I was just 'bout to water the garden and wondered if you'd help...."

"Sure."

I told myself nothing was happening, but it was. Little-by-little, thar was a tension growing with us—like when a hand lightly lingered over a passed sandwich or when we walked a bit too close and brushed an arm or a leg or a hip. I began to remember more and more how we were in the woods. I confess—one hot summer day, he called me to open the bathroom window and undo the screen latch. When I got thar, he put his lips to the screen like as if to pass a kiss through. It was so sweet and I didn't think twice—I kissed his lips through the screen. But that's all it took for desire to take over. I'm telling ya... I couldn't stop myself. I'm afraid I threw off my top and returned to the screen whar I pressed my breasts. Yes. And, he done pressed his hands on the other side and we stayed thar with our eyes closed. Then, I released the screen and retreated with my face bright red. We didn't look at each other for the resta the morning.

But Nene noticed as she walked up from the bus that afternoon. We were sitting on the back steps waiting for him to be picked up—sitting side by side with one knee touching. My face was flushed and I was laughing. Nene just knew something was different. We talked after Blue left. She told me she thought I acted young when Blue was 'round.

"Think so? Oh, I dunno 'bout that, honey."

"Well, yer not the same in the house with Daddy."

"Now look, young lady, don't ya go talkin' ta me like that. I admit Blue makes me happy. Yes, it's wonderful he done come into our lives. He makes us all happy. Thar's nothing wrong with that, is thar? Daddy's sick. That doesn't make me happy. You happy Daddy's sick?"

"No-o-o-o."

"'Course not, 'nuff said. And, just so you know, your chin's up in the air like what Gram used ta say—like a Donovan." Mark Twain flashed through my mind at that moment. "If you tell the truth you don't have to remember anything," but I let the screen door slam afore any more could be said.

This was a warning. I knew my kids loved their father—and also cared for Blue. And I wanted them to. I convinced myself, though. I hadda sacrifice my happiness to preserve theirs. So, I got busy in the house—mostly with Jason—whenever Blue was outside and outside when he was inside. It was hard. Also hard was that just 'bout that time, life got more complicated. Cee called with news from Forestland and apologized for bringing it while Jason was sick. She said she hadda let me know of Bud's fury. He done dropped in on her again—and with his gun, 'course. This time, she hadda call the sheriff to get ridda him.

Long days and nights started to give me headaches. My mind swirled with twisted and twisting thoughts. One moment I was reliving my forest ecstasy—next I was having flashbacks of Bud throwing plates against the wall 'cuz I didn't salt the vegetables or dumping dresser drawers on the floor 'cuz I moved the furniture or whipping his belt off and chasing me 'round the house 'cuz I asked for money. I remembered his drunken buddies called him "Big D" and when I asked why, he said it was none of my damn business. Only when one of the regulars in that smoke-infested bar shouted loud enough and I heard the word "devil," I put it all together. One minute I'd be sobbing over such things, then laughing the next at a silly recollection from the forest.

In all this mental confusion, though, my saddest thoughts were for Jason. Both guilt and anger came at me when I thought of the dear man who began to fail almost from the first. I realized I took him as my savior who rescued me from homelessness. And he was my anchor to Sophie. But he done turned into a burden way too quickly and I couldn't now find his charm. Seems life was more like driving a car outta control. Sometimes, I woke from nightmares whar I couldn't stop my car hurtling from one accident to another. I even began to fear driving again.

Then thar was Blue who brought only brilliant memories and hopeful wishes and happy moments. He popped into my mind all daylong, every day. Focusing on him was easy, but Jason and his needs were my main responsibility. After all, our life together was my very own creation. I went to bed repeating over and over a prayer from Sunday School: *God, grant me the Courage to change what can be changed, the Patience to accept what cannot be changed and the Wisdom to know the difference.*

Jason's health went downhill in the heat of that summer. At the end of August, he was put in the hospital again and, this time, the doctors said thar was nothing more they could do for him. They said he had "cardiac insufficiency." He lay on his hot hospital bed in his hot hospital room sucking oxygen while a fan turned slowly over his head. He took off his mask long enough to whisper he was miserable and didn't see why to struggle more.

I tried my best to console him. I read inspiring stories—usually from *Readers' Digest*—sometimes from the Bible. But seeing how he was suffering, I got taken over by religious doubt. I questioned God's all-loving nature—what I was taught. Why would God cause such suffering? I even began to think hell was here on earth. Then thar was that old abandonment thing, too. I sat at his bedside massaging his feet and saw my dear mate lying limp on the white sheets. His face was almost as white as they were and his kind, strong hands were still. The life I created that started in trauma was now full circle back thar and I was running outta patience for trauma.

That year, the song "Bridge Over Troubled Waters" done just came out and it was on the radio every day. Whenever I heard it I hadda leave the room. I remember being by his bed thinking as in a prayer, *Dear, dear Jason, father of our sweet Nene 'n Sparky 'n son of beloved Sophie, please don't leave. How're the kids gonna grow up without you? How'm I ever gonna find the strength to go on without you? I dunno how to do it. Please deny the power of this disease. Come back to us.*

God, please give Jason back his health. Please. Not forever, just let him go on livin' a few more years. He's a good man and should see his babies grow. Why're you punishin' me again? I tried so hard to be good this time. And our poor, innocent children—why are you punishin' them? I wanna trust you. I wanna love you, God, but this is too much.

Jason mostly slept or rested. One day at the beginning of September, he was propped up at a 45-degree angle to breathe easier, but he hardly opened his eyes all day and, when he did, the look in them was shuddering. He tried a whisper. Shushing him, I told him to rest more and we could talk later, but he knew there wasn't gonna be later—he had no more energy for later. Even though the medicine dulled his mind, causing him to drift in and out, he still knew. Sweaty, breathing hard, he put a grasp on reality for a few moments.

"Br-r-rig-g-g..."

"Yes, darlin', I'm right here."

"No more, ple-e-ase."

"You sure?"

"Mm-m-m-m."

"I understand, Jay, I do. I'm stayin'. Thar'll be no more suf-ferin'. I promise."

All that had been said afore 'bout the end of life was said already. I knew I could explain to the doctor what his wishes were and I did. The doctor said, "I understand, Mrs. Connors. There'll be no heroics." The hospital team measured Jason's fading energy as well as his increasing discomfort, then gave him the blessed medicine to take away his pain. A nurse stood next to me while I witnessed Jason's body go through the agonizing work of giving in to the almighty power of death. The ache in my heart as I watched my husband struggle for breath was more'n I could bear. I found myself watching the clock, timing his inspirations and expirations—words the doctor used. I always knew that my being younger meant I'd most probably have to deal with this, one day, but even so, it didn't ready me. I'm here to say thar's nothing worse than watching a loved one go from struggling to live to struggling to die.

It was early on September 6, 1971, that Jason labored his last. During his final moments, I saw his breaths come ever 'n ever slower 'til they stopped in one endlessly-long twitching sigh. I sat glued to my seat silently turning words over in my mind sorta like a poem or a prayer. My mind spoke from a fullness in my heart. Never afore was I aware of the wisdom of the ages that comes from some kinda wellspring whar human misery lives. Now, I was seeing that suffering is living as living is suffering. I realized that my feelings were mine and they made my life story, but they were also a part of all humans. I was coming to understood Sophie's wisdom—my head wanted answers to so many questions, but it was my heart that had got the meaning of life.

I wasn't the only one faced with awesome life truths. Nene 'n Sparky had their own difficult emotions during—first, Jason's loss of vitality—then, his hospitalizations—and now losing him. They begged me to explain. "Why, Momma, why?" I didn't have the answer, 'course. I could only manage a saying that gave me solace when I was little. With Nene hangin' on my arm, I pulled her up onto my lap and nuzzled her neck.

"Well, sweetie, thar's a simple answer in the *Bible*. Remember, when Job is most upset but he still finds the wisdom to pray and says, 'Naked I came outta my mother and naked I'll return, for only the Lord gives and only the Lord takes away.' Remember that, honey? Now that meanin' is for us. The Lord who put Daddy on this earth in the first place needs Daddy back now." These words seemed to satisfy the moment, but I think our holding onto each other was probably more important. I often felt the need to cradle the kids just to take in their warmth. That simple act meant more than any words.

When Sparky fell on Blue in tears the afternoon Jason died, Blue rubbed his head and forehead, gently whispering into his ear, "Mm-m-m, dear little *Chooch*, rest easy. *Unelanv'hi*, the Creator who made us all, decides when to call us home, whnh. We return to our Earth Mother, *Elohi*, and each of us must go when we're called. That's just the way of the world—the way it's always been—the way it's meant to be."

Sparky continued to have trouble accepting Jason's death, though, so a day or two later I overheard when Blue sat him down and repeated something he learned from the Crow people.

"Hey, little man, here's a question for you... what do you thenk life is?"

Sparky shook his head without words.

"Well, perhaps you could thenk about it like the flash of the firefly in the night or the breath of a buffalo in winter or that little shadow dancing across the grass only to lose itself in the sunset."

Sparky looked at Blue with a funny look, his forehead in a furrow—like this.

"It's beautiful, but it's short."

Sparky clung to Blue through the following days. Jason's body was taken to the town cemetery in the afternoon sun and we had a private burial. All four of his children stood together over his grave as Rev. Munson performed his second Connors burial. He led the family in prayer for the salvation of Jason's soul in the afterworld afore reading from the Bible.

Ecclesiastes 3:1-8

To all things there is an appointed time
And a time to every purpose under the heaven
A time to be born and a time to die
A time to plant and a time to pluck up that which is planted,
A time to slay and a time to heal,
A time to break down and a time to build,
A time to weep and a time to laugh,
A time to mourn and a time to dance,
A time to cast away stones and a time to gather stones,
A time to embrace and a time to be far from embracing,
A time to seek and a time to lose,
A time to keep and a time to cast away,
A time to rent and a time to sow,
A time to keep silence and a time to speak,
A time to love and a time to hate,
A time of war and a time of peace.

Afterwards, the whole Connors family and Cee's family joined hands 'round the open grave to sing—as best we could—Jason's favorite song, "Now the Day is Over." Blue came and read a poem he wrote. He asked to read it. 'Course I said yes, without even knowing what he was gonna say. I was touched.

Ending and Beginning

Sorrowful tears fall down
shaking the mighty ground
without a sound
breaking loose the bond

wresting a One from an Other
returning each to its Mother
Mother to Other to Mother
the endless circle of Life

Okay, so that's how those ten years came at me, but my throat needs a rest. You're probably wanting to think a bit now, anyways. Two especially important things happened after that I absolutely gotta tell you. I know you'll relate to them even more. Thar's a surprise, too. See you here in 'bout a half hour....

PART 6

Flying Sparks

de-ga-no-hi-li-do-hv tsu-da-we-la-di

I see y'all are back, so we gotta get going or we won't get done in time. During the break, some of y'all told me you missed seeing Blue. Well, I have news—he's the surprise! And, my kids, too! Wait... I see our car now. Good, I need Blue's help. Afore he gets here, though, a word 'bout language. I dunno that many words, so I gotta finish in English. I know how to say Osdineli hia—*that he's my husband—but not enough for story-telling. Anyways, here's Blue...*

S*i-yo, a-li-he-li-s-di, o-gi-na-li.* Hello and welcome, my friend. Howdy Shug and a big hello to everybody. Sorry I'm late—family matters, ya know. Hmm, can we squeeze these teenagers into the circle? That's good, that's good. Thank you. Just gotta say it's really, really great to be back. *O-s-dav-ga-lu-hi-s-di'-i.*

Blue, I was gonna tell what-all happened after we put Jason to rest, but maybe you could?

Okie dokie. Well, let's see... I didn't go back to the farm after the funeral. The social had worker stopped my placement. But I woke one Saturday thenking to see the family. I also felt bad the painting wasn't done. So, I went. I remember as I came up to the kitchen door, Ray Stevens was singing "Everytheng Is Beautiful" on the radio and it seemed so right. Peering through the screen, I saw a heavy discussion at the table.

Blue, excuse me—Nene and Sparky were following the debate going on in the country 'bout how school busing was gonna help solve the race problem by getting kids together. Their heads were swimming with how this was gonna affect them, ya know? And I remember we were busy making a big group doodle on shelf paper as we talked.

Yeah, right. So, just as I got there, I saw Sparky throw his crayon down and pound the table. All eyes were on him—even old Eeyo didn't notice me 'til I coughed.*

Oh, you shoulda seen my kids jump up and give Blue bear hugs. My heart jumped too. They'd missed him so much—almost as much as me. It wasn't 'til he got hisself a cuppa coffee that he came over and squeezed my shoulder. That mighta seemed like an everyday act, but it was really magic.

So, I jumped right in telling how I felt about integrating schools. I sure had an opinion—like I felt we could get a better education in our own schools without being bused off somewhere else. Eh, it's only my take. Then, after talking that to death, we started in on the antiwar movement. Those kids—I-I mean, their minds were exploding over world events. Sparky's the one who got me. His history teacher had them studying the Vietnam War, so he

---

* Some in the circle chuckle thinking they hear him say "Oleo."

said we should've invaded North Vietnam to end Communism once and for all. "To save the world," he said. After that, I guess I was—well—Sparky's foil while my little love pulled hamburg from the freezer and defrosted it in her new microwave. She wanted out of that discussion.

Yeah, I couldn't talk 'bout such; but it sure gladdened my heart to hear the kids razzing Blue like with Jason. I felt the walls of family—even if they weren't real. Later, Sparky set up the grill so Blue could cook the burgers while I put together a salad and Nene played ball with Eeyo. The day was turning out perfect. No negative anything. Just togetherness. It was heaven. We ate supper in the kitchen with the fan in the doorway moving the heavy air. But, while I was dishing out the ice cream and Sparky was hand-wrestling Blue on the table, Nene started to cough and I mean cough. She kept clearing her throat and giving her brother evil eyes. I was watching to see if she could breathe. Kids, I'm gonna tell this, okay?...

"Momma, Sparky's kickin' me under the table."

"Oh, Sparky, this sure has been one mighty good day all day long. Please don't ruin it. After you eat your ice cream, you can go watch TV."

"But, Momma, he's only kickin' me 'cuz we wanna talk 'bout something."

I asked her if it was family talk and could it wait 'til after Blue left. She replied, "It's family talk, but it includes Blue, too—only I dunno how ta say it."

Then Sparky piped up in a "brotherly" way, "Yes, ya do. Ya said ya could do it, so g'wan 'n do it, stupid."

"Mo-m-m-m, he called me stupid."

"Frankly, darlin', I don't give a dang. Eat your ice cream and you can leave the table."

Nene took her dish, set it down, looked at it, raised her eyebrows, stared bug-eyed first at Sparky, then at Blue and then back at the dish. Only after I sat down did she push her dish to the center of the table and speak. Looking back now, it was cute how the kids exchanged those looks, but I was totally confounded at the time. My spoon hung half way to my mouth as I stared.

"All right, I'll say just one thing, then *he* has ta do some talkin'... Sparky 'n I—we been thinkin'. It's mighty lonely 'round here now that—" She couldn't say more. She began bawling, her squinty eyes dripping tears onto the table.

My spoon began tearing onto the table, too. I sure didn't think this day could fall apart so fast. I reached my arms out and invited Nene onto my lap, murmuring in her ear and kissing her cheek. The room stayed quiet 'til Sparky, who was wiggling 'til he couldn't stand it more, chimed up, "She's right. We're missin' Dad so much. It's not right ta pretend it's okay without him."

"Indeed. You're both absolutely right. It's not okay. And so, let's not. I didn't think we were, but if we were let's not anymore."

Sparky's eyes were on fire, now. "Okay. But Nene 'n me both think the same. We want Blue back, like he was afore—not like Dad or anything. But like a friend, ya know? He made us happy and we miss him."

Nene gained courage from Sparky's words. She softly chimed in with her head on my shoulder and her arms 'round my neck, "He's always kind and good. We love him and," she hesitated, looking 'round the table from face to face to face afore finishing, "and we know you love him, too!" Now, look, you guys—remember, that's what happened and how it happened.

Shug, I remember that, too, and I also remember we couldn't resist laughing at what we thought had been our secret. Before we knew it, all four of us were laughing and tearing. What we did next was sweet—huddling, hugging and crying all at the same time.

Yeah. Blue and I promised the kids we'd think more on their suggestion. So, after diving into their soupy ice cream, they left to watch their favorite TV shows, *All in the Family* and *The Brady Bunch,* while we sat at that old table thinking on the next part of our lives.

That's when I confessed I'd been doing some thenking, too—how tradition would allow me to move into her clan house and keep custom with her. I admit, I also wanted to be in a family. I'd been impressed, watching, when Jason was alive. In my mind, I could be like an uncle to the kids and we could be together.

But for me? Well, thar was lots to consider. First off, my emotions had been on a roller coaster ever since I laid eyes on Blue. And then, even if my marriage wasn't based on passion, it sure was on love. After Jason done left, I lay in bed night after night tossing and turning 'til, one night, I got outta the dresser his winter underwear and stuffed it with tee shirts and socks and covered it all with his pjs then set it on the other side of the bed so I could snuggle up to it. After all, he was my partner for more than ten years and a wonderful father, too. I wasn't ready to let him go—or my link to Sophie. Being his wife was the very foundation of this life I created—and he was taken away from me. I was like in a vacuum.

... So, I put together my aching loneliness and the kid's suggestion and agreed to it. Blue stayed in the house that night and lotsa times in the following weeks—always sleeping on the couch. Talking of the future while we were painting the house helped me let go of the past. Joy and optimism drove all those haunting words of Cee's right straight outta my mind.... Say, Nene and Sparky, are you hungry? Why not go and grab something to eat? Everything on that table is delicious and getting cold. C'mon back when your plates are full.

... Okay, now they're gone, I wanna share something personal. One day, while they were in school, I invited Blue into bed for the very first time. Later, looking in the mirror at me with my head on his chest in the same bed and in 'bout the same position as I used to with Jason, it came on me—what I was doing to Jason's memory? I cried all that night and all the next day. No one could make me feel better. Remember, Blue, how I kept repeating it wasn't right to dishonor Jason by thinking of myself?

How can I forget? You made your case very well. I knew to leave and I stayed away f-for a week until you came and found me.

Uh-huh 'n I knew whar to find you, too—at the library reading the paper. I whispered in your ear how mad the kids were that I drove you away and how my distress was so much worse 'cuz I done hurt you and how much I needed you back.

So I went back. But I knew to finish off the loft in the barn, thenking to stay there 'til we knew what was ahead. I put up simple double walls at the top of the ladder and insulated them with newspapers and put together a platform bed, a few clothes hooks, an entry door and small window. It took less than two weeks and I had a place to sleep for the rest of the year—except in

the winter when I came inside and slept on the couch. I liked that
better—didn't have to deal with the mouse world or the buzzing
of the honey bees overhead. Finishing off the loft brought peace
into the house, that's for dang sure.

M-m-m. We fell into a habit of eating supper together every
night, then Blue went out back, so the kids and I could have our
family talk. This seemed to keep me satisfied 'til Cee hadda call.
She asked if I wanted the good news first—naturally, I said yes.
Seems Bud done lost his driver's license from drunk driving so
many times. That was the good news.

"Now, the bad news."

"It's alright, hon'n. I love ya anyways."

"It's jist Bud's been goin' 'round sayin' he knows yer livin'
'round here somewhars."

"Oh, yeah? How's he know that?"

"Seems his brother-in-law saw ya."

"No! Whar?"

"Somewhar's 'round Midway, I reckon. Coupla weeks ago he's
sure he saw ya."

"How'd he know it was me?"

"Well, he said it looked like ya. And, hon'n, he said the woman
was driving a blue Studebaker convertible."

"Crap."

My stomach dropped to my knees. So, now I hadda worry 'bout
Midway, too. Guess I wasn't invisible like I thought. This scary
news kept me near home 'til early fall when I came up with an
idea. I got Cee to go with me to the Ashville Five and Dime when
the kids were in school. We had a ball in the Halloween department with her telling me how I looked in different costumes. I

picked out two wigs and two types of glasses that gave me four different looks. After that, I used these when I was tempted to take a risky trip. I think they worked.

Hey, Nene and Sparky, didn't you think I was a riot?... Yeah, yeah, everybody thought I was just fooling 'round. Anyways, I think it worked. I was never discovered. Other than that, I guess you could say life settled a bit. Life does settle from time to time. Like beads on a necklace, thar're some jewels I wanna share with y'all.

Beaded Days

Like a strand of pearls
We wear the years 'round our necks
One lined up behind the other
Shiny, precious, numbered memories

One clear blustery day 'bout three months later, I was driving the high-speed lane on the new state highway to Midway, hightailing it to my 11:30 appointment to close out Jason's bank account. I asked Blue to go with me. Remember, Blue?

Ennit! It was little scary then, but sure is funny, now. When you told me to look back at the cars we passed, I saw t-two other cars weaving in what looked like... Well, a race with destiny—what I was thenking. By the time they caught up, we were cruising along with a bunch of other cars. Since we were all by ourselves in the high-speed lane, you coulda passed them and got outta their way, but you didn't. No, you hung alongside the car in the middle lane so you could block cars behind. I asked what you were doing and you said you didn't like what was going on.

It's true, I didn't. The first driver was a young guy looking like he was trying to escape the second one—and he was wearing a broad-brimmed hat. I kinda filled in the missing pieces.

I saw that, too, so that made both of us thenking we were in the middle of a law-enforcement act. I held my tongue and watched.

But I remember how nervous you were.

Yup, I was. And when the cars next to us fell back, it turned into a drama of just three cars—you holding the wheel tight, concentrating on your mirror as you slowed down more and more—and the state trooper behind, pulling up to motion the young guy off the road. But, nah, he stayed right on our tail.

Me? My head was with the trooper. It just seemed like my duty was to keep that driver trapped. Just when I mentioned we were 'bout to cross the Oconoluftee Bridge, the trooper pulled up to Blue's window and clearly mouthed we should "slow down and stop." Now, I knew we were a team! So I did. I eased my car ever-so-slowly to a dead stop with the trooper's car working to block the guy behind in the high-speed lane. I went and made a roadblock in the high speed lane of a highway on a bridge!

Yup, she did. Whnh, I realized I didn't know this woman like I thought. I asked, "What in tarnation made you go and do a thing like that?"

"Like what?"

"Instantly turn into a vigilante."

"I dunno, just seemed the right thing to do."

"But it was totally risky. You were so brave."

"I was? Wasn't tryin' ta be. Wasn't thinkin' of myself at all. I just—"

"You just what?"

"I-I dunno, just went and did it. Not thinkin' 'bout anything, just did it. Seemed right, that's all."

"Ah-h-h, now I see how wrong I've been. Thank you. This is a life lesson."

"Lesson?... 'Bout what?"

"Driving. Now I'm thenking it can be good for one's karma, after all."

And that's how Blue gained respect for lessons I could teach him. In fact—after that—he done got his driver's license renewed, which was a true blessing. See how we were teaching each other?

... Another example of jewel days was the time when both kids were in school and we were headed to the woods for a picnic. Strolling hand in hand, Blue asked me 'bout my life with Bud on the farm. I continued watching my feet touch the ground, "Nope. Some things I'm takin' to the grave and that's one."

Wow, did I ever get shot down. Kinda apologetically, I asked, "Okie dokie, then. So, do you wanna hear more about D-Dolores?"

"Sure."

"Well, I told you we had twelve good years and she was a good Gaduwa wife. Kept up with basket-making—sold 'em at benefits and the tribal holiday booth. Good cook, too. I liked the way she made our home welcoming. It was always good to come in with sometheng cooking on the stove. Remember, she died brenging our fourth into the world—way too soon. Whnh, both of them died. I-I heard it was horrible—but, I wasn't there; I was back here. It was the year after I met you. Didn't know anything 'til I got back. Her sister's husband—Hank—he took me to Carolee, and she explained. Dolores had been surprised with early labor pains, but she'd been gardening that morning and her waters had broke."

Oh, I say—when Blue told me how many of you women far outta town have your babies at home instead of at the Indian Hospital, I got it. I can understand why you don't wanna travel on bumpy dirt roads when you're in labor.

Yep, I told her how you women talk plenty about our roads. "And then, going into town to the government Indian Health Service? No-o-o, our ways are too different. But, well, the baby didn't come out right away and Carolee didn't thenk that all the while Dolores lay in bed she was getting infected. Next day, Dolores got hot and Carolee was alone with her. When Hank came in, he took one look and said she was going to the hospital. He carried her out to his truck. But thengs went downhill. I mean, he ran out of gas a few miles down the road and it was sometheng like seven o'clock at night and he had to run a couple of miles to a neighbor's and—well, it was t-terrible how it went. Anyway, he didn't get to the hospital in time and they couldn't save her or the baby, that's all. She musta died in great pain. Thenking on it always gets me upset, even this many years later."

Blue stopped, a blank look on his face. I said "Sorry," but that's all. Sometimes silence is best. After a while, he done brought up another subject that made a big impression on me.

"Sad as that was and after all the kids went through afterwards, they did okay, really. Dolores' brother, Harold, and his wife, Annie Lou—they took in Stormy and Lynnee Mae and little Sammy. And they're brenging them up on the Keetoowah path. I'm pleased how it's worked out."

As I spread out our big blanket at our favorite spot, a question came to me. "That's nice, but I don't get why they're raisin' them, not you." We were unpacking sandwiches and hot tea.

"Of course. Sorry, I forgot. Let's see, that goes back to before Europeans, when a Cherokee woman's life was quite different. Ya know, they had many rights the European women didn't and most women today don't."

"Well, then, I sure wanna hear 'bout that!" I shouted to the trees.

"Okay. In our tradition, a mother owns the home and controls everytheng in it—that means everytheng to do with the kids, too."

"That's not so different, is it?"

"That's just for starters." Blue's finger was pointing at me. "Ya see, it's true even today—fathers who follow tradition have no power over these thengs. None."

"That's different."

"Uh-huh. Fathers do have their role. But our families come from our mothers. There's a word for our kind of family—Matrilineal."

"I heard of it."

"For us, that means because I'm a traditional Keetoowah who observes clan laws, Lynnee Mae, Little Sammy and Stormy—th-they aren't my family."

"What-t-t-t? Get outta here."

"No. It's a big difference. And there's more. Our custom for dealing with kids who lose their mother is to have someone in the mother's family—usually her sister—take them in and bring 'em up. The mother's brother always has traditional responsibilities—mostly for teaching 'em."

Now I was the one to put a finger in the air—this time to stop Blue. I cleared my mouth of food afore I said, "I'll wait 'til you're done, but I have lotsa questions. And would you mind passin' the thermos?"

She caught me with my mouth full, but I eventually explained as I poured some tea into the thermos cover and handed it over, "In my case, Dolores' sister couldn't take the kids, so her brother took 'em. After all, they're family too. It's fine, because mother's brothers affect a child's life even when the mother and father are both alive and present."

"I'm tryin' ta be quiet, but I still don't see where-all the father comes in?"

My first sandwich gone, I wiped my hands on my pants before putting them on Brigit's shoulders. "Okay, okay. But, look, the basic theng you need to know is in Cherokee custom a father lets his kids grow up with their own family and clan, which—remember—the father is not part of. Sorry to worry your little head—I see you shaking it—but I'm here to say there's more ways to organizing a family than what you know."

Well, I done finished my sandwich and was rubbing a shine on my apple when he hit me with that. I couldn't hold back. "Now, just wait a bit. Settin' here in this space, I'm tryin' ta figure how my Jason coulda ever walked away from his kids. Ever. Why, he was ab-so-lute-ly devoted to his kids—al-l-l his kids from both of his families right up 'til the very day he went and lay down. He woulda no more left his two older sons with his first wife's relatives when his wife up 'n left—or Nene and Sparky, for that matter, if I was the one who left, than... he just wouldn'a done it. That's all. Wow, what you're sayin' is gonna take a good bit of time to sink into this head."

"I understand, believe me. But remember, just because Jason was like that doesn't mean that's the only way to be a father. Heavens, you only have to thenk back on your own."

This riled me so much I threw my apple as far as I could into the dry leaves whar it disappeared. Blue laughed as he bit into his second sandwich. I spoke as calmly as I could, "You hadda go 'n bring that up. Okay, I'll give you that. But, it's different here. I'm settin' you in Jason's class of men and I'm trying ver-r-ry hard to get how you done made a family with your wife, but your brother-in-law is thar for the kids after she up 'n dies—not you. And you're sayin' he was doin' for 'em even when she was livin'? And now that she's not, you're tellin' me they're his responsibility—not yours? This doesn't make sense of how things should work." I stared into the leaves, wondering where my apple went. I wanted it.

"You just proved you understand it perfectly. You said it just right. I know it seems strange to you, but remember this is *our* tradition. It goes back—far back, before Europeans—to the days when social order came from clans. Men were the hunters and warriors, always on the move, and they often had a number of wives and families in different places. The kids lived with their mothers and mothers raised the kids. Mothers owned and kept the homes, grew the gardens, made the food, clothing, baskets, whatever. Th-they were the settled parents. But the men? I mean, whnh, a good number of them never returned home from a hunt or a war. Their lives were dangerous, dealing with life-and-death matters."

"Yeah. So?"

Blue noticed me looking 'round for my apple, so he got up and fussed the leaves 'til he plucked it and gave it back to me, talking all the while. "They hadda find a way of taking care of the women and kids in case the men were lost. And they did. And if a man had more'n one wife, they hadda be in the same clan so all his kids were related. This amazing system worked really well for a long time. It was orderly and humane. Still is, if you practice it the right way."

I nodded a thanks, afore I took my first bite and said 'round pieces of apple in my mouth, "Hmm, I get what you're sayin'. I'll sure give it some consideration, but I can't see it workin' in today's world. But, then again, guess it explains why ya weren't thar for your wife 'n kids, 'cuz you were away playin' at being a brave warrior."

"You can make jokes, but you don't know what you're talking about. A warrior is a proud defender of his family, his clan, his ideals. He doesn't play. Didn't Jason go off and serve in the military? Wasn't he a warrior?"

I was feeling so silly when I spoke and I thought it showed in my voice, but when Blue answered, he was somber and serious. Clearly, I crossed a line. Thar was an awkward pause while I digested his words. Why is it that humor isn't always fitting? Why wouldn't it be a good idea to pop up with another Twain saying right then—like 'Don't put off 'til tomorrow what can be put off 'til day after tomorrow' or 'I'd rather have my ignorance than another man's knowledge because I have so much more of it.' Nah, I shook that idea away. Actually, I got a shiver from his truth. I lay back and wrapped the blanket 'round my shoulders. "So, how'd *you* grow up?"

When she brought this up, I knew we'd be there a while, so I lay down next to her and put my arms around her. That way, I could warm her as I looked into the chilly sky.

"Oh, my story's different. My father's parents—what you'd call my grandparents even though I don't—they brought me up after my mother died."

"When were you born... in '25 or '26 or something?"

"Uh, let's see... yeah, that's about it; I thenk it was in '27. I'm not good at dates, though—never paid much attention to clocks or calendars. Anyway, my father's parents made sure I grew up knowing of my father."

"That's nice. Wish I knew 'bout mine."

"Yeah, well, they were good folks. My father's family had a long history of following traditional Cherokee laws, but they couldn't with me."

"Why not? Were you such a difficult little tyke?"

"Hunh, there's a reason for my story, so don't be piddling. You should know by now that my family is my mother's clan and they were only real relatives I have, under tradition. They weren't around, so I grew up without a family. Still, my father's family brought me up in the Gaduwa way as best they could."

Sorry, folks, I gotta just put in here that I did think I understood what he was telling me, but I wasn't listening as carefully as I shoulda because I was distracted by the memory of not having a father to share relatives with and, then, that new concept of having a father but him not being family—so many strange ideas confusing me.

Blue kept going. "I know you don't get how I could grow up in my father's family and not feel they were my relatives, but listen…My father, Eli, was much older than my mother. They said she was something like sixteen when I was born and he was forty. His Cherokee name was *Da-nu-wa-a-na-li-hi*, which means 'warrior.' They said he took off for Arkansas after she died—went to tell her family, but he never came back. I heard folks who visited Arkansas learned he'd been there, but moved on to be with another woman. That's the last anyone knew."

I jumped up at that point waving my arms in the air. My voice rose as I paced back and forth. So much just didn't make sense. "Wait! Now, thar's more I'm not gettin'. Why don't Cherokee fathers even *wanna* see their kids grow? Why don't they *wanna* be a parta their lives even when they can? Please forgive me, but I can't figure why your father didn't *wanna* be thar for y'all or why you don't wanna see your kids grow up, neither. Yeah, okay, the uncle can be thar for 'em—that's nice. But shouldn't a father stick 'round for the ones he brought into the world? And why didn't your mother's family—what you call your only relatives—come take care of you if your family was followin' traditional ways?"

The smile he was wearing grew into a hearty laugh as he waited for me to stop railing. He was looking at the passing clouds, twisting his head from side to side as he waited his turn. Sometimes I think he looks at clouds more'n me. But this break plus the cold air coming in caused us to pack up. Blue continued talking as we headed on home.

"I really thenk I'm not going to have all the answers to all your questions, Shug, but let me tell you my history. Every time I asked elders, I got the same story. The grandfathers say my mother was a shy, young woman who showed up alone on the train from St. Louis with a heavy suitcase and a big box. My father's first wife had died from the flu the winter before. He just happened to be at the station thenking she was standing there looking lost. He offered her a ride in his pick-up and they started living together."

"Is that the Cherokee way?"

"Oh, yes, we do it, too. The story goes that they pretty much kept to themselves and she got pregnant right off. She was really quiet and my father's folks didn't get to know her much. Then, it became clear she was more'n pregnant—she was sick, too. She gave birth almost two months early, then died. I dunno why. Some folks said it coulda been TB, which was called consumption back then. Whatever. Apparently, she was from southwestern Arkansas and a full-blood *A-ni-wo-di*—that's the Paint Clan. No one ever learned much more'n that, so it doesn't serve me to worry about it."

"But that's so sad. What did ya say 'bout the Paint Clan—they the ones who adopted?"

"No, the *A-ni-wo-di* are healers and wise men—it's my clan. But, I've had a f-fine Keetoowah upbrenging with good people who loved me. I always felt secure and cared for in my father's family. His people, the *A-ni-wa-ya*—they're the protectors. And because my father was brought up by the same people in the same place, I've always felt connected to him. I grew up thenking what he must have been like at every age even though we never met. Funny, whnh, I still feel that way."

A quiet fell over us. I stopped and looked up into the branches of the pine tree over my head. The sunlight tinkling down made me shudder at the electric green that seemed to go right through me punctuating Blue's words.

"Blue, you have a terrific face on life, ya know? Some people, like me, we complain our whole lives long 'bout what we didn't get outta childhood instead of seein' our lives with such under-standing and its—well—imperfections. I wish I felt like you when I growed up."

"To accept what life offers is the right and true Gaduwa way."

We left off thar and didn't return to Blue's upbringing again until the kids asked him something 'bout his family at the supper table that night. He didn't speak to the same subject, though. He explained he was brought up by grandparents, same as me only different, afore the discussion got lively.

"My father's mother—her name was Nannie Bearclaw—she told me many stories of her childhood and what she knew of her mother's life. Nannie was born around 1861 when her father left to fight in the Civil War. Her mother was *Kanogisgi*—that means 'singer.' She was born after the Cherokees arrived from their march and before Oklahoma became a state. Do you know what year that happened, by any chance?"

Sparky jumped up and down outshouting Nene, "I do. I do. It was in 1907 and the state capital is Oklahoma City."

"Very good, *Chooch*," I said before I explained how the federal government declared that same land "Indian Territory" in the 1800s when they set it aside for the five tribes they labelled "civilized"—which was us, of course, and the Choctaws, Chickasaws, Creeks and Seminoles.

Blue's story impressed me. I didn't know anybody else who had a family with so much American history. Nene asked if Blue's family marched in the Trail of Tears and both Sparky and I looked at her. How come she knew to ask this? My kids amaze me. Blue described how thousands of Cherokees, and other tribes too, were forced to leave their homes and walk all the way to the western wilderness, lotsa them through the winter, just so's European settlers could take their land, back east. Like criminals, or cows even, they were locked up in dirty stockades for months, waiting on the government to decide when to move them. Different groups left at different times. *Kanogisgi's* mother's group was forced to start walking just as winter was coming on. I saw the kids' heads nodding. Seems they knew this. Blue went on.

"Remember, the weather was like it is now—cold. And back then, there were no roads where they were going, whnh, no motel or drive-through, that's for dang sure. It's interesting, though—on the day the f-first marchers set out, there was no rain and no clouds—only plenty of thunder in the sky. That's how the marchers knew, whnh, *U-ne-tla-nv'-hi* was angry." Nene asked who that was. "Sorry. *U-ne-tla-nv'-hi* is the Creator."

Me? I set thar putting in my thoughts how it must be terrifying to set out on any trip with winter coming on and the sky shuddering, but Blue continued, "Yeah. And it took five months to make that walk. Some even did it in bare feet. Different groups left at different times and took different routes—but any way they went—the weather got worse and worse. People came out to look at them or give them food or something to cover their feet. That's how the marchers named their path 'The Trail Where They Cried'."

We all look at Blue with confusion on our faces. He nodded afore explaining, "The Cherokees saw the locals crying at the soldiers' cruelty and they were ashamed."

"Ya know, I kinda remember hearin' something 'bout this in eighth-grade history, but I never gave a thought to the watchers—I always thought the Indians were the ones cryin'. Thinkin' now, I woulda cried watchin' 'em, too. I can't believe our government did this."

Sparky piped up, "It coulda been somebody in your family died on the way."

"You're right and perhaps they did. I'll never know. The survivors reached Fort Gibson many months later; I think the last ones were in March. They say my father's grandmother was one of those. She was alone, but coupla months later, she d-delivered *Kanogisgi*."

Woeful Tale

Westward walk
Following the sun
Chasing the future
Healing feelings
Step and step again
Over hills and plains
Rivers and swamps
Past and present
Pain and sorrow
Marching and trudging
Weeping for home
Weeping for justice
Crying for the dying
Crying for the dead
Wounded walkers
Woeful tale of tears

Nene's head popped up and she asked, "Blue, is havin' a baby without bein' married a Cherokee thing?"

"Sometimes, Nene, sometimes, but not always. Back then, marriage was different. As long as both families agreed and you were a good couple and none of the clans minded, you were married. But it was also true that when a woman decided she was done with her marriage, a man could come home and find all his stuff in the yard."

Nene was hearing more than her young mind was prepared for. "Seriously?"

"Yup. Women had lots of power. And having a baby was different, too—didn't always come with marriage. Traditional babies belong to the mother and her clan, so marriage wasn't the point then. But also, having a baby outside of marriage is really not the *A-ni-yv-wi-ya* right way. For the Cherokees who survived it to Indian Territory, though, life was—I mean—really d-difficult and confusing."

Sparky mentioned that his teacher had said a quarter of the marchers died on the march.

But Blue explained no one really knows—maybe as many as a third didn't make it. "And they were probably the weakest, whnh. Thenk—when the survivors got to Indian Territory, they'd already encountered so many life-and-death issues that no one was worried about having a baby. It was life-affirming. A blessing. Hope. You could say a birth should always be welcomed, ennit?"

We all agreed afore the room got so quiet I thought I heard Nene picking her fingernails. We were busy drinking in what Blue just said. Sometimes it takes a while to process ideas. I got up and hugged my babies afore getting some juice while Blue asked if we'd like to hear 'bout this baby. 'Course, we did. The kids said nothing while I talked back.

"The baby was welcome, but there was one little difference with *Kanogisgi*."

"What?" I wondered out loud.

"She had dark brown hair and bright blue eyes."

"Like yours! That's great, isn't it?"

"Well, I mean, intermarriage was never a p-problem for Cherokees—not then and not now. It wasn't—still isn't—bad if you're not full-blooded. But the traditional, correct—I mean right theng—for fathers is to claim offspreng, not shun them. This was especially important back then, when clans determined so much in every baby's life. Every Keetoowah needs to know the father's clan. Without it, there isn't the necessary information for a traditional upbrenging. And it's best not to marry into the father's clan, either, just like we don't marry into our own."

"So-o-o, what's that got to do with *Kanogisgi*?" I was prying, also maybe a bit dense.

"Well, there were too many possibilities. Her father coulda been an English soldier who took advantage of her mother in a stockade... or he coulda been a Frenchman at one of the trading posts who gave her sometheng in exchange for his pleasure... or possibly a Scotsman at a river crossing... or even a blue-eyed Cherokee of Viking ancestors. Who knows? Who knows?"

"Yeah? So? Whatta ya sayin'?"

"So, no matter if she came from any man anywhere, it didn't matter to her upbrenging. She had her mother and she had her clan family."

"Okay, but nobody knew anything for sure 'bout her father."

"Right. And that left her without a full knowledge of her heritage. Just that. Sorta like you."

That knocked me between the eyes. I got the point. You can bet on it.

... "Anyway, *Kanogisgi* and I shared the same eyes. Her daughter, Nannie Bearclaw—she got 'em, too. Our eyes were a family affair. I grew up with 'em staring me down all the time, reminding me old Nannie and I got our genes from the same unknown ancestor. But it never affected our being full-blood."

I was still foggy with all this blood stuff. I asked, "Why not?"

Nene chimed right up, "Mom-m-m, this was 'bout Blue's father's family. It was his mother who was a full-blood. Full-blood mothers have full-blood kids."

"Uch, okay. I get it now."

It can be a chore bringing up kids, can't it? After that, it seemed better just to listen.

"Thank you, Nene. So, I'm a full-blood, no matter what I look like. And I often wondered—I mean—I've done a lot of thenking on this and maybe it's 'cuz I look unusual for a full-blood that I try harder to be a good Keetowah. I dunno. Not to complicate things, but our tradition has changed over the years, just like everytheng else. Change happens and we adapt. Nowadays, laws passed in Congress make it so the father's blood quantum is considered, too. What's full-blood and mixed-blood has been redefined."

Blue and I had lotsa other discussions on blood quantum, but real blood hung 'round our house the whole next week. One morning, I was letting Oleo out and saw a small puddle of blood on the back stoop. Nothing else. No animal carcass. No sign of a struggle. Just blood—a bother to clean up. I even kidded Blue he left it as a reminder of our discussion. Next day, another one was thar—like as if I didn't clean up afore. This was a minor mystery. When it happened again on the third day, I got upset and Blue worked to make me feel better.

"Want me to come in and sleep on the kitchen floor? I can hear better inside."

"I dunno. What would ya do if you heard something?"

"Maybe nothin'. I could at least see who's doing this."

'Course, right off I suspected Bud. Who else would do this? And if it was Bud, my new life was over. I sure didn't want it to be him. I didn't even wanna know.

I could see she was terrified. And honestly, I was a bit concerned too. I didn't know about Bud then, but the symbolism wasn't good. I made light of it, offering to do sometheng little while thenking to do sometheng more. She agreed to let me sleep on the kitchen floor, but she didn't know I set a trap after she went to bed. I didn't want to scare her anymore'n she already was. Next morning, her fears were put to bed.

"Hear anything last night?"

"No, but go take a look outside."

"Oh, my! What's that over thar—a deer? You trapped a deer, Blue? Why'd ya do that?

"She's the one who's been coming to the stoop at night."

"What? Why's she been bleedin'? What's wrong with her?"

"She's really sick. I'm thenking she got caught in a bear trap and came here to be safe—maybe even wanting help."

"Oh-h-h, how terrible. How bad is it? Can we help her?"

"Nah, don't thenk so. Leg's bad 'n she's weak. I'll have to put her down."

"Oh, so sad. And, yet, I'm so-o-o relieved."

"I know, I know," is what Blue said, but he only thought he knew. He did take care of the deer—ya know, put her down. He wouldn't let us see him do it, though. And I never said anything to anybody 'bout this, but I always wondered why Oleo never barked to let us know an animal was nearby or how come a wounded deer came to our house. A great mystery. Ya know, the longer I live the more I think... us humans—we have a lot to learn.

But a deer bleeding on our doorstep wasn't the end of spooky things. Thar was always Bud. He made the newspaper that summer. Blue was out weeding the garden when Cee swung by with a little article she came across. Bud had been arrested for putting posters with my picture on telephone poles. After being warned three times, the cops were sick 'n tired of tearing down the "WANTED" signs, so they took him to dry out in jail. We first giggled 'bout it, but then got to talking seriously how this disturbed man couldn't let go of me. I asked Cee not to mention anything to Blue—I was embarrassed and still wanting this to all go away. Plus I didn't wanna upset him. After all, it wasn't his problem. Right?...

Whnh, me not knowing about Bud? Well, ignorance sure is bliss. I'd no idea what my dear girl was going through. She was too good at putting on a show. When I finally did learn about her years of terror, I came to admire her strength even more, but back then, it was her endinglessly-curious mind that got to me. She took in ideas like a dry sponge sucks water.

… Anyway, seeing that cloud over there reminds me of Spirit Wind. And thenking of my dear friend galloping over the trees, I'm distracted now, remembering how I used to ride these hills. So much nostalgia makes my heart full—and also reminds me of how much of a challenge it was to describe to my curious friend here what life was like growing up as a Gaduwa. Our next heavy discussion was about a week later. We were doing the dishes on a muggy evening. The fan was in the doorway, but still I was sweating like a pig in July.

"Remember I told you how I aim to be true to the old ways?"

She wasn't on my wavelength yet, "Yeah, so?"

"Well, speaking our language—what some folks call Tsalagi, even though the word doesn't really mean anytheng—that and keeping ceremonies like the Green Corn Ceremony and the stomp dance—it's how we come to thenk of ourselves as tradition keepers. We know if we let these go, we won't be any more."

"Uh-huh," as she grabbed more plates to set into the soapy water.

I kept polishing a glass, thinking how to tell her what I needed to say. "Ya know, back when the marchers arrived in Indian Territory, they brought old ways with 'em, but the ones who came earlier had already made their own government. New Cherokees brought old ways yet those already there had new ways. What was old and what was new was confusing."

Shug stopped what she was doing and looked at me, "Well, without knowin' what you're talkin' 'bout, exactly, I guess I can get it—thar can't be two governments for the same people."

"You're smart and everytheng sure is clearer looking back. But about t-twenty years after they got there, the ones who wanted to keep tradition decided to join up with Redbird Smith and breng back the Keetoowah Society... and it was kept a secret, at first."

"Why secret?"

"Because so many others were trying to fit into *yonega* society and be 'civilized' or Christian. They were two very different ways to live and not compatible."

Excuse me for stopping ya, Blue. I just wanna say that, at first, the lovely evening didn't seem a good time for a history lesson, but Blue's take on things always got to me—always showing me life from all sides and all that. I didn't knew 'til one of Nene's teachers told me what this kinda thing was—Blue was teaching me something called 'Multiculturalism.' I once told him I thought he was a good teacher and he answered, "Everytheng in life comes as a teaching. If we pay attention, we learn." Remember?

Definitely. I also remember telling you how important it is to learn to listen—or our tongues will make us deaf.

Yeah, we laughed then, too, but I knew I needed to listen more. It was while he was talking that it came to me how I once lived in a private world—like inside a bubble. Some people call that "*naivete.*" Blue's teaching 'bout another way of life was—well, refreshing... It opened a door to understanding, like—well, I can't find the words exactly.

So, as I was saying, "That Keetoowah Society was open to both full-bloods and mixed-bloods. Holding to tradition is what counted, not blood count. If you ask me, though, I thenk full-bloods have kept tradition b-better over the years. I mean, culture comes from the mothers and mothers' relatives have more influence on kids, so full-blooded mothers just have to pass on more tradition is what I thenk."

When I interrupted him, asking him if he'd take a big pot outta my hands, dry it and set it up high on the pantry shelf, he asked if I was listening. I told him I was, but was doing something else, too—what I just heard 'bout on TV—a thing called "multitasking." Guess we were multitasking along with multiculturalizing. Funny how life can get complicated.

"But getting back to that Society... It wanted thengs to be like before the Europeans came—back to when we put community before any one person—back to living off the land with hunting and trading, preserving harmony and balance and—of course—doing all this while keeping the physical and spiritual worlds connected."

Right then, he paused and I raised my finger in the air to tell him I needed a pause, too. I wanted to grab the broom from the pantry so's I could sweep the floor. He waited for me to return afore he went on.

"... And that's why they decided to keep our religious traditions—with the seven directions and keeping the interconnectedness of everytheng—as the core of Keetoowah living."

By now, I was done with the mess on the floor and was taking in all his words. My comment, "How beautiful that sounds" was all I could get out afore he done shook me.

"... But then, there were those other Cherokees who compromised on tradition in order to fit into *yo-ne-ga* society—even going so far as to take away women's rights. Whnh, that's when and how the two sides got violent—so violent it was like a Cherokee civil war."

What popped into my head right then was a vision of blood dripping over people—all people everywhere—and a bad feeling came on me. Guess I showed it 'cuz Blue came over and hugged me. I asked him to change the subject so I could stop seeing blood. Looking him in the eye, I asked him why was it so important to tell me all this. He teared up as he thought to answer.

"Because-because this is who I am. This is my background, my lifestyle, my ancestors, my heritage, my culture. I-I'm different from you and I want you to know *me*. I need to finish this so you can."

Well, that wasn't so much to ask and I knew it. I apologized and after I got holda my disgust with myself, I encouraged him to finish.

"Okay then, so it got even more complicated. The United States Civil War started about the same time and both North and South sucked Cherokees into that, too. We lost soldiers on both sides."

"They went and fought in the Civil War—like North against South?"

"We did. We even had a general in the confederate army."

"A general?"

"Yep. *Degataga.* Went by the name Stand Watie—had a lot of followers—even owned slaves. See, we were divided on just about everytheng and that worked against our getting together on just about anytheng."

"Oh, dear God. But whar in tarnation were your leaders? Didn't you have any?"

"Well, there was *Coowisguwi*. In history books he's called John Ross. Ever hear of him?"

"Oh, I dunno—we didn't make much of Indian history in school. I certainly didn't pay any mind. Maybe I did, maybe I didn't. My kids probably did."

I went on to explain how he was Principal Chief back east and worked to keep the people there, but couldn't change the government's decision. And he was the one to lead the march and help form a new government in Indian Territory. But then, I explained how Stan Watie and General Ridge of the Loyal League and his Pin followers wanted to do business with the new country and how the two camps went at each other. So much chaos for so long and no one able to fix it.

Me? I was sitting thar thinking how I always thought my country did things for people's good. How could this be true? When I asked Blue why the United States couldn't help, he told me all those treaties with Native nations said they hadda choose to either give up their land and relocate—that way they'd be on their own—or stay put, fit in and do like others did. And those Cherokees who chose Indian Territory didn't want interference, neither. They wanted to work things out by theirselves, in their own way. They didn't trust the government. 'Bout then, I began shivering from the dampness and we locked up.

… Hugging me good night at the back door, he asked, "Just one more little theng? You should know Cherokees had even more problems—worse ones—when white settlers started moving in on Indian Territory like they did in North Carolina and Georgia and Arkansas. It was like we were being chased right off the edge of the earth. Oh, *Yonegs* hear plenty about the sad Trail of Tears, but not about all the tragedy after—even though that's what really ended up in us being a displaced, broken people. Those Europeans with their relentless greed and laws, missionaries and boarding schools… they were the worst, the cruelest. Okay, I just wanted to finish off. See ya in the morning."

I shut the kitchen door and climbed the stairs with a heavy feeling. It came on me that thar was so much to know and Blue should put it all in a book so everybody could learn what *really* happened in the early days of our country. I hadda tell him it.

Anyways, besides Blue coming into my life, thar was plenty other stuff all happening at the same time. Worst was Bud. It got worser the day I was over at Lureen's house and a squall came up just as I was leaving. It was real good she loaned me her slicker for my walk home, 'cuz I was high-stepping it on the side of the road when I heard a car come up behind. I jumped back so's not to get splashed and that's how I saw Bud. I ran all the way home and called Cee in a panic.

"Cee, Cee, Cee," I cried when she picked up the phone.

"Wait a minute, hon'n," was what I heard afore she put her hand over the receiver and called, "Turn that music down!" then asked what was up.

"He's out here, now!" I screamed, stamping my feet.

"No-o-o. How'd ya know?"

"I just saw him fly by in Poppa's truck."

"Ya sure?"

"Yas-s-s! I can't mistake that stripe on the side, ya know. And more... thar was a big ole dog in the back, barkin' his head off."

"Lord-a-mighty. I heared he has a mean dog. Yep, that hadda be him. Did he come ta yer house?"

Oh, we commiserated plenty that day, but what could I do? Blue hadda right to drive county #4 just like anybody else. 'Course I knew his license was taken away, but that wouldn'a stopped him. You can believe I was glad I was wearing a hood and he couldn'a seen me. But it drove a knife in my heart to think I wasn't safe even a few steps outta my own driveway. In my mind, I could see that knife looking just like the one Bud useda stick into his belt afore going down to the bar—the very same he wanted to twist and turn inside my belly. The vision kept me awake for nights. Now I hadda worry 'bout a dog, too. I desperately wanted my old life to stay outta this one. I guess it was lucky the days ahead were gonna keep my mind busy.

... Nene was 'bout to turn thirteen so she was having a sleepover party the next weekend. That morning, I was making her birthday cake and we were in the kitchen talking 'bout her having her ears pierced and I was saying she should wait 'til she was sixteen to make sure it was for the right reasons while Nene was insisting *all* her friends were having their ears pierced and that was the right reason. Me? I could never have my ears pierced. Gram said only "bad girls" had their ears pierced.

... Our little talk increased in heat. Nene done asked why I worked so hard to make my kids different—why they hadda stand out weird. She said I laid on 'em strange customs and clothes, homemade haircuts, no pierced ears—that kinda thing. I knew fitting in was important and I remembered my painful teens, but her words put out a challenge. We left off, but I had second thoughts on how my attitudes and values were affecting my kids, like my grandparents affected me.

... Other mothers told me they just did as their parents did—that didn't help any. Blue and Cee gave some ideas, but nothing sat right in me 'til a few weeks later as I was reliving the discussion—I got a thought. Nene's voice eating at me—why wasn't I like everybody else? This time, I allowed as how values come to us not like a baked cake or a Jello salad with the ingredients all settled and stuck together. No, I decided values come more like in a soup—all the ingredients simmering 'til they marry. Yeah, I came to think this was more like it. I knew Nene wouldn't wanna hear my theory though—she'd wanna be a decorated, fancy cake more'n the best stew ever. No, better she figure it herself. Blue agreed—but then again, a lot he knew 'bout raising kids.

Now, now, mustn't get nasty. You always said you liked my style.

Yeah, I did and I do. I'm just trying to keep things light. Can't you tell who's the serious one, here? Mark Twain says he likes a good story well told—it's why he tells them hisself.

Yep—hope I never live long enough to tire of a good story.

Me too. I think a good story connects dots—makes sense outta crazy living.

Right. Sorta like the day I told you how Cherokees don't all agree on thengs and you asked me if I didn't agree on sometheng, would I kill because of it. Remember?

I sure do—it's when you made me admit you were human.

Yeah. I said, "Look how easy it is to break up families or nations or clans. Just thenk of what's happening in Vietnam. Right as we speak, villages and families are destroying each other. No matter—North against South, like in the Civil War—or Communism against Democracy in Vietnam—or Emigrants against Old Settlers—it's the taking of sides that blows up families and communities. History is the story of violence being used to settle differences—it's the way of mankind. Issues change, but human nature doesn't."

I could only get out an "Amen" afore Cee's car peeled up the drive.

Oh, that was funny. She came to a screeching stop and—since I didn't know her very well—I raised my eyebrows—like this.

My dear friend does have a way 'bout her—it's true. She was coming over because I wasn't answering the phone and she was worried. It was my fault—I wasn't thinking to keep in touch after Jason's burial, what with Blue being such a huge distraction. She brought some warm carrot cake—a recipe outta her new Betty Crocker cookbook—and some cold news from out in the world. She called it karma and was dying to share it.

... Ya see, thar was this Lila Crosby in high school—a real beauty queen who done married the star of the football team and he went on to become chief of police then county commissioner—all a big success story. Well, that morning, Cee heard a sheriff's deputy say on TV that Lila was found locked in the trunk of her own car parked at a scenic turn-off on the Smoky Mountain parkway. Yeah. Cee said the TV announcer reported Lila's crazy story 'bout driving home late the night afore, her getting kidnapped and stuffed in the trunk. No robbery, no ransom note, no sex, nothing—most suspicious story ever. But reporters said she'd been arrested twice in nearby counties for DUI and open bottles. Well, we had a good talk over our coffee and cake 'bout just how much all that beauty helped Lila in life and we came 'round to saying justice was done—with maybe a little bit of sarcasm.

I must say, I liked Cee right off. She seemed like a good and true friend. I guess I shook her when I said, "See how thengs can work with a Blood Law?"

"Whatta ya talkin' 'bout? That don't make sense."

"Well, Cee, Cherokees used to have that law when clans were honored. B-back then, when a crime was committed on a female, her clan had the duty to right thengs. Clans were responsible for all members and that meant punishing criminal behavior. It didn't have to be a life for a life or such as that, but clans kept the balance and the Blood Law helped—and women were the basis of that."

Cee and I both jumped. I was beginning to see women really did have more power back then. Blue just kept on talking. "These days, we call keeping balance "justice." Anyway, balance in society is very important—in case you never thought about it."

Cee and I looked into each other's eyes. We never did think on that afore, but we did agree that justice is important. I commented, "There's so much more to a community than I ever thought." After a moment, Cee observed it musta been hard for Cherokees to adjust to so many changes in their lives. I watched Blue pick some sweet grass to chew on afore he answered.

True, I do love sweet grass—hunh, almost as much as I love sharing my take on life. I explained to the girls how the old clan ways of keeping order were strict and everyone knew what to expect and our system knew how to settle disputes, but then the United States labeled us "savages" and government actions served to kill our clan system. And around the time Oklahoma became a state, the government insisted we get English names and start using our fathers' last names. These all made a huge difference in changing our identities and our sense of self.

Cee and I were staring at our dirty plates and couldn't think of anything to say. But Blue was only started. "Of course, th-that's when lawlessness increased, too."

Cee gave me the same look she used to in class when the teacher got going, but I stayed watching the table—avoiding her eyes or else I knew we'd get silly.

"Ya see, my people had to decide should they continue traditions now called 'savage' or adopt ways the new folks called 'civilized'—really nothing more than 'their ways.' We were forced to decide—to live as outcasts of the new country or work to blend in."

He took in a big breath, then spit out, "God, I hate that word 'savage'."

"Yeah, it's not nice," I said.

Blue jumped to his feet as his voice rose. "Not nice?" First, he pounded the table and then started waving his arms in the air as his eyes flashed fury. "Not nice? That's the least of it. In the dictionary it says 'savage' means thengs like wild, untamed, ferocious, even f-feral. How dare any person say that about another—especially one they don't even know? It's the worst insult. And it's just wrong to give that label to people whose ways you don't understand. And for us? Well, it's so far from the truth I can't find the right words—except... *wrong!*"

"Wow. Okay, okay. And now that you lay it out like that, I think I'm gettin' it. But I gotta say when I first met y'all back in the woods, I had a hard time figurin' out who or what ya were."

"You did, did you?" Blue took in a breath and cocked his head at me, his eyes dancing. I couldn't help but get up, go over and hug him. I invited him to sit back down.

"But I soon learned how wrong I was."

His response was calmer, "So, what do you thenk of me now?"

"That's easy. You're one of the three best persons the world's ever seen—countin' Sophie and that one over thar." Looking at Cee, I believe I saw tears in her eyes. It was a beautiful moment. Don't you just love those special times?

I didn't think Blue would say his next words with her in the room, but he did. "Shug, don't look through the eye of your heart. Thenk. Thenk hard. I'm the same p-person now as I was then. We both know I'm not a savage. I never was and my people weren't either. We've always had customs and rules and social organization. And I also know I'm not one of the world's best people, either. Perhaps you don't know the real me."

"You hintin' at something?" I got up to throw away the crumbs I'd been scraping with my hands. I needed to work off a bad feeling that suddenly came on.

"Nothing special. I'm just talking about perspectives—like who's peering through what glass and what color lens they have—that sort of theng. We all make our own realities—all day, every day. The real world isn't as we see it through our eyes. Our minds filter it. The perceptions and interpretations we arrive at are ours. It's not possible to know truth, capital T."

Blue went on to say this was like the confusion of the Cherokees when they found they couldn't see theirselves as the European settlers saw them or even theirselves as they were afore the Europeans got here. He said their lives were tested in all sortsa new ways... clothes, farming, money, language, laws, religion—all in "one huge cultural transformation that was foisted on them"—his words. It was quite a picture he painted. It reminded me of what happened to me and how I came to change so much, too. I knew it was impossible for me now to go back and be like afore Sophie.

I asked him, "How'd ya get to be so smart, anyways?"

"Well, the other day, I was looking at your Mark Twain book where it said, 'I've never let my schooling interfere with my education'."

Cee took off soon's we stopped laughing, saying thar was work to do afore her kids came home from school. I dunno, maybe she got enough. Not long after, Blue came up in backa me whispering in my ear he wanted to tell me something.

"We were laughing back there, but what you said made me wonder. Have you put me on a pedestal?"

I turned 'round. "Hunh? What'd I say?"

"Y-you made it seem I'm so smart and I don't want you to thenk like that. I'm not so smart. It's just that I pay attention to life's lessons. There was one time that taught me this."

"Whattaya mean?"

"Remember I told you how I used to be called Red and not Blue?"

"Yeah."

"Well, as I was told growing up, changing names the wrong way can bring bad fortune."

"Oh, no, hope that doesn't work for me, too!" Sometimes I can't stop myself.

"Yeah, well, anyway—if we wanna change our life, it's best to ask an elder about a new name, a new identity. Changing names does happen, but it should be done correctly."

Well, whatta you know, I done changed my identity and took on new names plenty of times and now Blue says Cherokees do it, too.

He went on, "Anyway, my grandparents' place was in the country so I went to a country school."

"Yeah...." I sat down. I could feel another story coming on.

"We were fifty to sixty kids from all around the county, but there were only three classrooms and three teachers for six grades. So, we had the same teacher for two years. In fifth grade, I got

Mr. Handcock. He was hired by the government—a free-spirit guy from California. He brought a woman with him I don't think was his wife and a boy who seemed hers. She was Mexican and Emilio looked just like her, not at all like Mr. Handcock. So, uh, I-I was in his class and it was a really good year. I was a good student. We hit it off and I was glad to have him for two years.

"Emilio was a year behind me—had a different teacher. He was shy, though. After about a month, Mr. Handcock asked if I'd buddy up with Emilio and be a big brother to him. Lots of other kids had a poor attitude about school. Not me. Mr. Handcock felt I could help Emilio. Anyway, thengs went fine until the beginning of December. Emilio seemed happier, but there was this one day we had a war with a few other boys. About four of them against little Emilio, another kid and me, whnh.

"We planned this by building bunkers out of persimmon branches lying around and we piled up old, rotting persimmons for our bombs. That day, we took positions like in a war and one kid shouted 'Go' for us to start throwing persimmons at each other. It was a boy theng—not mean or malicious or anytheng. But the problem was I got the bright idea of using a stick with an end shaped like a hook to hold a persimmon. I thought my idea was so smart—instead of lobbing bombs down from the sky and making sound effects like whistles and explosions, I could use the stick like a gun with a persimmon as my bullet. I was thenking it was such a great idea.

"I bent over and stuck a big, old persimmon into the tip, one of the firmer ones—not rotten. I made sure it was hooked on well, then stepped back for room to run a few steps for my swing. I can still see myself drawing my arm back and leaning back, my eyes shut. Yeah, I remember it so well. Then, after getting a quick f-fix on my target, I took a few fast steps forward and swung my arm in a big arc. But no, no, no, no… There was Emilio and he was right in front of me and he popped up just as I let my arm go. *Oh no,* I thought, *no, no.* But he came up from I-don't-know-where. Maybe he leaned over to pick up another bomb. I dunno, I just don't. And there was nothing I could do to stop my momentum. I mean, whnh—it was like, like slow motion, but it really wasn't. In a flash, I saw him rising up just as the persimmon took off. My insides turned icy cold and I heard in my head, 'Look out,' but the words never had a chance. With my persimmon flying high in the air, my stick swooped down on his head like he was my target all along.

"Suddenly, everything was whizzing and flashing. Emilio was on the ground, blood spurting from his eye and enemy bombs falling on my head and I was over him crying to him and also screaming to the others to 'Stop, stop, stop.' Next thing, everyone was all over us, wanting to know who did this and what happened. I-I couldn't stop crying. Mr. Handcock grabbed Emilio up and he woke—fortunately. It's also when he started screaming. Sometimes I still hear that sound in my head."

Excuse me everyone. I gotta stop Blue here. Ya see, I reached over to run my hand up and down Blue's thigh in sympathy and I could feel the pain of his words in his muscles. Yes, his old pain was alive again as he was talking to me. It stunned me. Sorry for interrupting, Blue, and that's what I did next—I apologized.

"I'm so sorry. You don't have to go and tell me more if ya don't want. I can tell it's troublin' you. It's okay not to talk 'bout this."

"But, this is the—it's, uh, the life lesson I was talking about. It's how I learned to pay attention to what life can teach us. Ya see, I put out his eye. He lived, ya know. It was j-just…his eye. Well, there was a question if he was ever the same mentally, but no one really knew.

"It made a big change in my life and I had a hard time with school after that. There was the rest of fifth grade to get through and then my relationship with Mr. Handcock, I mean—well, I could hardly enter his room, whnh. During summer vacation, I had stomachaches every time I thought of going back for another whole year with him. I only just made it through sixth grade—my worst year. Guilt, embarrassment, disappointment—they all haunted me.

"And I've had to work on those ever since. Only maybe now can I say I've worked them through. Now, I can look at it like the whole scene was objects moving in space without intention or emotion. Now, I understand thengs *can* happen without anyone wanting them to or being able to change them. I'm thenking now I know how to live life more like a Keetoowah—to accept the bad along with the good. It's only our minds that judge and, truth is, thengs just are. So, now I'm able to say this happened and it didn't make me a bad person."

Okay, I left off with Shug then, but I left out some details, too—like my grandparents so worried they sent me to Arkansas for a month the next summer—luckily not to a boarding school. I didn't want to tell her yet that this was when I developed my stutter and had to work with a speech therapist at the Indian Health Center. I saved that for later. But—well—everytheng comes out in the end, ennit.

See how Blue's life lessons done changed him, too? Seems it happens to everybody.

Well, Blue's gotta step out with the kids for a few minutes, but they'll be back. Thar's not much time left afore he has to get ready for the stomp dance, so we're gonna have to talk fast. While they're gone, lemme tell you 'bout my two babies.

A few months ago, I realized I didn't give my kids much of a Christian upbringing. It was when I was recalling how Poppa said I'd "incite the wrath of the Almighty" if I went against him in anything. To Poppa, his wishes and those of the Almighty were the same and these words were supposed to control me. It wasn't God Poppa introduced me to—it was the Almighty, the one who held all might and power to control and punish. And it came to me I wanted my kids to know this wasn't how I learned right from wrong. So, I sat them down and explained how as a girl I loved both gospel music and Johnny Mathis, but whenever Poppa came into the kitchen, he went straight for the radio, spitting out to change the station—said I was getting too fond of "nigras." Sometimes, he asked if I wanted to be a "nigra" more'n a "fine white girl." But I allowed that the Almighty loved all mankind— what I was told in Sunday School—and that was how I began to doubt Poppa's word was the same as the Almighty's.

I told 'em how my grandparents asked our neighbors—the Byrons—to take me to All Believers Presbyterian Church with them. I was taught Presbyterianism at the All Believers Sunday School, whar I struggled with the *Bible*. I did learn to accept it as the guide for living a good life and attaining grace. And, in my loneliness and rejection, I did find the idea of salvation most welcome. But these didn't make me a Presbyterian.

My third year in Sunday school I was twelve, old enough for the youth group—the True Believers—TB'rs for short. They were ten or twelve teens who went back to church, 6-8 Sunday evenings, and sat in the church basement for an hour of socializing afore holding a short worship service. You can bet I was most eager to get outta the house and the Byron boy three years older'n me sat next to me in the car. He was the cutest with curly, sandy hair and I had a crush on him. But these Sundays turned horrible. After I came in the house crying a few times, Gram said I better stay home. To be honest, it mighta been that the Byron boy didn't pay me mind. 'Course, neither did anybody else in the TB'rs.

Anyways, my church experience led me to believe in Original Sin and I was sure I was a product of sin, a perfect example of unworthiness. I told my kids I didn't want them to ever think like that. Botha them listened and asked a few questions, then said their hearts were full and they didn't need to learn more. I went to bed satisfied. That was good.

There are other beads on my necklace of memories, like when Sparky came into the kitchen with his dictionary. "Momma, it says here: '*To become* means to be what isn't yet but will be at a later time, i.e. after now, sometime in the future; transformation; an ongoin' nature of a state of bein'."

"Got that, hon?"

"Not sure. I guess I'm thinkin' that... it's sorta like life, isn't it? I mean, I'm a kid, but I'm becomin' an adult every day, right?"

"Yep, I'd say that's so. And I'm thinkin' that's the same for me. Seems it never ends."

So, that's how things were going with my two. Probably 'bout like with everybody else.

244

But, well, I see they're coming back. And—I see they brought the boxes. Good.

We did as you asked, my dear.

Okay. So, I want everybody to know that afore you leave, I want y'all to take one of my votives. I made 'nough so everybody can have one. Okay? I'm ready to go on now.

So, you been talking about me?

No, but I'd like you to do some talking, if that's okay.

Sure. Something in particular?

Yeah, but lemme set it up for you... A few years ago—think it was back in '72—I didn't know the tension I carried inside me was so tied to Cee until a certain phone call. You and I were coming in from collecting watercress and I rushed in the door with my hands full to catch Cee's voice saying, "Rats, she ain't home." It was lucky I caught her, but not lucky to hear the latest on Bud. She said he was now going 'round saying his former wife—me—that she was nothing but Spearfinger! I screamed into the phone, "Ohmygod, no-o-o-o! I can't believe this. Why'd he have to go and do that?"

"Dunno, honeykins, but this is serious. He's really out ta hurt ya. I'm gettin' wearied."

"Oh thanks a lot, Cee. I really gotta figure out what ta do. It's gettin' more'n bad. It's gettin' terrible."

The idea of me being Spearfinger sent chills up and down my spine. How could he do that to me? Growing up in Forestland, it wasn't possible *not* to know 'bout Spearfinger or to be scared of her—everybody knew and talked 'bout her. And, to think anybody would believe I was her... why, it sent me into a tizzy! I so wanted to ask Blue for help—I knew he'd have good advice—but Blue wasn't 'bout to have time for that. Wanna take it from thar?

Sure. So, I was changing my clothes from our walk—didn't wanna bring in any ticks. And before I could learn of Cee's call, I got my own phone call—this from Dolores' brother... Stormy's car accident. Perhaps you remember? Yes, drunk again and in Hastings about to go to rehab in Tulsa. He asked for me. I took it hard—I didn't know how serious his drenking was.

... So, my sweetie here drove me to the bus stop in Midway and never said a word of her new problem. When I got here, I found my boy in detox and facing his situation—out of school and no work. Like so many others, he was living in a sad way. The diagnosis they labeled on him was Alcoholism, whnh. When he got to rehab, they said it was Depression—from chronic hopelessness. What I think is he was a v-victim of *yo-ne-ga* poison. Anyway, before I went back to North Carolina, I made sure the Indian Health Service agreed to give him counseling. I wasn't sure how that'd go, but I'm thenking you know how it all turned out. That's all I have to say.

Thank you, Blue. I know it's difficult to speak of this. I'll go on now with what happened to me while you were away. First, I hadda face my fears. Nights, I lay in bed hearing Cee's voice, "He's out ta hurt ya and I'm gettin' wearied." I began locking my windows and doors and watching for cars in the driveway—anxious 'til the kids got home from school. I didn't let 'em go to friends' houses, neither. I started talking to myself. One of my favorite Twain sayings was "Of all the things I've lost, I miss my mind the most." That would give me a chuckle for a minute or two.

... It didn't help that Cee kept telling how Forestland was alive with Spearfinger talk. She repeated so many stories. Seems Bud's plan was to plant in folks' minds that Zena Firestone's stillborn was her first Spearfinger victim. This really made my blood boil. Losing my baby back then had been one of the low points of my life. Then, Bud's rumors were feeding the fears of the local mothers from two babies dying in North Carolina. Doctors were calling them "crib deaths"—whatever that is—altogether too mysterious, if ya ask me. Ya know, I understand the attraction of fiction and fantasy in our lives, but I also know any mother fears losing any child, so whatever feeds such fear must never be ignored. The mighty power of gossip got a grip on my heart. I was real scared and missed my strong protector. Oh, we talked on the phone, but I couldn't bring myself to lay this on him. After all, he was doing what a father should and I was prouda him.

And it was mighty kind of her to let me be, I must say. Couple weeks later, on a bright blue day—the kind we like to call my namesake—I surprised her at her back door. She flew into my arms and invited me into the bedroom.

Well, that sure was a big mistake.

Now, don't go saying that, Shug, It's just that y-you were on your monthly cycle and it took an emotional lesson on abstinence to convince you of the supreme power of women's lifeblood. I even had to remind you how we all respected you back in the woods. Folks, I had to tell her how women manifest one of life's most—well, maybe *the* most glorious medicine—one that sure surpasses any of a man. I don't thenk she knew that. Well, you can bet I slept on the couch. And then I was thenking it best to spend the next few days on other subjects. Can you guess which one I started with?... Yep, Cherokee stories.

... So many to pick from, as you know, but I decided to start with how I learned to follow my spirit guides back in the sixties as I watched brothers go off to Vietnam. I explained I couldn't be part of a cause I didn't believe in. I explained how we Cherokees have always been warriors and gladly serve in the military and how we take great pride and get respect for that. But I just couldn't be part of that war. I guess my decision was more like when the white chiefs abstained from political wars in the old days. I-I made sure the kids understood how such defiance isn't just wanting to go against authority—but more like listening to an inner authority—like a personal guide. That's when I started down the path I've followed ever since. I'm thenking the kids found this important. Right, guys?

... After that, I began nightly dinner talks about famous Cherokees. Nene, do you recall who impressed you most? Yes, George Guess—Sequoyah. I explained how, back in the 1800s, Natives were tolerated by white society if they acted "civilized"— which meant wearing *yo-ne-ga* clothes, working their jobs, speaking their language, attending their churches. Well, I told how Sequoyah was tolerated because he was a silversmith and how he figured that some of the symbols he used in his work could be adapted to make a syllabary—I dunno, maybe he knew of the Japanese syllabary—but anyway, he decided we Gaduwas could benefit if we knew what *yo-ne-g*-s were up to—that is, if we had a written language. His invention let Cherokees of that time learn to read and write in only a few days and transformed their lives.

Nene asked me why her school didn't teach reading English with a syllabary. I was laughing so hard I couldn't thenk of an answer.

... Oh, there were so many... On another night, I told 'em about the first gold rush in the United States that was back east near Dahlonega, Georgia. Even though Dahlonega was on Cherokee land, the discovery encouraged *yo-ne-ga* panhandlers to move right in. Trouble was, Georgia granted states' rights to them and the Georgia Cherokees fought back. They even took it to the Supreme Court, where it was refused because Cherokees weren't yet recognized as a sovereign nation. But I made sure they knew we returned to the Supreme Court after sovereignty was granted.

Blue's stories went on and on and I honestly think that's how I learned to accept the world as it is without judging. All my life up to then, I'd worked hard at shutting out the outside world if I didn't agree with it. With Blue's teachings, I was beginning to let the world in and accept life. This was one of my wishes when I started over and I was now doing it. It was the best gift Blue coulda gave me.

... I wished his stories kept my mind off Bud, though, but Spearfinger was eating me up. Finally, I just hadda take the bull by the horns. One day, I casually asked Blue if he ever heard 'bout that silly Spearfinger myth. He looked at me strangely, then said many Cherokees took the story seriously and feared for their babies. I asked if he personally believed in Spearfinger. Well, that got him into a strong lecture on the power of the mind, saying it didn't matter if he did or didn't—it was what *I* believed that mattered. He went on and on 'bout how the thoughts we carry in our heads interpret our world—it's our head that makes things real or unreal. Hunh, my own head was swimming, so I thought long afore I brought up the subject with him again.

... A week or so later, I chose when he was relaxing with a root beer float and the newspaper. I cleared my throat and asked if I could get his advice on something. After he said, "All I know is what I read in the papers" and laughed, he hadda go and tell me 'bout Will Rogers. I heard of him afore, but I didn't know he was Cherokee. Blue knew all 'bout him.

When he was done, I repeated what Cee said that scared me the worst—that business 'bout Spearfinger being me. Blue listened and nodded. He said he'd give it some thought. "Not to worry"—his words. That relieved me so much I actually put it in the backa my mind for a few days. At least I thought I did, 'til the Friday when Sparky's bus came and went without him getting off and the school secretary didn't know whar he was and his best friend didn't neither. I got hysterical. By the time Blue got home, I already had called the police. Thar were two possible things that coulda happened. Either Sparky was suffering in Bud's fat little fingers—that being most likely—or thar really was a Spearfinger. Remember, Blue?

Oh, yeah. When I got in, you were so upset you couldn't handle my calm. I guess I annoyed you. Apparently, I didn't care enough for Sparky—what you thought.

I'm not sure what I was thinking.

Well, my feelings were hurt. I headed for the barn. Then, when Sparky's advisor pulled up, you suddenly remembered Sparky mentioning that morning he'd be late.

Oh, I was so embarrassed. When I sent Sparky out to tell Blue supper was ready, he chose to stay out thar. Next morning, he was gone and I hadda face my overreacting. I was pretty upset with myself when Blue showed up 'round noon with a basket of strawberries. We pledged to each other to do better after.

Be-because of this, though, I realized how committed I was to this woman. Being accused of not caring made me see how much the whole family meant to me. That same night, a rare one in the mountains of North Carolina—clear enough to look at the stars—we stepped outside after supper. Lying on the ground, she set her head in the crook of my arm and recalled the night she spent alone in the cave wondering at the night sky's deep inspirations. That led me to explaining my theory of life. It struck her as a joke, at first, but she ended up saying I might have something on Einstein. Remember, Shug?

Yeah, 'course I do. That night stands out for many reasons.

It does, it does. Looking at the various constellations, I got inspired to share what I thenk life is about. I thought then—and still thenk—life can be condensed into the equation Life = Energy + Emotion. It can be reversed so that Energy + Emotion = Life, whnh. My equation is similar to Einstein's, but I believe it's true that everytheng—absolutely everytheng in the universe—is in constant motion. Vibrating. Everytheng actually is energy of some sort because of the vibrating. Some of the vibrating thengs aren't alive, though. Only those with emotions are alive. This makes sense to me and it's how I got to my equation. Well, I went on and on about this while pointing out the different star formations we could see. It was so beautiful that night it almost made me feel I was back here—here, where it's so easy to see the night sky. Suddenly, I bolted up and put my hands to my head. "Phoenix, Phoenix... Why didn't I thenk of it before?"

"Think of Phoenix? Who's she?"

"Phoenix is... Well, listen, when you were born you were named Zenobia, right?"

"That's what I was told."

"Yeah, okay. So, in the woods you renamed yourself Renee. Then, you were named Sylvie by Sophie and Brigit you got from Jason. Listen, I'm thenking Phoenix is the perfect name for you. Like in the myth—you're reborn from the fires of your past. Your spirit rises outta ashes over and over. And on top of everything, Phoenix lies at the core of Cherokee beliefs. We thenk of ourselves as the fire people. Even our newspaper is named The Phoenix. Th-that settles it. Because of the way your life has gone, you absolutely must be Phoenix. It's who you are. We'll get permission from an elder to change it right after we're married."

I was listening with joy to this little exploded suggestion 'bout changing my name and was nodding to his words, but my head popped up like a turtle when he said that.

"Married? That sounds an awful lot like a proposal. Is it?"

Blue smiled from ear to ear as he scrunched his shoulders, "Yeah, guess it is."

"Why?" I asked innocently.

"Why not?" was his answer that didn't seem romantic enough to me.

"I dunno. Just—" was all I said even though I woulda liked to say more.

"Just nothing, Brigit." Blue reached over and put his arms 'round me.

"Well, why not's as good a reason as any, I s'pose," I said, resting my head on his shoulder.

His next words were almost whispered, "You sound like you don't wanna marry me."

"That's not true," I insisted, shaking my head.

"Then, do you?"

"Oh, yeah. I dream 'bout it."

Blue pushed me far enough away to look in my eyes. "So, if we both want to get married, why don't we?"

"You're right—as usual," I nodded. "And Jason always said he wanted me to go on with my life after he went to sleep."

"You're not going to marry me because it's what Jason wanted, are you? If so, I'm rethenking." Blue dropped his arms and backed away.

"No-o-o, that's not it. I really do wanna commit ta you and have you 'round every minute of all my days. It's just that—I dunno, Jason's still with me, ya know?" I think I was pleading by now.

Blue nodded and brushed his hands through his hair. "Of course and I understand. Actually, I honor you for it. I'm not going to push you on this, not even going to breng it up again."

He stood up and waved his hands as he said, "When you're ready, you'll let me know, ennit? After all, it's up to the woman to ask. Seems maybe I jumped the gun here."

I got up and put my arms out. "See-e-e, that's why I love you. You're just perfect."

"Oh, Phoenix, come here. You're such an innocent—sweet, pure soul—eternal child of the universe. You're so good for me."

So, that's how I came 'round to being Phoenix. I can still see us thar, holding each other as we healed. It only took 'bout a day or two for me to go up to Blue and squeeze his hands 'til he got the idea I was trying to say something. He asked what I wanted and I said I wanted him. He asked if we should go find a special spot for a few minutes and I said we should find an official place for a lifetime. Blue let out a whoop, old Oleo started to yowl and the kids came running to find out what the matter was. They hooped and hollered when I announced we were fixing to get married. That night was a grand time in our house.

Something funny just came to mind. Hope it's okay to share... It was the very next day. This woman I love so much asked me to hand down the picnic bag from the top shelf. She was opening the ice box to grab the mayonnaise. Well, I was thenking she was making PB&J sandwiches for our rafting trip and saw how she was setting up to slather four slices of bread with peanut butter. I remarked I didn't thenk that'd be enough, since Sparky and I wanted two each and she should make one more for her. She replied she was leaving herself out, which was why she was getting the mayo—couldn't I see?

You sure ya wanna tell this?...

Why not? It's funny.

Okay then. So, I went and said, "It's an old one, hon'n. Goes back ta something stupid, but it keeps me from eatin' peanuts. Remember, how our family came together for reunions?"

She turned to watch me lean back against the counter, fold my arms and prepare myself. I knew this'd be good.

... "Thar was this one cousin of mine, Chip Wood. I think he—maybe—was the youngest of Uncle Bert's, closest in age to me and, of the boys, he paid me the most mind. He was a little different—maybe it was his one arm—I dunno. It was from when he was little and got it caught in the wringer helpin' his mom with the wash. The whole arm got sucked up in thar and you know how tight the wringer was to squeeze the water out." Blue nodded and said he remembered those old washers.

… "So, it took some neighbor to come take the machine apart and free his arm. I heard it was a year of operations to get it back workin'—sorta. Anyways, when I was 'bout four or five and he was 'bout ten or eleven, everybody was at the farm and I was washin' my hands in the bathroom and he came rushin' in zippin' down his fly. I could see everything and I asked what was that thing he was peein' from. He was shaking it up and down and gave me a look like I was from outer space sayin', 'Jerk, dontcha even know what a penis is'?"

So, when she told me this, she was holding her hands up, knife in one, mayo jar in the other, and turned to face me so I'd know the punch line was coming.

… "But, it goes on. Just at that very second, I heard Gram callin' out from the parlor, 'Okay, everybody, come get some freshly-boiled penis.' I got so very sick right then and thar, I went out back and threw up all what was in my stomach and then some. I stopped eatin' peanuts, in any way, shape or form—even buttered and boiled. So, here's my tomato-mayo, thank ya kindly."

And I stretched my arms over my head, laughing hard and yawning wide, before I murmured to the ceiling, "Well, we'll just have to work on that." It went right over her head at the time.

Yeah, well, while that was funny and all, we were in the car on our way to the river when the noon news wasn't funny. I remember how the announcer kept droning on 'bout the problems in the Southern Christian Leadership Conference—according to a Dr. Abernathy. My Sparky had a growing interest in civil rights and he asked how we felt 'bout both him and Martin Luther King. It was all Blue needed—he talked the whole way to the river.

I c-couldn't stop myself. I wanted him to know how strongly I felt. I told him it was long overdue for the country to face up to racism. Only after explaining my support for what Martin Luther King, Jr., stood for and describing my part in the March on Washington back in '63, could I calm down. Then, I declared serious talk was over for the day. We tied our tubes together and jumped into the chilly water. And it was really good we had that little break. It was the last time we'd be together for a long while.

Yeah, Blue's right. We were having such a good time, back then—waiting on our wedding and our future, while—all the while—the outside world was setting up to crash in on us. It was that very same night that Blue got a call shocking him into action. Setting the receiver down, he came to me with his head low and his voice even lower saying he hadda leave the next morning. He hadda join the sit-in at Alcatraz.

... I can't tell y'all how upset I was he chose California over me. Yes, we done discussed that situation and I knew he supported it. But now, he went and said he regretted not being part of the occupation of the Mayflower II, in 1970, or when the Legal Rights Center opened in Minneapolis or that takeover of the naval air station—and he was sick 'n tired of sitting out on all the Indian pride waking up 'round the country—while as they were all akin to his mission. He just hadda be part of the unity demonstration at Alcatraz. Well I got that, but I didn't know then he wasn't gonna come back for almost two years.

'Fraid she's right. It's what I did and why I did it. Remember, Alcatraz had been closed for six whole years. It was perfect for a unity protest. Maybe you don't remember that the Treaty of Fort Laramie says when federal property is no longer used, the Natives who once lived there can reclaim it. This was the perfect chance to take advantage of that. So, in November of '69, the Red Power movement tried to create on the island an American Indian spiritual center and museum.

... It was Jim Vaughn in the beginning, but then a group called "Indians of All Tribes" organized and said they wanted to buy the island for about $24.00 in glass beads plus some red cloth—sorta like the invaders did. Th-they also wanted an "American Indian Government" and a "Bureau of Caucasian Affairs" so they could hold in trust a part of the island for "as long as the sun shall rise and the rivers go down to the sea." I liked that. They wanted all ships coming into the harbor to see the island as a symbol of the *true* history of the country. Anyway, when I got this call, federal marshalls were already surrounding the prison, making life inside miserable.

... I couldn't resist. I flew to San Francisco and joined up with about fifty others in East Bay. We held a three-day sit-in at an old Nike missile plant until we were evicted. Our adrenalin was racing, though, and plans for more action were being made from coast to coast and I-I was in for the long count. I called Phoenix— still Brigit to everybody else. I told her I was thenking to go on to Seattle with maybe a thousand others to march cross-country to D.C. and didn't have much time to talk. I explained in few words that she should watch on TV for a Lakotan named Russell Means. He was heading up a new group called the American Indian Movement. Word was out that the group was gonna formally object to the government's ongoing violations of old treaties. They were taking these concerns to Washington.

Okay, y'all know by now that I was totally aware of the passion for justice that runs deep inside Blue. Some days, I even said he was living out his own Blood Law. But after he apologized for delaying our wedding and pleaded for my understanding, I hung up with my stomach in my mouth. Oh, I knew I was gonna miss him, but more'n that—I was hanging on his promise to fix my Spearfinger problem and that went off, too. I was scared and lonely.

… Seems Cee never brought good news anymore, either, and the silence in the house was weird. To me, it was just a matter of time afore something terrible was gonna happen. I was sure that without Blue's positive energy Bud's ugly, negative energy would find me. Whenever I heard hunters' gunshots in the forest out back, I jumped outta my skin. I was never like that afore. My kids thought I was being funny. I wasn't.

… I started having flashbacks seeing Bud after downing a six-pack, griping 'bout President Truman bombing Japan, shouting he shoulda bombed the whole country, then screaming Negroes were getting rights same as whites and how that was gonna ruin our whole country. I contrasted Blue's spirit out thar demonstrating for equal rights with Bud's sad soul. I heard, again, the downstairs sounds in the upstairs hallway of The Ordinary—talk of Robbie this and Robbie that—and loud laughing of "worryin' 'n warrin', hee-hee-hee." My mind always saw the regulars—scruffy men slouching on their stools, elbows on the bar, speaking in hushed voices 'bout their secret meetings and things Warren said. I wasn't able to put it all together 'til years later when I saw on TV a man named Robert Warren being taken into a court house. He was arrested for burning a cross on the front yard of a civil rights worker. A light went on in my head when I heard his voice… he was one of the regulars in the bar and Bud had been one of his supporters. It made me feel so scummy.

… Then, thar was the matter of who was I, anyways. Blue said I was gonna be Phoenix after we got married, But when? I had this new identity to wear, one I really, really wanted—and another I was done with, but which hadda be lived—and was less and less me every day. It was like I was living in limbo—not here, not thar.

… During this long, painful stretch, I did learn some important lessons. For one, I learned to budget. Jason planned well so I had a reasonable income from his life insurance and military pension, but I started to be real careful with money. I also got my teenagers to help finish the painting project. After that, thar was the porch and we did that together Oh, and I worked hard at being confident and unafraid—especially at telling myself thar was no sucha thing as Spearfinger. Sometimes, I wrote poems 'bout sinking deep roots and getting grounded. Once upon a time, I was drawn to Jason to be taken care of, but that turned into me being his caretaker too soon. Now, I came to see how I was taking care of myself. Blue, what were you doing?…

Well, I was on the march with 400 A.I.M. members—from many different organizations. In D.C. we broke into the Indian Bureau office just before the Presidential election—stuck it out a whole week. It was wild. I thenk it was… yeah, it was worth it. It led to a twenty-point position paper stating our most pressing claims that got to President Nixon the next year. Inside, we discovered how mismanaged the agency was and, as we were leaving, we took some documents for our records, whnh. I came on something Malcolm X had said and memorized it: "There is no better than adversity. Every defeat, every heartbreak, every loss, contains its own seed, its own lesson on how to improve your performance the next time." I liked that—still do.

Isn't Blue terrific? Look at how his eyes dance when he tells of his experiences. He sure burns with an inner fire, dontcha think? During this time, we talked on the phone as much as we could, but seems he was always in a public place and always in a hurry. I followed everything on the evening news—always looking for him. I never got a glimpse, but my heart swole with pride thinking of the conviction and determination driving him. I liked it when I asked him why he was doing this and he answered probably 'cuz he was his brother's keeper.

Well, that's the way I felt, but I worried what the consequences might be. After the B.I.A. was cleared out and we were only charged with trespassing, I couldn't call for two weeks, not 'til I got to Pine Ridge and not planning to come home soon. A.I.M. had made plans for us to join Lakotans already there for the next stand-off, which I'm sure you remember was against the latest government charge on Wounded Knee. This was my battle, now, too. I believe every one of us must hold the federal government to the First Amendment. After all, this is a democracy.

Me? I was glued to the TV. For seventy-one days, I followed the bloody body count at Wounded Knee. I saw government forces surround them—the helicopters and snipers—all that. And on every one of those seventy-one days, I was outta my mind with weary. The ugliness brought back the pain I had when Jason and

I worked so hard to keep Vietnam outta our lives, only this time thar was no way to avoid the outside world. This time, I hadda be aware of a hateful war. Blue was a warrior so thar'd be no peace for me. I thought of Cherokee wives with their husbands away so much of the time—and they had no phones or TV.

... One day, when he was able to make a quick call, he told me some Natives were saying if the white men won, they'd call it a great victory—if not, they'd call it a massacre. The Natives were getting nervous. I spent nights under my covers looking up at the ceiling, thinking, remembering—sure that hatred and war aren't good for any human soul. Ever.

My long-ago past barged and bumped into my present and I had no control over the memories that surfaced. Bud and his Spearfinger rumor were the worst. It was my very own internal war that seemed it was never gonna end. Then, Cee hadda go and tell me Bud had got old drinking buddies at the Rod and Gun Club to form a KKK posse. They were gonna scour the hillsides for me. Crazy man! 'Course, I never mentioned this to Blue. I knew if I did, he woulda come back afore his mission was complete or suffer terrible guilt. Cee and I sat for hours over cold coffee. She kept suggesting something ridiculous—she wanted me to meet with Bud to try and straighten things out. No way I'd have anything to do with that. Instead, I held onto what I knew Blue would say—to use the calmest approach possible. I told her when Bud got tired of feeding his stupid claim, it'd die of starvation Looking back, I think I was also kinda frozen with fear. And those hunters out back continued to scare the wits outta me.

... Then the *Ashland Times Gazette* went and published an editorial on "The Legend of Spearfinger," telling how it came outta the hills a long time ago. They called it "an old wive's tale," but ended up cautioning mothers to protect their kids from strangers. I couldn't believe it. When negative thoughts are put out thar, it's impossible to control them. I got more frantic. Mark Twain said, "The worst loneliness is when you're not comfortable with yourself." After that, I hadda read more 'til I found something to calm me down a bit, "Reality can be beaten by enough imagination." That man had such a way with words—almost like as if he was a mind-reader. Finally, a Saturday morning phone call got my mind onto other things for a good long while.

"Good mornin' Ma'am. Is this the party ta whom I'm speakin'?"

"Mm-m-m, 'tis." I recognized her, 'course.

"So, since yer the lady of the house, we'd like ta ask a few questions fer our survey. First off, we'd like ta know if yer refrigerator's runnin'—"

"Alright, for Pete's sake, if it's any of your business, yes, it is and I'll be sure 'n stop it from gettin' out the door, okay? What else is on your heavy survey?" I was giggling to myself.

"Well, thank ya Ma'am. Yer cooperation is most welcome. Next thing we'd like ta know is if y'ain't too busy today, would ya give us a lift ta the hospital?"

"Heavens, Cee, what're ya sayin'? No more foolin'."

"It's Jethro. He's done broke his back and now the car's broke, too. Don't know which is worse."

"You kiddin' me or what?"

"Nope, most serious. Last night, Jethro was helpin' ta load the delivery truck and, well, he slipped carryin' a sofa backwards— went 'n fell off the loadin' platform, so now he's flat on his back in the hospital."

"No-o-ooo. Say it ain't so!" I couldn't believe my ears.

"Okay... It ain't so. But fer real, he'll be thar fer sometime ta come, so I been thinkin' ta drop in on him 'n massage his private parts."

"Stop it Cee. This isn't funny. What're ya gonna do for money?"

"Steal."

"I'll be thar soon's I can."

I worried 'bout my dear friend. I knew of their money problems. Just so ya know—in the sixties, discount furniture warehouses moved into North Carolina and started selling directly to the public and that cut into lotsa family businesses. Cee's family store had been selling thar for over forty years and folks trusted it, but they were going downhill fast. Now in the seventies, they were barely in the black and only after Cee went and got a cashier's job at Piggly Wiggly. Blue pedicted it was only a matter of time afore they were gonna be history. I knew this accident could break both their backs unless they got help.

... I couldn't take on any of their bills, 'course, but I could bake, so I did. I posted notices in the library for a bake sale after Children's Saturday Story Hour. That turned out to be popular. The next month, I organized a sale at Little League practice. The third month, our sale was the day afore Mother's Day, which was nice 'cuz some moms got homemade goodies insteada making them. That was our most successful, I think, because I donated some of my popular lily-of-the-valley candles. Altogether, we raised over $1,000. Can ya believe it? It helped tide Cee 'n Jethro over 'til he could get back on his feet—literally. But they still hadda sell the business in the fall. Soon's he got well enough, he took a job at the new Walmart.

... By now, I knew Jethro pretty well. He was a plain-speaking man—mild-mannered but strong-minded. Never said much, but always considerate and thoughtful. Sometime afterwards, Cee told me Jethro's description of his back-breaking experience. Seems the very moment he fell, life took on a new reality and pain became his consciousness, his existence, his awareness. Just afore the accident he was happy-go-lucky, talking baseball with the guys, only half thinking of anything at all. Then, everything flashed to the present torture. His take on life became pain and only pain. His reality was brought down to each and every painful breath.

... That power of the present moment overwhelmed him so much he said he didn't think he could ever again plan for the future. For him, it was now only a dream. He learned that nothing is real and lasting, no matter what we think—that thar's only passing perceptions—that anyone's next second can bring a totally different reality—that it's best to give attention to the here and the now. Cee said this was the most profound talk they ever had. By the time Blue came home, they were in pretty good shape—just a whole lot poorer.

Meanwhile, I was still in Pine Ridge with that standoff. When the government finally got in, all 600 of us got arrested. Only 200 were indicted, but—luckily—not me. None of us knew it, but our actions would pay off a little bit. An International Treaty Council met in Geneva and the United Nations decided to pay attention to the rights of indigenous peoples around the world. What lesson did we learn?... Well, even if we don't know what the future holds, we know there're always consequences—some call it karma. Anyway, we returned to our homes feeling good. At last we'd taken a stand and we pledged from then on to not turn the other cheek when wronged. I especially felt good. It was like living under the old ways and felt right.

So, that meant it was just last June when Blue walked in the door with no more outside claims on him, no more causes, no more quests. We melted into each other and soon's as I stopped bawling we announced we were gonna hold a Cherokee wedding. Blue got Noah Powell, tribal leader for the Eastern Cherokees, to present our vows. It was a beautiful day in August, last year. We went down to the river and I wore a blue and white dress I made while he was away and draped a blue blanket over my shoulders. Blue wore a white shirt and jeans with a blue blanket over him. After we exchanged rings, Blue gave me a piece of meat and I gave him an ear of corn. Nene and Sparky were our attendants and they tied our blue blankets together and we were married. 'Course, Cee and Jethro and their six kids were thar. Right, partner?

Oh, yes, but don't forget both of Jason's sons were there too—real nice of 'em. Plus a few other friends. Everybody lined up to form an arch for us to run under before we began all the hugging and kissing. I thenk there were twenty-two people who witnessed our vows and stayed for the picnic. They were the lucky ones who got to hear my new bride announce she was gonna be Phoenix Redman soon's she could.

Oh, yeah, that's when and why Cee near fainted. Folks, my heart was so full that day and alls I wanted was to be happy, but my dear old friend hadda give me considerable grief. She complained up one side and down the other that when she just got used to one name, another one'd come along and how much I was asking of her. Later, when we were alone, she begged me to explain why was it so important to change names every few years. I didn't have a good answer 'cept that each name was a symbol of a new turn in life and—whenever I moved into a new stage—I saw myself differently and wanted to symbolize it. I told her others did that—like Cee's very own kids who dropped their nicknames and now used their birth ones. I reminded her she done changed her last name, too, when she married Jethro. Cee gave in, shaking her head.

… My kids made a joke outta the name change, too. They started going 'round the house saying I was a candle star. Was I gonna go on TV? They came up and ask for my autograph on napkins or scraps of paper. They even asked if they should still call me Momma or was I 'bout to change that, too. What else would you expect from teenagers? They think they're so smart.

… We planned our honeymoon during school vacation so we could leave the kids with friends and drive out here. Life took on a rosy glow. My heavy worries 'bout Bud and Spearfinger got buried under our blanket of joy and I was living in what truly was the moment. It was kinda like I was wrapped inside a pink cloud—so it was easy to let go that fear. Smells were sharper and the air crisper. Daily chores brought gratitude and I found myself asking, *How'd I get ta be so lucky? Even if Gram was right and thar's no such thing as luck, I'm feeling lucky just to be alive. My heart is full. What more could I ask for?* And I think that's a great thought to break on. I'm all goosebumps waiting to tell what more I could asked for, but Blue's time is up. Whar I was at then and whar I am now are two entirely different places.

Yup, she's right and I'm going to water, now. See everybody at the stomp dance.

Okay, I know you been smelling those wonderful aromas and your stomachs are growly like mine. "What more I could ask for" is coming up and 'splains a whole lot. Thar's two big revelations, too, so come on back....

PART 7

Glowing Embers

du-ti-s-du di-tsi-la

Okay, now we get to the big stuff. And with Blue gone, I can say whatever I want. Haha. By the way, have ya figured how I'm only telling 'bout transforming on my insides, like a spy mystery—"My Internal Adventures?" Anyways, lemme say a thing happened this morning. Waking up in one of Lynnee Mae's beds, I saw a spider over my head—maybe only a foot off my nose. Yikes, I couldn't help it—I screamed and Lynnee Mae ran in, saying it's that time when everything wants inside. I accepted that, but I'm here to say—and to you, too, Lynnee Mae—that was no regular spider. That was Sophie coming like she does every time I need her. I never kill spiders in my house. Always catch 'em in a glass and take 'em to the door and I dunno if it's the same one that keeps on coming back, but seems thar's always a spider in our house.

So, since this is gonna be Nene and Sparky's first stomp dance, I won't waste any more time afore telling how a coupla mysteries got solved. I'll start a year ago....

Waking up to a new sparkle in our yellow bedroom, first thing I saw was my spanking-new black suitcase that had zipper sides and wheels on the bottom. Imagine, wheels on a suitcase! It was Blue's amazing wedding present to me. He saw a TV interview of its inventor—some man called Bernie Saddow, I think. He knew right off he was gonna give me it. And it sure was a hit. It had two big pockets on the outside and tags and labels hanging on plastic rings so tight I hadda cut 'em off with scissors. It even had a small lock with two weeny silver keys plus a handle to trail it. I played with it like it was a toy. I even hauled zucchinis back to the house from the garden. One time, I used it to bring clothes in off the line. The kids kidded me, but I said I needed practice.

Owning a suitcase still stuns me. Why, even needing a suitcase—needing to travel—that was never mine afore. Poppa's satchel was good for my PJ's and toothbrush when I went for overnights at Cee's. And even though Bud had two brown leather valises that I packed for him when we moved from the tavern to the farm, I stuffed my stuff in a cardboard carton and pillowcase—same's when I moved into The Ordinairy. When my babies came? Jason brought my clothes to the hospital in his old duffel bag. So, I never did give a thought to how I'd feel having a suitcase. Well, lemme tell you, I was swept up in what you could say was a "tidal wave" of happiness—yawning and stretching and twisting my head to sneak another look at my new friend afore dropping back down to let my mind drift.

Don't remember why now, but I was recalling how Blue once asked me what I thought of him when we first met and I said I didn't know what to think. Then he asked what I thought of him now and I said he was the best thing ever came into my life. That's when he said he was not what I first thought and not what I think now. Well, that sure upset me and we argued. Blue mentioned he heard Mark Twain didn't look kindly on Natives and that's why he wasn't fond of him, but then he done quoted him. "Of all the humorous things in the world is the white man's notion that he's less savage than others." He eventually got me to agree on how we never do get to know others, really—how it's our perceptions that lead our minds and color our reactions and—since everybody's constantly changing anyways—it's pointless to judge. I settled myself under the covers again and put my hands over my heart to remind myself thar couldn't be a richer person in the whole wide world than me.

I sprang to my suitcase—my amazing symbol of freedom and independence—and packed what I was gonna use in the six days. I left just enough room on top for my house gift for Lynnee Mae. I smiled at how we were gonna head out early the next morning for the two-day drive, so the next night I'd be sleeping in a strange bed way out in western Tennessee. Then, if we stayed on schedule, we'd unpack in Lynnee Mae's house outside Tahlequah the next night and my new black friend would be with me all the way. I switched on my transistor. Helen Reddy was singing, *"If I have to I can do anything. I am strong. I am invincible. I am woman-n-n-n..."* I belted this out as joy showered me in my bedroom.

I was feeling true ecstasy. I was gonna meet Blue's kids—and no matter what he said—I was gonna think of them as if they's his family. I'd see places he talked of in his stories—real Cherokee life. Oh, thar was so much to look forward to. The car had new brakes and four new tires. My teeth were done cleaned, the kids were gonna stay at Lureen's house 'n they could feed the animals... everything was all set.

The only little bother was that visit to the dentist and the new forms that needed so much information. I done answered all the questions for the friendly receptionist, then regretted it when she followed up asking did I go to Forestland High School, by any chance? She was a friendly woman 'bout my age—trying to make me feel at ease—but I was trapped. She was figuring if we were in school together. Lordy, was I ever nervous. Hemming and hawing, I satisfied her 'nough, I guess. Then, she went and asked if I knew who Spearfinger was. 'Course I said no, but I hadda stand thar at her desk listening to her prattling all the latest—like mothers marching to the police station to demand protection for their kids. I hadda pretend to be shocked instead of revolted. I was in a total sweat afore I was called in. Things had gone way too far; the time was now. I hadda put an end to the old haunting in Forestland—it'd spread now to Ashland. The question was how was I or *we* gonna do it?

Blue pulled outta the drive at 6:30 next morning and we made it as far as a nice shady spot along Rte. 52 near Cookeville, Tennessee, 'round noon. At first, we rode in silence, then Blue wanted to listen to the top songs—like his very favorite "Bridge Over Troubled Waters." Another of his favorites was the Beatles' "Let It Be." Me? I was just happy I was gonna see Oklahoma. I popped my head up when Blue reached over and took my hand.

"I'm thenking I got you to thank."

"Thank me?"

"Yeah."

"Well, that's nice, but I'm settin' here, doin' nothing, sayin' nothing, so I'm missin' why you're thankin' me."

"And I'm over here doing the driving and the singing—feeling really good—just thenking on how you were the one who got me back to driving. So, thank you. It's real good to be the one to steer us into our future."

Yes, I heard these nice words, but I was stuck on my own feelings of being a passenger. I was thinking on how thankful I was Blue was doing the driving and guiding me into the future so I could enjoy the present—whar everybody sits on the edge of the future crushing the past, ya know? I thought 'bout how healing it was to have him with me on my life path. I squeezed his hand.

We decided to take a lunch break alongside a stream. Blue dropped a line in the water and—as we lay back against the tree trunks on the river bank—I shared some morning thoughts.

"I heard Mr. Harrelson's son's comin' back from 'Nam next week. He got his arm shot off. He's not gonna find a job real easy."

"Probably so."

"Wonder if we can help."

"It'd be nice, but how? We can't hire him."

"I know, I know. It's just that the country he's comin' back to is so different. I dunno how he's gonna make it. I hear a lotta vets are havin' a tough time. Wonder if Jethro could find a place fer him?"

"Ya know, you're right. Things are different now. It's different for me, too. Better actually. When I go into the kids' school now, I don't get a twangy feeling in my stomach any more. I can hold my head up higher. Maybe the mood in the country is changing. It's good, ennit."

"Blue, I think when they get to writin' the history of this time they're gonna make it seem like us alive, now—like we're like molecules of water bein' pushed along in a great big wave of change—movin' along together like in an enormous ocean of life. But I don't see it that way. Mark Twain says, "God created war so Americans would learn geography." Yeah, that's kinda funny. But, I don't see how my life's been so affected by war or what goes on in Washington. I don't reckon I done moved along with any wave. Really. In my world, it's true I'm way-y-y different than ten, fifteen years ago. But I'm different 'cuz of what happened on my inside. I came a long way on my own."

"You can say that again."

Yes, I did. I said, "I'm different 'cuz things in my life have changed me a lot," and sat thar smiling at the little joke—but also mulling another time when I had a different mindset. I saw it wasn't possible to figure how or when all the changes happened. *Change—how does it work anyways? It does—I know it. I think everybody does. All the time, change is going on 'round us and through us and to us. And even though we know it, we can't control it. It controls us… It's a mystery.*

We rode in silence for a while. Flashing through my mind was more from my Zena life—stuff I never wanted to lay on him. Suddenly, though, I just hadda release the biggest.

"Speakin' of change, I can't stop thinkin' how some things don't."

"Yeah. I get that, but what're you talking about?"

"I'm talkin' 'bout that old skeleton in my closet that's not goin' anywhar's." This slipped right out without my meaning it to.

"I know."

I done shared more pain than I thought I had from my time with Bud. I did it because I wanted Blue to know how much of an enemy I was battling, how much it hurt to have Bud's threats hanging over me and how important it was I get help to be free of it. And 'course, Blue's reaction was calm and tender and protective, like always. He said he already gave it lotsa thought and he hadda plan to deal with it in Oklahoma. When we got thar, we were gonna have a talk with an uncle of his. Wow! A huge weight lifted.

Traffic was light and thar was no construction, so the seven-hour drive was easy. Afore we knew it, we pulled into the Breezy Motel just outside Memphis. Chowing down pizza, Blue asked me how come my grandparents died and I shared the "bizarre" tale I never did tell.

First off, Poppa was sitting 'round cleaning his rifle and some-how managed to shoot hisself in the foot. Yeah. Well, he was embarrassed and didn't wanna go to the doctor. Coupla days later, thar was gangrene and he hadda go into the hospital for medi-cine through a needle in his arm. The very first day back home, Gram was rushing to finish her breakfast so she could tend to his wound—probably nervous 'bout her responsibilities—and, well, she forgot to chew her bacon—leastwise, that's what the doctor said. She lay gasping for breath on the kitchen floor and Poppa not able to get to her. Her dying that way just hadda be ugly and I don't like to think 'bout it. Poppa's health was already bad, so this horrible experience pushed him into a depression. He was put back in the hospital whar he died coupla days later. Heart attack. Everyone said the two of 'em were lucky to go home together. Guess so. I dunno.

At the end of our second travel day, we got in just in time to sit down to eat with Lynnee Mae and her five kids. Looking 'round now, I see y'all are here. I just gotta say I fell in love with ya the moment we met. We had a big happy meal together afore

Blue announced he wanted to touch bases with Sam Uncle the next day. No one asked why—they hadda know it was big.

Next morning, we drove out to Three Mile Road and found long-haired Sam rocking on his front porch mouthing an unlit cigar. Can ya picture it? Yeah. Right off, he asked me to paint a word picture of Bud, so I told him how Bud was a snake in the grass even though he claimed he was a "bright, smart-ass know-it-all little kid" who was forced to quit high school to go work and help his family. I suspected he probably hadda leave. He stole a car when he was twelve—just for the thrill. He done told me he liked "living on the edge," whatever that meant. After break-ins and shoplifting plus plain old drinking-to-get-drunk binges, he finally got caught emptying a cash register at a gas station— went to jail for eighteen months. It's whar he met a coupla KKK members. He never served in World War II—instead, he was in a Citizen's Watch keeping a look-out for enemy planes. He said he used to spend his duty time with his KKK buddies dreaming up schemes against local Negroes "just for the hell of it, to break up the monotony"—his words. I said Bud's being in the KKK musta fed his ego; he loved to conspire on anything. When his uncle left him The Ordinary, he made it a home for clan members. Later, it was also a hangout for returning soldiers so's they could be talked into the group. Oh, he was a crafty one.

I told him these things and more. Sam Uncle listened carefully, then asked 'bout the current situation. I explained Bud's obsession with me. He finally muttered some word that sounded like *ski-li*. I couldn't get what-all he said, but Blue did. He quickly fell quiet, rocking back and forth and reading the sky afore retreating into the house with a grunt. We waited on the porch and I got to worrying I done offended him. I whispered that to Blue, but he told me to be patient, so we sat more. Finally, Sam came out with a big smile on his face like he was most happy with what he was 'bout to say.

Seems Bud was suffering from a spell cast on him—maybe from a *ski-li*—and it was controlling his behavior and it spilled over onto me. Me. Sam's smile was a mile wide as he explained it was like a virus that got inside folks' brains that took over their thinking. He said Bud probably didn't know what was going on and couldn't break this spell hisself, but *I* could. In fact, *I* was the one to free botha us from the heavy negativity. Now, can ya imagine how that came on me? It fell so heavy on my ears I couldn't think. Learning I was under a spell that came from Bud made me wanna vomit. Yes, Bud was driving me crazy and I was feeling as a victim. But now I was to be his—and my—rescuer? Me? Sam said he could help. We worked out a plan.

Like I said already, Cee's been my lifelong friend and thar're so many stories I could tell of her and me—like our families sharing holidays and finding their family dog, Fifty-eight—from Heinz 57 varieties—dead on the highway. So many. But at a time like this, thar's nothing better'n a best friend. For my plan to work, I hadda call her.

"You're sure Bud's still livin' with his family?"

"It's what I'm hearin' anyways."

"Okay, then, I'm needin' ya to find out whar they're at."

"Gosh-a-mighty! I'm thinkin' they're all up on the Lucy Little Road."

"So, whar is that, anyways? Can't even remember."

"Over the other side of Lookout Pass—off Burreville."

"You know what's the mailin' address out thar?"

"Oh, could be Forestland or the Burreville Post Office, I s'pose."

"Probably. Could ya do me a favor, then?"

"Guess I could, kid. Try me."

"Could you find out and call me back? It's real important."

"Sure hon. But what's up?"

I told her the plan and Cee whooped how I was a ball of fire. When she called back the next day with the information I needed, I addressed my envelope to Budleigh Firestone, c/o Baxter Firestone, Lucy Little Rd, Burreville P.O., North Carolina, and I wrote:

Dear Bud,

I heard on the radio it's January 1, 1964. This is to tell you where I am. You must be worrying. I will get this to a mailbox soon as I can. I am ok in OK. I been here a very long time I don't know how long. I was kidnapped by Indians and Im a prisoner in Tulsa is all I know. Im now a sex slave. I know you would save me if you could. You are my husband and I hope we can work things out. I will write again if I can. Please pray for me.

Zena

First off, I can't tell you how strange it was to write Zena—like what I think they call an out-of-body experience. I was mighty happy with the plan, though. I knew Bud would fall for it. One of Blue's friends took the envelope to Tulsa for a postmark. It wasn't 'til I got home and talked to Cee that I learned what happened. I'll get 'round to that. But I gotta say, the more I think 'bout Sam Uncle, the smarter he is. He made it so thar was no need for the war I expected. After all I went through, the big bad spell was broken by a little white lie. Ya know, Mark Twain went and said something 'bout how "a lie well told is forever."

Hiss Turry and Miss Turry

Hiss Turry, born thousands of years ago
Miss Turry, as ancient as stars
together tell the human story
Fact, fantasy and fiction weave together
the fabric of human minds and hearts

Miss Turry and Hiss Turry marry
on the tongue like peanut butter and jelly
sandwich-layered, palatable ideas
for empty-bellied hungry souls
eager to be satiated, even if by illusion

After that, I relaxed and had a great time as we tooled 'round Tahlequah. It was nothing like what I expected. Every Okie promised me the rest of the state is different—that thar's flatlands and dry country and a desert—even cowpokes—and that show, *Oklahoma*, is true. But I was really struck with the country 'round these parts. Why, this northeastern part of the state is most beautiful! Now that I'm back again, I see how your trees and rolling hills make me feel I'm home. And the Illinois River outsida town—takes me back, too. Your land is friendly.

I think one of the things I 'specially appreciate is how y'all use the outdoors. It can be warm and humid, like at home, but you still eat outside—doesn't matter whar—home, church, stomp grounds. Not so much in North Carolina. It seemed at first when adults were in circle, kids ran 'round like they were unsupervised, but I can see now they sure are. And also, I noticed that if kids get hot and sweaty, they just jump in the creek and laugh as they're cleaning up and cooling off. Sure makes for a gentle, relaxed living.

Most of all, y'all done overwhelmed me with your warm hearts and open arms. You took me right in like as if I was one of y'all. In fact, both times I met Blue's past, I felt comfortable. So many of y'all look like me, talk like me, think like me. Oh, there's lotsa obvious full-bloods with glistening dark hair and big, round brown eyes and brownish skin walking the sidewalks and shopping the grocery stores and coming to stomp grounds. But it was only after I got here that I hadda change my mental image of Natives. More'n once, I thought the description of the United States, ya know, being a melting pot is—well—here.

One thing I found different, though—how quiet Blue's kids are. Yes, you guys over thar. I guess I'm used to my own is why it was such a surprise. Blue and I talked 'bout it in the car—how it was gonna be awkward for y'all to warm up to what I call a "sometime father" and his new woman—me. So, I learned to keep my words to myself, too.

And, oh-my-goodness, in every house I'm told to eat. Your tables are heaped with bowls of food, covered with tea towels or even a tablecloth—like it's meant to cover the food, not the table.

And the nicest women that ever lived are here. Always ready for guests. How different from my grandparents' house whar no one ever dropped in for food. Thar's so many little ways folks relate and a big difference those little ways make. Anyways, on our way back home, Blue and I decided our first family meeting was a good start.

Car rides are good for talks. We got to comparing our families. I told him of Gram's strange father—Peter *Donovan*. He was the son of Walter *Dunifon* whose father was named Mason *Doniphan*. Talk 'bout changing names—seems it's just a part of my family heritage! So, Mason came here sometime in the 1700s as something they call an "indentured servant"—which is actually a slave who can't be free 'til after he pays for his trip. Well, Mason never did and—when he died—his debt went to his son, Walter, and then on to Peter. But Peter, my grandfather, didn't feature the old debts were his. He bounced 'round the country, changed his name and settled in the Smokies. Gram told me he liked to brag to drinking buddies how he got outta his responsibility. I wouldn't know, 'course. I came along too late. But Gram spoke of him so much I growed up knowing him in a way. Gram'd say, "Thar ya go again, puttin' yer chin in the air jest like my daddy" or "Dontcha say such things, we'an, ya sound too much like my daddy when ya say such things."

Seems my family heritage includes some kinda passion for freedom. Gram used to tell 'bout this, saying how thar was some English king back in the 1600s who sent Protestants into a part of Ireland called the "King's Plantation." The Scots who went thar were called Ulster Scots and they settled on a particular Protestant religion called Presbyterianism. But they didn't get on well and they finally decided to look for freedom in this country. That's how they got called the "Scots-Irish." Blue commented on how today's Native American Movement shares this same wish for self-determination. Anyways—going back to the 1700s, Mason Doniphan was one of those Ulsters carrying inside a history of resisting authority. Blue said it was clear I carried his DNA and it was peculiar how many values my ancestors shared with his. Ya know, I got to thinking... our country is made up of people from so many different backgrounds but we're so much more alike than we know. Seems if we could learn more 'bout each other, we'd get that.

Blue was curiouser 'bout my family, so I done told how Gram and Poppa Wood had ten kids in all, but three died young and Uncle Willard died during World War I. The saddest stories were during the winter of 1918-19 when their twins died from the Spanish flu. Gram said they spooned special herbal teas into 'em night and day and soaked their little bodies with poultices of something called "carbolic acid." She said it was the best treatment, but they died anyway.

Of the ones living, Aunt Dora was somewhars outta state and more-or-less outta the family and my momma's wharabouts unknown—maybe not even alive—I dunno. Moira, Penny and Bert were scattered 'round Forestland—Moira the closest. Last was Jake, who came home from the army with both legs cut off and was living out his life at the General Military Hospital in Virginia. They were only able to visit him two times So, you can see how my family that started out big wasn't when I came along. I managed to recall for Blue names for eight cousins, but couldn't think of much to say 'bout them.

Even afore my precious suitcase was unpacked, I called Cee to hear 'bout Bud. 'Course she done had her ear to the ground. Seems Bud's reaction to the letter was to take it to the newspaper. Figures he'd think like that. So, they went and printed an article saying recent information had surfaced explaining the wharabouts of Bud's wife—me. They said they learned I was in Tulsa and this probably meant "the rumors 'bout Spearfinger didn't have any merit"—their words. All that ended up with Letters-to-the-Editor and phone calls to KISS radio from mothers claiming they never believed the nonsense anyways. So, that was all good.

Seems it wasn't enough for Bud, though. Coupla days later, Cee called me laughing and crying at the same time. Two Forestland police done just left. They came by to see what she knew 'bout me. Bud gave 'em her name. The police claimed my letter came from Tulsa and they wanted to give the Tulsa police as much information as they could to find me—a missing person. She said she hadda be the best friend ever—she played with the truth a bit—said the last time she saw "Zena Firestone" was the day the farmhouse burned—more'n eleven years afore. Well, that was true, wasn't it? Yay!... Cee and I wished the Tulsa police good luck in finding that sex slave house afore we hung up giggling.

It was in the *Ashland Times* one more time, when the Tulsa police decided the case closed. Seems the letter was written seven years afore and the last my best friend knew of me was four years afore that and so the case was cold. Forestland had gotten plenty sick and tired of hearing Bud's rants, anyways, and no one was paying him mind anymore. I was so relieved the police made him stop bothering Cee and Jethro. So, his energy got wore down and I hear he just quietly drinks these days. I'm hoping it's all he'll do for the resta his life. Blue observed the way it turned out was kinda like a fireman hosing down a fire. And me? Well, a lotta time had passed—I was looking different, had another name, lived in another place—I figured I didn't have to worry 'bout this poor soul anymore. Guess you can say I outgrew him.

The Studebaker came home needing only a new muffler, but Blue decided we better be looking to replace it. I agreed. So, we went and bought a brand-new pick-up. Blue said it hadda be a Mazda—anything carrying the name of the Zoroastrian God of Light hadda be good. He's a riot. And it sure is. Would ya look at that beauty over thar?

Anyways, that's the time when life started coming at me hard and fast—the biggest thing on what I call my "personal voyage of discovery." I saved it for last, but I just remembered a certain hot, humid night when thar was a light rain outside and the drops on the roof and in the trees were making music in our bedroom. I was lying in the crook of Blue's arm and botha our bodies were sweaty naked on toppa the sheets. We were lost in our thoughts afore I asked, "Hey, 'member that man I went into the woods with—that Brant Steele?"

"Mm-m-m."

"Well, thar was a time I saw him again."

"Really? Were you attracted to him then, too?"

"Cut it out. It wasn't like that. It was years ago. Jason and I and the kids went to the Fourth of July fireworks in Forestland. Doin' anything back thar was darin', ya know."

"Yeah."

"Well, we gathered ourselves on our blanket in the growin' dark, then I looked 'round and saw this man bein' pushed in a wheelchair."

"Oh, no."

"Yeah. A woman was wheelin' the chair, but I knew him right off. He looked much older. I did, too, 'course. Anyways, his head was down and he didn't look my way and once I saw him I didn't look again. But when I took the kids for drinks, Jason got to talkin' with him. He told Jason how he lost use of his legs when a car fell offa the lift in his shop. He was buried under 2,000 pounds of metal for hours afore gettin' rescued. Jason felt so sorry fer him—it wasn't fair."

Blue's philosophy came at me—'bout how life isn't just and there's no such thing as fairness—how it's so important to accept what comes our way—all that kinda thing. He fell asleep, but I lay thar listening to his breathing and snoring. I shivered 'bout what it must be like to live inside his skin and take abuse from stupid people and still be so smart and understanding and forgiving.

Now that I went and mentioned nakedness, I better tell what happened to my candle-making. I'm not sure when, exactly, but it was a rainy Sunday night when the kids and Blue and our dog— this one was Jigsaw—they were working on a puzzle upstairs. I was rushing 'round the kitchen making candles—just 'bout ready to take my clothes off. The house was quiet 'cept for my humming. My shape was kinda like a matron—like now—and my gray hair was hanging down. I musta had an eerie resemblance to Sophie. Jigsaw was upstairs—like I said—but according to Blue he was twitching in his dreams, then his ears came forward and he gently ruffed. I heard it and then I heard the porch floor creak and Jigs began loud barking, then came tearing down the stairs and I went to let him out and I saw a body jump in a car. Blue heard it and came down, put his arms 'round me and said it was probably time to start making candles with clothes on. 'Course I thought right off of Bud, but thar was no way he could trace me to this house, was thar? I didn't wanna listen to fear whispering in my ear.

Yeah, okay, I did start wearing a bathrobe. Ya see, I heard from Lureen the next day—she was working the checkout at the Five and Dime when a lady came in asking whar was her old husband, Jason Connors, Sophie's son. She was trying to find him and wondered if he lived at the Connors farm. Lureen said the woman made her feel weird so she told her nothing. It was kinda creepy, but I figured then who was peeking in my house. I gave Jigs extra treats.

I came ta see how life has a way of changing both our bodies and our minds in little what-you-call "increments." I came so far since I was a young'n, almost like a hermit crab shedding for a bigger shell. When I get old, I wonder if I can look back on all my other selves? I ask when will I ever get to be my own self?... Well, anyways, let's get to what happened this past spring that changed me into my newest self. This is big.

Heavy skies were hanging over me making the beds. My mind always fusses over this job—I was never one for straightening bedcovers. I was keeping myself distracted thinking how life can be divided into halves—one half for doing and the other for thinking and feeling. Me—I prefer that feeling-thinking side. Then I got to festering—how come women put so much time and effort into straightening sheets and blankets and bedspreads every single day of their lives? I dunno why you'd wanna look at a bed you couldn't ever tell was used—I wanna see messed-up covers whar I know my little ones lost theirselves in dreams. I love to imagine the crazy positions their bodies take in the dark by looking at how their bedcovers lie in the light. Oh, yes, when I tuck my babies in, I smooth 'em over so they're comfortable. It's just that unnecessary morning work that irritates. Anyways, this day was strange with me wanting to tidy up first the kids' beds, then ours. I didn't understand why the hanging clouds were so heavy on me as I jogged down to the mailbox.

The weight in my chest lifted when I saw Cee's return address on a big old envelope. What a nice surprise. By now, you get Cee's fresh way of living. She done sent me things in the mail afore, but never such a fat envelope. I tore it right open. Inside, thar was a piece of paper with a few scribbled words from her and a smaller envelope—this one from my Aunt Moira. Cee's note said Moira didn't know my address. I let myself down onto the lilies-of-the-valley and opened it. Afterwards, I couldn't move. I brought the letter to read to you:

Dear Zenobia,

I hope you get this. I sure you out there sumewhers. I want tell you what has been a secret all yur days. I dint not write you afor cuz I dint think you needed to no when you was young'n. Us grown folks getting older now + passing on I better start talking dont you think? I sure you don't no—I believe you wood of come to me. Its yur father. The 1 you never new. This is for you only.

When yur ma my sister got to 14 I asked her to sit for Henry + Rachel when I waitressed 3-11. She was fixing to watch them til their papa got home 8-9. She came direct from school made supper + put them down for a couple of months afore she got pregnant. She was happy with Rachel + Henry + it was a help for me + good for her to learn of we'ans. They was 3 + 4, cute.

This worked only couple months for couple reasons. All others thought why wuz I got pregnent with Baby-Lou + wuz sick being with food so I quit. But the real + secret reason was my husband was yur papa. I saw him on toppa her when I came home early 1 nite. I saw with my eyes. You understand I was 2 upset to go in. I let her go home afor I kicked him out. I wasnot gonna have him again. He was a very fisical man. I was a Christian. I couldnt accept him doing that. I told him he couldnt have yur ma or me or the kids no more.

Next day I stayed home for Mairi + told her she could not have him. we didnt no she was pregnent. We talked + she was very strong no1 else did that + she said she wasnt the 1 to start. I believed her. We cried alot + prayed + made our pleje (sp?) not to tell. When she was expecting and refuse to talk of the father I dint either so that's how you grew.

He went in the Army. died in 1932. a plane crash. O yes everone sed he was brave to serve his country + everone sed I was brave to raze 3 kids + not complain. It was ok. Henry + Rachel think he was a hero. That was ok. I hope you dont ruin their opinion of their papa now that you no he was running from his sins.

I dont no if Mairi was comfortable with our secret —Sometimes I think its why she left. I reckon if she hung round sumone wood find out + then who nose what. I dont no if Gram + Poppa new we never talked.

Now the docter say I dying so I need to gift you this story. You never new the mystery man cuz he was off to serve his contry + then dead afore I went + married Lester. if you have questions of this old lady afore she goes to sleep come fast. I turn 83 last Sunday + next day the docter say the reasun I cant breath is my lungs are bad. I can remember things if you want hear but my hand is tired. I don't no if you can read this. Please pray for me.

Yurs in familial love, Aunt Moira

P.S. almost forgot —Bo Boone is name. Maybe had Cherakee blood. I dunno. Sorry been meaning to tell you a long time.

So this is how I got to be the me you see. Please excuse me for a minute.

As you can imagine, the day that was heavy to start with then gave me this information and, well, it done thundered over me. I wasn't even sure if it was in the sky or inside my head, but I heard it both over my head and in the words. I read the letter three times and came up stunned each time. *How come I growed up not knowin' this? Moira's in serious shape, but why now, here, in this beautiful new life, is she tellin' me this?*

Thar'd been so many nights of asking my pillow for answers, back in my sad old life, nudging Gram for anything 'bout my father;

thar'd been so many remarks at school, so many painful moments when I felt abandoned, unloved, unworthy. I asked myself plenty of "whys" over the years 'bout having no father and my "elusive" mother. Only with the men in the woods and then Sophie and then in the life I created with Jason—that I eventually got to share with Blue—only then, did I get to feeling I belonged somewhar's and to somebody.

Next day, I went to Moira. She couldn't catch her breath. When she talked inside her oxygen tent, her garbled words didn't make sense and I couldn't get 'em. This upset me more'n anything. Thar was only one positive from the visit. Moira motioned me to a table drawer and encouraged me with her hand to read letters Bo Boone had wrote from the Philippines. I read the words of a frightened man telling his kids how excited he was to see the other side of the world and how he looked forward to learning strange-sounding foreign words that he could teach to them. He wrote a long paragraph describing how hard he trained in boot camp so he could be a brave and strong soldier who'd do his best to make the world a better place. In another letter, he urged 'em to help their mother and to please pray every night for his safety. He promised to come home fer Christmas.

She also kept a yellowed newspaper obituary from December, 1932. I read *"Army Sgt. Bradley 'Bo' Boone of Forestland leaves behind his wife, Moira Boone, a son, Henry and a daughter, Rachel. While engaged in honorable service to his country, Sgt. Boone died last month in a plane crash off the coast of Japan. After being stationed in the Philippines for the past two years, Sgt. Boone and two other soldiers were being transported to Japan on a special mission when their plane was hit by an air-to-air missile. The pilot reportedly made several attempts at recovery. It is confirmed, however, that the nose pitched down to vertical driving the airframe two meters into the ground.*" It went on. I read the whole thing twice, shuddering, then folded the tattered, yellowed paper and returned it to the envelope. Moira choked that she wanted me to keep it. I cried all the way home.

Her private funeral was the next week. I went as Zena and spent the day with my secret, never mentioning Moira's letter. Instead, I stayed inside my head—in another time, another identity, another life—as a young, insecure girl who wore pain and dis-ease. I felt the heaviness of Zena on my shoulders as I listened to the minister speak the word of God. I closed my eyes and saw another, long-ago reunion when all these same people were 'round me, trying to bring back how I felt 'bout each of them then. I wanted to insert into those memories the new and special warmth I felt now. I wanted to capture a closeness I never had.

In the middle of a prayer, I opened my eyes and looked at an older man in the pew in fronta me. I remembered this cousin from family reunions—when he was a mouthy, brash mass of boy muscle. His main interests then were football, hot dogs and wrestling. This profile was a mature man—a husband, father, perhaps grandfather—holding a sleeping baby. He had gray hair and bifocals and tears streaming down his cheeks. The last time I saw him was many years afore, just over the border in Arkansas, at a funeral for Aunt Minnie. We were talking at the coffee table while I was mentally trying to figure why he was paying me mind—he never did when I was a gawky kid. We were interrupted by an elderly lady who knew Aunt Minnie and went to the same church for "too many years to count"—her words. This sweet woman swept herself into our conversation, chattering 'bout good times through the years—how Minnie was a good soul—not one of those who outlived her God—and on and on. My cousin drifted away into the crowd and I never saw him again 'til my eyes fell on him here.

I tuned out the soloist singing "How Great Thou Art," grinning at the memory of his mother going to Gram's kitchen door calling for Eldridge. Me—little Zena—asked her who Eldridge was and she laughed, "Why that's Trumpet, Sugar" afore I asked why she called her son Eldridge when everybody else called him Trumpet and my aunt got quite a lotta pleasure from her chuckle afore she answered, "Close the screen, Sugar Baby, and come on in so's the flies don't," then walked 'cross the room calling back over her shoulder, "Dinna ya never know Trumpet likes ta toot his horn?" It took me the rest of the day to put that all together, but when I saw my cousin bend over and let gas out in his brother's face afore dissolving on the ground in laughter, I got it. So, here I couldn't stop myself from wagging my head that this distinguished-looking man was that same kid. My thoughts returned to the words "outliving her God" and what that could possibly mean: *How can anyone outlive God? Did those words mean anything or was that old lady just not able to say what she meant?* Then, all the mourners were standing up to sing the last hymn.

After the cemetery and sandwich reception at Moira's, whar everybody was so glad to see me, we were finally donning our raincoats to head on home when I heard my voice offering to host a family reunion. I also heard everyone giggling that was such a great idea—just like the good old days at Gram and Poppa's. But not a one of 'em knew who really made the offer. Someday, I'd like to try and do it.

That day was good, but the following ones weren't. Ya see, Moira's letter put a bright light on the dark insida me—whar I hadda explore. Now I knew who my father was, after all. I respected Moira's wish and decided to learn 'bout him on my own. Can you just imagine how it was to find out the one who fathered me might be a one to also give me Cherokee ancestry? I mean, wow! My bond to Blue suddenly got real deep.

Soon's as we could, we went to the Ashland Library with a mind to research locals with Cherokee blood. It was most fortunate the brand-new librarian, Mr. Youngblood, got interested in the project. He put a request into interlibrary loan for all Cherokee Rolls, then connected me up with the Cherokee Heritage Museum. By end of that day, we had some good leads. Little Zena who growed up hearing 'bout her Scots-Irish self was now Phoenix and Phoenix had many questions of a different sort. Thar was a new and very big hole to fill.

I don't think I need to tell you how important it was to have Blue with me. 'Bout then, though, he was onto a new interest— something called the Quantum Theory—and he loved going to the library to find out all's he could 'bout it. Blue feels the Quantum Theory explains what life is and knowing your energy is knowing yourself and all that—calls it quantum consciousness. He describes something like an aura of energy surrounding our bodies sorta like pieces of sand in a whirlpool. When he first started explaining it to me, I got reminded of Sophie and pictured Sophie's energy like I first did—swirling 'round her frail body—twinkling and sparkling with the essence of life. What Blue said made stunning sense to me.

But once Blue gets going, his ideas can't be kept in and he pours 'em onto me—or anybody else close by. Like his descriptions of the brain whar he says it's the thalamus, I think, that works like in a spiral binding together what's inside to the outside world in one continuous sweeping action that circles 'round and 'round in something like every 25 milliseconds. I have no idea what a millisecond is. He says these sweeping waves are part of a humongous quantum ocean and that our very thoughts—even the teeny tiniest ones—can change or even collapse the waves. He says this is all real, but I dunno. Sounds like voodoo magic to me. Anyways, I'm getting off the point. I just wanna say Blue's amazing energy kept me going.

So, when the government rolls came in, Mr. Youngblood suggested we start with the earliest. We first poured over the 1817 Eastern Cherokee Roll—ya know, the Reservation Roll. We came up empty-handed. Next, he showed us the Emigration Roll. That's the 1817 and 1838 list of Cherokee Old Settlers who first went on to Arkansas. Again nothing—no surprise thar. We finally got to the exciting Dawes Rolls that covered 1899 to 1907. I dunno if y'all know, but I found out the 1893 Dawes Rolls are the last for the Five Civilized Tribes wanting land in Indian Territory. These gave some hope—the first Boone was here. I wasn't satisfied, though, 'cuz these folks relocated. I thought we should search for North Carolina Boones. Mr. Youngblood agreed and suggested we pay special attention to eastern Cherokees on the 1908 Churchill Roll, the 1909 Guion Miller Roll and the 1924 Baker Roll. When we got to the Guion Miller Roll, I jumped outta my seat—I came on twenty-two Boones who went to live in Alabama, Indiana, Georgia and Tennessee. I copied the names Alexander, Charles, Columbia, Daniel Alijah, Evie, Frank, Gladdin, James, John, Joseph and William.

Hanging over our coffee cups the next morning, Blue and I worked up a plan, but the following days and weeks were harder than we expected—exhausting, in fact. Mr. Youngblood tried to help us with our investigating. He contacted the *Ashville Times*—it's the largest and oldest newspaper in our area so the one to have old records. Lucky for us, it was archiving old issues onto microfilm, right then, making it easier to read old papers. He spent hour after hour reading from the 1800s up to the present to find the name Boone. He came up with only a few articles. The one that got me most was 'bout a young man called Lightning Boone.

Seems he went to live alone in the Smoky Mountains at the end of the 1800s. He built a log cabin and lived in it for five years using ways he learned from some book called *Walden*. Guess it was popular in those days. Mr. Youngblood said I'd enjoy it, but I haven't got to it yet. After the five years were up, this Lightning Boone decided to come outta the woods and pick up his life again somewhars 'round the Big Cove area. He was shunned by folks allowing as he was crazy. A rumor got started he was only trying to copy Daniel Boone, maybe even steal his name. So, after 'bout a year, he done hanged hisself. I could relate to this Boone, but his story didn't help my search and thar truly wasn't any other.

That's how I got it—it doesn't matter how hard we try in life—not everything works out—and besides, a whole lot doesn't ever get wrote down or documented, neither. No matter how hard we try to know truth, it can slip right past us. And then, even if we think we know it, maybe it isn't. I poured my heart into this project for more'n six months and ended up knowing a human's take on truth is most imperfect. So, I hadda come to accepting I lived all my life up to then without a father—guess I can go on without one.

Moira's letter complicated my life by giving me a history that sure changed my feelings 'bout myself. Learning 'bout my birth also forced me to rethink my feelings 'bout my momma. Afore reading Moira's words, I was so sure she hadda be selfish and unloving. I rested on my resentment and hatred, feeling truth was mine. But I can't do that anymore. Now, I can see how my mother most probably didn't leave her own creation without considerable pain and I'm of a totally different mind. Recalling my momma's visits—the ones that hurt so much—I find myself thinking now how painful they musta been for her, too. After all, she was a runaway and that says to me "sacrifice." Now, my heart can't help but open up to that woman I never wanted in my life. Thanks for the tissue, ma'am....

So, I came to looking into the cold heart I gave to that stranger who popped into and outta my life when I thought I knew so much. But here again, it's another example of—no matter how I try to prevent it—the outside world always seems to move in on me. Last time I saw her was at the memorial service for Gram and Poppa. It was put off a coupla months so she could be thar. I was with Bud, back then, and in bad shape. At the farm afterwards, we were sitting together and got to talking 'bout how Gram and Poppa raised me. For some reason I'll never get, I asked why she didn't stay and raise me. Her answer never satisfied my feeling abandoned. She told me she "wasn't able to settle down"—her words. Oh, how little I knew. I didn't think this'd be our last talk. Today, I dunno even if she's alive and can't figure how to find her. Perhaps she thought I died when the farm burnt. Perhaps she never bothered to come back, assuming I was a happily-married woman who didn't wanna know her. Perhaps she couldn't face her guilt and embarrassment. Perhaps she did come back looking for me and was told I done left Forestville. Perhaps she died in somebody else's arms. I'll never know. Never. Sometimes, I think maybe she'll just pop up. I dunno how I'd feel 'bout that—just gotta wait and see.

Since Moira's letter, I've learned to turn my story—just like anybody could—I learned to consider what I mighta done if I was in my momma's place. I think the best thing woulda been what was best for my baby—probably what she thought. I even considered maybe Poppa's deal with Bud was his way of taking care of me and my future. I cry sometimes wondering what he'd thinka me now.

Seems truth has many sides. Now that a door to understanding feels wide open, I wanna walk on through into the bright light of forgiveness. I think this came on me not too long ago, really. It was a fine summer morning. I was hanging laundry on the line, mulling over what I was gonna say to y'all today. Putting it together in my mind, I saw how forgiveness could melt all the sorrow that's lived with me so long. Forgiveness came to me fast as lightning and then lightened the load I was carrying. What popped into my mind was what Sophie said to me 'bout whar truth lies... in the heart. Sophie's wisdom, again! Ya see, the bitterness in my overthinking 'bout myself had blinded me. I thank God a generous, barely-known relative helped my heart open up. Answers can come from the most unexpected places. Seems like I was taken by the hand of forgiveness right up to the altar of grace to let life flow through and 'round me—like I'm truly reborn—and this time for real.

So, I see the fire's dying down. That's good. I wouldn't bother stirring it more, sir. Just let me tie up a few loose ends....

On the way home from one of our visits to the library, Blue was driving and I let my head fall back. My eyes closed, I smiled. I-I was glowing.

"Ya know, Blue, it's amazing how many books thar're 'bout politicians and famous people—like Sonny and Cher or President Nixon's daughters or even that lulu, Dolly Parton—"

"Yeah?"

"Thar's just no end to people's curiosity 'bout their loves and their clothes, what they do for fun or whar they go on vacation. Ya know, no one'll ever write 'bout me or my dinky little life—but when you think 'bout it—my life story's pretty interesting, isn't it?"

'Course Blue agreed—that's just the way he is. I spent the resta the ride home lost in my head. *So, I could be part Indian or what they say nowadays—"Native." Whatta you know 'bout that! What does it mean, anyways? Am I different now? Does knowing it make me different? How much Cherokee blood makes a person different? What's different 'bout an Indian—or even a black person? 'Cept skin color. The color of their grandfathers' skin? Is thar a mathematical formula fer that? What makes any of us who we are? The way we talk? Walk? Eat? Think?*

What does it even matter what someone is called? Does a name make a thing or a person? If it does, then a name is everything. But it's silly to think I'm just a name—like a label. Aren't things

298

and people what they are—no matter what they're called—or even without a name or—for pity's sake, the wrong name? But how can a name even be wrong? Do people have a different life depending on their names or what label they carry? How would it be if everybody changed their labels and names with all the changes in their lives—like I did?

When things change, do they come to an absolute end, whar there's nothing more? No ripples, consequences, echoes? Isn't everything going 'round and 'round in one grand spin, like Blue says—all connected to everything else, like he says? Isn't he right that this is all one thing?

Why do we give babies names to make 'em special? Names—aren't they just little mental tricks to help us make sense of things so our heads don't get lost? We put labels on things just like we name babies and call 'em that to make that thing or that baby into what we decided it is—like as if we could. It's like we think we can control the continuous flowing of life. But that's all a mental game. The real thing—Life—is 'round us and in us, flowing through us, constantly changing, evolving—even when we're not paying attention. It's all flowing chemistry—it's the transforming fire and water and air.

By the time we got home, I figure I was a heavy thinker. I can't say anybody's ever heard such words come outta my mouth afore. Inside me, though, I gotta soul that's alive and kicking. And that's 'bout all what I wanted to share with y'all, today.*

Oh, one more thing… I just wanna say I'm real happy my family came for this Great New Moon Festival. It's like a homecoming.

---

* The circled Cherokees broke into applause until Phoenix asked them to stop.

Lynnee Mae and her family made my kids feel real welcome—soon's we were outta the car, they had mine playing stickball while Blue and I were under the tarp eating from their bounty. 'Course then he done mentioned right off how he read of Viking explorers in "The New World" and that "piqued his curiosity"—his words. He figures that since Vikings used slaves on their ships and sold 'em off to pay for their trips home, maybe his blue eyes come from them. Everybody laughed, 'course, then somebody mentioned thar's runic writing on Oklahoma rocks. So, we're going over to Heavener tomorrow ta take a look.

That's 'bout it, friends. I'm hoping to have time with each of you while I'm here. I'm more'n happy to talk 'bout anything. Thank you for listening to what I guess is really my "story of stories." I think the best gift folks can give a storyteller is ta be a good listener and y'all have been great. Dontcha think the world should stop being so busy and start caring for others? Anyways, it's good and dark now. Shouldn't we head over to the stomp ground and start dancing?

The Ketoowah Cherokees gathered around the warming fire this October day listened carefully to Phoenix's passionate tale while one elder—pain etched into his face—functioned as primary fire tender. As usual, the fire had been built in a cut 55-gallon barrel. Throughout, it had undergone various episodes—sometimes subsiding to a mesmerizing popping of sparks before falling wood incited the coals to spout new flames or curlicues of smoke.

Toward the end of her tale, Phoenix felt the fire need not last longer, but the tender wasn't ready to leave. In fact, everyone continued to sit silently searching the coals for inner illumination. As the energetic blaze gradually died down to a steady glow that fed a gentle trail of smoke lifting to the heavens, Phoenix smiled. Aware of being surrounded by empathy and understanding, she felt assured the ancestors would receive her fireside message.

One woman broke the silence to ask Phoenix if she could speak to her truest life moment—when she felt most authentically alive. The question returned her to when she was only five or six, before one of her mother's impending arrivals. For days, she'd heard "Momma's comin' so git ready" or "Don't let Momma find ya like that" or the like. Then, the day came when a car swept up the drive and a lively young woman hopped out and flew toward her with outstretched arms crying, "Zena baby, come to me." The image caused her to burst into tears. Regaining composure, Phoenix apologized and explained that this surprised her as her most vivid and real moment—for now she couldn't be altogether sure it had actually happened. It might have been only a dream.

This same woman then remarked how impressed she was that Phoenix had come around to accepting—even loving—her heritage, her life and herself. Phoenix hadn't thought of this before. Her eyes lit up as she recalled Jason's admonishment, "Ya gotta think the best of yer own or who can ya think the best of?" She agreed with the woman—she, too, was pleased she had come to accept and love herself.

With these words ringing in the air, an intense younger woman remarked on Phoenix's success at recovering from her breakdown. Phoenix's smile beamed across the fire as she replied that this continued to amaze her, too. Another person then wondered aloud how anyone knows if and when change has taken place inside. Phoenix referred to when she and her children were coloring and Blue surprised them at the kitchen door. She explained that it was when her kids were trying out new watercolors on that same shelf paper and Sparky ruined Nene's effort to create the color purple by dropping a big blop of yellow on it, transforming it to brown, that she got an inspiration. She realized Blue's return had changed the color of the family and wondered, since humans are mostly water, if perhaps life experiences affect our inner color. She suggested everyone examine their own color every so often. Some applauded her.

One elder opined that Phoenix was a self-made woman who had spent considerable time looking in a rear-view mirror. She smiled and thanked him before saying she thought of herself not so much as self-made but rather self-making, to which he laughingly agreed. She observed how driving a car had often reminded her of her life passage. He then asked how she wanted to live her life. It took no time to say she wanted to live the way Sophie had and to reach a ripe old age as full of life essence as Sophie. She then asked this elder if he felt she had been hard or soft. His response, "Both," confounded her. "Your hardness has given you the determination to go on—facing adversity over and over—and your softness... well, that's allowed you to adapt and change. You've been both."

Nodding, she mused, "Guess I bared my soul today."

The first woman spoke up again, "And it sure is grand, ennit? We really enjoyed spending time with you, Phoenix. Some of us have been wondering, though—do you know what your visions were all about?"

"No-o-o. I never did figure that out. Do you?"

"Why, so! At every step—when you were Zena, then Renee and Sylvia, and then Brigit and finally Phoenix—your mysterious and strange feelings were the future calling you. They were your spirit guides or protectors—messengers on your path."

"Well, I'll be. I didn't know that. I gotta think more."

All agreed she did have work yet to fully understand the meaning of her existence. Most knew she was well on her way to realizing what she'd been seeking all along—self-acceptance. They were sure she'd realize it—for in opening up her heart, Phoenix had opened a door to understanding that would continue to unfold in the years ahead—where her past would nourish her future.

She admitted to the warm-hearted Keetoowahs now standing around the fading fire that she regretted giving Jason reason to grieve. Although she was sure he'd loved her with all his heart and soul, she'd not returned the same level of devotion and feared he perceived only her loyal care. Someone piped up that she'd been wondering if Phoenix was ever going to get around to that. But, the first woman emphatically said Phoenix should not carry guilt, "A body can only ever give what one has to give. Besides, all marriages are trade agreements. In my opinion, there's nothing to regret." Phoenix appreciated those kind words more than the woman could ever realize.

An elderly man named Mosi—who wore a beautifully lined face and was a self-described history buff—asked to make some remarks. First, he complimented Phoenix for ridding herself from Bud's spell. He explained that in order for anyone to free themselves from the negative influence of *ski-li*—or what some call the "bogeyman"—it is necessary to first see through it and then be ever-ready to adapt and move on. Next, he emphasized the differences in how the Great American Holocaust is described to *yo-ne-gs* from how Cherokees hand it down. Lastly, he admonished everyone to remember that the Europeans who fled their homelands for life in "the new world" had themselves, no doubt, been victims of traumatic persecution and it was quite understandable they would end up treating the Natives as they had been treated. He said, "The most important thing to remember is that all people deserve respect, even if we don't agree with them or their ways. We must respect as we wish to be respected."

It wasn't until the next morning when the oldest member of the group, who'd been silent throughout, dropped by Lynnee Mae's house to compliment Phoenix on her courage in sharing her personal journey. After a short chat, he felt compelled to speak of his older brother, a Code Talker in The Great War. "He's gone on now, but Wesley was one of many Cherokees who went to preserve freedom for our country and the world—good men with good hearts. And our daddy, George, he was a Code Talker, too—back in World War I. You probably didn't know it, but the first Code Talkers in the American military were Cherokees—the 30th Infantry Division during the Second Battle of the Somme in 1918. My father was one of them. He talked Cherokee on field service phones and the enemy could never figure it out. Navajos, Comanches and Choctaws—they all served the same way." He asked her to tell her children things not found in history books, for the best and truest stories are handed down one to another.

Then, he admitted he couldn't put something out of his mind all night. "What was Grandma's song, anyway?" A big smile came as she burst out, "Mares-eat-oats-and-does-eat-oats-and-little-lambs-eat-ivy-a-kid'll-eat-ivy-too-wouldn't-you." They laughed all the way to the car and hugged as he got in.

The Cherokees circled around the fire that day had been busy with introspection and retrospection of the many stories shared there before. As they listened to Phoenix, they were weaving her information into the threads of their tapestry—refashioning their cultural legacy into modern legends—building stories for those to come. Some would go home as Lynnee Mae's husband did and say, "Let them be happy. May all beings be happy."

On the silent walk to the ceremony, Phoenix let out a gasp at another flashing image of her mother before a warm glow swept over her. She grasped her children's hands, her mind filled with thoughts of the elusive woman she never knew. Holding her head high a she was wont to do, she stepped out anticipating the sense of community awaiting her as she'd sing, pray and dance to the drumming of the men's hands and the jingle of the women's feet. She knew she'd spend comforting hours reflecting on her personal transformation—and how the evolving change had taught her self-reliance; how she'd found grace in forgiving life's imperfections; how she'd come to accept the essential transformative nature of life. Wisdom came in the discovery that not everything is as it seems. She knew that tonight she'd once again meditate on Sophie's words: "Tis the mind that seeks truth but the heart that finds it."

This prompted a recall of what Blue had asked before she attended her first stomp dance—if she'd like to feel a real fire.

"Waddaya mean? The one today felt warm 'n snug to me—"

He'd gone on to explain that there was a big difference between a warming or common fire and a Sacred Fire. She'd listened as he reverently reviewed the traditional story when *U-ne-tla-nv'-hi* handed down fire to the seven wise men atop Clingman's Dome and how ever since then there have been Firekeepers whose sole job was to maintain those special fires.

A few of them moved with the Cherokees when they went to Arkansas in the early 1800s and more with those who marched on the Trail of Tears.

"When you do the ceremonial dance around a Sacred Fire, you are sending your prayers to the Creator through the flames and the smoke. Don't thenk about anything else, not about your day or, whnh, what you'll make for dinner tomorrow. The more people pray as we go around the fire, the higher and stronger the flames will be. And just like you communicate with the Creator through the fire, the Creator communicates too. You'll see. You'll feel it. You'll feel the Creator through the fire."

The Chief of the Fire, wearing a black cowboy hat and eagle feather, welcomed her to the ceremonial ground. Looking into her eyes, he said, "*Si-yo,* Phoenix. The fire will tell you what the messages mean. You'll know your purpose because you've found your place."

Inner Fire

Life
a saga of heat and flames
atop black earth ash
visible glowing embers
colored memories
red, white, blue, yellow
kindling's potential
transformed into brilliance
Smoke's meaning manifest

Ashes

ko-s-da

As the twentieth century wound down, the Smoky Mountains continued weathering the years under their very own cloud blanket, harboring and nurturing a rich diversity of fauna and flora. The rolling hills also continued wrapping around the staunch Eastern Cherokees living in the Qualla Boundary, a land trust supervised by the United States Bureau of Indian Affairs—a mere fragment of the original homeland that Cherokees had to purchase back from the government through treaty cessions. Still, it is home. In 1984, Blue and his fellow warriors would have taken satisfaction—if they could have—in knowing that the Eastern Band and Cherokee Nation held their first joint council meeting in 146 years at Red Clay, Tennessee, and that it would become an annual affair. Unfortunately, Blue and his woodland friends never existed.

The United Keetoowah Band of Cherokees and the larger and more political Cherokee Nation, the other federally-recognized Oklahoma Cherokee tribe, continued to co-exist in Tahlequah.

Cherokee Nation reorganized under a Constitution and, in 1987, elected its first female chief, Wilma Mankiller, who had also attended the Alcatraz sit-in. One of its members, Brad Rogers Carson, was elected to the U. S. Congress as representative of the Second District of Oklahoma in 2000. And compassionate care for needy Cherokees, traditionally provided by the UKB, began to be developed by Cherokee Nation with community projects for the common good. The two organizations continued evolving, always with divergent views, complicated by competing casinos that they—like other tribes—considered vital sources of income.

Toward the end of the twentieth century, American Natives persisted in their survival saga. Not one tribe had yet been allowed to advance culturally to any significant degree under federally-controlled tribal functioning, resulting in what can best be described as a Korean *han* mindset. Because of continued reliance on the Doctrine of Discovery, minimal recognition was given to tribal authority; although Congress did amend the Indian Civil Rights Act to repeal a 1953 termination policy and did pass an Indian Self-Determination and Education Assistance Act to foster future tribal advancement. In 1993, President Clinton met with a 300-member delegation and Congress enacted the Religious Freedom Restoration Act to protect the use of peyote in ceremonies, then paid a visit of respect to the Pine Ridge Sioux Reservation in 1999—the same year the United Nations completed its Study on Treaties that declared treaties made between Indigenous nations and the U.S. government were to remain in effect as overseen by Congress.

After waiting years for a decision, the Supreme Court would affirm in 2020 that the nineteen million acres declared "Indian

Territory" to the five "civilized" tribes in the 1800s shall prevail as theirs. The huge implications are unknown.

Approaching the new century, Phoenix and Blue Redman were known as the quiet elders who lived in the Connors' family homestead. Assisted by widow's benefits and candle-making as well as Blue's cottage industry, they were able to maintain a modest and satisfying life. Recalling his father's family knowledge of smoking meats, Blue retrofitted Jason's smoke house in back of the barn and scoured the hillsides bartering with farmers for clean and slaughtered pigs. Motivated by a dream of replicating the Connor's reputation, he was soon recognized for putting out the best ribs in the area.

The Connors children moved on. Nene married, taught elementary school and lived halfway between Ashland and Midway. She and her husband had three children and vowed there'd be no more. Sparky, now known as Jasper, became a graphics design editor for an area newspaper and lived alone in an apartment in Midway. Junior and JJ both got married, but Junior's marriage failed soon after the wedding. Phoenix informed him at his father's funeral that since Jason had paid off the back taxes, he would one day inherit the family farm so to keep it in the family. JJ continued to pay on his father's Midway mortgage as it housed his office supply business. In the meantime, Junior dated lots of women in hopes of finding one as caring and kind as Phoenix—or whoever she might be called next.

Blue maintained a pleasant and distant relationship with his own children in Oklahoma, but was a dynamic *duda* to Phoenix's grandchildren. They filled his heart more than words.

After Jethro passed, Cee moved to Florida to be near her eldest daughter, which meant the once-close relationship of the two paled. Contact dwindled to Christmas cards and occasional phone calls. Yes, Phoenix had other friends, but none so dear.

The ugly memory of Bud continued to fade so that Phoenix merely lifted her eyebrows when Blue read aloud from the newspaper of his passing. Describing his life as ignominious, she quoted Mark Twain, "I did not attend the funeral but I wrote a nice letter saying I approved."

Mairi never appeared and Phoenix accepted that as another of life's mysteries.

The couple had fallen into a predictable routine through their many years together—one that successfully managed to avoid the world's travails that upset their friends and neighbors—by keeping to themselves, their children, their home and their garden. Mostly, they were lost in their own thoughts with little need for words. After all, their relationship had begun that way.

The Connors children concurred the staid couple needed to mark the millennium. For Christmas, 1999, they pooled resources and gave the couple a trip of their choosing—expecting Phoenix and Blue to visit Cee, but they were wrong. Phoenix's dental problems required extractions and consequent plates, while Blue finally gave in to a knee replacement and this put off all decisions for more than a year. By August, 2001, however, they were ready and the heat of summer enticed them northward. Phoenix said they would visit Cee in the winter.

Nene had initiated the tradition of annual Labor Day reunions for the Connors' clan—declaring this the one and only day when she was free from tending children—hers or others. After their reunion, the old couple stayed on to see the family's new computer in action. Nene suggested Blue ask Google how to seek information on his DNA, which prompted him to promise he would get tested when back home.

Early the next day, they took the bus into Charlotte to catch the Amtrak headed for Washington D.C. The Nation's Capital was a "must" for Blue after reading David Stannard's *American Holocaust,* his Christmas present from Lynnee Mae that revived his pride in his heritage. His heart had burned with rage reading page upon page of chronicled and referenced racial injustices wreaked upon his ancestors by generation after generation of *yonegs.* He needed to better understand what forces determined that his good, proud and competent fellowmen ended up living in shameful poverty within the boundaries of the greatest country on earth. The book made him feel thirty years younger, full of fire and ice and yearning to touch truth.

The first of their three fulfilling days was spent in the new National American Indian Museum where they were so enthralled that they signed up for a family membership, hoping to maintain an ongoing relationship. The rest of the time, they toured the monuments, the White House, the Capitol, the National Aeronautics and Space Museum and Arlington Cemetery. When time to leave, their heads were swimming at what had made them feel both pride and regret. The National Capitol spoke loudly of American history, while echoing whispers of an unrecognized history. The couple agreed the D.C. visit had given them a richer awareness of who they were and who they wanted to be.

They continued northbound as far as Williamsburg, Virginia, where they disembarked to visit historic Colonial Williamsburg for two days. Blue loved Williamsburg especially. He was enthralled by the herbs and potions in the apothecary shop named "Sign of the Rhinoceros" behind Dr. George Pitt's family home. Phoenix fell in love with the manicured gardens behind the Governor's Palace. She had never found the time, inclination or energy to make flower gardens look like these and it amused her how some felt it necessary to dress them up in such a formal way since flowers were nature's jewels all on their own.

They re-boarded the Amtrak for New York City and arrived at Penn Station in the late afternoon. A slow-moving and expensive rush-hour cab took them to the Belvedere Hotel on West 48th St. Totally exhausted, they were in bed by 8:00 p.m. But bright and early the next morning, they stirred to a fiery sun on their windowsill. They patronized a nearby Starbucks for two cups of the strongest coffee they'd ever tasted while eyeing many elders who seemed quite comfortable maneuvering the mind-boggling bustle of the city and who—with aplomb—walked miniature Schnauzers, Bishon Frises and Poodles along crowded sidewalks as if they owned them while navigating sidewalk puddles, delivery platforms and speeding cabs as if they were mere nothings.

Blue first watched other men hail taxis careening down the street before stepping off the curb and raising his hand for one to swish in and whisk them away. Destiny's Child blared "Bootylicious" in their ears—the female voices imploring, "I don't think you ready for this jelly." The turbaned Pakistani driver turned the radio off and competently steered the taxi down the West Side Highway for the christening of their three-day sightseeing jaunt—a climb up the Statue of Liberty. They almost lost their coffee in the back seat from the driver's one-handed steering as his other gripped a cell phone for an animated conversation in Farsi. Phoenix giggled nervously as Blue observed this rivaled some rides he'd gone on at the Oklahoma State Fair.

Relieved to arrive safely at the Harbor Park Visitors' Center, they discovered busloads of tourists had preceded them and the wait for the ferry ride to Ellis Island was now two hours long. Phoenix didn't want to waste a minute of their precious time. She insisted on Plan B, which required another but briefer cab ride to the World Trade Towers. There, they could have an enjoyable breakfast with what the guidebooks described as an unbelievable view. And besides, the morning's bright blue sky held no hindrance to perfect photos.

At 8:45 a.m. September 11, 2001, they held hands as they squeezed into the second-stage express elevator to the 78th floor sky lobby to then continue their ascent by escalator. Consumed with excitement, Phoenix whispered in Blue's ear that, in her opinion, the Belvedere should have such an efficient high-speed elevator as this—the one at the hotel had been so busy that morning they'd finally given up and walked down the four flights after fifteen minutes of watching the dial go down to the lobby and up to the top then down again with no stops in between.

The elevator was so crowded Blue had to hold his camera high in the air. Both of them were enormously pleased to have embarked on this grand adventure and to have remembered their promise to Nene—when they got to the 107th floor they would have their picture taken in the famous restaurant "Windows on the World."

Eternal Truth

Eternally pondering
the origin of Life
Truth
lies hidden in full view
Life begins in Passion
the lovers' well-known secret
Passion
the ultimate flame of life
fires the hearts of souls
driving Truth
into souls' potential
and smokes love's secret

THE END

Notes and Map

THE DOCTRINE OF DISCOVERY

As Roxanne Dunbar-Ortiz wrote in 2014 in *An Indigenous Peoples' History of the United States*, "In 1792, not long after the U. S. founding, Secretary of State Thomas Jefferson claimed that the Doctrine of Discovery developed by European states was international law applicable to the new United States government as well. In 1823, the United States Supreme Court issued its decision in *Johnson v. McIntosh*. Writing for the majority, Chief Justice John Marshall held that the Doctrine of Discovery had been established principle of European law and of English law in effect in Britain's North American colonies and was also the law of the United States. The Court defined the exclusive property rights that a European country acquired by dint of discovery: 'Discovery gave title to the government, by whose subjects, or by whose authority, it was made, against all other European governments, which title might be consummated by possession.' Therefore, European and Euro-American 'discoverers' had gained real property rights in the lands of Indigenous peoples by merely planting a flag. Indigenous rights were, in the Court's words, 'in no instance, entirely disregarded; but were necessarily, to a considerable extent, impaired.' The Court further held that

Indigenous 'rights to complete sovereignty, as independent nations, were necessarily diminished.' Indigenous people could continue to live on the land, but title resided with the discovering power, the United States. A later decision concluded that Native nations were 'domestic, dependent nations.' The Doctrine of Discovery is so taken for granted that it is rarely mentioned in historical or legal text published in the Americas." (pp 199–200)

In more recent years, there have been numerous condemnations of this doctrine that drove the taking of all American lands. Some who took this stand are: The United Nations, the Religious Society of Friends (Quakers), the Episcopal Church, the Unitarian Universalist Association, the United Methodists, the Anabaptists and the Disciples of Christ Church. As recently as 2016, 500 clergy from various denominations and nationalities who gathered to support the indigenous resistance at Standing Rock, North Dakota, joined in denouncing the precedent as racist and in violation of basic human rights. To date, there has been no condemnation from the Roman Catholic Church although a statement was issued in 2016 that it was under consideration.

STOMP DANCE AND STOMP GROUNDS

The traditional stomp dance of many Eastern Woodland Native Americans is practiced in North Carolina, Alabama, Mississippi, Florida and Oklahoma. Today, there are seven active Cherokee stomp grounds in Oklahoma. The term is English and refers to the dance movements of participants who circle around a ceremonial fire in a meditative state dancing, singing and praying. The location for the dance is a stomp ground, a patch of land held sacred and maintained for ceremonial use only. Outside the center are seven clan arbors where various families gather before the night's fire.

The day of the ceremony, a fire keeper and his assistant begin at dawn to build a fire usually deep in a pit below ground significant enough to last throughout the dance. It is built up from small slivers of wood using flint and a rock to make a spark and is tended continuously by these men only. The day is spent together in community, feasting on traditional foods and listening to elders' admonishments (unless Phoenix is invited to talk, that is).

Before the dance, men prepare and cleanse themselves by going to water and by smoking tobacco. The dancing begins well after dark and continues until dawn. It begins with the chief and elders, then a call goes out to all. Dancing continues in cycles of about four dances between rest breaks. Some participants may fast after midnight; many will take medicine made from roots and herbs. All will stay awake through the night. There is one male leader for the many melodies that are sung in the Tsalagi language. Women have turtle shell shakers attached to their ankles and they establish the rhythm for the circle of alternating males and females.

Alcohol and drugs are not allowed on the grounds and sometimes not for days before or after the ceremony. Since this is a religious ceremony, there is no rowdiness and photography is not allowed. Cherokees who choose to worship in churches or with other denominations are welcome to participate in stomp dancing.

CHEROKEE TREATY OF 1835

Lands ceded to the Cherokee nation in what was then called Indian Territory (and later declared Oklahoma)... "shall in no future time, without their consent, be included within the territorial limits of jurisdiction of any State or Territory. But they shall secure to the Cherokee nation the right, by their national councils, to make and carry into effect all such laws as they may deem nedessary for the governmcnt... within their own country."

LEGEND OF SPEARFINGER *(U'tlun'ta)*

Originating in western North Carolina and eastern Tennessee, this traditional Cherokee story is of an old hag named Spearfinger who is made of stone and whose right-hand forefinger resembles a knife. Parents warn children about entering wooded areas alone because she likes to beguile the unsuspecting into trusting her in order to cut their hearts out. Gory details of her appearance and behavior are enough to scare young listeners, but it is her magical ability to shapeshift and deceptively hide among unsuspecting people that is the most unsettling. There are a number of colorful versions of the Spearfinger myth and her ultimate enemy, Stone Man, available on the web.

PERSONALLY-IDENTIFIED INDIGENOUS PEOPLES
OF THE AMERICAS

Abipones, Abenaki, Acoma, Aguaruna, Ais, Akimel O'otam, Alabama (Alibamu), Aleut (Unangan), Algonquin, Alsea, Altamaha, Anishinabe, Apache (Tineh), Apalachi, Apalachicola, Apola, Arapaho, Araucano Mapuche), Arawak (Taino), Arikara (Ree), Aruak, Assiniboin (Stoney), Atakapa, Athapascans, Atsina, Aymara, Aztec (Mexica), Bannok, Bella Coola, Beothuk, Biloxi, Blackfoot, Blood, Bora, Brule, Caddo, Cahinnio, Cahokia, Cahuilla, Calusa, Carib, Carrier (Takulli), Catawba, Cayuga, Cayuse (Waiilatpu), Chakchiuma, Chane, Chatot, Chawasha, Chehalis, Chemakum, Chemehuevi, Cherokee (Tsalagi and Kituwah), Cheyenne (Tsistsistas), Chiaha, Chibcha, Chickasaw, Chimu, Chinook (Tsinuk), Chip, Chipewyan, Chippewa (Ojibway), Chiricahua, Chitimacha, Choctaw, Chorote, Chulupi, Chumash, Cocopah, Coer d'Alene (Skitswish), Cofitachequi, Colorado, Comanche, Conestoga, Conoy, Coosa, Coree, Costano, Coeur d'Alene, Coushatta (Koasati), Coweta, Cowutz, Cree, Creek (Muskogee), Crow (Apsaalooke), Cusabo, Dakota, Delaware, Diaguita-Calchaqui, Dine, Duwamish, Edisto, Erie, Faraon, Flathead (Salish), Fox (or Mesquaki), Gabrieuno, Gitxsan, Gosiute, Gros Ventre (Atsina), Guale, Guacara, Guarani, Guarita, Haida (Kaigani), Havasupai, Heiltsuk, Hidatsa (Minitari), Hopi (Moki), Houma, Hualapai (Walapai), Huarpe, Hunkpapa, Hupa, Huron (Wyandot), Iawakoni, Ilapi, Ichisi, Igloolik, Illinois, Inka, Innu, Inupiaq, Iowa, Iroquois, Itabi, Iuseno, Jeaga, Jemez, Joara, Jororo, Jumamo, J'varo, Ka'apor, Kahuawohl, Kalapuya, Kalispel (Pend d'Oreille), Kansa (Kaw), Karankawa, Karok, Kaskasla, Kauspel, Kayapo, Kichai, Kickapoo, Kiowa, Klamath,

Koasti, Kolla, Kootenay, Koruba, Kumik, Kusa, Kutchin (Gwich'in), Kwakiutl, Kwakwaka'wakw, Lakota, L'anero, Lemni, Lenni Lenate (Delaware), Lumbee, Mahican, Maidu, Makah, Maliset, Manacupuru, Manahoac, Mandan (Hidatsa), Manoki, Maricopa, Massachuset, Matses, Maya, Mdewkanton, Menominee (or Rice), Mescalero, Mesquakie, Methow, Metis, Miami, Miccosukee, Michigama, Micmac (or Mi'kmaq), Miskito, Missouri, Miwok, Mixtec, Mobile, Moche, Mochica, Mocovi, Modoc, Mohawk (Iroquois), Mohegan, Moingwena, Mojave, Monacan, Mono, Montagnais (Innu), Montauk, Mopuche, Muisca, Munsi, Muskogee, Nahua, Nanticoke, Napochi, Narraganset, Natchez, Nauset, Navajo (Dineh), Nazca, Neusiok, Neutral, Nez Pierce (Nimiipu), Nisgua, Nipmuc, Nipuc, Nootka, Nottoway, Nuth Chal Nuth, Nuu-chah-nulth, Nuxalk, Ocute, Ogala Lakota (Sioux), Ojibwa, Olmec, Omaha, Ona, Oneida, Onondaga, Opata, Orista (Edisto), Osage, Oto, Ottawa, Paiute, Palus, Pampa, Pamuco, Pamunkey, Paradeo, Passamaquoddy (Abenaki), Patwin, Paviotso, Pawnee, Payute, Pecos, Pehuenche, Pennacook (Pawtucket), Pend d'Oreile, Penobscott (Abenaki), Pensacola, Peoria, Pequot, Piankasha, Piegan, Pilaga, Pinal Arivaipi, Pima (Hohokam), Pitahauri, Pomo, Ponca (Quapaw or Arkansas), Potawatomi, Powhatan, Pueblo, Puelche, Purepecha (Tarascan), Quapaw, Quechan, Quechua, Querandi, Quinault, Roanoke, Sac, Salish, Sans Arc, Santa Clara (Pueblo), Santee (Hymahi), Saponi, Sarcee, Sauk-Fox, Sawoku, Selkiram (Ona), Seminole, Seneca, Serrano, Sewee, Shawnee (Shawano), Shipido, Shinnecock, Shoshone, Sioux (Dakota), S'Kallam, kan, Suquamish, Stono, Susquehannock, Swinomish, Taino, Tamaroa, Tapiete, Taposa, Tapirope, Tawakoni, Tawehash, Tehuelche,

Tekesta, Thomo O'Odham, Ticuna, Tilamook, Timucua (Utina), Tlingit, Toba, Tohome, Tohono O'odham (Papago), Toa, Tocobaga, Toltec, Tompiro, Tonkawa, Tsimshian, Tula, Tunica, Tuscarora, Tutelo, Umatila, Uninh, Uranina, Ute, Waco, Wahpeton, Wailaki, Waleapi, Wallatpu, Walla Walla, Wampanoag (Pokanoket), Wando, Wappinger, Washa, Wea, Weapemeoc, Wichi, Windover, Wintun, Yakama, Yamasi, Yankton, Yanacona, Yanomami, Yaqui (Cahita), Yaquina, Yayapai (Baja), Yazoo, Yokut (Mariposa), Yuchi, Yuma (Qyechan), Yup'ik, Yurok, Zapotec and Zuni (Ashiwi).

The following map of Indigenous Nations of North America locates more than the indigenous people I personally discovered in my readings when its beautiful and astonishing detail can be viewed full-sized on a wall. Regardless of the diminished size here, it clearly proves that the North American continent has been home to countless people for longer than we know. Researched and produced by Aaron Carapella of Tribal Nations Maps, this and many other maps of indigenous peoples around the world can be seen at tribalnationsmaps.com.

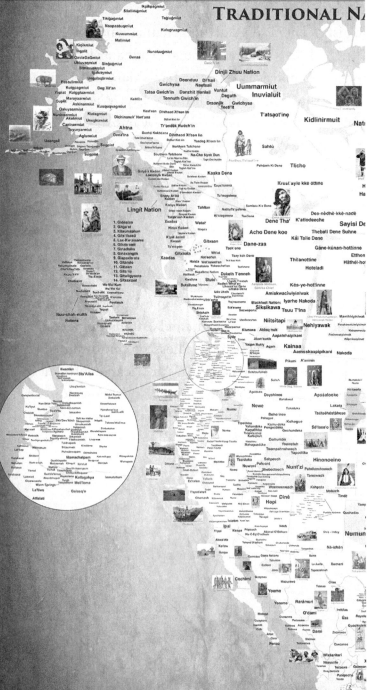

TRIBAL NA

TRADITIONAL N.

Ikpikpagmiut
Silalliñagmiut
Tikigagmiut
Tagiugmiut
Naapaabugmiut
Kuuvanmiut
Kuluguvagmiut
Malimiut

Kiñikmiut
Iiñgalit
OaviaGaGmiut
Ukivugmiut
Sitnasuakmiut
Iġalukmiut
Ungaligmiut

Denaa
Nunataagmiut

Pastulirimiut
Kuigpagmiut
Deg Xit'an
Yupiat Kuiggluarmiut
Marayaarmiut
Cupit Askinanmiut
Oaluyaarmiut Kusquqvagmiut
Nunivaarmiut
Kiatagmiut
Akulmiut
Caninermiut
Teyuryarmiut
Aglurmiut

Uoangss

Sugpiat
Sugpiat

Gwichyaa
Deenduu Dr'hail
Tatsa Gwich'in Danzhit Hanlaii
Tennuth Gwich'in
Dinjii Zhuu Nation
Vuntut
Deguth
Draanjik Gwichyaa
Teetl'it

Uummarmiut
Inuvialuit

Kidlinirmiut
Nat

Dichinanek' Hwt'ana

Ahtna
Dena'ina

Gehti Kokhtana Dihshaad Xt'een lin
Dena'ina
Tse'khaad tene
Didanetene
Northern Tutchone
Southern Tutchone
Na-Cho Nyak Dun

Oxfur Kiñ iin
Yandeg Xt'een lin

T'atsaot'ine

Sahtú

Pehdzeh Ki Dene
Tlicho

Kaska Dena

Krest'ayle kke ottine

H

Lingít Nation

1. Gideatso
2. Gitga'at
3. Kitsumkalum
4. Lax-Kw'alaams
5. Gitxas saw
7. Ginadoika
8. Ginaxangiik
9. Gispaxlo ots
10. Gitando
11. Gitxaan
12. Gits lip
13. Gitwilgyoota
14. Gitxaxsaat

Xaadas

Xaadas

Gitxsan

Tahltan
Wetar
Hiiya Kwaan

K'yak aánnii
Kwaan
Ts'msyen

Gitxaata

Nisga'a

Nat'eeten

Stl'eno

Nootka Tahltan
Ki'slagonna Taa'tona

Tsay kih Dene

Dene Tha'
Acho Dene koe

Dane-zaa

Des-nèdhè-kkè-nadè
K'atlodeeche
Sayisi De
Thebati Dene Suhne
Kái Taile Dene

Gâne-kúnan-hottine

Nuu-chah-nulth
Nations

Wei Wai Kum
Wai Wai Kai

Dakelh T'enneh

Tsilhqot'in

Uds Uhdih
Stuic
Kwatlina

Butsihne

Thilanottine
Hoteladi

Etthen
Háthél-ho

Kês-ye-hotlinne

Amiskwaciwiyiniwak
Iyarhe Nakoda
Siksikawa
Tsuu T'ina

Niitsitapi
Nehiyawak

Mamihkiyiniwak

Ktunaxa Akisq'nuk
Aapatohsipikani
Akan'suttk

Kainaa
Aamsskaapipikani
Nakoda

Pikuni A'aninin

Apsáalooke

Newe
Numu

Boha inee
Pohogue
Tipicdoka
Yahandeka Pengwideka
Kuyatikka
Toyapayuingi
Kotsabtull

Kamu-doka
Gwchutdeka

Ko'hogue

Tsétséhéstahese

Só'taco'o

Hinnoneino

Salpeech
Pahvant
Shebeetcech

Nuwuvi

Diné
Hopi

Tsoiduka
Nunt'zi
Tareowoah

Ipai
Tipai

Diné

Cochimi

Yoeme
Yoreme

Rarámuri

O'dami

Uza

Wixáaritari

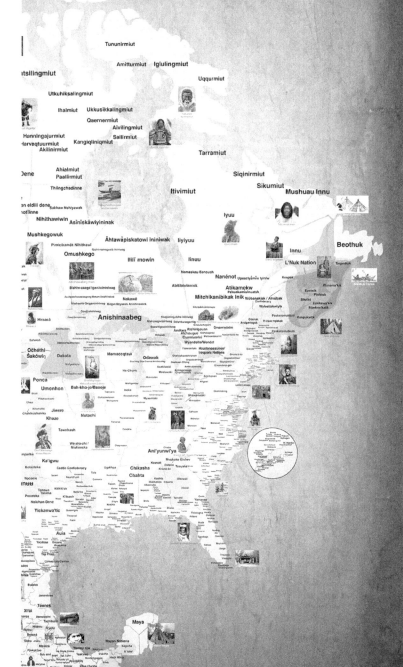

Tununirmiut

Amitturmiut   Iglulingmiut

tsilingmiut   Uqqurmiut

Utkuhiksalingmiut

Ihalmiut   Ukkusikkalingmiut

Qaernermiut

Hanningajurmiut   Aivilingmiut

Harvaqtuurmiut   Kangiqliniqmiut   Sallirmiut

Akilinirmiut

Tarramiut

Dene   Ahialmiut

Paallirmiut   Siqinirmiut

Thlingchadinne   Sikumiut

en eldili dene   Sakhaw Nehiyawak   Itivimiut   Mushuau Innu

ootline   Nihithawiwin   Asiniskâwiyininak

Iyuu

Mushkegowuk   Beothuk

Pimicikamâk Nihithawi   Gichi-namegosib Ininiwag

Omushkego   Âhtawâpiskatowi ininiwak   Iiyiyuu   Innu   L'Nuk Nation

Iliíí mowin   Iinuu

Nemaskau Eenouch   Nanénot   Upeeciyâmîw Iyiniw

Abitibiwinnick   Atikamekw
Mitchikanibikak Inik   Pekuakamiulnuatsh   Wôbanakiak / Alnôbak

Nakawê

Anishinaabeg

Hiraacá

OChéthi
Šakówiŋ   Dakota   Mamaceqtaw   Odawak

Ho-Chunk

Ponca

Umonhon   Bah-kho-je/Baxoje

Jiwere

Khaze   Nutachi

Tawehash

Wa-zha-zhi /
Niukonska

Ani'yunwi'ya

Ka'igwu

Kotsoteka   Caddo Confederacy   Ugakhpa   Chikasha
Chahta

Nocnele

Tenixted   Kïikik'ih

Penateka   K'íbash

Nsilshan Dene

Tickanwa'tic

Auia

Téenek

Xi'úí

Maya

Mayan Nations

Poems in BURIED SMOKE

Selected References

BANKS, William H Jr., *Plants of the Cherokee*, Great Smoky Mountains Association, Gatlinburg TN, 2004.

BLANKENSHIP, Bob, *Cherokee Roots Vol 1: Eastern Cherokee Rolls*, self-published, 1992.

CONLEY, Robert J., *Cherokee*, Graphic Arts Center Publishing Co, Portland OR, 2002.

CONLEY, Robert J., *The Cherokee Nation—A History*, University of New Mexico Press, Albuquerque, 2005.

CONLEY, Robert J., *The Witch of Goingsnake*, University of Oklahoma Press, Norman, 1988.

DUNBAR-ORTIZ, Roxanne, *An Indigenous Peoples' History of the United States*, Beacon Press, Boston, 2014.

DUNCAN, Barbara R, *Living Stories of the Cherokee*, University of North Carolina Press, Chapel Hill, 1998.

DUNCAN, Barbara and RIGGS, Brett H, *Cherokee Heritage Trails Guidebook*, University of North Caroline Press, Chapel Hill, 2003.

DWYER, Bill, *Southern Sayin's for Yankees and Other Immigrants*, APS, Charlotte, NC, 2004.

EHLE, John, *Trail of Tears—The Rise and Fall of the Cherokee Nation*, Anchor Books, New York, 1989.

EISENHOWER, John S.D., *Agent of Destiny—The Life and Times of General Winfield Scott*, The Free Press, New York, 1997.

GALLOWAY, Mary Regina Ulmer, *Aunt Mary, Tell Me A Story—A Collection of Cherokee Legends and Tales*, Mary Ulmer Chiltoskey, Cherokee Publications, Cherokee NC, 2001.

GARRETT, J. T., *The Cherokee Herbal—Native Plant Medicine from the Four Directions*, Bear & Co, Rochester VT, 2003.

GARRETT, J.T. and GARRETT, Michael, *Medicine of the Cherokee—The Way of Right Relationship*, Bear & Co, Rochester VT, 1996.

GLANCY, Diane, *Pushing the Bear—After the Trail of Tears*, U of Oklahoma Press, Norman OK, 2009.

HAMEL, Paul & Chiltoskey, Mary, *Cherokee Plants and Their Uses—A 400 Year History*, Book Publishing Company, 1975.

HERRIN, Alan, *Cherokee Calling—A Guide for Spiritual Growth*, White Bear Publishing, Tahlequah OK, 2004.

HIFLER, Joyce, *A Cherokee Feast of Days*, Council Oak Books, Tulsa OK, 2005.

HOBBS, Christopher, *Handbook for Herbal Healing*, Botanica Press, Capitola CA, 1994.

JOSEPH, Frank, Editor, *Unearthing Ancient America—The Lost Sagas of Conquerors, Castaways, and Scoundrels*, New Page Books—Division of The Career Press, Inc, Franklin Lakes, NJ. 2009.

KOENIG, Joel M.D., *Cherokee Chronicles 1540-1840*, Town & Country Publishing, 2003.

KOPPER, Philip, *The Smithsonian Book of North American Indians Before the Coming of the Europeans*, Smithsonian Books, Washington DC, 1986.

LEVY, Paul, *Dispelling Wetiko ~ Breaking the Curse of Evil*, North Atlantic Books, Berkeley, CA. 2013.

SELECTED REFERENCES

McLOUGHLIN, William G, *After the Trail of Tears—The Cherokees' Struggle for Sovereignty 1839–1880*, University of North Carolina Press, Chapel Hill, 1993.

McMASTER, Gerald, and TRAFZER, Clifford, *Native Universe—Voices of Indian America*, National Museum of the American Indian, Smithsonian Institution, Washington DC.

MAILS, Thomas E, *The Cherokee People*, Marlowe & Co, NYC, 1996.

MANN, Charles C, 1491—*New Revelations of the Americas Before Columbus*, Alfred A Knopf, New York, 2005.

MOONEY, James, Myths, *Legends and Sacred Formulas of the Cherokee*, Historical Images, Asheville NC, 1992.

PERDUE, Theda, *Cherokee Women*, University of Nebraska Press, Lincoln, 1998.

PERDUE, Theda, *"Mixed Blood Indians"—Racial Construction in the Early South*, University of Georgia Press, Athens, 2003.

SHARPE, J. Ed, *The Cherokees Past and Present—An Authentic Guide to the Cherokee People*, Cherokee Publications, Cherokee NC, 1970.

TWAIN, Mark, *The Wit and Wisdom of Mark Twain—A Book of Quotations*, Dover Publications, Mineola NY, 1999.

VERSLUIS, Arthur, *Sacred Earth—The Spiritual Landscape of Native America*, Inner Traditions International, Rochester VT, 1992.

WALDMAN, Carl, *Encyclopedia of Native American Tribes*, Revised Edition, Checkmark Books, New York, 1999.

WRIGHT, Ronald, *Stolen Continents—The Americas Through Indian Eyes Since 1492*, Houghton Mifflin Co, Boston, 1992.

YWAHOO, Dhyani, *Voices of Our Ancestors—Cherokee Teachings from the Wisdom Fire*, Shambala Press, Boston, 1987.

GOOGLE and the World Wide Web.

Made in the USA
Middletown, DE
21 February 2021